"How do you do it, Mr. Anders? Where do you begin looking for a missing child?"

Victoria's pulse quickened.

Philip laughed gently. "Really, Miss Carlin, you don't expect me to give away trade secrets, do you?"

Embarrassment colored her cheeks. "It's just so fascinating. If someone were looking for...someone," she persisted, "you would be willing to go out and search for him—or her?"

He studied her. "Are you looking for someone, Miss Carlin? A missing child?"

She averted her gaze, her thoughts drifting off to a familiar darkness. *Yes, I see a nameless, faceless child; my sweet little boy lost; heart of my heart, my very life. I never stop looking, and yet I wouldn't know him if I passed him on the street.*

Victoria's hands were trembling. "I never said that, now, did I, Mr. Anders?"

His gaze remained unflinching. "Sometimes a person's silences say more than their words."

CAROLE GIFT PAGE

writes from the heart about contemporary issues facing adults. Considered one of America's best-loved Christian fiction writers, Carole was born and raised in Jackson, Mississippi. She is the recipient of two Pacesetter Awards and the C.S. Lewis Honor Book Award. Over eight hundred of Carole's stories, articles and poems have been published in more than one hundred Christian periodicals.

A frequent speaker at conferences, schools, churches and women's ministries around the country, Carole finds fulfillment in being able to share her testimony about the faithfulness of God in her life and the abundance He offers those who come to Him. Carole and her husband, Bill, have three children and live in Moreno Valley, CA.

In Search of Her Own

CAROLE GIFT PAGE

Love Inspired™

Published by Steeple Hill Books™

STEEPLE HILL BOOKS

Steeple
Hill™

ISBN 0-373-87005-1

IN SEARCH OF HER OWN

Copyright © 1997 by Carole Gift Page

First published by Accent Publishing in 1985
under the title TO CHASE A SHADOW

Come now and let us reason together, saith the Lord: though your sins be as scarlet, they shall be as white as snow: though they be red like crimson, they shall be as wool.

Isaiah 1:18

Prologue

March, Easter Sunday

I went to the cemetery this cold, slate gray morning—had to, felt compelled, driven, as if the choice had been made for me. I stood with my back rigid, my hands doubled into fists, the wind whipping my hair, a torrent of tears dammed behind my eyes.

I had to be with Mother.

Hard to believe; the terrible reality still bombards me, like barbs in the flesh, sudden, unexpected, stealing my breath, leaving me reeling.

My mother is dead.

Nearly a month now since she died.

I stood in the light powdery snow for what seemed forever—yes, mud-rippled snow and frozen ground on this Resurrection Sunday; no sign of spring, no tree limbs budding with the promise of life. My feet and hands grew numb; my throat ached, raw with the cold.

I realize now I should have worn the heavy nubby coat Mother gave me when I began teaching at the university—a long, tailored, practical coat, a deep teal green, a color Mother said brought out the red in my auburn hair and accented the aqua-green of my eyes. I remember she got the coat on sale at Harris's, or was it Robinsons-May? Mother never paid full price for anything in her life. It was a wonderful buy, she said; it would last me for years, she said.

I accepted it gratefully, profusely grateful, as I accepted all of Mother's gifts. She shouldn't have, I told her; it was more than I deserved—I, the daughter who never measured up.

But not even Mother's marvelous coat could have warmed me today. I knew it as I approached the grave site. The coldness in my bones didn't come from winter's lingering chill. It was the coldness of death, like a rock in my chest, hard, frigid, unmoving. Today at her grave I noticed the earth was still scarred, not smooth and untouched like the land around it. It was the only sign, the remnant clue, that a funeral had occurred, a burial taken place.

Where my mother lies, the frozen earth still speaks of the deed, bears witness to it. In time it, too, will take on the bland, anonymous, impeccable look of a rich man's lawn. I accept that fact, as I accept the fact that my mother is gone; her soul is in heaven.

But can I ever accept her going?

This morning I knelt down and placed a perfect white lily on her grave. White on white, life and death blending into a milky blur— the smooth creamy flesh of the lily against the gritty, icy blue snow. There is no marker yet. The headstone will take several weeks to make. It will match my father's stone nearby—that proper, solemn slab of granite with his name precisely carved in large letters—James Edward Carlin, Beloved Husband And Father. Yes, that austere stone is a perfect memorial to a man as imperious in death as he was in life.

When I stood, my nylons were drenched; my knees revolted against the coldness. I wanted to do something or speak or walk somewhere. I wanted to feel some satisfaction in standing there, staring down at my parents' graves. But I felt as numb as my fingers. I wanted to turn and walk away or run to my car and drive somewhere where music was playing and people were singing—some lovely cathedral perhaps where spires rose heavenward and a man of God might declare triumphantly, *Death, where is thy sting; grave, where is thy victory?*

I wanted to be with somebody today. Not just somebody. I wanted to be with my mother. But there was no one around, except a stranger standing a short distance away by a large marble stone, his head bowed, his back to me—a tall, broad-shouldered man in a leather trench coat, a deep smoky gray color, his collar upturned against the cold. He wasn't wearing a hat and his thick brown hair looked wet from the snow.

"I'm here with you, Mother," I said aloud, but my voice came out too small, swallowed by the wind. I realized I, too, was being swallowed, but not by the elements—by something more immense and just as impalpable. For this time—for however long it lasts—I am as immobilized in life as my mother is in death. Perhaps worst of all, in spite of my faith, my life no longer matters to me. I know I should release my pain to God, but how? How can I surrender to the One I'm afraid now to trust?

It was irrational, I know, but I kept talking to Mother as if she could hear me. *"I've received so many cards and phone calls. Even people I hardly know have offered their condolences,"* I said, raising my voice against the whistling wind.

The stranger turned and glanced my way, as if he thought I might be addressing him. I caught a glimpse of dark mahogany eyes and chiseled, aristocratic features.

I looked down, abashed, then lifted my gaze as the stranger came my way. Our eyes met and held for a long moment as he passed by, his expression warm with sympathy and compassion. He had the most compelling eyes I had ever seen. He seemed to be telling me, *We are kindred spirits inhabiting the same emotional place. You're not alone. I understand your pain.*

Something leapt inside me, an instinctive response, a yearning to hold on to this moment of connection with another grieving soul. I wanted to say something, offer a smile. But as quickly as our fragile alliance formed, it slipped away. The stranger walked on through the fine blanket of snow, and I felt even more alone than before.

I turned back to my mother's grave and said, too brightly, *"Like I was saying, Mother, you wouldn't believe all the people who've phoned—dozens of your former students, and mine. People we haven't heard from in years, some even since Father's death six years ago."*

Six years.

It's hard to believe Mother and I have been alone, had no one but each other all that time. Even our colleagues at the university have maintained a polite distance all these years, comfortably insulated in their lofty bastion of academia. Convivial intellectuals, they are, who enjoy a good time as much as anyone, I suppose, but two lone women never quite fit their scheme of things.

Or perhaps we never tried—or cared to try—to fit their scheme. We kept to ourselves, pleased to dwell in peace, living quiet, orderly lives. And, of course, for me, a predictable routine was an immense relief after those earlier days, after that black hole of time seven years ago.

As my eyes returned inevitably to my father's headstone, memories swirled around me like a dark funnel cloud drawing me into its vortex. In its violent maelstrom I could hear my father's voice thundering, "How could you do this to us, Victoria? How could you let it happen? You've thrown away your future for some gypsy actor. You've shamed us all with his misbegotten child. Is this the kind of woman we raised you to be? Mark my words, daughter, you'll be the death of me yet...."

I was the death of you, Father. No one said an accusing word, but everyone knew the heart attack was my fault, my doing. If only I hadn't disappointed you; if only I hadn't broken your heart!

But it does no good to dwell on the past. Haven't I learned that by now? You're gone, Father. And now Mother is gone, too. I'm alone for the first time in my life, tied to no one, no bonds by blood, by birth, by affection. My last living relative has died.

No, that's not so.

There is another—blood of my blood, bone of my bone.

My child.

Somewhere in this vast world lives a little lost boy whose face I've never seen, whose voice I've never heard, except that day in the delivery room for a sliver of time before he was whisked away from me forever.

Where are you now, my son? Who do you call Mother? Do you have my eyes, my nose, my hair? My penchant for privacy? My love of books? When I lost you, my arms ached for months for someone to hold. I felt as if someone had plundered my heart and left me for dead.

But I denied my pain because I felt I had no right to grieve. For my parents' sake I bore my shame in silence and denied my son's existence.

But he lives.

He's somewhere, someone's child.

I've voiced the question over and over through a thousand sleepless nights, but now that I'm truly alone the question takes on an urgency I can no longer deny. I have to know!

Where is my son?

Chapter One

It was the first of May before Victoria returned to the cemetery—a gray, chill, cloud-heavy day with only faint streamers of sunlight to remind her it was spring. Her mother's headstone was in place now, surrounded by a lush green carpet of tender new grass. The imposing granite monument matched her father's marker, stately without being ostentatious. She stooped down and placed a potted plant in the grass—butter yellow chrysanthemums as bright as sunbursts, her mother's favorite; the house and garden had been filled with them when Victoria was growing up.

"I'm sorry I haven't come more often, Mother," she said, wincing with shame. Somehow, even from the grave, her mother could make her feel guilty! "I don't know why I haven't come. I guess coming here makes your death more real and stirs up the pain," she said, feeling the need to explain, to justify herself. "I'll do better, I promise."

God help me, I sound like a schoolgirl who's been caught cheating or skipping class! God, you've forgiven me; why can't I forgive myself?

Blinking back bitter tears, Victoria turned her gaze away from her parents' markers. Her eyes settled on the immense gravestone a few yards away where the tall stranger had stood, head bowed, during her last visit. The lowering rays of the sun breaking through the cloudy sky highlighted the inscription: Pauline Anders, Beloved Wife.

Victoria could barely make out the dates beneath the name. She squinted, silently calculating. Dear God in heaven, how tragic! The woman died at thirty. So young! Only a few years older than I am, Victoria noted, stunned, recalling the pain, masked but still apparent, in the furrows of the stranger's brow. She turned and fished in her purse for a tissue. I shouldn't have come. I can't handle this. My emotions are still too fragile.

Blotting the moisture from her eyes, she squared her shoulders and began walking back to her car. She was almost to the road when she noticed someone approaching—the mysterious man in the trench coat who belonged to Pauline Anders. Only now he was wearing a brown leather aviator jacket with a fleecy wool collar. And he was carrying flowers—red roses in a deep ceramic vase, a dozen at least. He offered Victoria an oblique smile as their paths crossed, and she obligingly returned it. In the fractional moment their eyes met she was reminded that theirs was a peculiar alliance—deep losses borne separately and in a sense shared wordlessly, beyond time and circumstance.

Too soon she looked away, breaking eye contact with the stranger, feeling suddenly self-conscious, almost flustered. The man's amber eyes were so vivid, so penetrating; it was as if he could read her very soul. She walked on, shivering, pulling her long, hunter green cardigan tighter around her, her cold fingers burrowing into the marled, slubby yarns. It was nearly dusk, and the chill air was already invading her bones. The overcast sky promised rain. Lots of it. Weren't April showers supposed to bring May flowers, not just more rain? Right now she wanted nothing more than to be at home in her little condominium, snuggling on the couch in her comfy flannel robe, sipping chamomile tea and watching the evening news on TV.

Unexpectedly, Victoria was aware of a sound behind her—heavy footsteps padding through the thick grass. She glanced around and felt a ripple of surprise. The stranger was striding her way, a shadowy form against the darkening skyline.

Victoria increased her pace, pretending not to notice him. Her automobile wasn't far—the gray compact parked just outside the cemetery's huge iron gate.

But the man's gait also increased. She sensed him just behind her, his breathing nearly as audible as her own. She walked faster now, her pulse racing, her ankle nearly turning as her stacked heels sank into the grassy, uneven ground. You hear such awful stories all the time, she thought frantically, breaking into a run. Women alone attacked by strangers, psychotics, madmen; women foolhardy enough to venture alone into dangerous desolate places like this one....

A deep masculine voice behind her shouted, "Stop! Wait!"

Was he kidding? She wouldn't give in without a fight. She bolted through the open iron gate, running to her car. She glanced over her shoulder and saw him running after her. Finally she reached the car. She leaned panting against the door. Now if only she could find her keys! She looked down at her empty hands. Her purse—it was gone!

"Miss, I think this is what you're looking for." The stranger hovered over her, surely more than six feet to her five feet six inches. She caught the clean fragrance of his spicy after-shave and the minty warmth of his breath. He held out her handbag, managing an amused, crinkly smile. "You dropped this back there in the grass."

She looked up at him, dazed, her pulse suddenly racing with something quite different from terror, and mumbled, "I did?"

"I'm sorry," he continued, those mesmerizing eyes holding her captive. She couldn't help noticing that he had an uncommonly handsome face, and at the moment he seemed almost to be enjoying her predicament. "I mean it," he went on seriously. "I really didn't intend to frighten you."

She took the purse and with trembling fingers found her keys. "That's all right," she murmured, fumbling with the lock. She opened the door and glanced back briefly. "I feel so foolish. It's just that this place can be a bit unnerving."

"Don't I know it," he said with a faint smile.

Feeling the need to say something more, she gazed up at the gray, drizzling sky and said, "This really isn't the sort of day to be out, is it? It looks like it's going to pour any minute now."

His voice was warm, almost a confidential tone. "I know. Some weather for May, huh? I was hoping to beat the rain, but no such luck."

She opened her palm to the sky. "You're right. It's already starting. I guess I'd better go."

He nodded and flipped up the large fleecy collar of his leather jacket. "Drive safely," he said, his candid brown eyes still boring into hers.

As the first large drops fell, she gave him a fluttery wave and climbed into her car. He returned the wave with a good-natured smile, then turned and walked quickly to his automobile. Victoria fastened her seat belt and turned the key in the ignition, but nothing happened. She tried again, and again, but there was only a dull click-click-click.

She heard a tap on her window and glanced over to see the stranger. "Release the hood and I'll check it for you," he told her.

A minute later he returned to her. "The water level in your battery's down. The terminals are corroded. You'll need a new battery."

"Oh, great." She sighed. "I'll have to call the auto club."

He leaned into the open window, his face close to her own. "I wish I had some jumper cables," he said with an earnestness that touched her. "I'll be glad to drive you to a gas station where you can make your call."

She stiffened. "No, thank you. I—I really couldn't impose."

"Please, I insist. It goes against my gentlemanly instincts to leave a lady stranded in this downpour. I'd really like to help." When she still looked doubtful, he offered a reassuring smile. "I know what they say about riding in cars with strangers, but I assure you I'm harmless."

Victoria weighed her options, and finally offered a noncommittal, "Thank you. I'd appreciate a ride." She picked up her purse and followed the man to a sleek, metallic-red foreign sports car.

As he drove toward the business district of the city, he glanced over at her and said, "I suppose this would be a good time to introduce ourselves. I'm Phillip Anders."

She smiled. "I'm Victoria Carlin."

"I'm glad to meet you, Victoria. Actually, I remember seeing you at the cemetery before."

"Yes. I remember seeing you, too. It was Easter Sunday."

He flashed an ironic smile. "There has to be a better meeting place than Rest Haven."

Victoria laughed faintly. She wasn't quite sure how to take this unpredictable man, Phillip Anders. One moment he seemed brooding and introspective; the next he was making droll jokes and offering the most disarming smile.

They drove to a nearby filling station where Victoria made her call. "It'll be at least an hour or more before the tow truck can come," she told Phillip when she returned to his car.

"All right," he said. "I'm in no hurry. Before I take you back to your car, let's stop by the little coffee shop next door."

"Oh, no," she protested. "You don't have to wait with me."

"I never leave a lady in distress." Laugh lines appeared around his eyes. "Like I said, I want to make sure you aren't stranded in this miserable weather."

In the Dew Drop Inn, a waitress showed them to a corner booth just off the kitchen. Several yellowed western prints decorated the mauve walls and an antique coatrack stood nearby. Phillip hung up their coats, then they sat down and ordered coffee. "Hot and black," he told the teenage waitress with backcombed, tangerine hair.

Victoria shivered involuntarily. "I didn't realize how cold I was."

"It shouldn't be this cold in May. We've had enough winter."

She nodded. "That's how I feel. It seems as if winter has lasted for years."

"It has," he murmured thoughtfully. "And there's no end in sight."

"I have a feeling you're not talking about the weather now."

"No." He paused. "Tell me, Miss Carlin—or is it Mrs.?"

She felt her face flush slightly. "Miss."

"Then that's not your husband's grave?"

"No. My mother's."

"I noticed two headstones."

"My father died six years ago."

"I'm sorry. I know how hard it is. I lost both my parents when I was young."

"And now your wife," she said softly.

He nodded, a tendon tightening along his jawline. "It's been nearly a year. You'd think it would get easier."

"She was so young. Do you mind my asking? Was it an accident?"

"Cancer. She never gave up. Bravest woman I ever knew."

They were both silent for several moments, sipping their coffee. Finally, in a lighter tone, he asked, "Just what is it you do, Miss Carlin—other than frequent cemeteries, that is?"

"I'm an instructor at the university. Contemporary American literature. I'm finishing my third year of teaching."

"Oh, one of those studious types—your nose always in a book?"

Victoria unconsciously lifted her hand to the back of her neck. "I suppose you could say that. I'm working on the thesis for my doctorate."

"I'm impressed," said Phillip. "My remark about studious types wasn't meant as an insult. I admire intelligent women. It's just that you don't look like any of the teachers I had in school—you know, the old-maid schoolmarms with their hair in a bun and spectacles halfway down their noses."

Victoria forced a laugh. "In just which century did you attend school, Mr. Anders?"

He accepted her mild rebuff. "All right, I'm exaggerating. But you look like you'd be more at home on the tennis courts or horseback riding in the country."

Victoria sipped her coffee, then said, "I've never played tennis or been on a horse. I've spent most of my life in libraries and classrooms."

"Even when you were a child?"

"Yes. My parents were both professors at the university and, for as long as I can remember, they stressed the importance of education. They naturally expected me to become a teacher, too."

"Doesn't sound like you had much fun."

"Fun wasn't one of my priorities." Victoria realized immediately how smug she sounded, so she added, "Learning was fun for me."

"Well, for me it was just plain hard work. I got through law school by the skin of my teeth."

"Then you're a lawyer?"

"Not anymore," he replied. "I passed my bar exams and set up practice as an attorney, but after a couple of years of sitting in a stuffy office, neck-high in paperwork, I decided I'd had it. I closed up shop and began working as a private investigator."

"Really? How exciting," said Victoria.

"To be honest, it's not as exciting as it looks on television," said Phillip. "I'm rarely into the shoot-'em-up cops-and-robbers stuff. In fact, sometimes my job is downright tedious. And I still get bogged down with paperwork, but at least there's a certain undercurrent of adventure that I didn't have as a lawyer."

"Exactly what do you investigate?"

"Missing persons. Kids mostly."

Her breath caught momentarily. "Missing children?"

"Well, there's always the husband or wife looking for a spouse who's left town. But most of my clients are searching for children— parents looking for runaway teenagers or divorced people whose mate has stolen their children."

Victoria's interest perked. "Really? You mean, someone just comes to you and says, 'My child is missing,' and you go out and find their child?"

"Essentially yes. But it's not quite that simple. Like I said, there's a lot of paperwork involved, and I run into my share of roadblocks and dead ends. And frankly, sometimes there's not a happy ending." His voice trailed off. "Some kids end up dead."

Victoria shuddered. "But most of the time you...you find the missing child?"

"Most of the time." He chuckled. "I'm a very persistent man. I don't give up easily."

She sat forward, her pulse quickening. She could feel the rhythmic pounding in her ears. "How do you do it, Mr. Anders? Where do you begin?"

He laughed, a gentle, warming sound she found most appealing. "Really, Miss Carlin, you don't expect me to give away trade secrets, do you?"

She sat back, embarrassment coloring her cheeks. "I'm not trying to pry. It's just so fascinating to think that you can go out and track down someone who's missing. You must make a lot of parents very happy."

He laughed again, mirthlessly. "And I've enraged a few, as well. But that's another story."

"But if someone were looking for someone," she persisted, "you would be willing to go out and search for him—or her?"

"Well, I would need to know the circumstances, of course. I may push the boundaries at times, but I stay within the law."

"Of course. That goes without saying."

He studied her with a disquieting frankness. "Are you looking for someone, Miss Carlin? A missing child?"

She averted her gaze, her thoughts drifting off to a familiar darkness. *Yes, I seek a nameless, faceless child—my sweet little boy lost, heart of my heart, my very life. I never stop looking, and yet I wouldn't know him if I passed him on the street.*

"Did you hear me, Miss Carlin? Do you know of a missing child?"

Victoria rotated her coffee cup between her palms. Her hands were trembling. "I never said that, now did I, Mr. Anders?"

His gaze remained unflinching. "Sometimes a person's silences say more than their words."

"I'm just very intrigued," she replied with a nonchalance she didn't feel. "I never knew a private investigator before. It must be a very challenging and rewarding occupation."

"It keeps me busy. In fact, too busy at times."

"Too busy?"

"Yes—when my wife was alive, anyway. Pauline and I didn't have the time together we should have. I was gone a lot." Phillip's words fell away, as if he realized he was saying too much, revealing more about himself than he intended. He drained his coffee cup. When the waitress walked by, he signaled her for a refill.

"Do you have children?" asked Victoria, knowing immediately it was a subject she shouldn't be broaching. What if he turned the question back to her?

Phillip grimaced. For a moment he said nothing. Finally he looked away, a glint of pain evident in his sable brown eyes. "No, we never had children," he replied somberly. "To tell you the truth, it's the greatest regret of my life."

Victoria looked away, discomfited by the man's unexpected confession. "Well, there's more to life than children," she murmured without conviction, her words unnaturally stiff and precise. She quelled the impulse to admit to Phillip that she, too, knew how it felt to regret something deeply, to live daily with a raw emotional wound that ruptured at the slightest inadvertent prick. But exposing her own pain would serve no purpose. She and Phillip were, after all, virtual strangers.

"Well, now that I've bored you with my life story, I think it's time for me to pick up the check," said Phillip offhandedly.

"Thank you, but I really wasn't bored," she assured him with a heartfelt smile. Suddenly, illogically, she didn't want their conversation to end, but she could think of no legitimate reason to linger, so she said dutifully, "I guess it is time to get back to my car."

Phillip nodded, reached for the check and tossed a crisp one-dollar bill on the table. A contemplative silence settled over them as he drove Victoria back to her stalled automobile.

Chapter Two

That evening Victoria couldn't get Phillip Anders out of her mind. His presence lingered like an afterglow, baffling, disconcerting and yet undeniably pleasant. As she rattled around her small, modern condo, sorting her mail, putting away dishes and browsing through her latest educational journal, his image was never far from her thoughts. She turned on the late-night news, but the newscaster's voice sounded so disturbingly similar to Phillip's, she quickly snapped off the set.

Even as she drifted into a restless slumber shortly before midnight, she saw his face in her mind, his classic features as solidly chiseled as a Michelangelo sculpture—and those eyes, so expressive and compelling, seemingly reading her very heart. And his voice—surely it wasn't the television now. In the hazy, rainbow reveries of her dreams she could hear the richness of his deep baritone and the mirthful ripple of his infectious laughter.

When she awoke the next morning, the image of Phillip Anders still occupied her mind, like some rare, esteemed object her consciousness had instinctively decided to accommodate. As she bathed and dressed and ran a brush through her cascading curls, fragments of her dream lingered. As she sipped her coffee and nibbled a slice of whole-wheat toast, she wondered where he was and what he was doing at this very moment. Even as she sat at her kitchen table grading test papers, her thoughts strayed inevitably to him.

She found herself absently tracing Phillip's features in her mind—

his long, distinctive nose, his generous mouth and that sturdy cleft chin. In her imagination she could picture his riveting, darkly lashed eyes, his sardonic smile and the thick umber brown hair that just touched his collar. The images appeared unbidden and left her feeling disconcerted, perplexed.

She wanted to see him again, but she knew she didn't dare.

What's wrong with me? she wondered. Had she taken leave of her senses, allowing this stranger to monopolize her thoughts? Surely it was a temporary aberration, perhaps even a predictable corollary of the grief process. After all, for the first time in her life she was utterly alone; perhaps her mind was simply filling the void with the first person who happened by.

"And if I believe that, I'm sure someone has a bridge somewhere they'd love to sell me," she mused dryly.

No, there was something about Phillip Anders that set him apart from everyone else she had ever known—a mysterious quality that attracted her and disarmed her at the same time. She wanted to see him again and learn more about him.

But she hadn't thought to ask for his business card, nor did she have the slightest idea where he lived. Surely he would be in the phone book, but she had no logical reason to call him. He might think her forward, even brazen. But, in fact, women did phone men these days and no one considered it unseemly.

But the thought of phoning him, of pursuing Phillip Anders in any manner, left Victoria with a knot of panic in her chest and a sudden dryness in her mouth. What made her think he would even want to see her again? They had nothing in common. Surely he had demonstrated no interest in her as a woman. And he was, after all, still grieving for the wife he loved so deeply and to whom he was obviously unswervingly devoted.

But there was more to her hesitation. Much more. And before her fantasies whisked her into the tempting arms of Phillip Anders, it was time to acknowledge the real reason for her reluctance to face him. Yes, already she could feel that old barrier resurrecting itself in her mind—the nameless, inscrutable panic that welled in her chest at the prospect of a man becoming close—any man.

There had been no man in Victoria's life since Rick Lancer seven years ago. In fact, there had been no man before or after Rick. And even now, because of Rick, there would probably never be anyone for Victoria.

Now, on this quiet Saturday just a few weeks before the end of the school term, Victoria allowed herself to think about Rick and about those days that still moldered in the deepest recesses of her emotions. She was standing before the bathroom mirror about to apply a hint of blush and a dab of mascara. Her long, natural red curls were pulled back from her forehead and spilled down the back of her neck. Her large green eyes were framed by thick, dusky red lashes. Her teeth were even and perfectly white. Her flawless ivory skin was marred only by a spattering of freckles that dotted her nose and cheeks. She didn't wear much makeup; she preferred the natural, clean-scrubbed look, the look her father had loved. It was that sweet, guileless naiveté of face and spirit that had prompted him to call her "Daddy's good-as-gold little girl."

She paused, the mascara wand in hand, and gazed critically at her unadorned face. It was no longer the face her father had loved, child-like and innocent, but the face another man had praised. Rick Lancer had called it a beautiful face, but he could have been lying even about that. Still, Victoria had been told, with a note of approval by an occasional student and an air of condescension by a fellow faculty member, that her natural good looks made her appear much younger than her twenty-six years.

But Victoria didn't feel younger. Sometimes she felt incredibly old. She wasn't sure she had ever felt young or attractive, except perhaps when Rick Lancer had called her beautiful. For a time he had made her feel beautiful. But not for long. Even now, when she thought of him, she felt ugly inside, damaged. She still wondered how Rick could have prompted such intense, contradictory emotions—love and hate, joy and despair, a sense of beauty...and degradation.

Thinking of Rick sent her spiraling into one of those dark moods that compelled her to reach for her thick, well-worn journal. She sat down at her desk and, in handwriting marked by quick, gracefully scrolled letters, she wrote:

Saturday, May 2

I keep going back to the past, reliving it, as if I've been sentenced to play it over and over again in my mind like a broken record, the sound always shrill and discordant.

I keep asking, How could I have been so foolish?

I was naive, I admit that, and overly protected by my parents. From earliest childhood my life followed a strict regimen—full days of classes and long hours of homework so that I could excel in every subject. Piano and voice lessons filled whatever free time remained. There were few opportunities for friends and recreation, and little chance to indulge in frivolous pastimes like shopping or telephoning, daydreaming or watching TV.

I remember vividly the most defining—and devastating—moment of my childhood. I was a young girl—seven years old. My parents threw a birthday party for me and invited my classmates. My father overheard me on the phone telling a classmate what present I wanted—a certain doll, or book, or game. Afterward, Father scolded me, saying, "You shouldn't ask your friends for gifts. It makes you look greedy, as if that's your only reason for a party. If someone asks you what you want, tell them you don't want a present."

"But I do want presents," I argued plaintively in my reasonable seven-year-old logic. "Why should I say I don't when I do?"

"Because a proper young lady is careful not to appear self-centered, as if gifts are all that matter," my father explained. "It's the company of your friends that counts. In fact," he added in that intrepid voice of his, "to teach you a lesson, I'm going to instruct all the parents not to send gifts, so you'll understand what's truly important in life."

So no one brought gifts, and I felt deeply shamed to think that everyone considered me a selfish person. That party was the worst event of my young life; all the children seemed to understand even without saying it that I didn't deserve to receive presents. As my classmates played games and ate cake and ice cream, I struggled to pretend that nothing was wrong, but I couldn't keep back the tears. At last I ran to my room and collapsed on my bed in deep sobs. My parents sent the children home and never mentioned the party again, but from then on I was known to my classmates as "the girl who doesn't get presents."

After that party, I made it a point never to ask for gifts for Christmas or birthdays; I simply showed grateful appreciation for whatever I was given. But Father's lesson had been too well learned. I found it difficult to ask anyone for anything—a favorite food, help with homework, a preferred television program. At all costs I would not be considered selfish.

My goal in life became to accommodate others, to make sure they were happy and content. I found a sort of spiritual satisfaction in sacrificing my wishes for another's, as if I could somehow atone for my childhood greed.

That attitude carried over into the rest of my life. I grew up feeling that my own needs and desires were somehow shameful and suspect, and that it was in bad taste, if not actually sinful, to let others know what I wanted. The proper thing was to pretend I had no needs or yearnings—better to acquiesce to the wishes of others and make them happy. So I grew up determined to please my parents by behaving like their perfect little girl.

I was careful never to vent my emotions around them—anger, fear, frustration, disappointment or sadness; rather, I always wore a smile and pretended everything was wonderful, so that my father would give me his smile of approval and praise me for being his "good-as-gold little girl."

My mother, too, seemed to love me most when I was on my best behavior, so I saved my tears and anger for moments when I was alone in my room, where I could sob into my pillow or pound my mattress with my fists when I was angry.

I realized as an adult that my parents had taught me, perhaps inadvertently, never to be candid with another human being, nor to express my own wishes and desires, but rather to bow to the opinions of others and deny in a sense my own personhood, my own right of expression, even my own right to make mistakes.

But when I turned eighteen, things changed. I was seized by the same sense of daring and rebellion that was typical of others my age. I found myself wanting to strike out against the limits imposed on me, to stretch myself, to do something bold and excessive, perhaps to begin walking down an unknown road and never turn back. I was obsessed by a restless yearning for something that had no name, no substance, no form. I dreamed of recklessly toppling my sane, sensible world.

It was during this period of inner conflict that I met Rick Lancer. He was playing summer stock at a little theater near the university. A classmate introduced us. I loved Rick immediately. He flattered me, courted me and carried me away with his dreams and schemes, only to eventually compromise me and cast me aside.

Rick was an actor with an actor's flair and sense of the dramatic. He prodded me out of my shyness, chided me for my rigidity of spirit and taught me to "loosen up." He promised me the world, the moon and the stars—or at least a wedding and a honeymoon, as soon as he saved up the money from his next gig. He gave me an inexpensive ring with diamonds no more real than his love for me. I still recall his words: "We'll announce our engagement when I get the lead in summer stock. Doll, we're as good as husband and wife. Don't let some silly little paper keep us apart. Let me love you the way a husband should."

I never actually said yes to Rick, but neither did I quite say no. I felt emotionally overpowered by him, mesmerized by his flamboyance and style. And, of course, I had been brought up to please without protest those I loved...and so I let Rick Lancer take what he wanted.

By the time I realized I was pregnant, Rick had already journeyed to New York with a local acting troupe. My letter telling him about the baby was returned marked Address Unknown.

My pregnancy devastated my parents and put an irreparable chink in their carefully laid plans for my life. They told me I had betrayed the long years of nurturing and intense devotion they had invested in me. My father considered my pregnancy an act of rebellion against him. "After all I've done for you, to think you could do this to me—heap shame on the family name!" But he had a remedy for every situation, even the tragedy of an unwanted pregnancy.

"You made a mistake, but we'll take care of it," he told me, his voice edged with contempt. "It's all arranged. Your mother will go with you. No one will ever need to know. Your life will be back on track before you know it."

I burst into tears and for the first time in my life stood up to my father. "No, no, no! You can't make me kill my baby! It's mine and you can't have it!"

When I refused the abortion, my parents sent me to a private university in another state where no one knew me. I completed my sophomore year and earned a straight-A average, but I was going through the motions, dazed and numb. I was painfully alone, except for my baby growing inside me—my wee, constant, unseen companion. At night I would lie in bed and talk to my child, pouring out my hopes and dreams for the two of us. I would feel him kicking, a foot here, an elbow there. We played a little game: I'd press the spots where he kicked and he'd nudge me back. Kick and nudge, kick and nudge. I vowed I'd let him grow up to be his own person, but even as I made the promise, I knew I could never keep it...because I couldn't keep him.

My parents made it clear I couldn't come home with a baby, and *when I threatened to go elsewhere, my mother told me the awful news. My father was seriously ill and needed me at home. "He asks for you constantly, dear. You're the only one who can comfort him."*

Two weeks later I delivered my baby—a pink, thrashing, bawling seven-pound boy I saw only briefly as he was taken from my body and placed in a bassinet. I wanted my son more than I had ever wanted anything in my life, but in my mind all I could hear was my father's voice denouncing me: "You've sinned. You don't deserve to keep your child!"

So I signed the papers for his adoption, convinced my life was over at the tender age of twenty. I never anticipated the emotional upheaval I would experience by giving up my child. After he was taken away, I felt a physical ache for him—my arms ached to hold him, my breasts ached to nurse him. It was as if my very heart had been torn from my chest.

Three days later I returned home, desolate, my arms empty, to offer my ailing father what little comfort I could muster. But without a word or a glance he'd delivered his ultimate rebuke. He'd died of a massive heart attack hours before I arrived home, and somehow I knew it was my fault; my weakness and selfishness were to blame.

As I settled in at home and began my junior year at the local university, my father's death struck me with its staggering reality. His desk was cleared, his chair empty, his possessions gone. The walls were silent, the rooms enormous without his voice, his presence. Worst of all was the growing conviction that I had caused his death. My shame had killed him.

"No," Victoria said aloud with a decisiveness that startled her. She dropped her pen on the desk and slammed her journal shut. She was trembling, the memories assailing her as if it had all happened yesterday. "No, it wasn't my fault! Dear God, why can't I put it behind me?"

She ran to the bathroom and splashed cold water on her face and blotted the wetness with a towel. She stared soberly at her reflection, a dark accusation clouding her eyes. "I didn't kill Father," she told herself severely. "God has forgiven me. The guilt is gone...if only I can someday forgive myself.

"I've got to get out of here. Maybe some fresh air will clear the cobwebs of memory from my head."

Victoria went to her closet and took out a suit, a double-breasted blazer and pleated trousers in powder pink crepe wool. She dressed quickly and left her condominium.

Her car was still in the shop, but the local mall was within walking distance, and she could use the exercise. She would walk to Elaine's Fashion Boutique, a chic little women's shop she frequented on occasion; she liked their styles, and their prices weren't exorbitant. Yes, she would go there and buy herself something frivolous. No, not frivolous. The annual faculty tea for graduating seniors was scheduled for next weekend and she needed something new to wear—perhaps a pretty pastel dress, something delicate and springlike.

But later, at Elaine's, as she browsed through a rack of high-priced garments, she had second thoughts. Maybe I'd better make do with what I have at home, or I could try the rack of sale dresses, she mused, then chided herself for always giving in to her practical nature.

I'll just try on a couple of these expensive dresses, she decided, just to see how they look. She walked over to the dressing rooms where several women stood waiting. She noticed a little boy sitting in a straight-back chair near one dressing room. He sat stiffly, frowning, obviously fighting an advanced case of restlessness. Something in his features made Victoria take a second look. He had thick, obstinately curly red hair, large green eyes and a turned-up nose lost in freckles.

Victoria's heart began to beat faster. He looks like me as a child, she marveled silently. Her thoughts raced. He's about the right age. He could be my son!

Victoria struggled to remain calm. This had happened before—a chance encounter with a child who looked as if he could be her son. The likelihood of meeting her own child was remote at best, so why did she always react this way, with such a flash flood of emotion? Why couldn't she put her child out of her mind as she had intended six years ago at his birth?

She knew the answer. Too much had happened since then. Since her conversion three years ago, Victoria had been plagued by the question of her son's eternal destiny. Did he have Christian parents? Would someone tell him about Jesus? Would he listen? How Victoria yearned to find him and tell him herself.

Since her mother's death, she admitted it had been even more difficult to quell the desire to see her son, to touch him just once, to share her faith with him and assure herself he was happy and healthy.

Now, staring at this child—a stranger's child—fidgeting in his chair, Victoria realized the desire had become an obsession.

She had to find her son.

And, as if she had found the missing piece of a long-troubling puzzle, she thought of Phillip Anders. "Of course! I've got to call him! He's the answer! He'll know what to do!"

That evening, with trembling fingers, Victoria riffled through the telephone book and found Phillip's number. But now that she was actually dialing him, she was assailed by misgivings. "I shouldn't be doing this," she said, her voice barely audible. And when she heard him say hello, her throat refused to emit a sound.

"Hello? Is anybody there?" he questioned. "Who is this?"

"It's...Victoria Carlin," she said at last. "You came to my rescue yesterday at the cemetery."

"Well, hello, Miss Carlin."

"I don't mean to bother you—"

"Bother me? To tell you the truth, I was hoping I might hear from you again."

"You were?"

"Yes, I enjoyed our chat at the coffee shop."

"So did I. And I was thinking..." Her voice trailed off.

"Thinking about...?" he prompted.

"About you being a...a private investigator, Mr. Anders."

"Yes, Miss Carlin? Is there something I can do for you?"

"I'm not sure." Her voice faltered again. "You said you...you find people...children."

"Yes. Like I said, I do my best," he replied. "Is there someone you want to locate?"

"Yes," said Victoria, her tone growing decisive. "I would like it very much if you could help me find a little boy."

"A boy, you say?"

"Yes. He just turned six."

"What's his name, Miss Carlin?"

"I—I don't know."

"You don't know?"

"No. I'm sorry. I don't know much about him."

"Well, we'll work with whatever you have, of course," he replied patiently. "Just who is this boy, Miss Carlin?"

She closed her eyes; it seemed to take her forever to force out the words. "He's...he's my son."

Chapter Three

Phillip Anders suggested they discuss Victoria's case over dinner on Tuesday evening. He met her at seven at the Dingho Chinese Restaurant just north of the university. It was a quaint place with intimate tables and soft lights, accented by jade carvings, porcelain vases and wall scrolls depicting squat Buddhas and towering pagodas.

As Phillip settled back in his wicker chair opposite Victoria, the delicate china on the linen tablecloth gave his brawny good looks a rough-hewn texture. He looked out of place, this tall, square-jawed man with hands too large for the tiny teacups.

Victoria smiled impulsively. "I'm surprised you picked this place, Mr. Anders. You look more like a steak-and-potatoes man to me."

He grinned. "I am. But I thought this atmosphere would suit you."

"I'll consider that a compliment," she replied.

"It is."

Their gaze held for a moment. She felt a velvety warmth steal over her and she quickly dropped her gaze to her menu. Wait a second, she reminded herself. This is a business meeting. Not a date.

"I suggest their Peking duck or steaks Manchurian," said Phillip with a smile.

She looked at him in surprise. "You've been here before?"

"With clients a few times."

"Then I'll defer to your judgment."

"Peking duck," Phillip told the round-faced Oriental waiter. "With egg flower soup and sautéed snowpea pods."

"It sounds like a culinary delight," said Victoria.

Phillip leaned across the table confidentially. "What I like best are all the little take-home cartons to warm up the next day. It beats my usual frozen dinner fare."

"I know what you mean. I hate cooking just for myself."

Phillip's eyes crinkled with amusement. "I hate eating my own cooking. No matter what I fix, it ends up tasting like overcooked cardboard."

"Perhaps you should invest in a cookbook."

"I have dozens around the house. My wife, Pauline, was a gourmet cook. She collected recipes like some women accumulate jewelry. There was nothing she couldn't make."

"She must have been a very remarkable woman."

Phillip's burnt-sienna eyes took on a distant sheen. "She was the best." He looked up and blinked as the waiter brought their soup.

"Very hot," warned the man.

As Phillip picked up his china spoon, Victoria bowed her head and silently offered a quick prayer of thanks for her food. She looked up, embarrassed to see Phillip watching her.

"My wife and I used to do that," he said. "She never let a meal pass without saying grace."

"It's still a bit new to me," Victoria murmured self-consciously.

They ate in silence for several minutes. Then Phillip cleared his throat and said, "You telephoned me about locating a child for you, Miss Carlin. Would you like to tell me about your son?"

She dabbed a corner of her lips with the linen napkin. "Please call me Victoria."

"If you'll call me Phillip."

"Of course...Phillip." She touched the back of her neck nervously. Her face felt uncomfortably warm. "I must tell you, Phillip, I've never talked about my son to anyone. It's very difficult for me. Now that both my parents are gone, no one even knows I have a child...except you."

"I can understand your reluctance to share something so personal."

"It's just not the sort of thing I want people to know about."

"But surely there's not the stigma there once was..."

"Perhaps not. But wrong is wrong. I know it no matter what anyone says, no matter how people try to whitewash it." She didn't add that she could still hear her father's voice in her head condemning her for her actions. Lamentably, his voice was often louder than the voice of God in her heart.

Phillip's expression softened. "You sound like you're still struggling with guilt feelings."

Victoria sipped her tea before replying. "I know I've been forgiven. I'm just not sure I've forgiven myself."

He flashed a wry smile. "Self-forgiveness can be a hard-won battle. Frankly, I haven't quite managed it, either." His words were throwaway. With a change in tone, he was quickly back to business, but he had stirred Victoria's curiosity. I want to know more about this cryptic, contradictory man, she acknowledged silently. But he obviously doesn't want to talk about himself.

"How can I help you, Victoria?" he asked in his professional, take-charge voice.

She told him sketchily about her strict upbringing, her whirlwind romance with Rick Lancer and the child Rick still didn't know about—the baby she had carried and loved but never held, the child who belonged to strangers now.

"Did you consider keeping your baby?" Phillip wondered.

"No," Victoria replied without hesitation. Then she relented. "Of course I did. Every day of my pregnancy. It was all I could think about. I wanted my son more than I've ever wanted anything in my life. But it was out of the question. My life was already predetermined—my education, my career. My parents had everything planned. There was no room for a mistake, especially not one resulting in an illegitimate child."

He eyed her curiously. "Are you bitter about that?"

She shrugged. "I don't know. I suppose on some level I am, but I remind myself that my parents had my best interests at heart."

"Did they?"

"I like to believe they did. At the time I felt too overwhelmed to go against their wishes. And my father was ill. He needed me. So I did the only thing I could do."

"You gave away your child."

"It was the hardest thing I ever had to do. I regretted it the moment I signed the papers."

"And now? Do you still regret it?"

"Now it's too late. It doesn't matter how I feel. What's done is done. I'll never know what might have been."

Phillip sat forward, his elbows resting on the table, his fingers interlocked. "Yet, now you want to find your child. After six years, you want to intrude yourself on his life."

"Is that what you think I'm doing?"

"Isn't it? Your son has his own life now—parents, a home, a future that has nothing to do with you. Are you prepared to interrupt all that and change the course of your son's life?"

"That's not what I want, Phillip. I don't intend to hurt my son. I just want to know how he is. I need to see him, just once."

Phillip poured more tea. "Have you considered the consequences?"

"What do you mean?"

"I mean, the unpredictable events you may set in motion, the problems you could cause your son and his adoptive family?"

Victoria's voice was tremulous. Was she hearing right? "Are you saying you won't help me?"

"I'm saying I want you to think this through very carefully, Victoria. Do what's right and best for your son."

She stiffened, her defenses flaring. Was she wrong to think she had found a friend in this man? Obviously he had no intention of helping her. "Do you talk this way to all your clients, Phillip?" she asked coolly.

"You bet. And if I believe the child isn't a client's first concern, I don't take the case." He paused while the waiter served their Peking duck. They helped themselves to several slices of the crisp, golden meat. "You know, Victoria," he continued between bites, "there are a lot of distraught people out there who want to use their children as pawns or weapons against their mates. I refuse any part in such cases."

"My case isn't like that at all!" she protested. This wasn't going the way she intended. She never should have come. Maybe she should just get up and leave and forget she'd ever met Phillip Anders.

"I know your case isn't the same," Phillip assured her. "But I can't help wondering whether your emotions aren't clouding your judgment."

"My emotions?" She stared incredulously at him. How ironic that he would accuse her of letting her emotions cloud her judgment when she had lived a life so devoid of emotion-based decisions.

"What I'm saying, Victoria, is that perhaps the best gift you could give your son is to stay out of his life."

She was trembling now. "You don't understand, Phillip. I'm not going to tell my son who I am, nor do I intend to alarm his parents. I just want to see my child from a distance. I want to know he's well and safe.''

Phillip nodded soberly; he still wasn't ready to concede his argument. "I must warn you, Victoria. You may have to go through an awful lot of trouble for that one distant glimpse.''

She lowered her gaze. "There's more, Phillip,'' she said quietly. Talking about something as private and personal as her faith wasn't easy, but it had to be done. "Three years ago I made a commitment. I don't know quite how to explain it to you, but I put my faith in Christ.'' Her eyes met his. "Since then, I've felt a deep burden for my son, for his eternal destiny. I'm not trying to sound like some religious zealot, but what if no one ever tells him how to find God?''

Phillip studied her for a long moment. He seemed to be weighing his response. Finally he said, "I made that same commitment some years ago, Victoria, before I was married. Pauline was a Christian, too, although I must admit my own faith is rather rusty these days.''

"Then, being a believer, you must understand my concern for my son.''

"I understand, but I don't necessarily agree. Can't you trust your son to God's care and get on with your own life?''

"You don't think I have a right to find out about his spiritual upbringing?''

Phillip heaved a disgruntled sigh, as if he knew what he was about to say would get him into hot water. "Okay, Victoria, let me put it on the line. I think you've got other motivations going on inside that you're not even aware of, but it feels safe to put it all under a spiritual umbrella.''

She bristled. "Are you suggesting I'm not being honest with you about my motives for finding my child?''

"Maybe you're not being honest with yourself,'' said Phillip.

She reached for her purse. "If you won't help me, Mr. Anders, I'm sure there are other detectives who will.''

"Wait, Victoria.'' He reached across the table and seized her hand. His touch sent a warm ripple of pleasure through her, touching off pinwheels of emotion she hadn't experienced since she was in Rick Lancer's arms. For a long moment neither of them spoke. It was as if they had connected on a new, unexplored level that neither had anticipated, and neither of them knew where to go with it from here. At last he released her and her heart rate slowly returned to normal.

"I didn't say I wouldn't help," he told her solemnly. He looked as shaken as she felt.

"But you said..."

He averted his gaze and picked absently at his Peking duck, as if he weren't ready yet to say more. After a moment he looked up at her, his eyes crinkling wryly. "What I'm trying to say, Victoria, is that I never take a case I can talk a client out of. The road ahead is too tough for the weak-willed or faint of heart."

"Are you saying...you will take my case?"

"I'm saying you'll have to search your motives as we go along and make sure your head is on straight, okay? Do a whole lot of soul-searching. And then, if you're willing to put yourself in my hands and trust my judgment—"

"Oh, I will. I do!"

"Even then," he cautioned, "I can't guarantee a happy ending."

"I don't ask for any guarantees, Phillip," she assured him. "Just help me find my son, and I'll do whatever you say."

"Then I guess we've got ourselves a deal. I'm your man." He shook her hand vigorously and once again their eyes locked with a riveting intensity. Goose bumps prickled her skin. She was excited, of course, about finding the son she had never known, but if she would admit it, she also felt a heady exhilaration at the prospect of spending time in the company of this remarkable man, Phillip Anders.

Chapter Four

Wednesday, May 6

I keep thinking about what Phillip said last night about my motives. What if I'm not being honest with myself? What if I'm just using my spiritual concerns about my son as an excuse to indulge my maternal yearnings?

What if I find my son and all I care about is getting him back? Am I opening a Pandora's box? Am I just inviting more heartache? Maybe Phillip's right. Maybe I should just trust my child to God and get on with my life.

But what life?

How can I go on with my life when such a big part of me is missing? When I walked away from my son six years ago, I thought that was as bad as it got; everything after that would be easier, and the pain would lessen with time. Instead, the emotional wound has festered and spread, infecting even the healthy parts of my life. I don't know how I could have survived these years without God's strength and comfort.

But now new concerns taunt me. What realities will I have to deal with when I find my child? What sort of life did I release him into six years ago? In my mind I've concocted a perfect world for my boy—loving parents, a happy home, a future any child would envy. I've consoled myself with the fantasy of an ideal life for my son. If I can't have him, at least he has the best of all possible worlds with his adoptive family.

But does he?

Surely reality can never match my dreams.

Will I be able to accept a less-than-perfect situation for my child? If the life he's living now is less than what I could have provided, then what was my sacrifice for?

Dear God, I'm so afraid of what I'll find, of how I'll feel. What if this all blows up in my face and my life is more messed up after I find him than it is now?

What if I find him and I can't let go? Will I become one of those crazy, obsessed women who won't stop until they've destroyed their child's life?

To be honest, I don't know what my motives are. Yes, I want to be sure someone tells my boy about God. I want someone to be there to answer his questions and point him to faith in Christ. I admit, I would give my life to be that person. But I know how improbable that hope is. So I will be satisfied just to know that someone will be there to help him find the answers.

It's still not real to me what I'm doing. Looking for my son. Starting the process in motion. My baby! Only not a baby now. A little boy. Six already. Will I know him? What will he look like? Will I feel that connection I felt when he was in the womb and we played our silly little bumping games?

The questions bombard my mind. Will I be able to transfer the love I feel for this fanciful child of my imagination to my real flesh-and-blood son? Or will he be a stranger to me? Surely I will feel a mother's love for him. If only he could feel a son's love for me!

When I let myself think about it—all the possibilities—my excitement bubbles up and spills over and colors everything I do, every waking hour. No matter how many doubts and anxieties—and yes, at times, stark terror!—I feel, still, my overriding emotion is pure joy. To think that I may actually, on this earth in this lifetime, lay eyes again on my child. Perhaps even hear the sound of his voice. I can ask for no greater gift.

But for now I must play this waiting game, waiting for Phillip to call with news, waiting, praying. How long will it take? Dear God, please don't make me wait too long!

* * *

The following Tuesday Phillip telephoned Victoria and said, "I have some information. When can I see you?"

Her pulse quickened. This was the call she'd been rehearsing in her mind for days. "You found my son?"

"I'd rather discuss it with you in person. Are you free now?"

"Yes, of course. I'm just grading final exams."

"I'll be there in a half hour."

Victoria found waiting for Phillip an excruciating exercise in patience. She touched up her makeup and ran a comb through her hair. She straightened her tiny living room, replacing the stack of test papers on the coffee table with a bowl of fresh fruit. She returned several partially read books to the large oak bookcase. As she busied herself with incidentals, she sensed she was running purely on nervous energy.

When Phillip finally arrived, Victoria greeted him with clammy, trembling hands. Her mouth was dry; her throat ached. "I haven't felt so anxious since my student teaching days," she told him as he took the velvet wing chair she offered. "I feel almost as if you're giving me back my son."

"Not so fast," said Phillip. "I told you before, a search like this is likely to have its ups and downs."

Victoria sat on the sofa across from Phillip. She clasped her hands to keep them from shaking. "What are you trying to say, Phillip? Is it bad news?"

The tendons in his neck tightened; his eyes took on a shadowed, thoughtful expression.

"Please, Phillip, tell me. I've got to know."

He sat back, his muscular frame filling the lime green chair. "Your son was adopted by a couple in their mid-twenties named Frank and Julia Goodwin."

She pressed her fingertips against her lips. "You already know their names—the couple who adopted him? Oh, Phillip, I think I'm going to cry. Tell me all you know about them."

"Not a great deal, I'm afraid. They lived in a small town in Oregon, not far from where your baby was born."

"Lived? They aren't there now?"

"No." Phillip's brow furrowed. "There was an accident, Victoria. Over six months ago."

"An accident?" She sat forward, her muscles suddenly tense.

"A car crash," said Phillip.

Her pulse quickened with alarm. "Oh, no! Phillip, don't tell me—!"

His deep voice was somber, almost a monotone. "Frank and Julia Goodwin were both killed."

Victoria's breath caught. Dear God, she didn't want to know, and had to know, but how could she cope? To find her child and have him immediately snatched away? She couldn't stand it if—please, God, don't let it be! "And my son?" she barely whispered.

"He survived," said Phillip quickly. "He was injured, but my sources indicate that he recovered."

Relief radiated through her body. She sank back, every muscle like jelly. "Where is my baby now?"

Phillip removed a slim notebook from his vest pocket. He thumbed through several pages. "Your son was released into the custody of his maternal grandparents—Julia's parents—Maude and Sam Hewlett. They live in Middleton, a farming community north of San Francisco."

"San Francisco?" Victoria repeated carefully. "That's not far. Maybe half a day's drive."

"No, it's not bad," Phillip agreed. "The boy could have been in some remote city halfway around the world."

"Middleton, you said? North of San Francisco? All right, wonderful. That's where I'll go to find my son." Impulsively she added, "Would you like to go with me, Phillip?"

"Hold on," he said, reaching over and touching her hand, a cautionary gesture. "There's more, Victoria."

"Bad news?" she asked with apprehension. She didn't want to hear anything that would dampen her spirits. She knew now where her son lived. What more did she need to know?

"Not exactly bad news," said Phillip. "It's more puzzling than anything."

"What do you mean?"

"I had a colleague of mine from San Francisco check your son's neighborhood and the local school system for some record of the boy. So far he hasn't been able to uncover any evidence of your son's existence."

Victoria shook her head, baffled. "Wait a minute, you're confusing me. No record of his existence? How can that be?"

"I don't know. I'm just telling you what we've found."

"My son is six years old now. He should be in first grade, or at least kindergarten."

"I agree. But there's no record that a Joshua Goodwin or a Joshua Hewlett was ever enrolled in any public or private school in the area."

Victoria's heart stopped in mid-beat. "Joshua, you say? That's my son's name?"

Phillip nodded.

"Joshua." She repeated the name several times, marveling. "Joshua. It sounds strange and wonderful all at once." Tears welled in her eyes and spilled over. "I always wondered what he was called, my son, what name he answered to. Joshua. I like it. Don't you, Phillip? It's a good, strong name. A biblical name. If I recall correctly, it means 'Jehovah is salvation.'"

Phillip sat forward and rubbed his hands together methodically, as if marking time until her emotional outburst subsided. At last he cleared his throat and said, "Unfortunately, Victoria, it's a name we can't trace past the accident that killed his parents."

Victoria looked back in stunned silence, trying to make sense of Phillip's words. "That can't be," she said, shaking her head. "Surely you've missed something, some clue. Have you checked with his grandparents?"

"No, not yet. That could be a ticklish situation, especially since we don't want them to know Joshua's natural mother is looking for him."

"You think there could be trouble?"

"It's happened before."

"Have you talked to the Hewletts' neighbors?" She tried to keep her voice under control, but couldn't help hearing the nervous, urgent edge as she questioned Phillip.

"My colleague contacted every house on the block," he replied. "No one has ever seen the youngster."

Victoria's voice rose with a shrill desperation. "But that's impossible. Little boys play outside. They have friends. Surely someone has seen him."

"No one," said Phillip. "Everyone says the Hewletts are very private people. Not much is known about them. But all the neighbors agreed on one point. The Hewletts live alone."

Victoria stood and walked to the window, hugging herself protectively. She felt a chill inside, like a clammy hand crushing her heart, making it hard to breathe. "Something's wrong, Phillip. Something's terribly wrong."

He joined her at the window and placed a sympathetic hand on her shoulder. "That's the way I read it, too, Victoria."

She turned to face him, tears wetting her cheeks. "I'm scared, Phillip."

Impulsively he drew her into his arms and gently stroked her back, a friend offering comfort. He whispered against her hair, "It'll be all right, Victoria. I promise."

Hearing him say those words, she believed him, as if he truly could make everything right for her—this man of such strength, integrity and sensitivity. She wanted to stay in the warmth of his arms and savor his consolation; she had never felt so safe before. But as he held her she sensed the stirring of something more between them, not just comfort, but a physical attraction. It was the same delicious rush of adrenaline she had felt with Rick Lancer, only better, for she had always been on her guard with Rick. In Phillip's arms she felt almost as if she were home where she belonged.

She lifted her face to his and for an instant she thought he might kiss her; but even as his lips parted, he released her and stepped back abruptly. "I'm sorry, Victoria. I didn't mean to— I promise, that won't happen again."

She brushed back a stray lock of her burnished hair. She felt flustered, breathless...and disappointed. "Don't apologize, Phillip, please. I'm sure you were just trying to calm a distraught client." She laughed feebly. "I suppose it's all part of the job description, isn't it?"

"Not until today," he murmured, smoothing his hair back and straightening his jacket.

It was obvious they both felt at a loss for words, so she said with forced lightness, "What are we going to do, Phillip?"

His brows arched quizzically. "Do?"

"About my case."

"I knew that," he said with a sheepish smile. When he spoke again he was all business. "I think we'll have to confront the Hewletts and see what they have to say."

"*We?*"

"I thought you might want to drive down the coast with me and meet them for yourself."

"Do you think that's wise?"

"We have no other leads. And frankly, I think the situation warrants a face-to-face meeting with your son's grandparents."

"When should we go?"

"I'm free next weekend."

"All right. That works out well for me, too. The school term is over. I'll be finished with my duties at the university and have my grades turned in by then." She paused and searched Phillip's eyes. "What will we say to the Hewletts?"

He shrugged. "Let's see what happens when we get there."

She nodded, then patted Phillip's arm in a gesture of camaraderie. As anxious as she felt about her son, she was grateful that God had sent her a man like Phillip, a man she sensed she could trust to help her with her quest. She gave him a pleased, slightly abashed smile and said, "I just realized you've been here an hour and I haven't even offered you a cup of coffee."

He grinned and squeezed her hand, the warmth of his touch as pleasurable as a kiss. "Thank you, my lady. I thought you'd never ask."

Chapter Five

Early Saturday morning, Phillip and Victoria drove down the coast to Middleton through a slanting, presummer rain. After lunch at a local pancake house, they drove to the Hewletts' home on Blackberry Street. As Phillip pulled up beside the shingled, Victorian-style house, Victoria emitted an exclamation of dismay. "Oh, Phillip, it looks like one of those frightful haunted houses from a horror movie!"

The rambling, slate gray house sat back from the street on a steep, grassy incline. Beveled crystal windows, dark green shutters and gingerbread-gothic trim gave it a remote, turn-of-the-century aura. Even in the mid-afternoon sunlight, it seemed to possess a life of its own, an ominous presence that tightened a knot of foreboding in Victoria's stomach.

"Can you believe it, Phillip? To think that this is the home of my child's grandparents!"

"Not the most inviting place I've ever seen, but no use sitting here letting our imaginations run wild." He pulled the door handle. "Guess we'd better go up to the house and see what's waiting for us inside."

"Wait," said Victoria. "Both of us going may arouse suspicion. Maybe I should go alone."

"Do you think you can handle it?"

"I've got to, for Joshua's sake."

"Are you going to tell them who you are?"

"I don't know. Right now I just want to meet them and see if I can find out something about my son."

"They may not take well to a prying stranger."

"I won't pry. I'll be very subtle."

Phillip took her hand and held it for a long moment, his eyes searching hers with a mixture of concern and admiration. "You're quite a courageous young lady, you know that?"

She flashed a grateful smile. "You really think so?"

"I know so."

"I've never considered myself a brave person," she admitted. "It must be my maternal instincts taking hold. I need to protect my son, whatever the cost."

He squeezed her hand. "You know I'm in your corner, Victoria."

She nodded, a pleasant warmth flushing her cheeks. "You don't know how much that means to me, Phillip. You're the one who's given me the courage to look for my son."

With obvious reluctance he released her hand. "But if you're not back here in ten minutes, my brave lady, I'll come looking for you."

"Pray for me," she murmured as she slipped out of the car.

"My prayers haven't got past the ceiling lately, Victoria," he called after her.

She looked back at him. "Pray, anyway. My knees are knocking."

As she approached the massive door with its arched windows and frosted-glass panes, Victoria noticed a small, hand-lettered sign tucked in the molding: Room For Rent. An idea formed as she knocked soundly. A full minute passed before she heard a scuffling sound inside. As the door swung open, a large-boned woman in a flowered, ill-fitting housedress glared out at her.

"Yeah?" the woman grunted, her shrewd, hazel eyes narrowing. Her brows were thick and unattended; her white, wispy hair was pulled back tightly from her full-lobed ears.

Victoria squared her shoulders and drew in a sharp breath. "Hello," she said with a buoyancy she didn't feel. "I—I'm Victoria Carlin—"

"So?" the woman interrupted. She stepped back, a beefy hand on her hip as she gazed appraisingly at Victoria. She had a long horse face with sagging cheeks and a rippling neck. "You selling something?"

"No," Victoria said quickly. "I—I saw your sign about the room for rent."

The woman's thin lips twisted into a smile. "You're looking for a room? Why didn't you say so?"

Victoria chose her words carefully. "I'm very interested in finding just the right place."

"Well, I'll tell you right up front I'm very particular," said the woman. "I just put the sign up a few days ago, and I already turned down a couple of drifters. I don't take kindly to strangers in my house, but with times so bad and the pittance we get from Social Security—well, a body has to pay the bills somehow, and my Sam can't work anymore with his lame back."

"I know how it is," said Victoria with genuine sympathy. "It's very hard to make ends meet these days."

"And getting harder all the time," said Maude. "Anyways, you look like a decent sort. Come on in." She held out her hand. "I'm Maude Hewlett."

Victoria shook the woman's hand, then followed her into the dimly lit living room with its antique cherry wood furniture. The heavy drapes were closed, and the flower-print walls were cluttered with primitive paintings and knickknack shelves. Scattered randomly were several artificial plants and wicker baskets overflowing with yarn.

"The room is fifty dollars a week," said Maude. "Twenty more for meals. I want references and a month's rent in advance."

"I'm really not sure I..." Victoria began. She looked around, flustered. The television set was on, distracting her—a game show blaring with overeager contestants laughing, clapping, shrieking.

Victoria's gaze moved to a framed photograph on top of the TV—a large picture of a young woman and child, their heads together, smiling, the boy's arms wrapped adoringly around the woman's neck. Something in the child's face clicked in Victoria's memory—the recollection of a photo of herself at age five. The same curly red hair, freckled cheeks and laughing eyes. My son! she thought with a sudden swell of emotion. She felt tears gathering, rimming her eyes. She knew she was staring, but she couldn't pull her gaze away. She wanted desperately to reach out and touch the picture, pick it up, caress it, but she sensed she was raising Maude's suspicions, so she glanced away before the woman saw her face.

But Maude Hewlett had already followed Victoria's gaze. "That's my daughter and grandson," she said matter-of-factly.

"It's a lovely portrait," Victoria managed to say.

"They're both dead," Maude continued in her detached monotone.

Victoria stared incredulously at her. She felt as if the woman had struck her with a two-by-four. "*Both* dead?"

"A car accident six months ago." Maude's mouth contorted slightly. Her expression hardened as if she were defying Victoria to pity her. She turned abruptly toward the hallway. "You wanna see the room now?"

Victoria clutched the back of a chair. She felt faint; her mind was reeling. Surely it wasn't true. Her son couldn't be dead. Oh, God, please, no! Not after I've come so close to finding him!

"You coming or not?" inquired Maude sharply.

With great effort Victoria found her voice. "Yes, I—I'm coming."

The room was small but pleasant enough, with chintz curtains, a polished oak floor with rag rugs and a patchwork quilt on the bed. The dresser mirror was dim with age, the wallpaper yellow and peeling in spots around the mahogany cornices.

"How long you planning to stay, Miss Carlin?" queried Maude.

"I don't know," Victoria replied distractedly. How could she carry on a rational conversation when her mind registered only one appalling thought—her son could be dead! Somehow, God help her, she had to convey a semblance of normalcy. "I—I'll be staying just for the summer," she said with forced brightness. "I teach up north at a state university. I'm working on my doctorate in contemporary American literature. I need a place with lots of peace and quiet to write my thesis."

"This is the place," said Maude. "I don't like lots of people coming and going. My husband and I keep to ourselves. We don't mind nobody else's business and they don't mind ours."

"That sounds fair enough," said Victoria. She inhaled sharply, gathering her courage. "I'll take the room, Mrs. Hewlett."

"All right. If your references check out, you can move in first of the week."

When Victoria finally left the Hewlett home and climbed back into Phillip's waiting automobile, she felt stunned, emotionally drained. She was trembling and her legs were unsteady. She had held back her feelings with such fierce resolve that now the dam of tears threatened to break. She collapsed into the seat beside Phillip and covered her face with her hands. The anguish tore from her throat in dry, racking sobs.

For an instant Phillip stared helplessly at her, then instinctively he gathered her into his arms. "Victoria, talk to me. Are you okay? What happened?"

She swallowed her sobs and pulled away from him. "I can't talk yet. Just go. Drive. Get out of here."

Phillip started the car, merged with late-afternoon traffic and drove in silence for several miles, the pulse in his jaw throbbing with tension. Finally he pulled off at a rest stop and parked. "We've got to talk, Victoria," he said, swiveling in the seat to face her. "You were gone so long, I was about to come in after you. I never should have let you go in there alone."

She found a tissue in her purse and blew her nose. "No, Phillip, I had to do it. I—I just didn't know how hard it would be."

He slapped his palm against the steering wheel. "I let you down. I'm sorry. I've seen enough in this business to know when things aren't what they should be. I was a jerk sending a woman in to do a man's job."

"No, Phillip, you did the right thing."

He grimaced. "Do you feel like talking now? Can you tell me what you found out?"

Her tears started again. "Mrs. Hewlett—she told me—oh, Phillip, she said my son is dead!"

He slipped his arm around her shoulders and gently massaged the back of her neck. "She came right out and said it?" he asked with a catch in his voice. "You mean, she knew you were Joshua's mother? How could she—?"

"No, she didn't know. But I saw a picture of Joshua, and Mrs. Hewlett noticed me looking at it. Out of the blue she came right out and told me about the accident. She said her grandson died in the crash."

"To tell a complete stranger such a thing—that's strange."

"She seemed like a strange woman. But she was fairly blunt about everything," Victoria told him. "Phillip, is it possible your sources made a mistake? Do you suppose my son really is dead?"

"It's possible, Victoria, but not likely. My gut feeling is that the Hewletts are hiding something."

"I have that feeling, too," she said, finally regaining a measure of composure. "That's why I took the room, Phillip."

He stopped rubbing her neck. "You did what?"

"There was a room-for-rent sign on the door. It seemed like the perfect excuse for my being there. Then when Mrs. Hewlett told me

Joshua was dead, I knew I had to stay. I have to find out what happened to my son, Phillip."

"That's *my* job, Victoria." His expression took on a stony grimness. "There are a lot of crazies in this world. I'm prepared to handle them. You're not."

"What are you saying, Phillip?"

"I'm saying I want you to telephone Mrs. Hewlett and tell her you've changed your mind about the room."

"I can't. I won't."

"You must," Phillip said levelly. "I'll continue the investigation. I'll keep you apprised of every detail. But I can't let you get personally involved like this."

"I'm already involved," she protested. "I won't give up the room. Don't you understand, Phillip? The Hewletts are my only link with my son. I've got to find out what they're hiding, no matter what it costs."

"It could cost you everything," he warned, his tone edgy, almost accusing. With a nervous energy he drummed his fingertips along her neck to her shoulder. Then he pulled her against him and pressed her head against his. Neither of them spoke for a long time. His breathing was ragged; perhaps hers was, too—she couldn't tell. She could smell the spicy fragrance of his after-shave and the tangy, masculine aroma of his skin. His chin was already showing the faint stubble of a five-o'clock shadow.

He was holding her almost too tight, but it wasn't a romantic embrace; it was as if he wanted desperately to protect her but wasn't sure he could. "I won't risk losing you," he said at last, his voice raw with feeling.

She didn't reply, didn't ask what he meant by such a cryptic statement, but she understood now that a powerful connection was growing between them that went beyond their professional relationship. Perhaps even beyond friendship.

Chapter Six

Monday, May 18, 2:00 p.m.

Believe it or not, I'm packed and ready for the drive to Middleton—ready outwardly, but inside I'm filled with doubts, terrified of facing Mrs. Hewlett again. I keep wondering what horrible secrets she's keeping. And what if she guesses the truth about me? Could I make matters worse for Joshua by blundering into his life like this, by playing this bizarre charade?

I've always been such a cautious person, conscientious to a fault, never stepping outside my boundaries, never testing the limits, except once, of course, with Rick Lancer—and look at the trouble that got me into! But I can't compare this situation with that one. I'm doing what I have to do to find my son. I must keep reminding myself of that. I can't rest until I know what happened to him.

The thought that he might be dead haunts me. What kind of mother was I to let him go without knowing what kind of life he would have and what kind of people would raise him? How could I have trusted others so completely to do what was best for my son? And how could I have had so little faith in my own ability—and right—to care for him?

Not that I have great reserves of faith in myself even now. When my parents were alive my life was so simple and straightforward. I tried relentlessly to be their obedient daughter, to make them proud of me; and even though I often failed, I was consumed with trying.

Now that I'm alone, my life is in chaos. I don't know who to try to please, except God—and all too often He has my father's voice, so that I can't distinguish between the two; I can't tell what God wants for me and what my father would have wanted. I don't want to hear my father's voice anymore, but it's there; I can't get it out of my head.

I know I ought to think about pleasing myself for a change, but even that idea is distressing, because I don't know what I want. I've spent too many years denying my desires. I want my son, but I have no idea where my search for him will lead me, nor what it will cost— not in dollars, but the emotional drain.

And to complicate matters even further, there's Phillip. Without meaning to, he's turned my life upside down and thrown my mind into the worst sort of turmoil and confusion. Even as I value his help and friendship, I find myself longing for more from him—yearning for him to see me as a woman, to cherish and caress me and make me feel loved. And at the same time, the idea of a romantic relationship strikes terror in my heart. In the very same breath I want to pull him close and push him away. How can I give my love to another man after what Rick Lancer did to me? How can I trust him? Or myself?

Even though I'm filled with doubts, I can't let Phillip see my misgivings, or he'd never let me drive to Middleton alone. When he comes to say goodbye this afternoon, I must put on a brave, smiling face and pretend that I have every confidence in the world.

Dear God, help me to put my confidence in You!

"I still don't like you going," Phillip told Victoria shortly after four o'clock as he carried her suitcases out to her car. "It's just too risky."

Victoria followed with her pillow, makeup case and a sack of crackers and cheese. "Really, Phillip, you're thinking like a detective now. What risk is there in spending a few weeks with an elderly couple who just happen to be my son's grandparents?" Now if only she felt as brave as she sounded! She prayed Phillip wouldn't see through her bravado; if he guessed how frightened she was, he'd never let her go.

"It's not that simple and you know it," he told her, his dark umber eyes shadowed as he looked at her.

Victoria felt warmed by his concern. If only he were going with her! She had known him for such a short time and already she felt lost without him. "I'll be fine, Phillip, believe me," she assured him. And if he believed that, she was a better actress than she thought. "I'll keep in touch, I promise. And if I find out anything at all, I'll let you know."

He pulled her into his arms. "I—I can't let you go."

Softly she said, "You can't stop me, Phillip."

His brows furrowed. "I wish I could go with you."

"You can't. You have your work. I'm sure you have lots of other clients needing your help."

"You're the only client on my mind right now." He pushed her hair back gently from her face and moved his knuckles slowly over her cheekbone. He lowered his face to hers and she had the impression that he wanted to kiss her goodbye, but instead he brushed his lips against her forehead and released her. "Be careful, you hear?"

She managed a tremulous smile. "I will."

He squeezed her hand tightly as she slipped into the driver's seat. "Call me when you get there."

"It'll be late," she warned.

"That's all right. I'm a night owl at heart."

As she waved a last goodbye and pulled out of the driveway, she felt a disconcerting reluctance to go. She dreaded the long drive down the coast alone, but even more so she hated leaving Phillip.

"I can't let myself feel this way," she chided herself as she turned onto the freeway heading south. "My involvement with Phillip was supposed to remain strictly professional. All right, who am I kidding? We've become friends, but that's all it's going to be. Neither Phillip nor I are ready for an emotional entanglement. It's the last thing either of us wants."

She sounded so certain, so positive. Why then wasn't her heart listening?

The drive down the coast was longer than Victoria remembered. It had seemed so short last Saturday riding with Phillip. They had been so engrossed in conversation that the miles had flown by. Now the miles dragged with a dull, grudging sameness.

The closer Victoria got to Middleton, the more her son weighed on her mind. Would she be able to solve the mystery of Joshua?

Would she find him? And what would she find? Dear God, please let me find my boy, and please let him be all right. Let him be alive! Give me a chance to see him, and know him, and love him!

When at last Victoria pulled into the Hewlett driveway on Blackberry Street, her head throbbed and her back ached. Was it the long drive or the anticipation of her stay with the Hewletts? In the heavy, fog-shrouded darkness, the rambling old house looked more ominous than ever. Victoria shuddered. If Phillip were with me, I wouldn't be afraid, she thought, and immediately cast the idea aside. Forget Phillip, she scolded silently.

As she climbed out of the car, she arched her shoulders, then strode purposefully up the walk to the porch. Lights were on inside, so someone was home. She knocked soundly, her heart pounding. It was ridiculous to feel so nervous. There was nothing to fear. She had come to find the answers about her son. Nothing else mattered now.

After a minute the door opened and a tall, angular man in glasses and a striped work shirt stared down at her. He was bald except for a patch of gray-black hair on each side of his head. His long, thin, hangdog face merged unceremoniously with his neck. "Miss Clarkin?" he muttered.

"Carlin," she corrected.

"In your letter you said you was arriving today. I didn't expect you meant after dark."

"It was a longer drive than I remembered." She looked past him into the living room. "May I come in?"

He stepped back slowly and nodded, but his small, dark eyes remained fastened on her through his thick lenses. "Make yourself at home." His voice was monotone.

"You must be—" she began.

"Sam Hewlett." He looked over at the heavyset woman in the kitchen doorway. "You already met Maude."

Victoria nodded and forced a smile. "It's good to see you again, Mrs. Hewlett."

"You missed dinner," snapped the woman. "It's at six sharp. I can't keep things sitting, getting cold."

"I picked up a bite on my way," Victoria told her. "I'm really very tired. I'd just like to bring my things in and go to my room."

Maude's expression softened. "It's too late for dinner, but I got some herb tea brewing. It's called Almond Pleasure. Smells real good, don't it?"

Victoria smiled relentingly. "It smells wonderful."

Maude gestured to Sam. "You go help her bring in her stuff. I'll pour the tea and set out some glazed doughnuts."

With Sam's help, Victoria quickly transferred her belongings from her compact car to the old-fashioned bedroom that would be hers. Now, sitting across from the Hewletts in their cozy, Early American kitchen, Victoria wondered why she had felt so nervous. Although the Hewletts were rather gruff, unschooled people, they seemed like decent, unpretentious folk. Perhaps it had been nothing more than Victoria's overactive imagination that had aroused her suspicions about them in the first place.

"You want another doughnut, Miss Carlin?" asked Maude.

"No, thank you," said Victoria. "But I will have more tea. It's delicious."

"It's just tea bags I get at the grocery. They got all kinds of fancy stuff these days."

Sam sat back and rubbed his large hand over the fine network of bluish veins in his forehead. The pouches under his eyes puffed slightly as he worked his mouth into a curious grin. "You an authoress, Miss Clarkin? The wife says you came here to write a book or something."

"Not exactly a book," said Victoria. "I'm a university instructor in American literature. I'm working on my doctoral thesis."

"That sounds pretty highfalutin to me," he replied. "What you writing about?"

Victoria hesitated. Should she tell him or get by with an evasive answer? "I'm doing a comparison study," she said.

"Whatcha comparing?"

"The lives and works of Flannery O'Connor and Sylvia Plath."

"Never heard of them," he scoffed.

"They were American writers who died in the early sixties," she explained patiently.

"So why bother about them?"

She felt as if she were back in her lecture hall at the university. "They both wrote intensely and perceptively about the dark side of human emotion."

"The dark side?" Maude echoed suspiciously. "Sounds like devil talk to me."

Victoria shrugged. "I suppose you could put it that way. Both women explored the dark, disturbed or evil side of human nature. I want to demonstrate how their God-consciousness, or, in one case, lack of it, influenced their lives and work.''

''God-consciousness?'' Sam grunted, as if she had said something stupid.

''Yes,'' replied Victoria, wishing she hadn't pursued this very personal subject of her thesis with the Hewletts. Her thoughts and ideas were still in an embryonic stage, fragile, vulnerable. She didn't want to damage them by exposing them to the Hewletts' scorn or contempt. Still, she had begun this conversation; she might as well finish it. ''O'Connor embraced God heartily,'' she explained, ''and her faith shows in her work just as it showed in her life. In spite of a long, debilitating illness, O'Connor managed to achieve a fulfilled, abundant life.''

''So?'' snapped Maude. ''What was she? Some saint? We all got our crosses to bear, you know.''

Victoria cleared her throat irritably and pressed on. ''Plath, on the other hand, desperately longed to believe in God, but ultimately she rejected Him. In spite of career success, marriage to a famous poet and two healthy children, Plath succumbed to despair and committed suicide when she was thirty.''

''That don't mean nothing,'' said Sam. ''Lots of people do that. What's your point?''

''My point is,'' persisted Victoria, quelling her exasperation, ''a person's God-consciousness affects and, in fact, determines his or her earthly and eternal destiny.'' She considered adding a word about Christ and redemption, but witnessing about her faith was still a new and terrifying prospect for Victoria. She had already said more than she intended. She didn't want to come across as a pious prude or a bookish, intellectual boor.

''It's all a lot of hogwash, if you ask me.'' Maude snorted. ''The way I see it, the devil's the one you gotta watch out for. I learned that at my mama's knee.''

Victoria managed a smile. She carefully pushed back her chair and said, ''I'm really tired. I think I'd better get to bed.''

Maude stood, too. ''Suit yourself, Miss Carlin. I'll show you the way.'' She led Victoria down the hall to her room and opened the door. ''Everything's ready. There's extra bedding in the closet. Sam plugged in an extension phone for you. Of course, you pay for any long-distance calls you make.'' She looked around as if trying to recall something else, then added, "The bathroom next door is yours. You get fresh towels and sheets twice a week."

Victoria gazed appreciatively around the neat, homespun room. How inviting the bed looked with its fluffy eiderdown quilt! "Thank you, Mrs. Hewlett. I'm sure I'll be very comfortable here."

Maude nodded. "You should be. It's a good, comfortable room. Belonged to my daughter when she lived at home." She stepped back out of the doorway. "I'll leave you be now. Breakfast is at seven sharp."

As soon as Victoria shut the door, she sank down on the bed with delicious relief and let her aching muscles relax. If she wasn't careful, she would fall asleep in her clothes. *I promised to call Phillip when I arrived,* she remembered suddenly. *He'll worry if he doesn't hear from me tonight.*

She sat up and reached for the phone on the night table. Phillip answered on the first ring. The sound of his voice sent a tickle of excitement through her. She missed him already. "Were you sitting on the phone?" she inquired lightly.

"Just about," he admitted. "Frankly, I was beginning to think I should have driven you, after all."

"I was beginning to wish that, too."

"The trip that bad?"

"That long."

"I'm sorry. I really would like to have been with you."

"Me, too. You have a way of making time pass more quickly."

"I'm not sure that's a compliment, but I'll take it as one." His voice lowered a notch as he asked, "Have you found out anything yet?"

"No, nothing. It's too soon. I had a rather interesting chat with the Hewletts tonight, but I'm afraid I did most of the talking."

"Is that wise?"

"Probably not. But they asked me about my thesis. Once I get going on that, I—"

"Victoria," Phillip interrupted.

"What is it?"

"That sound in the phone. Do you hear it? Sort of a hollow, airy echo."

"I hear you fine, Phillip."

There was a sudden click and the echo was gone.

"Someone was listening in, Victoria," said Phillip.

"You mean someone here...the Hewletts?" asked Victoria incredulously.

"You bet. We've got to watch what we say. If you have something to tell me, go to a pay phone somewhere."

"Are you saying the Hewletts suspect something?"

"Who knows? But we can't take a chance. Everything you do and say must be above suspicion. That's the only way I'll let you stay there."

"This was my decision, Phillip," she reminded him gently. "And I alone will decide when I leave."

"All right, Victoria," he replied coolly. "But let me remind you, this isn't a game you're playing. The stakes are very real. Your life could be in danger."

Phillip's warning played jarringly in Victoria's mind later as she slipped into bed and pulled the covers up around her neck. Even though her body was exhausted, she wasn't sure her mind would let her sleep. She argued silently with herself. Surely Phillip doesn't really believe my life is in danger. But how trustworthy are the Hewletts? They're an odd sort, but certainly they wouldn't harm me. Nor can I believe they would do anything to hurt their own grandchild. But then, where is Joshua? One thing for sure, he's nowhere in this house, or Maude never would have rented me this room. But why does she claim he's dead? Is he? she wondered. The idea was unbearable. After all these years, when Victoria had finally dared to reach out to her son...he couldn't be dead!

She thought about the photograph in the living room of Joshua with his adoptive mother. She traced his features in her mind—his soft red hair, his little impish smile, the darling freckles on his upturned nose. She imagined herself holding him in her arms the way the woman in the picture held him. Then a wrenching thought gripped her. Who was comforting Joshua now that his adoptive mother was dead? Who was wiping his tears?

Dear God, please—where on earth is my son?

Victoria found that more than her anxieties over Joshua kept her awake. Being in a strange, new place made sleeping difficult, too. She heard peculiar noises—water running through the pipes, the constant scritch-scratch of a tree limb on her window and the chill wind creaking through the weathered timber of the old house.

At last she fell into an uneasy slumber punctuated by garish dreams and heart-pounding nightmares. Shortly after midnight she woke with a start and looked around wildly. The room was dark except for the green glowing hands of the alarm clock. She had heard a sound, something more than the steady ticking of the clock. Lying still, her body tensed, she listened, waiting, scarcely breathing.

There was nothing but the rhythmic scratching of the branch on the windowpane.

Just as she was about to sink back into her dreams, Victoria heard the sound that had yanked her bolt upright out of sleep. An agonized, ear-splitting scream.

Victoria jumped out of bed and flung on her robe. She crept silently across the dark room. Trembling, she opened her bedroom door and peered out into the hall. Nothing but silence, darkness.

What do I do now? she wondered.

As she stood in the doorway, she heard the scuffling of slippers from the far end of the house. The hall light went on and Victoria blinked against the brightness as her eyes gradually focused on Maude Hewlett.

The robed woman scowled at Victoria and snapped, "What's the matter?"

"I—I heard something," said Victoria. "It sounded like a scream."

"Naw," grunted Maude. "It was them cats in the backyard. When they get going they sound like a bunch of banshees. Don't worry. I shooed them away."

"I see," said Victoria, hesitating.

"Go on back to sleep," Maude ordered.

Victoria slipped back into her room and shut the door. Even as she lay back down, she couldn't quell the alarm she felt. It wasn't a cat she had heard. The sound hadn't come from the backyard. The terrible, flesh-crawling scream had broken from somewhere in the very soul of the Hewlett house.

Chapter Seven

At breakfast Victoria waited to see whether the Hewletts would mention the scream she had heard last night. Neither Maude nor Sam said a word. Victoria decided not to bring up the subject, either. "Is the library near here?" she inquired as she finished her coffee.

"Coupla miles." Sam snorted. "On Pine Avenue, north of here."

"More scrambled eggs?" asked Maude, offering Victoria the bowl.

"No thanks," said Victoria. "But everything was delicious."

"You don't eat enough to keep a flea alive," scoffed Maude. "Our Julia was like that. Always on a diet. Always afraid of putting on a few pounds."

"You mean the girl in the photograph?" asked Victoria, perking up.

Maude nodded. "Yeah. Our daughter. I told you that before." She handed the bowl of eggs to Sam. "Here, you finish these. No sense them going to waste."

Victoria waited, hoping Maude would continue talking about her daughter. I need all the information I can get, she reflected, but I don't dare probe. Asking questions will only arouse suspicion. But if Sam and Maude are the closemouthed types they appear to be, how will I ever find out what happened to my son?

"You gonna go work on that book of yours?" queried Sam.

"What?" Victoria asked absently.

"The library—you going there to write your book?"

"My thesis? No, I'm still in the research stage. I need to check out books written by the two authors, plus whatever has been published about them by other writers."

"Sounds like a heap of work," said Sam, swallowing a mouthful of coffee.

"Yes, it is," Victoria agreed. "But I enjoy it." She stood and carefully replaced her chair. "I probably won't be back until early this evening."

"Dinner's at six sharp," Maude reminded her.

"I'll be here," said Victoria. She returned to her room for her briefcase and sweater. As she passed back through the living room, she paused. The Hewletts were still in the kitchen. Quietly she walked over to the television set and picked up the photograph of Julia and Joshua. With Maude always in the room, Victoria had given the picture only a cursory glance before. Alone now, she stared hard at the photo, hungrily memorizing every feature and angle of her son's soft, pliant face. He was beautiful, with dreamy, vulnerable eyes and a gentle, trusting expression. Unruly, reddish-blond hair fell over his forehead and curled around his ears just as Victoria's had done when she was a child. He had the same button nose, round, chipmunk cheeks and finely carved mouth she had at five. There was no doubt about it: This was her son.

Sudden tears filled her eyes and a painful lump formed in her throat. All of the unspoken yearnings of seven long years threatened to surface. Victoria blinked quickly and replaced the photograph, but not before her eye caught a glimpse of Maude in the kitchen doorway. The woman's expression was cold, cryptic, severe; her lips remained tightly pursed.

"I was just looking at your daughter's portrait," Victoria stammered as she moved awkwardly toward the door.

"Dinner's at six sharp," Maude answered, her tone unmistakably menacing.

Victoria was grateful for the vast anonymity of the public library. Here she could relax and be herself, without being on guard for every deed or word. For her, research was always an invigorating mental exercise. It did for her mind what she imagined jogging accomplished physically for Phillip, who had once mentioned he loved to run.

If Victoria admitted it, delving into the lives of Flannery O'Connor and Sylvia Plath gave her an opportunity to forget herself and her own problems. Their very different, difficult lives reminded Victoria she had no room for complaint about her own lot.

Victoria's hours of study passed quickly. At five she returned to the Hewlett home with an armload of books. Sam opened the door to her and whistled appraisingly. "You actually going to read all those, Miss Clarkin?"

"Victoria," she puffed. "Please call me Victoria."

"Long as you call me Sam."

"I'd be pleased to, Sam." She adjusted her load. "I'm going to put these in my room and freshen up a little. Then I'll help Mrs. Hewlett with dinner."

"Don't bother," said Sam. "She don't like no one else puttering in her kitchen. Just be at the table at six—"

"Sharp," Victoria finished with an amused smile.

Sam flashed a crooked grin. "You learn fast, girl." He followed her to her room and opened the door for her.

"Thanks." She sighed and closed the door behind her. She dropped her bundle of books on the dresser, then sank down wearily on her bed. Aloud she murmured, "Even if I never find my son, this little adventure is forcing me to dig into my thesis and get it done. Whatever happens, the summer won't be wasted."

She returned to the dresser, removed her pendant necklace and gently laid it in the velvet jewelry box her mother had given her. She looked again curiously. Her jewelry was in disarray. Was I in that much of a hurry this morning? she wondered. Usually I keep everything so neat.

An uneasy feeling crept over her. She opened her dresser drawers, one after another, surveying each one. Nothing seemed to be missing, but somehow she sensed that things weren't exactly as she had left them.

Someone's been in this room, she thought with a shudder. There's no lock on the door, no way of keeping the Hewletts out. But what were they looking for? And what did they find?

She thought suddenly of her journal. If they read that, they would know everything! She ran to her bed and reached under the mattress where she had tucked the journal after writing in it this morning. Thank heavens, it was still there—and she had remembered to lock it. She reached for her purse and checked her key chain. The key was still there. But from now on she would have to keep her journal with her. She tucked it into her roomy handbag.

By the time Victoria had showered and changed into a comfortable slacks outfit, she had nearly convinced herself that she was mistaken about someone searching her room. *My nerves are on edge and my imagination is playing havoc with me,* she decided as she took her place at the dinner table.

"You get a lot of work done?" Maude questioned as she set a platter of ham and fried potatoes on the table.

"Yes, I did," said Victoria. "Did you and Mr. Hewlett have a nice day?"

"Same as usual," said Maude, sitting down. "Sam fixed a broken shutter out back. I worked on my soap crafts and watched my game shows on TV."

"Are you retired, Mr. Hew—I mean, Sam?" Victoria asked politely.

"You bet. I worked nearly forty years for Brownlin Utensils on the east side of town. Retired three years ago. Since then I done some part-time work—carpentry, manual labor—till my back gave out this spring."

"He worked in that awful factory, same job all those years," Maude said bitterly. "He shoulda been a supervisor, a foreman, but no, he set back and let the young fellas snatch up all the promotions."

Sam cleared his throat irritably. "I was happy doing my job, Maude. I didn't wanna be no boss of nobody, making decisions about this or that. I liked things fine the way they was."

"No backbone, that was your trouble," she snapped. "You got the backbone of a jellyfish." Maude looked narrowly at Victoria. "You find yourself a man who can stand up for what he wants, not some spineless fella who lets everybody walk all over him."

"Miss Clarkin ain't interested in your opinion, Maude," snapped Sam. "Specially of me."

There was an uneasy silence until Victoria, grasping for a safe topic of conversation, said, "You mentioned doing soap crafts, Mrs. Hewlett. Just what are they?"

Maude brightened immediately. "Oh, you probably already seen them around the house—in your bathroom and on my knickknack shelves. They're bars of soap inside crocheted turtles and fish. I've made them for years. Sold a lot, too. The novelty shop downtown carries them for me. So does the little boutique up north, near our summer cabin. For years I've taken them a supply every time we go up there on vacation, haven't I, Sam?"

"Sure have. No one makes them things quite like Maude. They're pretty enough for rich folks' fancy houses."

"I'd like to see them," said Victoria. "Did you do all the paintings in your living room, too?"

Maude's complexion blanched. She looked away.

"No, our daughter, Julia, did them," replied Sam quickly. "She was the artist in the family. She could make anything look beautiful."

"She woulda been a famous artist if she'd lived," muttered Maude. "If that blasted drunk driver hadn't killed her. It was murder, plain and simple." She shook her head mournfully. "My beautiful little girl, gone just like that, no warning, nothing."

"It must have been terrible for you," murmured Victoria.

"I'll never get over it, never!" said Maude under her breath. "She had so much promise. She shoulda been the one to live."

"Didn't you say her husband was killed in the accident, too?" ventured Victoria.

"The whole family, wiped out in one fatal blow. Killed instantly. They never knew what hit them."

No, that isn't true! Victoria wanted to scream out. My son's alive! The hospital records showed that he survived. But she forced her voice to remain calm as she inquired, "Your grandson died, too?"

"They all died, that's what I said," replied Maude, her eyes narrowing. "Sam and I lost everything that mattered to us. It's been over six months, but it seems like yesterday."

"It'll always seem like yesterday," agreed Sam quietly.

"I blame it on the devil," declared Maude. "The devil and his devil water!"

"The fella that hit our Julia was soused on whiskey. Don't even remember what he did." Sam's voice cracked. "He walked away from the accident without so much as a scratch."

"It seems it always happens that way," observed Victoria, holding her emotions in check. She couldn't let the Hewletts see how shaken she was by talk of the accident. She poked idly at her potatoes. Somewhere during the course of their conversation, she had lost her appetite.

After dinner, in spite of Maude's protests, Victoria helped clear the table. As she returned the salt and pepper shakers to the pantry, Victoria spotted a basket of toys on the bottom shelf. Her heart skipped a beat as she realized they were undoubtedly Joshua's toys. She stooped down and examined them lovingly—miniature race cars, plastic building blocks, action figures and a worn brown teddy bear with a single button eye. Impulsively she picked up one of the little cars and tucked it into her pocket. I just want to hold it and look at it for a while, she told herself. It's something Joshua played with. I'll put it back later.

"What're you doing?" growled Maude. She was suddenly hovering over Victoria, her beefy hands on her enormous hips.

Victoria stood guiltily, her hand covering her pocket. "I just noticed the toys. I suppose they belonged to your grandson."

Maude promptly shut the pantry door. "They were Joshua's, all right. I never had the heart to get rid of them."

Victoria nodded. "I'd feel that way, too," she said softly. "It must make him seem nearer, having something special that belonged to him."

Maude looked thoughtful. "Yeah, I guess it does."

"I felt that way when my mother died this past year," said Victoria. "I felt better just having a few of her favorite possessions nearby—books, jewelry, photo albums."

For a moment there was the faintest hint of vulnerability in Maude's face, then the expression vanished. Maude's defenses resurrected themselves as she snapped, "You scoot outta here now. Let me finish my work."

"Very well," said Victoria. She hesitated. "I noticed a drugstore near here. I thought I'd drive over and pick up a few items. Do you need anything?"

"No, nothing." Maude snorted, turning her back to Victoria.

Victoria remembered a telephone booth just outside the drugstore. She went there first, praying as she dialed that Phillip would be home. She sighed in relief when she heard his deep, warm voice.

"Victoria? That you?" he asked in response to her hesitant hello. "You calling from the Hewletts'?"

"No, I'm at a pay phone. I just had to talk to you."

"Trouble?"

"No, not really. Oh, I don't know. There's nothing specific, but several things happened that bother me."

"I'm listening," he said seriously.

Victoria caught her breath as she gathered her thoughts. "Well, Phillip, first there was the scream last night."

"Scream? Who was it?"

"I don't know. Maude said it was just some cats howling out back, but I'd swear the sound came from somewhere inside the house."

"Can you describe it? Did it sound like someone being hurt?"

"I don't know, Phillip. It was like nothing I've ever heard before—human and yet not quite human. It wasn't the typical scream of someone hurt or afraid."

"What else happened?"

"This may sound silly and maybe I'm making too much out of it, but I found a basket of toys—Joshua's toys. It really threw me, seeing his playthings, as if he'd just left them there hours before. Maude said she never had the heart to give them away."

"I suppose that makes sense," said Phillip.

"Something else," said Victoria, "more ominous than the toys. I think the Hewletts went through my belongings today while I was gone. I can't prove it, but I had the feeling that things were just slightly out of place."

"Anything missing?"

"Nothing I'm aware of. But it gives me the creeps thinking of them pawing through my belongings. I don't know if they could have found anything incriminating or not. I've got my journal in my handbag, so they won't find it."

"Have they said anything to suggest they're suspicious of you?"

"Not exactly. But I sense them watching me closely—I suppose just as I'm watching them."

"Is there anything else?" Phillip queried.

"Just that the Hewletts still insist their grandson died in the automobile crash that killed his parents." Victoria paused. "Are you sure it couldn't be true, Phillip?"

"Positive," he replied. "I checked everything out again, more thoroughly than before, if possible. I reread the accounts in the newspaper morgue, checked the hospital files and the death certificates. The Hewletts' daughter and her husband were killed instantly. Unfortunately, they weren't wearing seat belts. But Joshua was in one of those child safety seats. He was treated for a head injury and released from the hospital ten days after the accident."

"Released to the Hewletts' custody?"

"Right. One interesting fact I did uncover—Joshua was scheduled to return to the hospital for a follow-up checkup. He never showed. The doctors have no medical record of him following his release from the hospital."

"That's not especially reassuring," said Victoria.

"But everything indicates that Joshua survived the accident. Now we just have to find out whether..." His voice trailed off.

"Whether he survived the Hewletts?" Victoria finished heavily. Her voice broke and a sob tore at her throat. "Oh, Phillip, I'd give anything to know where my son is right this minute."

"I'm doing all I can from here, Victoria, but I suspect the real progress will come from your end as you get better acquainted with the Hewletts."

"In that case, I'd better get back," said Victoria soberly. "Pray for me, Phillip. This isn't exactly how I planned to spend my summer vacation."

"Just give the word, Victoria. You can come home anytime you wish and I'll assume full responsibility for the investigation. I'll even drive down and pick you up."

"No, Phillip, you don't have to do that. I have my car, remember? Besides, what I've got to find out can be learned only by gaining the Hewletts' trust, and that takes time. It's something I doubt you or any other private investigator could do as well as I can."

"As much as I hate to admit it, I think you're right, Victoria. And as long as we have no evidence that a crime has been committed, there's little action I or any other legal agency can take."

"Even though Joshua is missing?"

"At this point that's merely conjecture, a stranger's unfounded claim. The Hewletts could come up with any number of explanations. Joshua could be at summer camp or living with another relative or attending a private school somewhere out of state."

"You're depressing me, Phillip."

"I don't mean to, Victoria. It's just that I'm worried about you, and I want you to be aware of the need to proceed with caution."

His concern warmed her. "I'll be careful, Phillip. I promise."

"Good. I'll hold you to it." His voice deepened. "I really don't like leaving you there alone, Victoria. I miss you."

"I miss you, too, Phillip."

"Those aren't idle words," he assured her. "I really do miss you."

The sudden tenderness in his voice made her heart do a somersault. "They weren't idle words for me, either, Phillip," she said softly. She had to admit, despite her reluctance to get involved, her feelings for Phillip Anders were deepening into something much more than friendship. "Listen, Phillip," she said, trying to sound nonchalant, "I'll call you again when I find out any news at all."

He was momentarily silent, then said with a note of resolve, "You do that, Victoria. Call me. But I'm driving up this weekend to see you and check out the Hewletts. You tell them you're having a visitor—you know, just a harmless old friend from back home?"

"Oh, Phillip, I'd love to see you!" she cried, realizing she didn't care in the least how eager she sounded.

"Great! Then it's a date. I'll drive up Friday night. I'm afraid I can stay only Friday and Saturday. I promised Pauline's parents I'd spend next Sunday with them. I've owed them some time together for a long while, but you know how easy it is to put things off. Anyway, Victoria, I'd like to take you out to dinner somewhere nice on Friday evening. So you pick the place, okay?"

"I don't know any restaurants around here, Phillip."

"Okay, then we'll find a place when I get there, somewhere nice and private, with lots of atmosphere."

"Atmosphere?"

"You know. A little moonlight and romance."

There was something in the way he said "romance" that sent Victoria's heart soaring and singing at once. Breathlessly she said, "Until Friday night, then, Phillip. I can't wait to see you."

"Same here, Victoria," he replied, his voice resonant with feeling. "I'll be counting the hours until we're together."

Chapter Eight

On Friday night Victoria met Phillip just outside Antonio's, a small Italian restaurant on the outskirts of town. The moment she saw him walking toward her across the parking lot, she felt something special. A rush of feelings that surprised her with their intensity. Excitement, anticipation and something more—a desire for his embrace. He looked taller and more athletic than she remembered—his stride vigorous and sure, his muscular physique evident even through his blue sports jacket and his sturdy face handsomely chiseled by the interplay of moonlight and shadows. It seemed like ages since she'd seen him; had it truly been only a matter of days?

To her own surprise, she found herself running to him and being swept up into his arms, as if they belonged together, as if being together were the most natural thing in the world. He held her close, his chin nuzzling her hair, and whispered, "I've missed you, Victoria. And the truth is, I've been more than a little worried about you."

"I'm fine...now that you're here," she replied as she nestled her cheek against the nubby fabric of his jacket. She felt breathless, even a trifle weak; her heart raced as if she had run many miles. After a moment she looked up at Phillip and smiled. He was smiling, too, that familiar smile that made those crinkly lines appear around his eyes. She could tell by the way he looked at her that he was debating whether to kiss her; she settled the matter by rising slightly on tiptoe and planting a kiss on his cheek.

Phillip touched the spot where her lips had been and said, "With a greeting like that I'll be sure to visit more often."

"I was hoping you'd say that," she replied with just a hint of flirtation in her voice.

Arm in arm they entered the restaurant and Phillip told the hostess they'd like a table with some privacy. The waitress led them to a back corner table in the quaint, dimly lit room. As they sat down, he told Victoria, "I'm glad we decided to meet here instead of at the Hewletts'. Let's face it. We wouldn't gain anything by having them meet me yet."

She nodded. "I agree. Everything about you shouts law and order."

"I'm not sure how to take that." He laughed mildly, reaching across the table for her hand. "I would hope I'm not so obviously transparent."

"Of course you're not, but then again, your demeanor does convey a certain sense of authority and...propriety."

He grinned. "Okay, Prof, you got me with your fancy words. I give up."

Victoria felt the color rise in her cheeks. "I'm sorry, Phillip. I guess I've spent too many hours this week immersed in my studies."

His gaze was approving. "You're much too pretty to be a walking dictionary. But don't worry. I'm not intimidated."

Victoria raised her chin slightly. "Thank you for that vote of confidence, my dear Mr. Anders."

He squeezed her hand. "You'll get my vote every time, Victoria. I admire your spunk...and your courage."

She met his gaze. "I'm not sure whether it's courage or foolishness."

"Only time will tell, but you've got my vote for courage." With obvious reluctance he released her hand, sat back and scanned his menu. "Before we talk shop, check out the dinner selections. Order what you like. It's my treat."

"I should pay," she protested. "After all, I hired you—"

"When we mix business and pleasure, it's my tab. And this is definitely pleasure. Tell me, what looks good to you?"

She hesitated. "Maybe the veal hollandaise."

"I think I'll try the shrimp scampi."

After they had ordered, Phillip settled back in his chair and gazed intently at her. "So how have the past few days gone? Any more screams in the night or other unexplained incidents?"

Victoria absently turned her water glass. "I don't know, Phillip. I'm at the point where I'm not sure whether the, uh, occurrences are real or a product of my overactive imagination."

"Try me," he said.

"All right. The other night, sometime after midnight, I thought I heard someone sobbing—horrible, racking sobs that chilled me to the bone. But they were muffled, too. I couldn't tell where they were coming from. By the time I gathered my courage to investigate, they had stopped. I left my room and walked up and down the hall. I even went to the kitchen and got some warm milk. Needless to say, my stomach was churning by then."

Phillip's brows furrowed, shadowing his eyes. "That must have been a frightening experience."

"It was." Victoria still absently twirled her water glass, her voice wavering now with emotion. "When I didn't hear the sounds anymore, I sat down at the kitchen table and—I couldn't help myself— I began to weep. I thought maybe I had imagined the sobs. Or maybe they were the cries of my little boy, all alone somewhere. Maybe he was sobbing because he needed my help and I couldn't get to him, I couldn't help him. I felt so helpless and frustrated, Phillip. Even now, the memory of those sobs just twists my heart. What do you think it all means?"

His expression softened, his gentle eyes warming her. "My dear Victoria, I think it means you are a very sensitive, tenderhearted person who would do anything for her son. And I promise I'll do everything in my power to give you that chance."

"But do you think the cries were just my imagination?"

"What do you think?"

"They seemed so real."

"Then let's assume they were. How can we explain what you heard?"

She shrugged. "I don't know, Phillip. You're the detective."

"Did you see anyone? Was there any activity in the house at the time?"

"No, nothing at all. It was as still as a tomb. I tell you, it really gave me the creeps. When I finally went back to bed, I couldn't get back to sleep for hours. And I'm not usually one to overreact to ghost stories and things that go bump in the night."

"Did you ask the Hewletts about the sobbing?"

"Yes. The next morning at breakfast. And I was ready if Maude came up with another silly story."

"Did she?"

"No. As calmly as you please, she told me she couldn't sleep and was watching an old movie on her bedside TV."

"And you don't believe her?"

"Do you?" challenged Victoria. She was silent as the waitress served their dinners. As soon as they were alone again, she said urgently, "I know what I heard didn't come from any television set, Phillip." She paused for a long moment and drew in a deep breath. "And in my heart of hearts, I know it wasn't just my imagination."

Phillip speared a plump, sautéed shrimp and dipped it into the drawn butter. "Just what are you saying, Victoria?"

She shook her head in frustration. "I don't know what I'm saying—"

"It sounds like you're suggesting that there's someone else in the house."

She looked up intently. "I am, and yet...I don't see how there could be, Phillip. I've been all over the house. None of the rooms are locked or guarded or anything. In fact, yesterday when the Hewletts were out shopping, I looked in every room. I felt guilty doing it—like someone out of a cheap spy thriller. But I had to know. I had to prove to myself that it was only the Hewletts and I in that big, drafty old house."

"You proved that to your satisfaction?"

"I found absolutely nothing, Phillip. No sign that anyone else, child or adult, occupied the house."

"Then we're back where we began. How do we explain the strange sounds—the screams and sobs?"

She shrugged. "I don't believe in ghosts—at least not the kind that haunt old houses and play pranks on unsuspecting humans."

"So, like I said, we're back to square one," he remarked.

"Which leaves us absolutely nowhere," she lamented. She glanced down at her plate and sighed. "Not only is our mystery still unsolved, but after all my talking, my veal is stone cold!"

"That's one problem I can remedy," Phillip said in his take-charge voice as he signaled their waitress.

Later, as they left the restaurant, Victoria told him confidentially,

"I really didn't intend for you to order me a whole new dinner. I felt terribly foolish."

"Why? I'm the one who should have felt embarrassed. I devoured my entire dinner as well as yours...and I would do it again."

"You poor thing. You ate the cold meal. The hollandaise was hard and yucky."

"Yucky? Did I hear 'yucky' coming from an English teacher? I can't believe my ears!"

"It's the influence of my freshmen students. Everything's yucky to them. Or gross. Of course, by fall they'll have some new word, equally yucky, no doubt."

Phillip took her arm as he walked her to her car. "Tell you what," he said. "I won't complain about your saying 'yucky' if you ignore my occasionally fractured English."

"Deal," she quipped as they reached her vehicle. She fished in her handbag for the key and handed it to Phillip.

He unlocked the door and opened it, then pressed the key back into her hand. Slowly, gently, he drew her to him. "Now about tomorrow, Miss Carlin. I'd like us to spend every minute together. What do you say?"

She smiled and said teasingly, "You don't sound very business-like, Mr. Anders."

"Oh, I'm all business," he murmured. "In fact, what I'm feeling right this minute is very serious business."

"Phillip, please—" Her heart was pounding again, the way it did before when he was close. His nearness made her head spin. But as pleased as she'd felt when they'd met and he'd held her in his arms, now it felt as if things were moving too fast. She couldn't think straight, couldn't think at all.

"Phillip," she stammered, "I'm glad we've become such good friends. I respect you and enjoy your company immensely, but—"

"But I'm rushing things, right? Don't worry, I understand." He released her and held her elbow as she slipped into the driver's seat.

She looked back up at him. "Phillip, I didn't mean... It's just that I can concentrate on only one thing at a time. And right now that's my son. Please understand."

He gave her a cavalier nod, as if to say it was no big deal. But she could see the disappointment in his eyes as he shut her door and stepped back from the automobile.

She rolled down her window and looked back at him. "Phillip, I'm sorry."

"Don't be. I'd probably panic, too, if the situation were reversed and you were making moves on me."

"I didn't say you were making moves," she protested, flustered. "I just said I...I need to take things more slowly. Surely you understand, Phillip. My emotions can handle only so much at a time."

He bent down and looked in the window at her. "I do understand," he said sincerely. "I'm really not trying to complicate your life, Victoria. But something's happening here between us, whether you admit it or not. Something very special. But I won't push, okay? For now, as you say, we're just...friends."

She gave him a lingering smile. "Thank you...friend. Now tell me, what are we doing tomorrow?"

"I'm going to make you my assistant, and together we're going to do some sleuthing."

"Really? Do you have anything specific in mind?"

"Yes, I do." He lowered his voice a notch. "Do you think you can get hold of a photograph of your little boy, one as recent as possible?"

She searched his eyes. "I might be able to. Why?"

"I'd like to show it to some of the local merchants, see if they recognize him."

"I don't understand."

"Places like the local toy stores and ice cream parlors, even kiddie shoe stores where they keep records of their customers' birthdays and shoe sizes and stuff. If Joshua has lived here for six months, we should be able to find a trace of him somewhere."

"You really think we'll find something?"

He reached into the car and nudged her chin encouragingly. "Who knows? At least we can try."

"Oh, Phillip, my hopes are soaring already."

His strong hand still cupped her chin. "Dear Victoria, let your hopes rise, but keep your feet firmly planted on the ground," he cautioned, "because we've got a lot of territory to cover." He reached into his shirt pocket, pulled out a business card and slipped it into her hand. "This is where I'll be—the Starlight Motel. Call me if you need me, no matter how late it is."

She gazed at the card and winced inwardly, unexpectedly remembering Rick Lancer and another motel seven years ago. It had a similar name—the Starlighter. She could still see those bright yellow neon letters flashing brilliantly in the night from the window of the room she had shared with Rick. For an instant, the pain of her sin came back full force. She recalled sitting alone by that window after they'd been together; like a little lost waif she had sat trembling and cold, hugging herself as she rocked back and forth, her shame burning with each flash of that garish neon sign. She shuddered even now, thinking of that night, momentarily forgetting God's forgiveness.

"Are you all right?" Phillip asked when she didn't reply.

She swallowed hard over the sudden dryness in her throat. "Yes, I'm okay," she said, rallying, forcing a cheery tone. "I'm sure I can manage until tomorrow. Where shall we meet?"

"The Starlight has a little coffee shop. Meet me at eight for breakfast?"

"Make it nine. I'll need time to get hold of Joshua's picture."

"Okay. Nine it is." He took a lock of her hair in his hand, held it for a moment, then released it. "Drive carefully, Victoria."

"I will," she replied, a bit too breathless. "You, too."

"See you in the morning," he called as she turned the ignition and shifted into drive.

As she headed toward the freeway, she thought, I won't just see you in the morning, Phillip. I have a feeling I'll be seeing you tonight, in my dreams!

At nine-thirty the next morning Victoria entered the Starlight Coffee Shop and found Phillip already at a table, reading the newspaper and downing his second cup of black coffee.

"Sorry I'm late," she said, sitting down. "It wasn't easy getting Joshua's picture."

"But you did?"

"Yes. I found it in an album in one of the spare bedrooms. I had to wait until the Hewletts went outside to work in the yard before I could look for it."

"Let's see."

She pulled the photo from her purse. "It's not as nice as the one Maude keeps on the television set, but Joshua's face is clear and sharp. I didn't dare take the other one. They'd miss it right away."

"This is fine," said Phillip. "He's a cute kid. Looks like you."

Tears sprang to her eyes. "Do you really think so?"

"I wouldn't say it if I didn't mean it. He's the spitting image of you, or at least what I imagine you looked like as a child."

She brushed the wetness from her eyelashes. "I thought he looked like me, too—after all, he's part of me. But then I realized I couldn't possibly be objective. I'd see myself in him no matter how he looked."

"Well, take my word for it. He's every inch your son." Phillip shifted his position. His expression grew intent. "Here's our plan of action for today, Victoria. I warn you, we have a lot of ground to cover in a short time. I've got to get back home early tomorrow morning, so we've got to do all our sleuthing today."

"I'm with you," she assured him. "Just tell me what to do."

"Like I said last night, we're going to check out every place around here where a young child might be seen—the fast food restaurants, toy stores, local amusements, clothing shops."

"You mean you're just going to ask people if they've seen Joshua?"

"I'm going to show them his picture and see if they recognize him. If they ask any questions, I'll tell them we're looking for a missing child." His voice lowered. "But under no circumstances will we give anyone information that could get back to the Hewletts. That means, not your name or my name or Joshua's name. So far Joshua isn't legally missing. I don't want to do anything that's going to put this case on the front page of the papers before we have a chance to personally confront the Hewletts."

"Are you actually thinking of confronting them, Phillip?"

"I don't want to. I doubt we'd get anywhere with them. But if we don't locate Joshua soon, we may have to." He paused meaningfully. "And if they refuse to cooperate, then it becomes a police matter."

Victoria didn't reply, but a shiver went through her. She was glad when the waitress finally brought her coffee and took their orders. She had skipped breakfast with the Hewletts and felt famished.

As the waitress left, Phillip leaned across the table confidentially. "Listen, Victoria, today you'll have a chance to see how I operate as a private investigator. At times you may be confused by what I say or do, but just follow my lead and you'll be okay."

She gave him an ironic smile. "What you're being too kind to say is that I should let you do the talking and keep my mouth shut."

"Something like that." He grinned.

The waitress was back with their breakfast specials—bacon, eggs, toast and jam. Victoria bowed her head for a moment and prayed silently. When she opened her eyes, she was startled to see Phillip's head bowed.

"I decided to take *your* lead in this one," he said softly.

She smiled, feeling suddenly warm inside.

They ate in silence for several minutes. Then Phillip said, "I think I'd better share some of my procedures with you so you'll know how I handle things."

"All right," she said. "I'm eager to learn."

He cleared his throat, as if what he was about to say had never been articulated before. "As a Christian," he began "—howbeit, a rusty one—I refuse to lie, even in my investigative practice. I figure there's always a creative way around it. For example, when I arrived in town yesterday afternoon, before I met you, I telephoned all the pediatricians within ten miles of the Hewletts. Now I could have said I was a detective looking for information, in which case they would have told me they weren't at liberty to give out details from a patient's records. Or I could have lied and said I was Joshua's father and needed my son's records for school. But I wouldn't do that."

"Then what did you do?"

"I simply told the truth without offering any explanations. I said I wanted a copy of Joshua Goodwin's vaccination records. In every case, they told me just a minute while they checked their files. Each one returned and told me they had no file at all on Joshua Goodwin. So, you see, I found out just what I wanted to know."

"But if they'd had something, do you really think they would have told you?"

"I think so. I sounded like someone who believed he had the right to know, and I've found that most of the time people are willing and even eager to give out information. They like to be helpful. They like to feel as if they're doing you a favor. And if the information seems innocent enough, like vaccination records, for example, and the questioner appears direct and straightforward, well, let's just say information isn't all that hard to come by."

"It's amazing," said Victoria. She hesitated, sorting her thoughts.

"You look troubled," said Phillip.

She stared at her plate, then looked up urgently at him. "I feel the same way you do about lying," she said, "but what you've just told me makes me wonder about something—"

"What is it, Victoria?"

Her voice came out uneven. "Do you think I'm living a lie because I'm staying at the Hewletts under false pretenses?"

He almost smiled. "Well, some people might see it that way, but you're using your real name and you *are* working on your thesis. If the Hewletts have nothing to hide, then your stay can't possibly hurt them. But if they've done something wrong involving your son, you have a perfect right to find out what it is."

She smiled in relief. "Since you put it that way..."

That evening as Phillip drove Victoria back to the Starlight Motel to pick up her car, she sat in silence, her feelings mixed. She was exhausted. How, she wondered, did Phillip ever keep up such a pace?

Still, in spite of her weariness, she had enjoyed being with him. He was good company, a true friend. He had proved that over and over again today. She was fortunate to have his capable, wholehearted help in seeking her son.

But even as she sat beside him in the automobile, she had to admit they were already more than friends. She wasn't even sure what that meant. *More than friends.* What had he said last night? *Something is happening between us...something very special.* Out of fear and uncertainty she had discouraged his attentions, so perhaps he would back away from pursuing any sort of romantic liaison with her. And wouldn't that be best, after all? Her one relationship with a man had proven to be the disaster of her life; she couldn't risk such a calamity again.

And yet she couldn't deny the tender sprigs of emotion taking root in her heart. She cared for Phillip more than she had a right to. And he seemed to care for her. But then, perhaps all men behaved this way around women without the slightest serious intentions. She had so little experience to go by. How could she know whether Phillip was serious or merely engaging in a mild flirtation to make their business association more palatable? And surely a large part of his heart was still reserved for Pauline, the wife he had loved and lost.

Whatever Phillip felt for her, she was painfully, deliciously aware of his physical presence and found herself at the most surprising moments yearning for his closeness. But then she was back where she had started; it was a vicious circle, for such emotions, such desires, had gotten her into terrible trouble. She couldn't risk losing everything she cherished—her honor, her integrity, her fragile, struggling personhood—that way again. She had to keep her mind focused on what really mattered here—finding her son.

But she was beginning to realize that even Phillip's help wasn't going to be enough. They had found no new clues today, no one who recalled ever seeing Joshua. They had reached a dead end, and that realization, as much as the day's activities, had left Victoria weary beyond words.

Phillip, apparently sensing her dark mood, remarked, "I'm sorry we didn't get any leads today. But don't give up hope."

She looked over at him and realized she was pinning too many hopes on him, hopes without substance. Wasn't it foolish to hope when the situation was hopeless? "Maybe it's time I faced the fact that my son is dead," she said gloomily.

He eyed her sharply. "Where's that coming from?"

"Isn't that what you're thinking, too, Phillip? The Hewletts claim he's dead, and he's nowhere to be found. What else can I believe?"

"This is one time I don't want you believing anything until we have the facts."

She couldn't keep the frustration out of her voice. "We may never have the facts, Phillip!" She lowered her gaze and sighed audibly. "I'm sorry. It's just that all these years I've longed to see my son. Now, finally, I've come so close, but suddenly I realize it may never be close enough."

"I won't give up on this, Victoria, until we have the answers," said Phillip, reaching over and taking her hand.

She smiled, accepting the warmth of his palm. "I appreciate you, Phillip, I really do, and I don't mean to take my frustration out on you. It's just that, before the investigation, even though I knew I'd never see my son, I believed he was out there somewhere, happy and healthy, with a family that loved him." There was a catch in her voice. "Now that we can't even trace him or prove that he's alive, the pain is almost unbearable."

Phillip's tone was somber. "I know, Victoria. I never had children—Pauline wasn't able—and next to losing my wife, having no children has been the deepest regret of my life. Pauline and I both wanted a house full of kids. Neither of us grew up with brothers or sisters, so when we married, we both wanted to have the biggest family on the block."

Victoria turned her hand over and linked fingers with Phillip. "I apologize," she told him. "I've been so wrapped up in my own problems, I've ignored your feelings completely. Forgive me for being so insensitive."

He smiled. "I can't forgive what doesn't need forgiving. You're such an easy person to talk with, Victoria, someone I can honestly share my feelings with. That's a rarity for me. I really don't like talking about myself, but you make me feel comfortable. I like that."

"So do I," she said. They had arrived back at the Starlight Motel and Phillip was easing his sports car into the parking space beside her compact. Already she was dreading the drive alone back to the Hewletts. She didn't want to leave Phillip.

The realization startled her. She had always been such a private person, finding her pleasures and satisfactions in solitary pursuits. But now the idea of being alone prompted feelings of sadness and anxiety. "It must be the Hewletts," she said aloud, knowing even as she said it that it wasn't entirely true.

"What?" asked Phillip.

She felt herself blushing slightly. "Nothing. It's just that I hate going back to the Hewlett house tonight. The place really makes me uncomfortable."

"I've told you before, you can go back home anytime you—"

"I know, I know, but I'm not giving up until I find out the truth about my son." She opened her door and stepped out, and waited as he climbed out of the vehicle and unlocked her car.

He turned to her, and their eyes met and held for a long moment. "I don't want to let you go," he murmured, taking her face in both his hands, his fingers sinking into her thick curls. "Call me crazy, but I don't want to let you out of my sight."

"I don't want to go, either," she admitted. "I feel so safe with you, Phillip. I love that feeling. I've never had it with anyone else."

He leaned his face close to hers, his lips mere inches from hers. His breath was warm, inviting. "I wish I could take care of you, Victoria," he whispered. "I wish I could make everything come out right for you and your son. I wish—"

"You're doing everything you can, Phillip, and that's all I could ask for," she murmured. His closeness was so sweet and intoxicating, she couldn't quite concentrate on what she wanted to say. "I—I don't know what I'd do...without your help."

"I guess I'd better let you go," he said, his eyes searching hers, his mouth nearly touching hers now.

"Yes, I—I'd better go," she replied, just before his lips came down fully, gently, on hers. It was a tender kiss, warm and wonderful, but all too brief. As he released her, she saw concern written in his eyes. He's afraid he's offended me, she realized. She reached out and touched his cheek. "You're a very special man, Phillip. You've lifted my spirits. Thank you."

He smiled. "The pleasure was all mine."

She fumbled for her car door handle. "I guess you'll be getting an early start home tomorrow. You said you'll be spending the day with Pauline's parents."

"Right. But you can reach me at home tomorrow evening."

"Great. Good night, Phillip." She turned away abruptly, before she changed her mind about going, and slipped into her car. She drove away from the hotel feeling light-headed, her senses reeling, the taste of Phillip's kiss still on her lips.

It was after nine when Victoria arrived back at the Hewletts'. She had missed dinner and had neglected to telephone. Sam and Maude were both obviously peeved with her. They sat sullen faced before the TV, watching a sitcom rerun. "The library closed hours ago," Maude complained.

Victoria couldn't contend with this strident woman tonight. She had experienced enough emotional upheavals for one day. So, while Maude sputtered, she promptly excused herself, went to her room and gratefully shut the door behind her. She was too tired to shower or even to remove her makeup. She undressed, pulled on her nightgown, crawled between the covers and stretched languorously.

"Lord, so many emotions are churning inside me," she whispered into the darkness. "Feelings for Phillip, my own unsettling desires and misgivings, and so many worries about my son. Help me, Lord, to know what You want for me, and please help me find my son." She wanted to say more, but within moments her words faded into slumber.

Sometime during the deepest hour of night, Victoria woke with a start. She lay tense, listening, as a gossamer moon cast pale shards of light across one wall. She hadn't heard a scream; in fact, she couldn't recall hearing anything. Yet something was amiss. She sensed it, felt it to the very marrow of her bones. Her muscles were rigid, unmoving. Her eyes searched the darkness. Then she saw it. Her door was open. An elusive shadow moved in the doorway!

She stared hard, her breath caught in her throat. "Who—?" she tried to whisper, but no sound emerged.

For an instant, the moonlight caught the figure in the doorway. It was a child. A pathetic little voice said, "Mama?"

Chapter Nine

Victoria sprang from her bed. "Joshua?" she cried. Is it possible? My baby, my boy?

The child fled.

Blindly Victoria ran to the doorway and grappled for the light switch. "Wait, please! Don't go!" She flipped the switch and, blinking against the brightness, stared up and down the hall.

It was empty.

"But I saw him. He was here," she whispered to herself, baffled. "He called me Mama! Oh, God, can it be?" She reached for her robe, pulled it on and padded quickly down the hall to the Hewletts' room, her heart pounding fiercely against her ribs. She stopped and steeled herself outside their door. What was she going to say? She could ruin everything if she raised their suspicions. But surely the old rules didn't apply now; the circumstances had changed. She had actually seen him, her boy. First, catch my breath. Get control of my emotions. She inhaled sharply and knocked.

After a moment Maude opened the door. "What is it?" she said thickly, tying her robe around her.

Victoria's voice was ragged, her emotions erupting in spite of her best resolves. "I—I saw someone...in my doorway—"

"You musta been dreaming again," scoffed Maude. In the pale light her cold-creamed face looked bloated, pasty.

"It wasn't a dream," insisted Victoria. She carefully gathered her words. "A child opened my door. He—he was just standing there."

Maude's face registered alarm. "A child?" She bustled over to her bedside table and snatched up a shiny object. Victoria caught just a glimpse of a chain and what appeared to be a key. Maude returned and said, "You go back to bed. I'll look around and make sure everything's okay."

"I'll come with you," said Victoria.

"No. Go to your room. I just wanna check the locks."

"But the child—?"

Maude's eyes narrowed. "There wasn't no child, Miss Carlin."

"But I saw him. He was standing there as real as you are."

"I'll say it again," said Maude through clenched teeth. "There wasn't no child in this house. It was your imagination, and that's the end of it, is that clear, Miss Carlin?"

Victoria relented under the force of Maude's sinister gaze. "Maybe you're right, Mrs. Hewlett," she replied. It wouldn't help to pursue the matter now; forcing Maude's hand might put Joshua in physical danger. "Maybe it was just a dream," she said as she turned back to her room.

For the rest of the night Victoria lay wide-awake, a blizzard of questions bombarding her mind. Who was the child? Was it Joshua? Surely it had to be. Where has he been all this time? Where is he now? she wondered. Is he okay? Is he real? Surely he wasn't just the product of my imagination!

"He said Mama," she marveled aloud. "I actually heard him say Mama." It was the most beautiful sound she had ever heard.

Shortly after dawn Victoria telephoned the Starlight Motel. "Please connect me with Phillip Anders's room," she told the operator.

"I'm sorry, ma'am," came the brisk reply. "Mr. Anders checked out half an hour ago."

Victoria's heart sank. She should have known. Phillip had told her he would get an early start home. He was spending the day with Pauline's parents. She hadn't thought to ask for their number. "Thank you, anyway," she said dully, and hung up. Now what? she wondered.

At breakfast that morning both Maude and Sam seemed edgy and preoccupied. As Maude passed Victoria the scrambled eggs, she said, "I been thinking, Miss Carlin. It ain't working out so well, us having a boarder. Sam and me like our peace and quiet, and, well, to be honest, you're the nervous sort, always getting spooked in the night by noises and such and stirring up the whole household. Maybe it'd be better all around if you moved out."

Victoria nearly dropped the bowl of eggs. "Move out?" She felt as if the bottom had dropped out of her stomach. "I—I can't move out. I've just settled in. I like it here."

Sam peered at her over his spectacles. "That not the way we see it, Miss Clarkin. The missus and me figured you wasn't fitting in so well. You been as skittish and high-strung as a filly. Seems you'd do better back where you come from."

"That's not true!" protested Victoria, alarm tightening her throat. Stay calm, she warned herself. Don't blow it now! Put on the show of your life. Your son's life may depend on it! "Really, I've been very happy here, Mrs. Hewlett," she went on in her most convincing tone. "And I've accomplished so much on my thesis. I could never have done all this work back home, with all the interruptions. You know how it is—the phone always ringing, students and colleagues dropping by, everybody making demands. But your home is perfect for me. No one knows where I am. I can work in absolute peace and quiet."

Maude glowered at Victoria as she rubbed her thumb over a dab of grape jelly on the red checkered oilcloth. Victoria had a feeling the granite-faced woman wished she could get rid of Victoria as easily as she wiped away that dollop of preserves. "I'm sorry, Miss Carlin. You best be looking for another place."

"Oh, I would," Victoria assured her, "but I just can't take the time right now. I have only another week or so of research to do and I'll be ready to write my thesis. Please let me stay until I've finished my research."

Maude's expression remained dour as a persimmon. "Don't you understand English? I've made up my mind, Miss Carlin."

"Please, Mrs. Hewlett, I'll pay you double the rent. Just give me another week or two."

Maude's eyes narrowed and one shaggy brow arched with interest. Victoria could see the wheels turning. Maude was counting the dollar signs in her head. "Double the rent, you say? Does that mean double what you're paying for meals, too?"

"Yes, of course. Double everything."

"That's mighty generous of you, Miss Clarkin," said Sam.

"Oh, it's worth it to me, Mr. Hewlett, just to be able to work on my thesis in peace."

Sam and Victoria both looked expectantly at Maude. A grudging smile flickered on her pursed lips. "Double the rent and you stay two weeks at most," she muttered, "but you gotta pay it all up front. Cash in hand."

"You've got a deal," said Victoria, sighing with relief.

That evening, as soon as she could slip away from the house without arousing suspicion, Victoria drove into town and telephoned Phillip from the drugstore pay phone. As soon as she heard his voice she broke into tears, startling both Phillip and herself. "Oh, I'm so glad you're home," she cried. "You don't know how glad!"

"What's wrong?" he asked, his voice rising in alarm. "Talk to me! Are you in danger, Victoria?"

"No, it's nothing like that," she assured him. "Oh, Phillip, it's actually something quite hopeful."

"Tell me."

"Listen, Phillip. I saw *him*."

There was silence for a moment. Then Phillip said, "Your son? Are you sure?"

"I—I can't be positive, but I woke up in the night and saw someone standing in my doorway."

"You saw him clearly—recognized him?"

"Not exactly. I saw his shadow. I got up, but by the time I reached the doorway he was gone."

"You're sure it wasn't just a...a—?"

"A figment of my imagination?"

"I didn't say that, Victoria. I'm just trying to get the facts."

Suddenly she felt irritable and full of doubts. "I expected skepticism from Maude, Phillip, but not from you."

"I'm not doubting you, Victoria."

"I know you're not," she relented. "It's just that I spent a sleepless night, then I had a confrontation with Maude this morning. She told me to move out. Why would she ask me to move out if she isn't hiding something?"

"She actually asked you to leave?"

"Yes, but I handled it just fine, Phillip—like you would have done. I bought myself some time. You would have been proud of me.

"Anyway, now my emotions are as taut as rubber bands. But the important thing is, I came within inches of touching my son! But I must admit, I don't see how even the Hewletts could hide an active, noisy little boy anywhere in that house without me knowing it."

Phillip's voice grew intent. "Listen, Victoria, I want you to try to remember every detail of that incident. Did the Hewletts say or do anything suspicious?"

Victoria shifted her position in the cramped phone booth. "Yes, now that you mention it, there was something I noticed."

"Tell me."

"When I told Maude I saw a child in my doorway, she looked alarmed. She went immediately to her bedside table and picked up something. It looked like a long chain with something shiny—a key, I think. She wears a chain around her neck, but she always keeps it tucked inside her housedress, so I never really noticed a key on the chain before."

"Do you think you could ever get hold of that key?" asked Phillip.

"I don't know. She apparently takes it off only when she sleeps. But what good would taking a key do when I don't know what it opens?"

"You're right, Victoria. Besides, it's too risky. Forget the key for now."

"Then what should I do?"

"Continue working on your thesis, and keep your eyes and ears open. I'll drive back up on the weekend, or sooner, if I can get away."

"Would you, Phillip?" She hesitated. "What about your other clients?"

"It's not my other clients I want to be with, Victoria. It's you. I miss you like crazy."

"Oh, Phillip, I miss you, too."

"Listen, I'll work something out and drive down as soon as I can. Meanwhile, watch your step."

"Don't worry, Phillip. I'll spend the entire week in my research. I may even begin writing my first draft."

"Great. I'm eager to hear all about it. I'll see you Saturday, if not before." Almost as an afterthought, he added, "Listen, Victoria, I'll come directly to the house. I think it's time I met the Hewletts myself."

"What shall I tell them about you, Phillip?"

"Just say I'm a friend from home. Your best beau. I'll handle the rest when I meet them."

"They're terribly nosy, Phillip. We won't be able to talk privately."

"Don't worry, we'll manage just fine. You can always tell me all about your thesis. No harm in that, right? And while I'm there, I'll be making some observations of my own."

"Thank you, Phillip. I feel better already."

"That's my girl."

"Oh, Phillip, I just thought of something. I never asked you about your visit with Pauline's parents. I'm sorry. Did it go well?" Why was she asking? she wondered. Was it for Phillip's sake or her own? Was she hoping he would say he was completely over his wife's death?

"No need to apologize," he said offhandedly. "And, yeah, it went okay. It was one of those things I had to do. I hadn't seen her folks for several months."

"Do you feel like talking about it? I'm a good listener." Please say you've gotten past the hurt, that someone new is taking her place.

"There's really not much to say. It went as well as could be expected. We spent a lot of time talking about Pauline."

"That must have been painful for you."

"Yeah, it was."

"I'm sorry, Phillip." I can't say the words, but it's painful for me just knowing you're still hurting.

Phillip's voice lowered a notch. "Seeing her folks brought a lot of things back and stirred up some feelings and memories I've tried to suppress for a long time. But, hey, I'll survive."

"It's good that you saw them, Phillip. It's all part of the healing process." She knew that process as intimately as anyone.

"Yeah, you're right," he conceded. "What do they say? Two steps forward, three steps back."

She sighed, thinking of her own losses. "Grieving is the pits, isn't it? Just when you think you're on solid ground you fall into a black hole and have to start digging your way out all over again."

He grimaced. "I couldn't have said it better myself."

"You loved her a lot, didn't you?" Just saying the words wrenched Victoria's heart. How could she ever have thought Phillip was ready to move on to a new relationship?

Phillip made a little coughing sound low in his throat. "The irony is I loved her more than I ever realized when she was alive. I'll never forgive myself for not giving her the attention and appreciation she deserved."

"Never is a long time, Phillip. But I know what you mean. I'm still having a hard time forgiving myself for breaking my father's heart."

"I guess we've both got a long way to go, but we'll get there," Phillip reassured her. "They say time is the great healer."

Victoria wondered if that was true. Sometimes it didn't seem so. Time had never healed the loss of her son.

"Speaking of time," she said finally, "it's getting late. I'd better get back to the Hewletts'. Besides, I'm starting to get claustrophobia in this phone booth."

"All right, drive carefully. And, Victoria, you go back there and hold your chin up high. Don't let the Hewletts get to you."

"I won't, I promise. I know we're on to something, Phillip."

"I think so, too. Now let's make the most of the time we have."

"I intend to." In more ways than one, Phillip! I want to make the most of the time I have with you, too!

"We'll get the answers to your son's whereabouts, whatever it takes," said Phillip.

"I won't leave Middleton until we do," she replied.

"You're one gutsy lady, Victoria."

"Thanks to you, Phillip." It was hard to tell him how much hope he inspired in her. And courage. "You don't know how much I need you—your help," she confided, her tears starting again—happy tears and sad ones mixing together. "I really do miss you."

"Believe me, dear girl, it works both ways. I can't wait to see you again."

"Same here." She dabbed her eyes with a tissue. "I'll be waiting, Phillip. Please...don't change your mind about coming."

"Are you kidding? Nothing could keep me away," he assured her fervently.

Chapter Ten

Thursday, May 28

*M*y life is a paradox these days, filled with baffling contradictions. I've found my son; I haven't found my son. I'm falling in love with the most wonderful man I've ever known; I'm terrified of falling in love with anyone. And I think Phillip may be falling in love with me, yet he still grieves deeply for the wife he lost.

I dwell in a house full of silences so loud I can never relax. I am surrounded by the most prosaic and mundane of furnishings, yet I live in the heart of a mystery. And every day I play this bizarre game of cat and mouse; I watch the Hewletts and they watch me. And we wait, watching and waiting, filled with our separate silences, waiting for what, I do not know.

Time only brings more questions, never answers. Just when I think I know my own mind, a new door opens and reveals rooms I never knew were there. Dear God, every day You reveal bits and pieces of my soul to me. You make me examine my motives, my perceptions, my goals.

I am already asking myself, What will I do when—not if!—I find my son? Will I be a mother to him? What does it mean to mother a child, especially a son I've never seen or known? Isn't parenthood difficult enough when you've raised your child from birth? What audacious folly to entertain the idea of becoming someone's mother *overnight! And even if I were to raise my son, how could I possibly pursue a relationship with Phillip, as well?*

What am I thinking? How reckless and foolhardy I must be to covet the love of someone who had the perfect wife; for surely, by all accounts, Pauline Anders was impeccable. How can I—a bookish, naive schoolmarm knowing nothing of the male psyche—expect to compete for a virile, worldly man like Phillip Anders?

And yet my hopes rise in my heart like flags, and my dreams are filled with him each night.

My heavenly Father, where will this odyssey take us, and when will the mysteries be revealed? This coming weekend, Lord? I pray that You will go before us in the way and make our paths straight and honorable in Your sight. And whatever comes, may I be strong enough to face it with dignity and grace!

Phillip arrived at ten sharp on Saturday morning. Sam opened the door with a tentative nod. "You must be Miss Clarkin's gentleman caller," he drawled, eyeing Phillip closely as he showed him inside.

Victoria and Phillip exchanged amused glances. Gentleman caller? Phillip mouthed on the sly.

"They just assumed..." she whispered with a smile.

Maude greeted Phillip with the same stolid reticence she reserved for door-to-door salesmen and other uninvited solicitors. "Come on in and shut the door," she muttered, "before that summer heat gets in and melts us all."

Phillip ignored Maude's clipped tone. Turning on his charm, he shook her hand warmly. "Victoria has told me so much about you," he said with an enthusiasm that prompted Victoria to roll her eyes heavenward. "I understand you're something of an artist, Mrs. Hewlett."

Within moments Maude was showing Phillip her entire collection of crocheted soap fish and turtles. Then, when he complimented her on the original paintings on her walls, she told him, "Oh, my daughter, Julia, painted them. She woulda been a famous artist...if she'd lived."

"I'm sorry," said Phillip, his gaze meeting Maude's. Then, looking back at the paintings, he remarked, "They're nicely done. Reminiscent of Grandma Moses's primitive style, but fresher, more refined."

Maude beamed. "That's what I always told her. She never liked to push herself on people. She wouldn't sell herself. Just liked to sit and paint and pay nobody no mind. I tried to tell her there was places out there would pay a mint for her work, but no, she was happy just sitting at home painting and minding the baby.''

"Baby?" questioned Phillip.

"My grandson, Joshua." Maude's expression turned glum. "He wasn't even her own, but that girl sacrificed her whole life for him. I told her she could be somebody important, didn't I, Sam? She could make people stand up and take notice, but no, she was bound and determined to stay home with that boy. He was so busy and active, he didn't give her no time to paint."

"Was he a problem child?" ventured Victoria, keeping her tone even and detached.

"Not so's you'd notice. Not then, anyways." Maude pointed to a small landscape of a rough-hewn mountain cabin. "That's my favorite of Julia's paintings—our vacation cottage up north. Julia loved it there."

"It sounds like you and your daughter were very close," said Phillip conversationally. "You must have spent a lot of time with her and your grandson."

"No." Maude snorted. "That hubby of hers moved them out of state when the boy was barely two."

"He never liked Maude and me." Sam grunted, his lips curling in disgust. "He took our girl away just to punish us, if you ask me. We hardly saw her after they moved away."

Maude's voice quavered. "Then the accident took them all away for good." Her face contorted slightly as she gathered up her crocheted soaps and placed them carefully back in their box.

In the uneasy silence that followed, Phillip glanced around the room and remarked easily, "You know, Mrs. Hewlett, I love these old Victorian homes. They have so much more charm than modern houses. Don't you think so?"

"Sure do," she agreed, recovering her composure. "Them new-fangled houses look like cracker boxes to me—all cut out the same. Real ugly, if you ask me."

"Absolutely," said Phillip. "But your house reminds me of my grandmother's home back in Boston. I used to visit her every summer when I was a kid. Man, do I miss that place!" He paused, his expression suddenly animated. "Would you mind if I looked around your place a little—just for nostalgia's sake, Mrs. Hewlett? I don't know when I'll come across a house like yours again.''

Maude's thick jowls flushed with pleasure. "Help yourself, Mr. Anders. It ain't nothing fancy, but Sam and me like it.''

"And well you should," said Phillip approvingly as Maude led him off down the hall.

They were back ten minutes later, Maude beaming with pride. "Sam, Mr. Anders thinks our house should be on one of them snooty society lists—you know, the ones that promote tours of old historical spots. He thinks our place belongs right up there with the best of 'em. Wouldn't my granddaddy sit up in his grave if he knew the house he helped build got on that list?"

Sam sat back and chewed thoughtfully on his lower lip. "Aw, your granddaddy's probably sitting up in his casket regardless. He was too stubborn to lie down, even for his own funeral."

"You could take a lesson from him, Sam Hewlett. You got gelatin for a backbone," Maude snapped. As she glanced up at Phillip, her shrill tone turned back to syrup. "What do you think of Mr. Anders's comments about the house, Sam?"

Sam pretended to be absorbed in his television show. He poked his tongue around inside his cheek, trying to extract a bit of food from his teeth.

"Sam, you answer me now! Mr. Anders likes the house. What do you say?"

As he explored a back molar with his index finger, Sam's eyes remained fixed on the TV. "Sounds like the man knows good stuff when he sees it, Maude," he drawled.

Maude looked around at Phillip and Victoria. "Don't pay that man no mind. He's got the manners of an old hound dog." But her tone sweetened as she looked up benevolently at Phillip and said, "We've kept Miss Carlin's gentleman friend long enough. I figure you young folks want a chance to visit. Go sit yourselves in the kitchen and have some tea and muffins. The fan's on out there, so it ain't bad. Sam and I'll stay here in the living room and watch TV."

"Not much on the tube Saturday morning," grumbled Sam.

"There's Ernest Tubb and an old 'Lucy' rerun," said Maude, settling back on the sofa and flicking the remote control button.

Victoria went to her room for her research materials, then she and Phillip retreated to the kitchen and shut the door with muffled laughter and relief. She loved being with Phillip again, pleasantly aware of his nearness, hearing the pleasing lilt and timbre of his voice.

"I think Maude likes you," she whispered mirthfully, "and the way you finagled that invitation to see the house! You're a smooth operator, Phillip Anders."

"Flattery will do it every time."

"I'll remember that," she noted.

"In your case, not flattery, but truth," he corrected.

Victoria ignored the compliment and asked instead, "Did you notice anything suspicious around the house?"

Phillip glanced back at the swinging door that separated them from the rest of the house. "Not a thing," he whispered, "except the Hewletts themselves. They could be distant cousins of the Addams family."

Victoria frowned. "The Addams family? Who on earth are they?"

"Never mind. I forgot your forte is Melville and Maugham, not Morticia and her brood."

"Actually, this summer I'm concentrating on Plath and O'Connor, but I really want to talk about my son—"

He put a finger to her lips, his brows furrowing, and said softly, "Not here."

At his touch, her heart caught in her throat. Their gazes locked and his fingertips remained poised near her lips. She thought he might draw her to him and kiss her; she could see by the expression in his eyes that the idea had occurred to him, too. "Not here," he repeated with a tenderness that made her desire his kiss all the more. But she understood. They had to remain circumspect. Sam or Maude could walk in at any moment. She nodded agreement. Louder, more deliberately, Phillip said, "I want to hear all about your thesis, Victoria. How is it going?"

Carefully she spread her papers out on the checkered oilcloth-covered table. "I'll tell you all about it," she whispered, "but it's not my thesis I need help on, Phillip."

He nodded. "I know, but at the moment it's a safer topic than your son or the Hewletts."

"But I'm dying to hear your theories and opinions about this house and—"

Again, he touched her lips, his fingertips remaining for a long moment, his dark eyes drilling hers. "The thesis, Victoria." His tone was persuasive.

She reached up and clasped his hand against her cheek and gave him a resigned smile. He returned the smile and gently caressed her hair. "Don't worry," he murmured. "We'll talk. Later."

Victoria got up and poured two glasses of iced tea and set a basket of blueberry muffins on the table. "You're absolutely sure you want to hear about my thesis?" she asked as she sat down across from him.

"Positive," he replied. "Just trust me—as long as you don't mind talking while I eat."

She managed a laugh. "I'd rather talk than eat anytime."

He reached for a muffin. "You mentioned O'Connor. You don't mean as in Flannery, do you?"

"Yes, I do. Flannery O'Connor. Have you heard of her?"

"You bet. When I was in college, my lit professor assigned me a paper on her."

"Are you serious? But you studied law—"

"I had to take lit classes in college like everyone else," replied Phillip. "At the time, I wasn't too thrilled about the assignment. I wanted to write about some rough-and-ready author like Hemingway or Faulkner. Then I started reading O'Connor and I was fascinated."

"You mean you liked her? Not everyone does."

Phillip chuckled. "Her characters are so earthy and real, flaws and all, and sometimes they're pretty weird. But they're never dull. After writing that paper, I became something of an O'Connor fan."

Victoria broke into a spontaneous smile. "My dear Mr. Anders, you never cease to amaze me!"

"You think I'm teasing, don't you? Go ahead. Ask me about any of her stories—'The Displaced Person,' 'Good Country People'..."

"I believe you, I believe you!" She stifled a laugh. "It's just that you don't know how refreshing it is to find someone I can talk intelligently with about my thesis."

Phillip raised his palms in a cautionary gesture. "Now, now, I'm not promising anything intellectual. Just a good listening ear."

"Just finding someone who's acquainted with O'Connor's work is a blessing," said Victoria.

"Actually, I've even seen her family home," said Phillip, warming to the subject. "Pauline and I visited Milledgeville, Georgia, one summer. It's beautiful country."

"You're one up on me," said Victoria. "I've never been to Georgia."

He paused and looked at her. "I'm sorry. I'm getting you off track. Go ahead. Tell me about your thesis." Before she could respond, he stood and soundlessly crossed the room. She watched as he put his ear to the door and listened. After a moment he returned to his chair. "Thought I heard something," he remarked. "Just wanted to make sure we didn't have an eavesdropper."

Victoria cleared her throat uneasily. "Thanks for checking."

"Go on with your thesis," he urged.

Her voice grew serious, even a bit tentative, as she said, "All right, well, since I became a Christian three years ago, I've been fascinated with the role faith plays in our lives, and specifically the role it played in the lives of two widely acclaimed authors. You already know about O'Connor. The other author is Sylvia Plath."

Phillip shook his head. "I'm not familiar with her."

"That's okay. You will be. Actually, I believe the *lack* of faith played as significant a role in Plath's life as the *presence* of faith played in O'Connor's."

Phillip helped himself to another muffin. "I suppose that makes sense, although I'm not sure that what you're suggesting is grounds for an entire thesis."

"That's what I'm going to have to prove this summer," replied Victoria. "You see, I realize there were many complex issues that affected the lives of both Plath and O'Connor, quite separate from their personal beliefs. But I'm convinced their attitudes toward God and faith ultimately carved their very different destinies."

Phillip shrugged. "I hate to rain on your parade, Victoria, but can you sell it to your professors? I mean, what difference does it really make what these two authors believed?"

"It makes all the difference in the world to me, Phillip." Victoria sat forward intently, invigorated by the subject. "You see, before I met Christ, I *was* Sylvia Plath in so many of my feelings and attitudes. I've shared with you a little about my teenage years, how I was such a loner and an overachiever. I felt I had to be perfect for my parents. It was almost an obsession. During those years I read Plath compulsively and fantasized that we were somehow the same person. I even romanticized her suicide and brooded about taking my own life."

Phillip's brows arched. "Hey, that's heavy stuff."

"I know." She shifted uneasily. "Now, since my conversion, I realize how mistaken I was about so many things. But I still feel a kinship with Plath, and I believe if she could have found what I've found—and what Flannery O'Connor knew—it would have changed everything for her.''

Phillip looked dubious. "You're sure your ideas aren't just based on wishful thinking? How do you know faith played such a big part in O'Connor's writing? I've read most of her stuff and never considered it especially religious.''

"I admit, the spiritual message in her work is extremely subtle, Phillip, especially if a reader doesn't know what to look for. You've got to examine her life and her personal writings to understand what she was trying to accomplish in her stories.''

Victoria reached for a large paperback and opened it. "This book, *The Habit of Being,* is a collection of O'Connor's letters. Listen to what she wrote to a student. 'Let me make no bones about it: I write from the standpoint of Christian orthodoxy. . . . I write with a solid belief in *all* the Christian dogmas. I find that this in no way limits my freedom as a writer and that it increases rather than decreases my vision. It is popular to believe that in order to see clearly one must believe nothing. This may work well enough if you are observing cells under a microscope. It will not work if you are writing fiction. For the fiction writer, to believe nothing is to see nothing.'''

Phillip sat back and smiled. "All right, I admit that's a pretty powerful statement of faith.''

"There's more, Phillip," said Victoria, flipping several pages. "In another letter O'Connor states her essential purpose in writing. She says, 'You do not write the best you can for the sake of art but for the sake of returning your talent increased to the invisible God to use or not use as He sees fit.''' Victoria was breathless now. "Do you have any idea, Phillip, how that blesses me, how affirming it is to know that's how she felt?''

"I can tell by the glow in your cheeks and the light in your eyes," said Phillip.

Victoria reached for another book. Her tone sobered as she said, "But listen to what Edward Butscher, Sylvia Plath's biographer, wrote about her in his book, *Method and Madness.* 'Behind it all, as usual, as part of the gnawing fear, was an absence of belief. The...poems end in nothingness or hardness because that was all her devouring mind could rationally discover; it was the oblivion logic could not avoid. Belief is what she craved—the slightest sign that events had an ulterior significance. She lit bonfires and kept totems of black magic in her study drawer, but more was needed—a positive system of spiritual meaning. She wanted desperately to commit herself to religion, as she had committed herself to politics and art, but found no salvation in the Unitarianism of her upbringing.'''

Victoria closed the book and looked at Phillip. "I don't know what that says to you, but I believe if Plath had found the faith she was seeking so desperately, she would quite possibly be alive today."

"That's a powerful claim," remarked Phillip seriously. "You may be right. Personally, I wouldn't even want to risk an opinion."

Victoria inhaled deeply and sat back in her chair. "Of course, there's no way to prove it one way or another, but I do want to explore that search for meaning that both authors pursued in such opposite directions. If I accomplish nothing else, I'll have a better understanding of what my own faith means to me."

"That's very important to you, isn't it?" noted Phillip.

Victoria sipped her tea, then replied, "Yes, extremely important, especially now. It holds me together. Gives me hope." She paused. "Isn't your faith important to you, Phillip?"

A muscle in his temple twitched slightly. He glanced out the window, as if distracted. "It has a place," he said noncommittally. "Frankly—" he looked back at Victoria "—since Pauline died, I try not to think much about my faith."

She gazed back at him, her eyes probing his. "Oh, Phillip, how can you face the terrible pain of grieving and not think about your faith?" she asked gently. "Christ was called a 'man of sorrows.' Scripture says He carried our griefs and bore our sorrows. Phillip, doesn't that make Him our sympathetic partner in mourning, not the perpetrator of our pain?"

Phillip pushed his chair back from the table. Victoria had the sensation that he wanted to flee. "I don't look at it the way you do," he replied, his tone clipped. "I think God could have kept Pauline from dying, and since He didn't bother, I'm not too keen on making time for Him in my life."

She reached across the table and put her hand over his. "I'm sorry, Phillip. I can't imagine what my life would be like without His comfort."

He interlocked his fingers with hers. "I'm glad it works for you. Maybe someday it'll work again for me."

Feeling suddenly ill at ease, Victoria withdrew her hand and began gathering her papers. "I suppose I've rattled on long enough about my thesis," she told him, her tone apologetic. "You were polite enough to listen. I won't take advantage of your kindness by boring you further..."

Phillip reached out and retrieved her hand and pressed her fingers against his lips. "You weren't boring me, Victoria. You fascinate me...baffle me...infuriate me at times. But you never bore me."

"Nor do you bore me," she replied quietly. "But you do infuriate me from time to time."

"And do I fascinate you?" he asked with a mischievous wink.

You're the most fascinating man on this earth, she thought, and immediately the color rose in her cheeks. Aloud, she said, "May I claim the fifth amendment on that one?"

"Now you're playing my game," he noted. "Maybe I should throw myself on the mercy of the court." He pressed her hand against his cheek and gently moved her fingers over the faint stubble along his chin. Victoria sat transfixed, savoring the warm, prickly feel of his skin over the solid line of his jawbone. If only the kitchen table weren't separating them; if only the Hewletts weren't lurking in the other room. She wanted nothing more than to go into his arms, no matter what obstacles lay ahead, no matter how unlikely it was that they would ever find freedom from their pasts to love each other.

Phillip seemed to read her thoughts; his eyes said it all, and surely he read the same yearning in her eyes. Several moments passed and neither of them moved, lest they disturb the fragile spell that held them. Still caressing her hand against his face, Phillip murmured, "Maybe God's not against me, after all."

"What do you mean?" she asked, the words barely audible.

His dark eyes crinkled. "Look what He's done."

"What, Phillip?"

"Isn't it obvious? He brought you into my life, Victoria."

Chapter Eleven

Phillip had impressed Victoria with his clever scheme for getting Maude to give him a full tour of the house. But his ploy for getting a tour of the grounds from Sam was also quite admirable. "I noticed lilacs out your back window," Phillip remarked casually. "Do you know how rare it is to find beautiful lilacs like that in this part of the country? My grandmother raised them like that."

"No better'n those," declared Sam. "Come on outside and take a look."

Phillip winked privately at Victoria as he followed Sam out the back door. Finally, around 5:00 p.m., after a thorough tour of the yard, Phillip said a cordial goodbye to the Hewletts.

"If you wanna stay till six, you're welcome to eat a bite with us," said Maude, sounding more hospitable than she had ever been to Victoria. "It won't be much—some leftover meat loaf and rice—but you're welcome to it."

"That's very kind of you, Mrs. Hewlett," said Phillip in his most gallant voice, "but it's a long drive home and I have clients to meet early in the morning."

"On Sunday?" queried Victoria.

"That's the only day some of my clients can meet me."

Sam peered curiously at Phillip. "I don't recollect you telling us just what it is you do, son."

"No, I didn't," Phillip replied casually. "You might say I help people solve their problems."

"That sounds a mite vague to me," mused Sam. "You some sort of counselor or one of them newspaper fellas that dishes out advice?"

Maude elbowed Sam and tossed him a condescending glance. "Don't you know nothing, Sam? It's women that write them advice columns. I bet Mr. Anders is some sort of business consultant."

"Very perceptive, Mrs. Hewlett," replied Phillip, easing his way out the door. "Thank you again, both of you, for your hospitality. I'm sure we'll meet again."

Victoria walked Phillip to his car. "I wish we had time to talk privately," she told him.

"We can talk right here before I go."

Victoria glanced back at the house. "The Hewletts are watching."

Phillip smiled wryly. "They're waiting for our romantic farewell."

"They don't want to miss a thing."

"All right, they won't." In a grand, sweeping gesture, Phillip drew Victoria into his arms.

"Phillip, what are you doing? I told you they're watching our every move."

"We still have talking to do," he told her confidentially. "I don't want the Hewletts to think we're exchanging anything more than harmless lovers' endearments."

Victoria allowed herself to relax in Phillip's embrace. His arms felt amazingly good around her, so sure and strong and capable. And he seemed taller somehow, larger than life. The lowering sun was too warm on her face and hair, too bright, making her feel a bit feverish and light-headed. Or was it Phillip's closeness that made her mind whirl? "What...did you want...to tell me?" she asked, finding the words somehow elusive.

"I just wanted to say, I didn't notice anything suspicious in the house or in the yard, Victoria. Just as you observed before when you looked around, all the rooms are empty. There are no stairs to an attic, and Sam even took me into the garage and down into the fruit cellar. The house is clean. As far as I can tell, there's no place they could be hiding the boy."

"Are you sure?"

"If they were hiding him here, I don't think they'd be so willing to show me around. Besides, now that I've actually met the Hewletts, I have a theory about Joshua. I think they may have given up custody of him after the accident."

Victoria searched Phillip's eyes. She had never noticed their exact color before—not just dark brown, but a russet brown flecked with gold lights. "What makes you think they gave up custody of Joshua?"

"Several things," said Phillip. "Maude exhibits a great deal of antagonism toward the boy. She obviously never accepted him as her grandson. She saw him as a hindrance to the sort of life she felt her daughter deserved. I suspect she saw Julia's husband in the same light—as someone who had come between her and her only child."

"She said as much when she mentioned him taking Julia out of state to live."

"If Joshua had been Julia's natural child, I imagine Maude and Sam would have bestowed on him the same devotion they heaped on their daughter—"

"But he wasn't her child. He was someone else's, so they saw him as perhaps an interloper, a problem—"

"We can't be sure," said Phillip, "but that's how it looks to me."

"So what does that mean in our search for Joshua?"

Phillip pressed his cheek against hers. "I hope you don't mind, Victoria. I want the Hewletts to think we're having a long and tearful goodbye."

"Phillip, I—" She felt suddenly breathless. She could concentrate on nothing at the moment except his nearness.

Phillip was silent, too, as if he had forgotten the Hewletts as well as his reason for holding Victoria in his arms. A minute passed before he spoke. His voice sounded husky as he murmured against her hair, "My darling Victoria, I'm trying to maintain my professional integrity, but what you do to me!" He gazed at her with a mixture of solicitude and desire, and spoke her name again, as if he had never said it before. Before she could respond, his mouth came down on hers firmly, insistently, with a passion that left her weak and trembling.

Years before, she had received Rick Lancer's kisses meekly, passively, with almost a naive detachment. But Phillip's kiss was another matter. She found herself responding with heartfelt ardor and desire; she was kissing him back, unleashing her own long-repressed yearnings. So this was what it was like, she marveled, to love someone with all your heart, mind and soul!

After a moment Phillip released her, too abruptly, and held her at arm's length. "I'm sorry," he said.

"What's wrong?" she asked, scarcely finding her voice.

"Nothing," he replied. "I—I forgot myself. This little charade of ours probably wasn't a wise idea."

Victoria felt herself stiffen. "Charade? Is that what it was?" Had she misread him so completely? Hadn't he just poured out his soul to her as she had relinquished hers to him? How could he reject her now so swiftly? "I suppose you're right," she said shakily. She felt embarrassed, mortified, angry. His kiss had been only another ploy to outwit the Hewletts. But he had fooled her, as well. "Perhaps you'd better go, Phillip."

His tone softened. "Wait, Victoria." He drew her back and caressed the burnished curls that cascaded over her shoulder. "Before I leave, I want you to know my plans."

"I'm listening," she said coolly, her mind still spinning. What had just happened between them? For her, the whole universe was different now. How could Phillip ramble on as if they were still the same two people they had been an hour ago?

"I'm going to start checking every orphanage in this state and neighboring states," he was saying, his tone professional, pragmatic.

She stared up at him, trying to make sense of his words. "Check orphanages? Why, Phillip?"

"Like I said, it's possible the Hewletts relinquished their custody of Joshua—to an orphanage perhaps."

"But wouldn't it be in the official records?"

"Not if they did it on the sly or under a fictitious name." Phillip stole a glance back at the house. "You see, I think the Hewletts are too proud to publicly forsake their own legal grandson, but they may have found some covert way of removing him from their lives."

Suddenly Phillip's words were starkly clear. "You think Joshua may be stuck in some orphanage under another identity? Or adopted by another family who has no idea who he really is?"

"It's possible, Victoria. That's all I can say for now."

She tried to quell a rising panic. "Phillip, it can't be true!"

"Another thing," said Phillip.

She shook her head; she was feeling too emotionally thin to cope with more bad news. "What is it, Phillip?"

"I've reached a decision," he said solemnly. "If we don't uncover something definite about Joshua this coming week, I think we'd better confront the Hewletts directly with our suspicions or else turn the whole matter over to the police."

"Oh, Phillip," she cried. "What if our accusations force the Hewletts to do something desperate? What if they harm Joshua or see to it that no one ever finds him?''

"That's why I've put off confronting them or involving the police. But we can't let this thing drag on forever. They've given you only another week to stay here. And we've exhausted nearly all our resources. We've tried every tactic, and we keep coming up empty-handed.''

"Something will break for us this week, I'm sure of it. Whatever it takes, Phillip, I'll make it happen.''

"Nothing foolhardy," he warned with concern, his hand still caressing her hair. "I feel responsible for you, you know.''

Victoria smiled faintly. She wanted his consolation. She felt a ray of hope that he felt somehow responsible for her, and yet she still felt rebuffed. "I'm a grown woman. I think I can take care of myself.''

He wound one of her curls around his finger. "I'm sure that's true, but somehow, when we're together, I have the unmistakable feeling that *I* should be taking care of *you.* I must confess, it's a rather disconcerting sensation.''

She glanced around self-consciously. He was confusing her again—taking two steps forward and one step back, or vice versa. What was he trying to tell her? She wasn't skilled at reading a man's mind, let alone his heart. Perhaps it was safest not to take too much for granted. Keep your expectations low, she told herself, and you won't be hurt. "You'd better go, Phillip," she said, "before the Hewletts get suspicious. I'll call you this week—from the drugstore.''

He gave her a brief, almost perfunctory embrace this time, as if he had resolved not to let his guard down again. She felt a keen stab of disappointment. He had given her such a sweet taste of romantic intimacy; she couldn't help wanting more.

As he walked around to the driver's side of his sports car, he called back, "I'll telephone if I learn anything new. Take care, Victoria. And please, don't take any chances.''

"I won't," she promised. She stood watching, blinking back tears as Phillip drove away, a groundswell of emotion nearly overwhelming her as his car disappeared down the street.

But, moments later, as she walked back up to the house, her mind was already churning, grasping for ways to persuade the Hewletts to reveal their grandson's whereabouts.

* * *

On Monday afternoon Victoria returned home early from the library with a splitting headache—more, she realized, from her anxiety over Joshua than the pressure of her studies. As she entered the house, she was surprised that the Hewletts weren't in their usual spot, watching TV game shows. She called their names, then looked briefly outside. Their car was gone; everything was strangely silent.

This is my chance, she realized, the moment I've been waiting for!

Her headache felt better already. She had a few precious minutes to check the house, to inspect each room for clues that might lead to her son. Quickly, her heart racing, she put her books in her room and headed for the stairs. She had been upstairs twice—once when Maude had invited her up to see the crocheted soaps and another time when Victoria had privately explored the house during the Hewletts' brief absence.

Maude had made it clear that upstairs was out of bounds to anyone except Sam and her. Yet, as Phillip had noted, too, there was nothing upstairs to hide. There were four rooms—two bedrooms sparsely furnished and dusty with disuse, a cozy sewing room and a storage room filled with old clothes, cardboard boxes and stacks of magazines and yellowed newspapers.

Where to begin? Victoria decided to check the storage room first. She peered carefully into one of the large cardboard cartons. It was filled with flattened cereal boxes. Another box held egg cartons and empty coffee tins; another was brimming over with grocery box tops.

Victoria's agitation grew. Only a few precious minutes to search the house and she was wasting her time rummaging through trash—stuff that should have been discarded ages ago. What did Victoria expect? Maude was an ardent coupon collector. She took advantage of every manufacturer's free offer she could get her hands on. Her knickknack shelves spilled over with the cheap trinkets and baubles that years of collecting had reaped.

Victoria sighed, keenly disappointed. There was nothing here of her son. She went to the sewing room. She felt as if she were on a bizarre TV game show, running from room to room to find the door that held the prize—something, anything, to prove her son's existence.

The sewing room, too, looked harmless enough with its old-fashioned sewing machine, baskets of yarn, cloth remnants and sewing materials. Nothing here of her son. Dear God, help me! There has to be something in this house to lead me to Joshua!

With growing trepidation, she moved on to the bedrooms. The first appeared to be a guest room. It had an unused, anonymous quality about it. On the double bed was a quilted spread and two velvet throw pillows. The dresser and bureau were cherry wood; the large mirror was faded with age. Julia's bright, primitive-style paintings lined two walls.

Suddenly Victoria jumped, her heart in her throat. She had heard something—a noise outside. A car in the driveway? The Hewletts returning home? Her mouth dry as sandpaper, she stole a glance out the window that overlooked the front yard. An unfamiliar vehicle rumbled by. Thank goodness, it wasn't the Hewletts. She turned to the dresser and with cold, trembling fingers carefully opened each drawer. They contained clothes—blouses, nightgowns, undergarments—that could have belonged to either Maude or Julia. Victoria shuddered. She felt a stab of shame; she was violating the privacy of strangers.

Lord, forgive me! I have no choice. I've got to do this!

She felt underneath the clothes and ran her hand along the inside perimeters of each drawer. Again, nothing that belonged to a little boy.

Victoria sighed audibly. Beads of sweat had formed on her upper lip and her silk blouse felt damp against her skin. She was running out of time. The Hewletts would be back any moment now, and she had found nothing of consequence. She might never have this chance again. Please, God, give me something, even the smallest of clues!

She looked around again and noticed the closet door near the rocker. She hadn't had time to inspect the closets before. With clammy fingers she opened the old varnished door and peered inside. Her shoulders sagged as she gazed at the shelf of hat boxes and the row of overcoats, jackets and raincoats. Still nothing belonging to a child. Not even a little boy's coat or rubber boots.

Victoria went on to the other bedroom. Her legs were feeling rubbery and her breathing was ragged with anxiety. The upstairs was warmer than downstairs, with an airless, stale, closed-in quality. This room, too, was empty, except for an oriental rug on the floor and more of Julia's paintings on the walls. But there was something different about these paintings. They were all of small animals—puppies, kittens, lambs and baby chicks. They possessed an appealing charm—warm, bright and lively, something a child would like. Then it struck Victoria. Julia must have painted them for Joshua. Perhaps sometime in the past this had been his very own room.

Oh, Joshua, you must have loved these darling animal pictures. Did Julia show them to you and teach you the animals' names? Did you clap and laugh with glee over each little puppy and kitten? If only I could have been the one to share them with you!

Thoughts of her son brought waves of sadness and regret. Victoria pushed the feelings away and sniffed back the sudden tears. Impulsively she walked to the closet and turned the knob. It was locked. She tried again. The door wouldn't budge.

"What are you hiding in here, Mrs. Hewlett?" she said aloud. She turned in frustration and walked to the window. This room, too, overlooked the front yard. Thank heaven, the Hewletts still hadn't returned. Victoria gazed curiously at the window frame. It was square. Yet she recalled looking up at the front of the house and seeing a small arched window. Where was the room with that window?

Victoria seized on an idea. She rushed from the room, ran downstairs and hurried outside to the front yard. She stared up at the second-story windows. Yes, there were the rooms in which she had stood just moments ago. She looked above the double windows and spotted it—the small arched window above the others. "That's it," she cried. "There's an attic."

But how could it be? There were no stairs leading to an attic. Phillip had noticed that fact when he had looked around. If she had thought of an attic at all, she, like Phillip, had assumed it would be a small crawl space, nothing worth investigating. "But this attic is big enough to have a window," she marveled. "That must mean the locked door doesn't open into a closet at all." She shivered in spite of the heat. "Is it possible? It must be a stairway to the attic—a room I haven't seen!"

Victoria returned upstairs and tried the door again, futilely. It would take a key to unlock it. A key? A bolt of comprehension struck. "Maude's key! That's it! The one she wears around her neck!"

Victoria was trembling now, her pulse throbbing. The clue to Joshua's whereabouts lay behind this locked door. She knew it, felt it to the very marrow of her bones. Somehow, if it was the last thing she ever did, she would get that key.

Chapter Twelve

My hand is shaking as I write, but I've got to get these thoughts down now, while they're fresh and vivid in my mind. I'm convinced I'll find the answer to the mystery of Joshua behind the Hewletts' attic door. Don't ask me how I know; I just do.

In my imagination I picture myself opening that door and Joshua rushing into my arms and calling me Mama, the way that shadow-child of my dreams called me Mama that dark night weeks ago. But I realize how irrational my thinking is; Joshua can't be in the attic, or I would know. There's no way he could be there; no little boy would accept such cruel treatment without putting up a monstrous fight. And yet I have this feeling there's something up there that will lead me to him.

This afternoon I managed to get back downstairs before the Hewletts arrived home, and I don't think they suspect anything, but I've been walking around on pins and needles since discovering that door. I'm afraid I'll say or do something to give myself away. I want so much to blurt out my suspicions and demand that they unlock that door and let me unravel this terrible riddle. Then I catch myself and tighten my lips so I won't spill out all my anger and frustration. Phillip will want me to play this by the book. I've got to let him know what I've discovered, and yet I don't dare phone him from here.

When I think of Phillip, my mind feels unsettled, confused. I keep reliving that kiss and the feelings it prompted—the stunning realization that I love Phillip and will surely never feel this way about another man. But then I remember for Phillip that kiss was just an act for the Hewletts; he still has only one love in his life—Pauline. So I am filled with elation and despair all in one delirious, heartshattering emotion—elation to at last experience genuine love and despair over knowing it will never be returned.

But I don't dare think about Phillip now, except in a professional sense. My involvement with him must be limited to our pursuit of my son. I can't handle more than that right now. It's all I can do these days to cope with my fears and questions about Joshua.

No matter where else my mind takes me, my thoughts keep going back inevitably, chillingly, to that attic door. What lies behind it? I keep thinking I'll find something there that will lead me to Joshua. Strangely, I feel him so close to me; it's as if he's just within my grasp. And yet my logical mind insists a healthy six-year-old boy could never be housed in an attic without everyone within shouting distance knowing. And that realization leads me to a possibility I dare not even entertain. But the fear haunts me nevertheless—nearly convulses me, like an icy hand compressing my heart.

Dear God, please don't let Joshua be dead! Not after all this way I've come to find him! I trust You with my life; I know I must trust You with Joshua's, too. Help me to have the boldness and perseverance I need to get into the attic and see what's there. And give me the strength and grace to deal with whatever I find.

Victoria telephoned Phillip from the drugstore that evening and again the next morning, her sense of urgency growing. Each time she succeeded only in reaching his answering machine. Her information was too important to trust to a machine, so she replied with a formal, "Call me when you have a chance, Phillip. It's very important."

She hated talking to a machine; her voice always grew stiff and unnatural and her words bunched up and tumbled over one another. She suspected half the world hated answering machines as much as she. It was small comfort.

Secretly she found herself feeling almost relieved that Phillip hadn't answered her call. He might have insisted she leave the attic alone and let him handle it. Victoria had no intention of doing that.

She felt too close to uncovering the evidence of her son's existence and—she prayed urgently—his whereabouts.

For the next two days Victoria stayed home from the library and waited with growing tension for an opportunity to seize Maude Hewlett's key. The chain was always there around the woman's neck. Did she never take it off or leave it unguarded?

Finally, on Wednesday afternoon, Victoria saw her chance. Sam had gone to the hardware for lumber to replace several rotted fence posts. After lunch, Maude sat down to watch her game shows and promptly dozed off. Victoria considered removing the key from Maude's neck but immediately dismissed the idea. It was too risky. Maude would surely awaken. Besides, taking the key from her person seemed too much like stealing.

Even as Victoria stood debating what to do, Maude roused and glared up at her. "You want something?" she snapped.

"No," Victoria said quickly. "I was just on my way to my room."

"You ain't going to the library?"

"No, I've finished my research. I've got my laptop and I'm ready to begin writing my thesis. I thought it would be easier to work in my room where it's quiet and private."

"Don't let me keep you." Maude grunted.

Victoria hesitated. "If you'd like to go take a nap, I'd be glad to answer the phone and take any messages."

Maude heaved herself out of the chair. "I might do that. Even 'The Price Is Right' can't keep me awake today." She shambled off to her room and Victoria went to hers.

Ten minutes later Victoria stole down the hall and stealthily opened Maude's door. The woman lay sleeping, snoring loudly. Victoria turned her gaze to the bedside table. Sure enough, there was the key! She tiptoed over and wrapped her fingers painstakingly around the chain.

The slightest sound could awaken Maude. Victoria shuddered to imagine the woman's wrath if she caught Victoria in her room. With the key securely in hand, Victoria slipped out, closing the door carefully behind her. She glanced outside the front window to make sure Sam hadn't returned, then nearly flew up the stairs to the bedroom that held the mysterious locked door. With trembling fingers she inserted the key and turned the knob. The door opened!

She drew it back slowly, cringing with every silence-shattering creak of the old varnished wood. She peered inside and stared with a mixture of dread and anticipation at the steep, narrow steps leading up into a musty darkness.

I was right! These stairs lead to the attic! For a moment Victoria couldn't move. She waited, barely breathing, as if something—or someone—would spring at her from the black hole at the top of the stairs. What did she expect? Was it fear that gripped her now? Surely not a fear of ghosts or even the threat of bodily harm. It was something more elusive. She felt a sudden, unbidden terror of the unknown. What would she find in the attic?

A sour taste formed at the back of her throat as she allowed herself to articulate her deepest apprehension—that in this dark and lonely attic room she would find her son's lifeless body.

Victoria's skin prickled. Her palms felt clammy even in this airless room, oppressive with summer heat. Gingerly she began to climb the rough-hewn, dirt-encrusted steps toward the door at the top of the stairs. Already the air was stale and heavy with mildew.

Victoria reached the top step and turned the knob. The door was unlocked. As it opened, the pitch-black of the narrow stairwell gave way to a dim, golden-hued light from the high, arched window inside.

The shafts of afternoon sunlight effused the room with a burnished glow, like a photograph yellowed with age. But something else caught Victoria's eye—a startling image that flashed like an electric shock in her mind and would forever leave a wrenching, indelible imprint. A child sat on the floor in the corner, rocking slowly back and forth, his face expressionless.

A long, low moan escaped Victoria's lips. She covered her mouth with her hand and stared, transfixed. She felt her own body rocking unsteadily, as if responding reflexively to the child. "Oh, my dear Lord," she murmured. "What have they done to him?"

Victoria tried to move, but couldn't. It was as if she and the boy and everything surrounding them had been suddenly caught in a freeze-frame of time. He continued rocking, oblivious of her, his red curls damp on his forehead, his pale, freckled face blank, his large, unblinking eyes apparently unseeing.

"My son, my baby," she cried, the words nearly a sob. "You're alive. You're real! Thank God, thank God!" But, oh, she thought, dear Joshua, what kind of hellish existence have the Hewletts forced you to live?

She stood watching him, unmoving, hardly daring to breathe. Dear Father in heaven, I want to run and gather my child up in my arms and comfort him. I want to kiss his face and hair and rock him and soothe his hurts, but I don't dare. Something's wrong with him, very wrong. I've got to approach cautiously; I don't want to frighten or alarm him.

She gazed in stunned fascination around the attic room. It was nearly as large as the bedroom downstairs, but the low ceiling beams and the steep pitch of the roof made the space seem unnaturally compressed. Brown outdoor carpeting covered the floor; the walls were nothing more than unfinished wood. A youth bed occupied one side of the room; a small dresser and toy chest stood against the opposite wall. The air in the room was stale, tainted foully with must and urine. Victoria noticed a large plastic garbage bag beside the door, stuffed with soiled bedding. She had often seen Sam going out to the Laundromat carrying such bags, but she had never given them a second thought. Surely she had never imagined they contained her son's dirty laundry!

Victoria looked back at the boy and marveled that he still wasn't aware of her presence. Tentatively, her voice almost a whisper, she called his name. "Joshua?"

He continued rocking.

"Joshua," she said again. She took a step toward him, then crouched down and crawled until she was close enough to look him full in the face. She sat and gazed at him, fascinated. He was beautiful, with delicate, finely carved features and deep, dark, thickly lashed eyes. He sat gazing into space, apparently caught up in some fragile, ethereal vision only he could perceive. He looked like a perfect, expressionless doll, barefoot, dressed in a T-shirt and faded jeans.

Victoria felt tears rise in her eyes. She blinked them back but they spilled out, anyway. My baby, my baby, the last time I saw you, you were a helpless infant, a tiny pink angel with hair of spun gold, needing a mother's care. Now you're a boy, all elbows and freckles and patches and knees, and still desperately in need of a mother's care! I should have been here for you! All these years I should have been here!

She reached a cautious hand toward the boy, just short of touching him, and said tremulously, "You are my Joshua. I've waited six long years to look into your face."

Still, he rocked, silent, unseeing.

Victoria sat beside him on the hard floor and wept, yearning to touch him, yet terrified that one wrong move would scare him away.

Suddenly she stiffened. There was a noise on the stairs. Footsteps! The door behind her clicked—not open, but shut! A key turned in the lock. Victoria jumped up and sprang to the door. She wrenched the knob hard. It refused to open. "Maude—Mrs. Hewlett! Sam! Is that you? Please, unlock the door! I'm in here with Joshua!"

She stopped and drew in a breath. Of course they know I'm in here, she realized with a start. They deliberately locked me in! She hammered on the door with her fist and shouted, "Open this door! Let me out! You can't do this to me!" She called again and again. There was no response. At last she gave up, breathless, her throat raw, her body warm with perspiration.

She returned to the boy and sat beside him. He hadn't noticed a thing. His eyes held a dreamy detachment.

Victoria felt a wave of anger and frustration wash over her. "The Hewletts can't do this," she said aloud again. "People can't hurt other people like this. They must be insane!"

She reached over and gently touched Joshua's arm. He stiffened and stopped rocking. Alarm registered faintly in his eyes, but otherwise his expression remained blank. Victoria withdrew her hand and he began rocking again.

"What did they do to you, Joshua?" she cried. "How did they make you this way? You were a normal, happy little boy once, I know you were." She moved closer to him and gently slipped her arm around his shoulder.

The boy reared back and emitted a high-pitched scream. Victoria sat back, stunned. It was the same unearthly sound that had awakened her in the middle of the night weeks ago.

Then, without warning, Joshua threw his head back against the wall and battered it repeatedly—a sickening thumping sound against the musty timbers that tore at Victoria's heart. She reached instinctively for the boy, but he collapsed on the floor, his body rigid, his jaw clenched, his eyes rolling, his face contorted.

Within seconds Joshua's body began to jerk convulsively. "Oh, dear God!" Victoria cried in horror. This couldn't be her child; this broken, twisted shell of a boy was more animal than human! But somehow she had to help him, had to keep him from destroying himself. She leapt forward and grappled with the small thrashing body, dodging his flailing arms and legs as she tried desperately to hold him.

She struggled with the writhing child for what seemed forever, at last wrapping her arms around his warm, squirming torso and holding him tight against her to keep him from striking his head. Finally, gradually, Joshua's movements lessened and his perspiring body relaxed against hers.

Victoria was sobbing now, her own chest heaving as she rocked her exhausted son in her arms. Oh, God, what am I going to do? What sort of nightmare have I stumbled into? Please, help me! Help my boy!

At last Joshua slipped into a deep sleep, his abdomen rising and falling with each noisy breath. Victoria leaned down and pressed her cheek against his damp face and wept uncontrollably, her tears wetting his soft, pale skin. ''Oh, Joshua,'' she cried, ''what terrible traumas have you been through, my baby, to make you this way? Dear God, what have I done to my boy, letting him go, deserting him? Please bring Joshua back to me. Please bring back my son!''

Chapter Thirteen

Joshua slept so soundly in Victoria's arms that she feared he had slipped into a coma. She lost track of time. The sun's rays through the narrow window lowered and turned a burnished orange. Victoria's arms ached, but she refused to move lest the child awaken and be gripped by another seizure. She wept and prayed intermittently and raged in silence against the Hewletts. She didn't dare think what they might do now that she had uncovered their dark secret. Would they hold her captive just like Joshua? No. Phillip would come looking for her.

He wouldn't give up until he found her.

That was comforting—the idea that someone cared enough about her to seek her out and find her. The Lord had done that, and now God had led her to her own little son. Joshua was—if not well—at least alive. Somehow, now that she had found him, she had to believe her heavenly Father would make things right.

My Father God, please wrap us both in Your loving arms, protect us and send Phillip to find us soon. I've come this far for my son; don't let the Hewletts defeat us now!

As the last rays of the sun faded and evening shadows lengthened across the attic room, Victoria awkwardly lifted the sleeping child and carried him to his bed. She stretched her aching muscles and paced the little room, scouring her mind for a way out. Surely the Hewletts would open the door soon. It was past dinnertime. They would have to bring Joshua something to eat.

Victoria recalled the little plastic dishes she had often seen drying on the drainboard in the kitchen. She had assumed they were from the Hewletts' frequent TV snacks, but now she suspected they actually belonged to Joshua. Why hadn't she been more alert, more observant, more questioning?

Victoria located a light switch and turned on the single bare overhead bulb. She explored the attic room, stooping down where the roof lowered. There was a small alcove with a child's plastic potty-chair, a rusty, makeshift sink with a single, old-fashioned spigot on a pipe that meandered off into the darkness.

So this had been Joshua's home—for how long? Weeks? Months? Victoria shivered involuntarily as the anger surged back into her consciousness. She strode back to the door and pounded and shouted until her fists stung and her voice cracked.

Minutes later Victoria heard footsteps on the stairs. Her pulse quickened. She waited, scarcely breathing. A key turned in the lock and the door opened. Sam's tall, angular, loose-jointed frame filled the doorway. His dark, beady, ferretlike eyes burned through her. His nostrils flared and his pale lips contorted as he growled, "Git downstairs, now!"

Victoria squeezed past him and fled down the narrow steps to the second floor. At the foot of the stairs she looked around and asked, "Aren't you bringing the boy down, too?"

"He stays where he belongs," said Sam, locking the attic door behind him. He nearly pushed Victoria out of the bedroom and down the stairs to the living room.

Maude waited for them, stern faced, her hands on her enormous hips, the folds in her fleshy arms rippling with her every breath. She glared at Victoria, her thick, unattended brows arched menacingly. "What you got to say for yourself, Miss Carlin?" she snapped.

Victoria stared her down. "I think you're the one who has some explaining to do, Mrs. Hewlett."

Sam gripped Victoria's arm. "Don't get smart with us, girl. You been snooping around this house, getting into things that ain't none of your business."

"That boy upstairs is my business," Victoria retorted. "He's your grandson, Joshua. You said he was dead, but you've got him imprisoned upstairs in your attic." Her voice became a sob. "How could you do it to him? He's just a little boy. How could you lock him up like that?"

"I said, it's none of your business," warned Sam. "Now you git your stuff packed and git out of here."

"I'm not going anywhere without that child," cried Victoria.

Maude's bosom swelled with indignation. "How dare you threaten us! You come in here, a stranger, and start telling us what to do. You got your nerve, lady!"

"How long has Joshua been in the attic?" demanded Victoria.

"Get your stuff packed," ordered Sam.

Victoria searched his marble-cold eyes entreatingly. "What's wrong with the boy, Mr. Hewlett? What happened to him? Was it the accident?"

"Out! Now! No more questions!"

"But he's terribly ill. He needs treatment. He needs help. A doctor!"

"If you won't pack up, Miss Clarkin, I'll do it for you."

Victoria turned beseechingly to Maude. "Surely you must be concerned about Joshua's condition. He had a seizure just now when I was with him. It was horrible! There must be something someone can do."

"We done all a body can do." Maude snorted. "Ain't nothing will help that boy. It's too late."

"It's not too late," Victoria insisted. "Just let me take him and have him checked by a doctor—"

"That boy ain't going nowhere," declared Sam. "He stays put and that's final."

Victoria wiped the perspiration from her upper lip and inhaled deeply. She stepped back, squared her shoulders and looked evenly at the Hewletts. "Listen to me, please. I don't want to cause you any trouble. I just want to talk to you about that boy upstairs. Can't we sit down and have a calm, sensible conversation?"

Maude and Sam exchanged stony glances, then looked back grudgingly at Victoria. "What goes on in this house is our business, Miss Carlin," said Maude. "We don't owe you no explanations."

Victoria forced her voice to remain steady. "How can you think that locking a child in the attic is an acceptable thing to do? What would your daughter say if she knew?"

"She'd do the same thing if she knew the truth," said Maude.

"What truth?"

Maude looked away. "Never mind."

"Tell me, please. What truth? What terrible thing could make you lock your own grandson away like a wild animal?"

"That's just what he is," snapped Sam. "Wild as they come. Only half human, if you ask me."

"You mean because of the spell he had? Has he had them before? Is that what you're trying to hide?"

"Don't tell her, Sam," cautioned Maude. "We swore we'd die with the secret."

"If you don't tell me, I'll go straight to the police," Victoria threatened, her voice tremulous. "Then everyone will know what you've done."

"We done what we had to do," Maude lamented, sinking down onto the sofa. "We tried, but we couldn't handle him. Not Sam, not me. Sometimes he was okay—"

"At first, after the accident, he seemed okay," interjected Sam, "except he didn't talk—"

"Never said a word again after we brought him home from the hospital," continued Maude. "Not a word. Just sat and rocked, like a zombie, staring straight ahead, spookylike."

"Then the tantrums started," said Sam, his voice gravelly. "Not like most kids have. Joshua threw himself around, hit his head against the wall—"

"You must be talking about seizures, not tantrums," cried Victoria. "It's a medical problem, not a behavioral problem!"

"Call it what you will. He acted crazy," said Maude. "We couldn't hold him down or make him stop. He was wild as a wounded animal." She sighed heavily. "That's when we knew."

"Knew what?" coaxed Victoria, her voice ragged.

"We knew what was wrong, didn't we, Sam?"

He nodded, his high, bald forehead furrowing. "And we knew there was nothing we could do for the boy but hide him away."

"Tell me, please! What was wrong with him?" demanded Victoria, fighting back hot tears of frustration.

Maude fixed her gaze coldly on Victoria. "We knew Joshua had the devil in him, that's what."

Victoria stared at Maude in disbelief. "Devil? What are you saying?"

"The devil took Julia and let the boy live, simple as that, Miss Carlin. And the devil's not about to give up that boy."

"The devil doesn't have anything to do with this," cried Victoria. "That child needs medical care! Have you taken him to a doctor?"

"He was hospitalized after the accident," Maude replied. "He had a bad bump on the head—a real ugly gash—but it healed and went away. The doctors sent him home."

"But has he seen a doctor recently?" persisted Victoria.

Maude shook her head. "What's a doctor know about casting out devils?"

Sam stepped between Maude and Victoria. "We've said enough. Now it's time for you to git."

"Not without Joshua," said Victoria.

"You're crazy as the boy." He grunted. "What's a stranger like you want with a kid possessed by the devil?"

"He's not possessed! He's a sad, hurting little boy."

Maude stood and approached Victoria. "Don't you see? He wasn't our own. He wasn't Julia's flesh and blood. He was cursed from the beginning. He was a love child, a sin child—illegitimate. He wasn't wanted. He never should have been born." Her voice took on a high, intense whine. "It was him and his curse that killed our Julia. Why else would he live and she be the one to die?"

Maude's words struck Victoria like a clenched fist. She groped helplessly for words. She was shaking uncontrollably now. Her tongue felt thick in her mouth as the familiar barbs of accusation pierced her heart. In distant chambers of her mind she could hear her father's austere voice indicting her. *You've betrayed us, daughter, violated everything we raised you to be! This child never should have been conceived. It's a mistake only you can remedy; don't let an unwanted baby be a blight on your life!*

"It wasn't like that," she sobbed, her face in her hands. "I always wanted him. I never wanted to let him go!"

Maude and Sam stared at her. "What're you saying, Miss Carlin?" Maude drawled suspiciously.

Victoria shook her head, shattered, immobilized, as tears and pent-up emotion spilled over an invisible dam. "Don't you understand? I'm Joshua's mother," she told them brokenly. "I'm his natural mother and I've never stopped loving him!"

Chapter Fourteen

$\mathbf{F}$or the first time since Victoria had met them, the Hewletts appeared speechless. They stared at her, dumbfounded, their mouths gaping. Finally Maude found her voice. "You think we're fools enough to believe a story like that, Miss Carlin? Ain't no way you could be Joshua's mother."

"But I am," she insisted, her voice rising urgently. She had never stood up before and shouted to the world that Joshua was her son; now that she had, they didn't believe her! "I can prove it. Joshua's birth date—April 13. The hospital he was born in—St. John's, a beautiful old building with Spanish-style architecture. Dr. Daniel Palling, a gray-haired man with a stubby mustache, delivered Joshua. Dr. Palling's the one who first made contact with the adoptive parents, your daughter, Julia, and her husband. The lawyer who drew up the papers was Sidney—" she paused, gasping for breath "—Sidney Darnell. So you see, I have every right to speak in Joshua's behalf. I am his mother!"

An odious expression clouded Maude's face. Her eyes seemed to strain in their sockets. "Joshua's mother?" Maude scoffed. "A tramp's more like it!" Her cheeks puffed and the veins in her temple bulged as she demanded, "Just what is it you want, Miss Carlin?"

Victoria shrank back involuntarily, then steadied herself and met Maude's gaze squarely. All of his life she had denied her son and abdicated responsibility for him; now it was time to stand up for him and protect him, once and for all. "I want my son, Mrs. Hewlett," she said unswervingly.

Sam stepped forward, hovering over her, his eyes narrowed to malevolent slits. "He ain't yours no more. He's ours. That's the law."

"I think the courts will want to take another look at the situation," said Victoria. "They take a very dim view of child abuse."

"That boy's not abused," declared Maude. "Sam or me never once laid a hand on him. Joshua gets fed and clothed and taken care of just fine."

"That's right," Sam agreed. "You let some fancy doctor see how Joshua acts and he'll shut the boy up in some loony bin for sure."

Victoria reached out and clasped Maude's wrist. "Please, let me take the boy. I love him. I'll get the help he needs. No one would take better care of him than I."

Maude bristled and jerked her hand away. Her mouth twisted into a contemptuous sneer. "Go away, Miss Carlin, and don't you ever come back here again."

"We'll call the police," warned Sam. "You got ten minutes to pack your stuff and get out of here. Then I start throwing you and your belongings out on the street."

Victoria stiffened, her hands clenched so tightly she thought her knuckles would break. "I'll go, Mr. Hewlett," she said, "but I'll be back." She turned and ran to her room and shut the door behind her. As she swung her suitcase up on the bed, her muscles turned to jelly. She sank down weakly on the plush eiderdown quilt and tried to steady her breathing. "Oh, God, dear God," she whispered aloud, but her prayer was beyond words.

She forced herself to move, but she could scarcely fold her garments or pick up her jewelry from the bureau. In a numb frenzy she emptied entire drawers into her suitcases and dumped her books and papers into cardboard cartons.

Before she had finished packing, Sam burst into the room, grabbed her bags and began carrying them out to her car. "Time's up," he said. "Now out you go!" Gruffly he stuffed her things into the trunk while she loaded the back seat with some of her more fragile possessions.

With a final, menacing, "Stay away from here," Sam stalked back into the house and slammed the door.

Victoria sat in the driver's seat of her car, trembling, her emotions skittering wildly. *Lord, how can I leave here knowing my son is still* caged in the attic like an animal? Please, God, I can't just go away without Joshua. I feel as if my heart is being torn from my body! Help me to know what to do! Should I go to the police? Call some child protection agency? But who? And will they even believe me? She closed her eyes and gripped the wheel. Stay in control, she told herself sharply. Don't fall apart now. Call Phillip. He'll know what to do.

She drove to the drugstore phone booth and breathed a sigh of relief when Phillip answered on the second ring. "Thank goodness, you're home," she exclaimed.

"Victoria? What's wrong?"

She began to cry.

"Honey, what happened? Are you okay?"

"Oh, Phillip, I found him. I found Joshua. He was there in the house all the time!"

"In the house? Where? How?"

"It's a nightmare, Phillip. He's locked in the attic!"

"The attic? You can't be serious. I never saw any stairs to an attic. I figured there was just a crawl space."

"That's what I thought, too, but it's an actual room. The stairs are behind what looks like a closet in one of the upstairs bedrooms."

"Well, thank God, you found him!"

A sob caught in her throat. "I found him, Phillip, but the Hewletts found me, and they locked me in with him. Then they made me leave. They were so furious. They're insane, Phillip. They wouldn't let me take Joshua. He's sick. He needs a doctor. He's still there, locked up like an animal."

He made a low whistling sound. "I can't imagine it. You must be devastated."

"I am. I don't know what to do. I need you, Phillip."

"Darling, I wish I was there with you right now. I'm sorry you've had to face this alone. Listen, I'll do anything I can to help, but even if I leave now, I'm still hours away."

She pulled a tissue from her purse and blotted her eyes and nose. "I know, Phillip, but just hearing your voice helps."

"Now tell me about Joshua," he said with concern. "Do you think he's safe for tonight?"

"I—I suppose so. They haven't harmed him physically."

"All right, I'll leave tonight and be there before dawn. You say they made you get out of the house?"

"Yes, literally. Bag and baggage, out the door."

"Okay, listen to me. Go check into the motel I stayed in when I was in town. The Starlight Motel, remember? Get some sleep and try not to worry. I'll be there by sunup."

"I can't wait to see you, Phillip."

"Same here. Don't worry, Victoria. I'll do everything in my power to work this out. I won't let anyone harm you or your son."

"I know, Phillip. I'll be waiting. Good night."

"Good night, dear girl. God be with you. I'll see you in the morning."

Victoria numbly did as Phillip instructed. Even as she settled into the strange motel room and distractedly prepared for bed, she drew comfort from Phillip's words. *I'll see you in the morning.* Yes, Phillip would be here, and somehow he would make everything all right. As she lay down and stared up into the darkness, an image formed unbidden in her consciousness that would never be erased—the fragile, winsome face of her own silent, unreachable child. Joshua.

At six the next morning, Victoria was already dressed in jeans and an olive-green sweater and running a brush through her red, shoulder-length curls when Phillip arrived. Instinctively she ran into his arms and received his embrace. He held her for a long while, pressing her head against his chest. She could feel his heart beating as rapidly as her own. He caressed her hair and tilted her chin up to his. "Dear girl, you're crying," he murmured. "Your tears rend my heart."

"These are tears of joy and relief to have you here with me," she said.

"Then let's see a smile, not tears," he said, wiping away the wetness on her cheeks with his thumb.

She managed a teary smile, grateful for his tenderness. "I—I don't know what I'd d-do without you," she stammered. "I've never felt so helpless in my life."

He led her over to a quilted love seat by the window and they both sat down. "Now tell me everything that happened. Take your time. Don't leave anything out."

In halting words she told him her story. Somehow she managed not to cry again, although the tears remained in her throat in one great sob that ached for release.

Phillip's expression remained inscrutable as she spoke. He asked brief, pointed questions and merely nodded when she replied. When she had finished, he took her hand, pulled her to her feet, and said, "Come on, Victoria. Let's go."

"Go? Where?"

He picked up her overnight case and opened the door. "We'll stop by the coffee shop, grab some breakfast to go and head for the police station downtown."

"Then you do think this is a matter for the police?"

"Absolutely. The sooner we report this, the better."

At the coffee shop, Phillip ordered one coffee and a doughnut. Victoria wasn't hungry, but she held Phillip's coffee and fed him doughnut morsels as he drove. Shortly after he pulled onto the freeway heading for Middleton's commercial district, she asked him the question that burned in her mind. "Is there any way I can get custody of my son?"

Phillip kept his eyes on the road. Almost reluctantly, he said, "Maybe. But I don't want to get your hopes up."

"Why not?" she pressed. "The Hewletts are guilty of child abuse and neglect. How could the court let them keep him after the terrible things they've done to him?"

"First of all," said Phillip, accelerating as he pulled into the fast lane, "we've got to prove they did those things. And even if we prove the Hewletts are unfit guardians, that doesn't mean the court will give you custody of Joshua."

Victoria sank back in her seat. "I'm getting my hopes up for nothing. Is that what you're saying?"

He reached over and took the paper cup she held. "I just don't want to see you hurt, Victoria," he said, sipping his coffee. "That soulful look in your eyes just about does me in."

She smiled in spite of herself. "Now you make me sound like a cocker spaniel."

"No." He grinned back. "You're a lovely lady in every way, and I'd just hate to see what the ravages of an ugly custody battle might do to you."

"Well, that's a bridge I may never get a chance to cross," she said solemnly.

He handed her the coffee and said, "Have some. You look like you could use it." She started to refuse, then realized he was right. She took the cup and sipped slowly. It seemed a pleasant, almost intimate thing to do, to share the same cup. "I suppose, being a lawyer, you've been involved in many custody battles."

"More than I care to remember. But it's more than the court battle I'm concerned about."

"What else?"

"Well, there's...your reputation."

She nodded. "You mean, the public will know I had an illegitimate child?"

"There will likely be publicity. Can you live with that?"

She thought about it for a moment. She had been raised to consider appearances—what others thought of her—more important than anything else, even her own happiness, but that wasn't the way she wanted to live now that she was on her own and making her own choices. She had to be true to God, to herself and to her son, and if that meant publicly acknowledging and accepting responsibility for all her actions, past and present, then somehow she would find the strength to do it. "Yes, Phillip," she said, "I can live with publicity. I think I could do anything to have my son with me."

Phillip drummed his fingers on the steering wheel, as if he were already making plans. "Here's what we do, Victoria," he began. "We'll file a report of suspected child abuse with the police and Child Protective Services. You tell them just what you told me."

"Then what?"

"The police will dispatch a couple of officers to the Hewlett home to investigate the charges."

"They'll get Joshua out of there right away, won't they?"

"Yes, if the situation is as you described it."

"Phillip, are you doubting my word?"

"No, of course not. I'm just saying that the Hewletts are shrewd people. They may try to cover up what they've done."

Victoria tensed. "Are you suggesting they may harm Joshua?"

"No, I don't think so. I'm just saying that it's up to the police to decide whether or not the child should be removed from his home."

"Do you think they'll arrest the Hewletts?"

"I doubt it. But they'll begin an investigation to determine whether a crime has been committed."

"Will I be able to see Joshua?" she ventured.

Phillip's dark brows furrowed slightly. "I doubt it, Victoria. At least not right away."

"Where will they take him?"

"Probably to the hospital first for a routine checkup. From the way you've described him, I imagine they'll want to run tests to determine what caused his seizure and his apparent emotional trauma.''

"Being locked away in the attic has certainly contributed to his problems,'' Victoria declared under her breath.

"Well, I'm sure the Department of Social Services will recommend therapy and see to it that he begins some kind of special schooling." Phillip reached for the coffee cup and took another swallow.

"What happens then?" asked Victoria, taking the cup back and automatically sipping where Phillip had drunk.

"Then Joshua will be placed in a state home for dependent children until a court hearing determines whether he should be returned to the Hewletts.''

"Where do I fit into all of this?" she asked, turning the cup in her hands.

"You may petition the court for custody of Joshua, but you'll likely face a grueling battle with the Hewletts.''

"Will you represent me, Phillip?"

He gave her a dubious glance. "I'm a private investigator, Victoria. My days as a lawyer are behind me.''

She looked imploringly at him. "Please, Phillip. You've seen me this far. I can't imagine facing this thing without you.''

"Please, Victoria, don't ask me—"

She seized his arm with a desperation that startled both of them. "I've got to ask, Phillip. You're the only one I can trust. Please, do this for me.''

The tendons in his neck tightened, then relaxed. His lips moved slightly, as if he were silently arguing with himself.

"Well?" she coaxed after a minute.

"You've got me over the proverbial barrel, you know. My instincts tell me I can't let you stumble into this thing alone. For what it's worth, I guess I'm your man.''

She broke into a smile, relief sweeping over her. "Thank you, Phillip. Thank you! I owe you one, okay? In fact, if you win this case for me, I'll owe you everything.''

"I'll remember that.'' He smiled and reached for her free hand and pressed it against his lips; his lips were still moist and warm from the coffee. "We're here,'' he told her. "That big fortresslike building on the corner is the police station. Are you ready, honey? This is going to be one long day.''

"I'm as ready as I'll ever be," she replied with a tight little smile, "as long as you're beside me."

He winked supportively. "I promise, I won't leave your side."

Inside the station, with more nervousness than she expected, Victoria filed her complaint against the Hewletts. After an hour of answering countless questions, she sighed with relief as she and Phillip left the huge, gray stucco building.

"Now what?" she asked as they slipped into his sports car.

"We wait," he replied as he pulled out of the parking lot. "I asked the officer to telephone us at the motel as soon as he's filed his report."

"But that could be hours."

"You're right. Meanwhile, we go have some lunch, take a walk around town, go window-shopping, whatever."

"I almost wish we could have gone with the police when they confront the Hewletts," said Victoria.

"Our presence could make things volatile, Victoria. The officers will be very low-key and businesslike. They'll examine Joshua and check out the situation thoroughly without unnecessarily inciting the Hewletts. Believe me, that'll be best for Joshua, too."

"I know you're right," she agreed, "but I can't tolerate standing around doing nothing when my son's future is at stake."

Phillip gave her a thoughtful, sympathetic glance. He cleared his throat and said, so softly she could barely hear him, "You know, you might try praying."

She looked up quickly into his eyes. "Oh, Phillip, why is that always the last thing I think of?"

"I'm rusty in that department myself," he remarked, "but when Pauline was alive, no matter what happened, prayer was the first thing she always thought of."

Victoria winced at the mention of Pauline. She shrugged off the feeling. It was silly, reacting negatively to Phillip's wife, a woman who was dead. One would think I'm jealous, reflected Victoria. Maybe I am!

"Well, what will it be for lunch?" asked Phillip, slowing the vehicle and gazing around. "It looks like we're on Restaurant Row. Take your pick. Mexican or Chinese? Or we could settle for a plain old cheeseburger and fries."

"I don't think I can eat a thing," she told him.

"Then I'll pick the place, because you're definitely going to eat.

You can't survive on a few sips of coffee. You need some nourishment.''

She laughed. ''Are you saying I should have had some of your sweet, gooey doughnut? If that's your idea of a healthy diet—''

''That delectable doughnut was my idea of fine cuisine,'' he corrected. ''The perfect marriage of sugar and fat. But no, I won't inflict my dietary predilections on you.''

She beamed. ''Oh, I like that word.''

He grinned back. ''See, Professor, my vocabulary isn't as rudimentary as you suspected.''

''I never said—''

''No, I just saw it in the smugness of your expression.''

''Phillip, I never—!''

''I know. I'm teasing.''

She laid her hand lightly on his arm and said, ''Phillip, I like you just the way you are.''

His dark eyes crinkled, gleaming with unexpected tenderness, as he replied, ''And I love everything about you, Victoria.''

She looked away as the warmth rushed to her face. Was it just a casual remark, or was he trying to tell her how he felt about her? If only his sentiments matched hers! But this wasn't the time to analyze their feelings; that would only complicate the task at hand. ''Now, about that restaurant, Phillip—''

''We can go anywhere you say, Victoria.''

She felt a flicker of disappointment. He didn't sound as if he minded her changing the subject at all.

''I'll even suffer through tofu and yogurt,'' he said, ''if I can get you to eat something. I won't have you fainting dead away on me.''

''Don't worry, Phillip. I'd just as soon pick up something at a fast-food place and get right back to the motel. I don't want to miss that call.''

Phillip looked pleased. After buying some fish and chips at a nondescript beanery called Seafood Sam's, they returned to Victoria's motel room. After they had eaten, Phillip watched the news on TV while Victoria flipped mindlessly through her thesis notes.

From time to time she looked at her watch, and then at Phillip. Each time he gave her a sympathetic smile and reached over and patted her hand or squeezed the back of her neck. ''It shouldn't be long now,'' he told her.

But when two hours had passed, she tossed her notes aside and told Phillip, "It's taking too long. What if the police don't do anything? What if the Hewletts convince them nothing is wrong? Shouldn't we call and see what's happening?"

Phillip slipped over beside her, drew her close and stroked her hair. "I know it's hard, but we've got to hang in there, Victoria. Give it a little more time. We'll hear something. I promise. Meanwhile, talk to me. Tell me the story of your life. I want to hear every word."

She elbowed him playfully. "You're just trying to get my mind off Joshua."

"Is that so bad? Come on. Tell me what you were like as a little girl."

She laughed cynically. "You don't want to know."

"Sure I do. Cute as a button, I bet."

"You never would have noticed me, Phillip. I always had my nose in a book. I was the quiet, shy, studious type."

"You must have had fun sometime. Didn't you skate and jump rope and go to parties like other little girls?"

A scene from the past flashed in Victoria's mind—the disastrous seventh birthday party with no presents. She had never overcome the shame of being the little girl who deserved no gifts. In fact, she had never shared that humiliation with another living soul. She looked up at Phillip and searched his eyes; they were filled with compassion. "There was a party once," she ventured, "a very important one, but I don't think you'd want to hear about it."

He smiled down at her. "If it was important to you, I want to hear every detail. Don't you see? I want to know everything about you— the good and the bad—everything that has made you who you are today."

"It's not a pretty story, Phillip."

"Let me be the judge of that."

She smiled. "All right, you asked for it. I'll tell you a story I've never told anyone." The words came slowly at first, but before she knew it she was spilling out all the hurts and struggles she'd felt growing up—the fateful birthday party, her father's condemnation, her parents' strict discipline and the suffocating upbringing that caused her to flee at eighteen into the arms of a free-spirited renegade like Rick Lancer. She found herself pouring out feelings she hadn't even realized were in her heart. And all the while Phillip listened, watching her with eyes of love, acceptance and understanding.

She and Phillip were so immersed in conversation they were both startled when the phone rang. It was after 4:00 p.m. when the call came from the police. Phillip jumped up and answered on the first ring. Victoria stood beside him, dry mouthed, her body tense. She tried to make sense of Phillip's monosyllabic responses. Finally he returned the phone to its receiver and gazed soberly at her, his brows shadowing his eyes.

"What did the officer say?" she asked, her voice barely a whisper. "Tell me. I've got to know."

Phillip rubbed his jaw in a gesture of frustration and bafflement, then pummeled his fist against his palm. "Blast it all! I should have anticipated it. The Hewletts are nobody's fools."

Her heart pounded in her throat. "What are you saying, Phillip?"

His gaze was piercing, direct. "You were right to be concerned, Victoria."

"What happened? Tell me!"

Phillip raked his fingers through his hair. "The officers found no sign of abuse or neglect in the Hewlett home," he told her, heaving a sigh of exasperation. "Joshua was peacefully napping, surrounded by his own furniture and toys, in the upstairs bedroom, the one with the animal paintings on the walls."

Chapter Fifteen

"**O**h, no, Phillip!" Victoria gasped. She felt her eyes fill with tears. "Are you saying the police left Joshua alone in that dreadful house?"

Phillip clasped her shoulders to steady her. "No, Victoria. They took Joshua with them. The boy's out of the house for now."

"But how—if there was no sign of abuse?"

"The officer tried to talk with Joshua. He quickly saw that the boy has medical problems. He took Joshua to the hospital for tests. I imagine he'll be there for a couple of days."

Victoria reached for a tissue on the bureau and wiped her eyes. "What happens after that, Phillip? Will the Hewletts get him back with no questions asked?"

"Not at all," he said, drawing out the words for effect. "Because of your report, there will be further investigation. And I'm sure the doctors will do a thorough workup. So, you see, Joshua's condition will be carefully scrutinized from different vantage points."

"You're trying to cheer me up," she mumbled, "but you don't think I stand a chance of getting custody of Joshua."

"You don't know that and neither do I," he soothed. "Like I said before, we'll petition the court for a custody hearing. We'll do the best we can."

Victoria clutched Phillip's arm. "I want to go to the hospital," she said urgently. "I want to hear what the doctors say about Joshua."

Phillip looked doubtfully at her. "The Hewletts will probably be there. Are you sure you want to risk seeing them now?"

She walked over to the dresser and picked up her purse. "I've got to find out about my son. Do you want to drive me, or shall I take my car?"

He reached in his pocket for his keys. "Come on. I'll take you." He paused and held up a warning hand. "But no matter what happens, I don't want you saying a word to the Hewletts. It could jeopardize our case."

Her eyes lingered on his. She almost smiled. "*Our* case? That's the best thing you've said all day."

Fifteen minutes later Phillip pulled his sports car into the visitors' parking lot at Mountainview General Hospital. He and Victoria made their way upstairs to the pediatric wing and stopped at the information desk where a crisp, silver-haired nurse told them no information was available, except to family members. When Victoria blurted that she was Joshua's mother, the nurse looked skeptical.

"I was told that couple over there are the boy's parents," she said, pointing to the Hewletts in the waiting area.

"They're his *grand*parents," Victoria corrected, hardly masking her indignation. "Now, please tell me, where's my son? I need to see him. I want to be sure he's okay."

"I'm sorry, ma'am, if you want information, you'll have to talk with the boy's doctor," the starched matron announced. "That's who his grandparents are waiting for now."

"Please, I just want to take a peek at him," Victoria persisted. "I promise I won't disturb him or even let him know I'm there. Just one little look. I'm his mother. I need to know he's all right."

"I told you, ma'am, you'll have to talk to his physician."

Phillip clasped Victoria's arm and said confidentially, "Come on, we're not getting anywhere here. Let's go sit down and wait for the doctor."

Reluctantly Victoria allowed herself to be led over to the waiting area. She sat down, forcing back her tears as Phillip sat beside her and held her hand. "I've got to see my son, Phillip," she whispered. "Maybe I could just sneak down the hallway and find his room. No one would have to know."

He gently squeezed her hand. "No, Victoria. For Joshua's sake, we've got to play this completely by the book." Glancing across the room, he warned, "Don't look now, but we've got company. Maude Hewlett has spotted us."

Already Maude was storming toward them, her corpulent frame shuddering as she spewed her wrath for all to hear. "Well, if it ain't the flimflam lady and her snoopy friend! Ain't you a pretty sight! Pretending to be a prissy schoolteacher and acting so goody-goody while you was double-dealing us! How dare you show your lying face around here?"

Phillip's signaling glance told Victoria to ignore the woman's rantings—an order Victoria found almost impossible to obey. With trembling fingers, she picked up a magazine and pretended to scan it while Maude raved on.

"Listen up, Miss Fancy Schoolmarm, just because you sicced the police on us don't mean you're going to get that boy," the woman trumpeted. "He's ours and ain't nothing you can do to change it, you hear? You go back where you come from and leave us be!"

Victoria's pulse raced and she felt the color rise hotly in her cheeks, but she forced her eyes to remain on the page before her. Phillip cast her a sympathetic glance from the corner of his eye and tightened his grip on her hand. Then he flashed a mockingly chivalrous smile at Maude and said, "Have a nice day, Mrs. Hewlett."

Sputtering like a stalled engine, Maude stalked back to her seat. She sat, alternately glaring at Victoria and whispering loudly to Sam, until a tall, dark-haired physician approached and called their names.

Phillip nudged Victoria. "Come on. This is it—the doctor's report. We'll go over and listen from the sidelines."

But as Victoria and Phillip drew near, Maude turned on them and growled, "Get out of here, you troublemakers. This ain't your business."

The physician gave Victoria a swift, appraising glance, then looked back at the Hewletts. "You are the boy's legal guardians?"

"His grandparents," Sam said firmly.

"I'm Dr. Paxton." His expression was grim. He squared his shoulders slightly and made a low, rumbling sound in his throat.

"Mr. and Mrs. Hewlett, would you please come with me to my office where we can talk privately?"

As the Hewletts followed the physician down the hall, Victoria stepped forward, too, but Phillip placed a restraining hand on her arm. "Wait, Victoria."

She stared at him in surprise. "Why? I want to hear what the doctor has to say."

"I know, but I doubt the doctor will let us in his office."

"Then I'll tell him who I am. Surely he'll—"

"Maude will make another scene. We can't risk it, Victoria."

She searched his eyes in desperation. "Then how can I find out about Joshua?"

"I have my sources. We'll get the answers, but not at the risk of endangering your case against the Hewletts. For now, let's keep a low profile."

Victoria couldn't hide her exasperation. "Then what am I supposed to do now?"

He wrapped his arm around her shoulders. "It won't be easy, I know, but we're going home. For the next few days you need to try to get on with your life and forget the Hewletts."

Hot tears scalded her eyes. "And forget my son, too? That's easy for you to say."

"No, it's not easy," he countered softly. "Don't you know how much I want to make this situation right for you? If I thought staying here and confronting the Hewletts would help our cause, I'd be the first one to give Maude Hewlett a hefty piece of my mind. But that's not the way to win custody of your son."

"How can I leave the hospital without even seeing Joshua?"

"There's only one way," he said, drawing her against him. They were standing in the middle of the waiting room, embracing, Phillip's chin nuzzling the top of her head, when she heard the halting, deep-felt words erupt from his lips. "Father God, I don't ask You for much these days, but Victoria and I could sure use a favor right now. Will You please let Your guardian angels surround little Joshua and protect him every moment he's out of our sight? Help me to find a way to bring Joshua back into Victoria's life so she can be the mother to him she's always wanted to be. I'm praying this in Jesus' name. Amen."

She looked up at him, tears clinging to her lashes. "Thank you, Phillip. That's the most beautiful prayer I've ever heard."

"Now let's hope the Almighty thinks so, too." He released her and took her elbow. "Come on. Let's head back to the motel and get your stuff. We've got a long drive home."

She held back. "You really do think Joshua will be all right?"

"The boy's getting the best care he's had in a long time," he assured her. "He's in the capable hands of the medical profession and the Department of Social Services. There's nothing more we can do for your son now, except pray...and prepare for our day in court."

"When will that be?"

He looked thoughtful. "The custody hearing could be weeks or months away. I'll do all I can to get the earliest date possible."

Victoria hugged his arm and gave him an appreciative smile. They left the hospital and walked arm in arm out to the parking lot, both of them silent until they were back in the privacy of Phillip's car. "It's going to be okay, Victoria. You've got to believe that," he told her as they headed back to the motel.

"I know, Phillip. I'm trying to keep my hopes up." But even as she said the words, she felt a heaviness in her heart. Over and over again she seemed to be saying goodbye to her son without ever quite saying hello. *I feel as if I'm forsaking Joshua again, turning my back on him in his hour of need, going away when he desperately needs a mother to comfort him.*

As he drove, Phillip tried to make conversation, but her responses were abbreviated and tinged with the gloom and disappointment she felt. Just before they reached the motel, she rummaged in her purse for a tissue, but her fingers wrapped around something else instead. She held the tiny object up to the light streaming in through the windshield.

"What's that?" asked Phillip.

Fresh tears started. "It's one of Joshua's little toy cars. I found it in the Hewletts' pantry and kept it, just to have something of his to hold on to."

"Well, you hang on to it real tight," said Phillip, "and one of these days you'll be able to give it back to him yourself."

"Do you really believe that, Phillip?" she asked.

He nodded. "This is one of those times, Victoria, when we've got to hang on to more than a toy car. We've got to hang on to our faith in God's goodness."

"I'm hanging on for dear life," she murmured. "Joshua's life." She pressed the little metal car against her cheek. "You know, I've never given my son a gift," she said wistfully, "except a flannel receiving blanket when he was born. It had cute little puppies on it. But I don't know if he ever got to take it home."

"You gave him more than that," said Phillip. "The best gift possible."

"What's that?"

"You gave him life."

She flashed a grateful smile. "Dear Phillip, you always know just what to say to cheer me up."

After Victoria checked out of her motel room, she and Phillip headed for their cars. "I wish we were traveling together," she told him as they approached her vehicle.

He caressed her shoulder. "Me, too. It's a long drive and I could use some good company."

She looked around distractedly at the motel, the coffee shop and the parking area filling already with early-evening travelers. "I feel as if I'm leaving everything so unfinished, so unresolved," she told him, her voice cracking with emotion.

He embraced her for a long moment and kissed her forehead, then released her. "We'll be back, Victoria. I promise you, we'll give this fight everything we've got."

She blinked back tears. "Do you always go all out like this for your clients, Mr. Anders?"

He grinned. "You know me. I've got a soft spot in my heart for kids." He paused and added meaningfully, "And to tell you the truth, I've got quite a soft spot in my heart for you, too, Miss Carlin."

She managed a teary smile and said, "What a coincidence, Mr. Anders. It sounds like the same soft spot I've got for you."

He nudged her chin affectionately. "We'll have to talk about these soft spots one of these days."

He gave her a brief kiss on the cheek and held her door as she slipped into her car. She drove behind Phillip all the way home, stopping at a gas station when he stopped and joining him at a twenty-four-hour truck stop for coffee and a late-evening snack. He drove directly to her condominium and checked it briefly in spite of her halfhearted protests that she wasn't worried about intruders. His face sagged with exhaustion when he said good-night. "Get some sleep," he ordered good-naturedly. "I'll call you in the morning to see how you're doing."

"And you'll let me know as soon as you find out anything?"

"Absolutely. In fact, I'd stop by tomorrow, but I'm going to plow through my workload and clear the decks, so we'll be ready to head back to Middleton as soon as we get the word."

"That's fine with me, Phillip," she told him solemnly. "After all that's happened, I think I need some time alone to get my bearings."

"All right, but if you find you need a little company, just say the word and I'll be there."

"No, Phillip, I mean it. I could use some space."

He leaned down and kissed her lightly on the lips. "I'll give you all the space you need. But don't take too long. I'd like to come around and offer a comforting word now and then."

"Thanks," she said simply.

Victoria spent the next two days alone in her condo, sleeping late, pacing the floor and weeping without apparent reason. She nursed cup after cup of strong herb tea and listened for hours to melancholy songs she hadn't played since college. Both her body and mind rebelled against the emotional turmoil of the past several weeks. She couldn't bring herself to examine her thesis notes or write a single comprehensible sentence. She found herself watching TV as mindlessly as the Hewletts had.

She was depressed. There was no other word for it. She lived for Phillip's phone calls, but each time that he called to tell her he had no news she felt her emotions sink deeper into a dark abyss.

In her journal she wrote:

All of my son's life, people and circumstances have conspired to keep us apart—first, my parents and my own weakness and shame, then a legal document I never should have signed, and now the Hewletts and a court system that may never know the truth about Joshua's abuse.

My life, like Joshua's, hangs in limbo, buffeted by the whims of others who do not understand or care. I have never felt so powerless, so helpless, so alone. God, where are You? You promised to be with me always, but right now You seem so far away. Surely it's not Your idea of justice to rob a mother of her son or let a little boy be victimized by monsters like the Hewletts. Show me the way through this terrible maze, and help me to be strong enough to win back my child.

And yet, Lord, I must confess, even as my supplications for Joshua soar heavenward, my doubts loom greater. Dare I give voice to these silent forebodings? I must: What if I win him back; what then? What sort of life lies ahead for a wounded child like Joshua? Just because I'm his mother doesn't mean I'll be able to meet his needs. I'm a woman alone without the slightest idea how to be a mother, even to a healthy child. Oh, Lord, who would have dreamed there'd be so many obstacles to overcome when I decided to go looking for my son?

Finally, on the third day, Phillip telephoned again and said, "I've learned this much. Joshua is still in the hospital undergoing extensive testing—CAT scans, X rays, psychological evaluations, the works. As far as I can tell, the results aren't all in yet, but I'll let you know the minute I hear anything more." He paused, then asked, "How are you holding up?"

"Not well," Victoria confessed. "I can't seem to break out of this lousy mood."

"Want some company?"

"I'm afraid I'm not much fun to be around."

"Let me decide that. I'm coming over."

"It's not necessary, Phillip."

"Yes, it is. I don't care whether you've had enough space or not, I want to be with you. I'll be there in an hour."

Victoria caught a glimpse of her straggly hair and faded bathrobe in the antique mirror and said quickly, "Better make that two hours."

"Don't fuss," he told her. "Just throw on an old shirt and a pair of jeans."

When Phillip arrived, he took one look at Victoria and did a double take. Her hair was styled in soft, flowing curls and she was wearing a pair of designer jeans and a plaid shirt with the tails tied at her waist. He whistled approvingly, then exclaimed, "You look great!"

"You said to throw on a pair of jeans."

"And you threw them on just right. A perfect fit!" He touched her curls lightly as his gaze appraised her. "In that outfit, with your flaming red hair and freckles, you look like a gorgeous Huckleberry Finn."

"Am I supposed to be flattered by such a comparison?"

"Forget Huck Finn. You're just downright gorgeous!"

She felt herself blushing and changed the subject. "Are you hungry? I was thinking of throwing a salad together."

He clasped her hand. "No, I think it's time to get you out of the house for a few hours. Let's take a walk and maybe pick up a pizza somewhere."

"A walk? Are you sure?"

"Doctor's orders," he said, escorting her to the door.

"So now it's Doc, is it?" She chuckled as he led her down the stairs and onto the sidewalk.

"Let's just say I'm prescribing some fresh air and a change of scene for my best patient—uh, I mean, client."

As they walked, they linked hands and fell into a steady cadence. The air was warm and smelled of magnolias and honeysuckle. The lawns were a verdant green with neatly kept houses and apartment buildings nestled among gnarled oaks and towering sycamores. It was a pleasant neighborhood, with a certain settled, homey, yet anonymous look to it; it could have been any neighborhood in a hundred American suburbs.

They were silent at first, taking in the pleasant scenery and balmy air. But after a minute or two, Phillip looked over at Victoria and said, "It seems like weeks since I saw you. I've missed our times together."

"Me, too, Phillip. I've gotten used to having you to talk with. Since my mother died, I haven't had anyone to share things with— you know, the ordinary, everyday events."

"But from what you said, I thought you and your mother were never very close."

"We grew close in the years after my father died. We were both teaching at the university and sharing the condo. In some ways, we became more like sisters than mother and daughter. I have to admit I miss that, especially now. You just don't realize what you've lost until the person you love is gone."

"I know what you mean." Phillip's voice grew husky. "There were days after Pauline died when I'd give my right arm to be able to sit down and talk with her again—just to relive an average, uneventful day together."

"That's how I've felt the past couple of days about my mother," said Victoria. "It's almost as if I just wanted to be a child again and draw strength from someone else. Let someone else make my decisions for me, the way my parents always did." She smiled wryly. "I suppose that sounds like I'm trying to run away from my problems."

Phillip met her smile with his own. "It just sounds like you're trying to deal with a lot of deep, painful things. And like I said, I have a listening ear."

Victoria was silent for several minutes, her gaze taking in the homes and yards and greenery around her. Without quite looking at Phillip, she murmured, "To tell you the truth, I feel guilty."

He looked quizzically at her. "Guilty?"

"It goes back to what I said before. I've really never been able to forgive myself for what happened with Rick Lancer. I'll always believe that it was my pregnancy that caused my father's heart attack and killed him."

"That's pretty heavy stuff, Victoria."

"That's only half of it, Phillip," she confessed. "Maude Hewlett brought the rest of it home to me when I confronted her about hiding Joshua in the attic."

"What are you talking about?"

Victoria's voice wavered. "Maude told me she believes Joshua is cursed because he's illegitimate. She blames his natural mother— me—for his problems. She thinks that because he's a child of sin, he's possessed."

"That's a lot of baloney and you know it," said Phillip.

"I know it in my head, but in my heart I still feel guilty," she lamented. "Joshua *was* born because of my sin, and I feel responsible for everything that's happening to him now."

Phillip cleared his throat—a low, guttural sound. "Victoria, we've talked about this—how we both feel guilty over our past mistakes. I feel guilty every day for not giving Pauline the time and attention she deserved. Sometimes I think that, since she died, I've made her a saint in my mind. I've forgotten her faults and the problems and arguments we had. But making her a saint makes me feel even more guilty for being only a part-time husband."

"So what are you saying, Phillip?"

"I'm saying I know all about guilt feelings. Rationally, I know I'm being ridiculous to feel so guilty about Pauline, but emotionally—well, that's another story."

"Exactly," said Victoria. She raised her shoulders questioningly. "So what's the answer?"

He squeezed her hand. "I don't know, but the first one who finds it tells the other, okay?"

She nodded. "I feel better just talking about it, Phillip. Thanks." She flashed a smile while blinking back unshed tears. "In fact, I don't remember when I've enjoyed a stroll through my neighborhood as much as this one with you."

He draped his arm over her shoulders and pulled her against him as they walked. "I'll tell you a secret, Victoria," he confided. "I've never enjoyed anything as much as I enjoy being with you."

Chapter Sixteen

Phillip and Victoria had walked about halfway to town when Victoria had second thoughts about dining out. She looked up dolefully at him. "Could we skip the pizza, Phillip? I think I'd just like to head back home."

"Tired?"

"I just don't feel like mingling with people tonight. I guess I'm in one of my solitary moods."

"Does that mean you don't want my company?"

She clasped his arm. "It means I want *only* your company."

He smiled. "Then, by all means, let's head home."

"I could whip us up a mean omelette," she suggested, "with cheese, mushrooms, olives, the works."

"Now you're talking, lady."

A cool breeze was wafting through the sycamores as Phillip and Victoria climbed the steps to her condo. She was about to unlock her door when Phillip stopped her. "Let's stay out on the porch for a few minutes and enjoy the evening."

She nodded. "It'll be stuffy inside anyway, no matter how many windows are open."

They sat down on the wrought-iron love seat and were silent for several moments, comfortable, relaxed, his arm circling her shoulders. As he gently massaged her neck, she felt the tension easing and an aura of peace slipping over her. It was a perfect night. Even the ordinary sounds of the neighborhood seemed somehow subdued, remote. Crickets chirruped somewhere in the dewy grass, a television droned several doors away and a dog howled in the distance, but in the darkness of her little porch, Victoria felt a remarkable silence surrounding the two of them.

"That feels good, Phillip," she said softly. "It's just what I needed. I'm starting to unwind."

"I hope so," he replied as his fingertips continued to knead the tense cords in her shoulders and neck. "Your muscles are as tight as a drum."

"It's all the tension over Joshua. I never dreamed our search would end up like this, with so many problems and unanswered questions."

"You're not sorry we went looking for the boy, are you?"

She turned and looked at him. "Oh, no, not at all. Think where Joshua would be now if we hadn't found him!" She paused contemplatively. "Besides, if you hadn't taken my case, we never would have become friends. I can't imagine not having you in my life."

"My feelings exactly," he told her. "You've changed my whole way of looking at things."

"I have? How?"

"How do I put it?" He thought a moment. "I'm not buried in the past anymore. I know now I can survive without Pauline. I'm coming to realize it was her life that ended, not mine."

Victoria studied his face in the shadows. He was so strong, his sharply honed features as stalwart and dashing as a general's, and yet his eyes shone with such compelling warmth and tenderness.

"Do you suppose that's why God brought us together," she wondered, "so we could help each other at a difficult time in our lives?"

Phillip gazed at her, the moonlight reflecting in the dark wells of his eyes. "Victoria," he said softly. "Sweet Victoria. I think God may have had even more in mind than that."

"Phillip," she began, but she couldn't recall what she was about to say. Even more disquieting, she couldn't pull her gaze away from those captivating eyes.

He drew her close, the fragrance of his after-shave mingling with the cool evening air. "Victoria," he whispered, "at this moment I feel as if there's no one else in the world but us...and no other time but now." He ran his fingertips over her forehead, her nose, her chin. He traced the outline of her lips. "You are so beautiful, Victoria."

Slowly, gently, he gathered her against him and his lips sought hers, moving over her mouth with a tenderness that left her feeling weak, dazed…and wonderfully exhilarated. She wanted to lose herself in his kiss, the warmth of his embrace. Let this moment last forever; let me spend the rest of my life in Phillip's arms!

Time passed. Seconds perhaps, or minutes. Or perhaps she and Phillip were suspended in time, Victoria couldn't be sure. She couldn't be sure of anything right now, except that she had never felt so at ease with anyone, so connected, so in sync, her heart beating as one with Phillip's, her deepest yearnings mirrored in his eyes.

Deep shadows cut across his face, his eyes glistening with raw emotion. "I had forgotten how alive a man can feel when he's with a woman he loves," he told her huskily.

"Phillip, please—" She tried to speak over the eager pounding of her own heart, but his closeness had scattered her thoughts to the stars. What did he mean by "a woman he loves"? Do you love me, Phillip? Or are you thinking of Pauline? God help me, I'm not experienced in matters of the heart!

"Surely you don't…love me," she murmured at last.

"Don't I, Victoria?" he challenged, his mouth warm again on hers. After a moment he drew back and studied her with a slight scowl. "Did I assume too much? Perhaps you don't feel the same way."

"It's not that," she protested weakly. "I care very much for you, Phillip. I feel so many things, but I—I don't know what they mean. How can I trust what I don't understand?"

Phillip released her, sat back and sighed heavily. He shook his head and rubbed his hand over his face in a gesture of futility. "I'm sorry, Victoria. I don't want to spoil what we have together. It's just that it's been a long time since I've felt free to truly share myself with another person."

"I understand that. I feel the same way."

"And frankly, I miss the intimacy of marriage," he confessed. "Not just the physical aspect, but all the little commonplace things a person takes for granted when he has them. Things I took for granted in my wife. Falling asleep in her arms. Knowing she was beside me in the darkness. Reaching for her in the morning before I'd even opened my eyes. I miss those things."

Victoria winced inwardly. She didn't want to hear the intimate details of Phillip's marriage. Obviously he was still very much in love with his wife. "You and Pauline must have had a very special relationship," she murmured uneasily. "I've never had those things. I can only imagine what it would be like."

"But I'm not talking about Pauline now, Victoria. Don't you see? What I shared with her is gone, in the past. I'm talking about what I feel tonight with you."

Now Victoria really was confused. "With me?"

"Please, don't be alarmed. No matter how I feel, I would never pressure you, Victoria. If you're not looking for a romantic involvement—"

She stared helplessly at him. "But I didn't say that, did I? I—I don't know what to say." She wanted to cry, I don't know what I feel, Phillip. I'm drawn to you and terrified of you all at the same time! I don't know whether to run to you or away from you!

He smoothed her hair back from her face. "Talk to me, Victoria. Tell me how you feel."

How could she tell him what she hadn't even articulated for herself? The ideas were jumbled in her mind. "Phillip, I love being with you, being close to you," she began, choosing her words carefully. "But I'm afraid, too. I've never had a real relationship with a man. There was Rick, of course, but I was a young, naive girl. I never guessed his motives. I was swept up with the idea of romance, and then it all came crashing down on me when I learned I was pregnant. By that time Rick had skipped town and my life was in shambles."

"But that was years ago, Victoria," argued Phillip, gently tucking one of her curls behind her ear. "You've grown so much since then. You're not the same person."

"Are you sure? In some ways I feel the same."

"More importantly," said Phillip, "I'm not Rick Lancer."

Victoria cupped Phillip's cheek in her hand. "I know you're not Rick. But I can't help how I feel. The thought of getting close to a man—any man—strikes terror in my heart."

"Then you're saying we have no chance—?"

"No, Phillip, I'm not saying that, because what I feel for you feels an awful lot like love. Do you see the dilemma I'm in?"

"The dilemma we're both in."

"It's true," she agreed. "Neither of us knows whether what we're feeling is love. How do you know you're not just lonely and reacting to the first woman you've been close to since Pauline died?"

Phillip lightly kissed the tip of her nose. "You are so insufferably practical, Miss Carlin."

"And there's Joshua," she said softly. "Right now all of my energies must be spent in getting custody of my son."

"Yes, my dear Miss Carlin," said Phillip philosophically, "you are pragmatic to the core. But you're right. Our first concern has to be Joshua, his safety and his future. Then perhaps, when all of this is over and you have your son, the two of us can sit down and determine whether we have a future together, as well. Is it a plan?"

She smiled, her eyes filling with tears. "Yes, Phillip, it's a plan. And thank you for understanding."

He stood and pulled her up from the love seat. "Now if my memory serves me right, you were going to fix me the best omelette this side of the Mississippi."

The rest of the evening passed quickly for Victoria. Cooking for Phillip was fun and he praised her simple efforts to the sky. She felt relieved to have had their talk; in fact, felt closer to him than ever.

Phillip's last words to her before saying good-night were, "I'll call you tomorrow. We should have some news about Joshua by then."

Victoria slept fitfully that night, waking at the slightest sound. Her dreams were filled with a kaleidoscope of images: Phillip and his kisses, the Hewletts ranting and raving, Joshua crying for his mother. In one dream she and Phillip were on a roller coaster. She could feel the wobbly car groaning up the steep incline, then plunging dizzily down the other side, only to face another monstrous hill, another dark valley. And as the tiny car surged around the coiling track, she screamed and gripped the handlebar with every whiplash thrust. In the dream she saw a montage of faces before her eyes: the Hewletts, laughing maliciously; Joshua, his haunted eyes wide and vacant, a single tear on his cheek; and Phillip, his arms wide open, saying, "Come—no—go back!"

The telephone woke her at ten the next morning. She jumped out of bed, horrified that she had overslept. It was Phillip. She tried to sound bright and alert as she greeted him, but her tongue felt thick and her mind was still sluggish from slumber.

"Did I wake you?" he asked.

"Oh, no," she said quickly, then caught herself and admitted, "Yes. I should have been up hours ago."

"Well, while you were dozing, I've been busy. I found out there's going to be a hearing today in juvenile court to place Joshua."

"So soon?" she cried. "I've got to be there, Phillip."

"Hold on, Victoria. It's just a formality. The judge will place Joshua temporarily in the state home for dependent children while an investigation is made."

"I mean it—I want to be there, Phillip."

"No, Victoria. Our day in court will come in a few weeks if I can manage to get us on the calendar that quickly. Usually these things take months."

"Phillip, I can't wait months. Neither can Joshua."

"I know, and that's going to be my point. With Joshua's serious physical and emotional problems, he needs a stable family life as soon as possible."

"He won't get it with the Hewletts!" she exclaimed, her anger already rising to the boiling point.

"Well, that's what we have to prove," said Phillip. "I have an appointment with Joshua's caseworker today. I'll try to get the scoop on his hospital report."

"Please let me come with you, Phillip," she pleaded.

"My instincts tell me this isn't the time, Victoria. We've got to handle things on an objective, businesslike basis. Believe me, I think it'll be best for your case."

"It's hard, Phillip, but I'll defer to your judgment. When will I hear from you?"

"I'll probably get back late tonight. I'll call you tonight or first thing in the morning."

"No, Phillip. Please come directly here. I don't care how late it is. I've got to know what you find out." She paused and said, more lightly, "I'll have your favorite coffee brewing."

"How can I resist a good cup of coffee?" He chuckled. "You win. Keep the home fires burning. It may be midnight before I get there."

Phillip arrived at Victoria's apartment that evening shortly after eleven, looking weary, his hair mussed, his tie loose around his neck. He gave her a bear hug of an embrace and kissed her soundly on the lips. "Made it with time to spare," he quipped dryly.

Victoria shook her head pitiably and smoothed his mussed hair. "Oh, Phillip, you look awful!"

He gave her an appraising glance. "And you look terrific, my darling."

"Sit down," she said. "I'll get the coffee." She was back in a minute with a pot of coffee and a plate of bagels and cream cheese. Phillip had dozed off in the recliner. She shook him gently and handed him a cup of coffee. "It's black and strong," she said.

He roused, stretched and took the cup. "Just the way I like it."

She sat down across from him and waited until he reached for a bagel. Then she asked, "What did you find out, Phillip?"

He chewed slowly, sipped his coffee and looked at her, his eyes gentle with compassion. "Some of the news is good, Victoria, and some of it may be hard to take. I just wanted to let you know ahead of time."

She steeled herself. Whatever he had to say, knowing was better than not knowing. "Go on. I'm listening."

He cleared his throat perfunctorily. "Joshua was released from the hospital and placed in the state home. He'll be there until the custody hearing. With a few strong-arm tactics and some friendly persuasion, I was able to get the case on the dockets three weeks from now rather than the customary three months."

"That's good news, Phillip. Thank you for all your hard work." But she sensed this might be the only good news he had. She didn't want him to stall for her sake; she wanted the truth. "Did you find out what's wrong with Joshua?" she probed. "Did you talk to his doctors?"

Phillip took another swallow of coffee. "No, but I did talk at length with Joshua's caseworker. She's a pleasant lady named Mrs. Ramsey. I have a feeling she's sympathetic with our position. Of course, her main concern is what's best for Joshua."

"That's what we want, too," said Victoria. Was Phillip never going to get to the point? "Please, tell me. What did she say?"

Phillip sighed audibly. "She told me Joshua's problems stem from two sources—one physical, the other psychological."

Victoria caught her breath. "It's serious, then?"

"Joshua sustained a massive cerebral contusion in the accident six months ago that killed his parents," said Phillip solemnly. "He was in a coma for several days—"

"But he recovered. You told me that before."

"Yes, he came out of the coma and seemed normal enough at first. But he apparently passed into a second stage the doctors call 'cerebral irritability.'"

Victoria shook her head. "What does that mean? He became— what?—an irritable child?"

"More than that, Victoria. The doctors suspect he became easily disturbed by any form of stimulation—noises, light, even voices."

Victoria's stomach recoiled sharply, as if she'd been walloped across the middle with a broad beam. "Oh, Phillip, no! You can't mean— Surely the doctors aren't suggesting that Joshua's...crazy?"

"No, not at all," Phillip said quickly. "It's just that with a serious head injury, recovery isn't always complete at once."

"Not complete? What do you mean?"

"There's a lot to digest here, Victoria. The truth is, there may be residual headaches, vertigo, impaired mentality and even occasional seizures as a result of what the doctors term...'irreparable cerebral damage.'"

Victoria stood and walked over to the window. She was trembling, chilled to her very spirit. Her mind kept screaming, Not my son, this can't be my son! He's already been through too much, and I've waited too long for him. God, don't do this to us now! She felt sudden, irrational anger against both Phillip and God. Was Phillip trying to erase all her hopes? Was God trying to make her give up and forget about her son? More and more, the obstacles seemed insurmountable. "What you're saying is that Joshua is brain damaged," she stammered, tears brimming. "He'll never be a normal little boy."

Phillip rose and went to her. He wrapped her in his arms and rocked her like a child. "I'm *not* saying that, Victoria, darling. I'm saying that Joshua needs care. He needs treatment. He may need months, maybe even years, of therapy. But the brain has incredible compensatory powers."

Lost in his arms, she fought waves of despair. "This is too much. I can't take it all in, Phillip."

"Listen to me, darling," he whispered against her ear. "It's not hopeless. Even though part of Joshua's brain may be damaged, the doctors think he'll be able to live a full, active life."

"They *think,* but they don't *know,* do they? Nobody knows!"

"God knows," said Phillip quietly.

Victoria drew back from Phillip and covered her mouth with her hands. "My poor baby!" she cried. "He's been through so much! The accident. The loss of his adoptive parents. The horrible treatment he's suffered at the hands of the Hewletts! And now this! How can I help him? What can I do? I feel so helpless, Phillip."

He rubbed the wetness from her cheeks. "You'll do whatever you have to do, Victoria. He's your son."

She gazed up wistfully at him. "You have more faith in me than I have in myself." She sighed and shook her head in frustration.

"Listen to me. I don't even have custody of Joshua. I may never even have a chance to help him with his problems."

They settled on the sofa together. "That's where my job comes in, Victoria. I'm going to see to it that you get your chance. But first, how about a refill on the coffee?"

Shakily she got up and poured more coffee for Phillip and herself, then sat back down in the circle of his arm. They sipped their coffee in silence for several moments. I've got to get myself together, she told herself. I won't be any good to Joshua if I fall apart now. Help me, Lord, to think clearly and keep my emotions in check so I can help my son. "You mentioned something about Joshua's seizures," she said between swallows of hot coffee. "He had one the day I was with him. I told you, didn't I? Anyway, what I need to know is, can the doctors prevent them?"

Phillip held his coffee cup balanced in his right hand. "Yes, they can prevent them, Victoria," he assured her. "The doctors believe Joshua's had relatively few seizures, but they've put him on anticonvulsant medicine."

"For how long?"

"Maybe for the rest of his life."

Victoria shook her head ponderously. "I'm beginning to understand now where the Hewletts got their weird ideas about Joshua. If he suffered terrible headaches, acted strange and even had convulsions, as superstitious as the Hewletts are, it's no wonder they thought he was possessed."

"Only a warped mind would think that, Victoria," said Phillip. "A normal person would realize he was suffering from prolonged head trauma. They'd get him to the doctor fast for treatment."

"You're right, of course," she agreed. "Imagine how much Joshua has suffered these past six months because the Hewletts were too ignorant to help him!"

"I suppose, in their own twisted way, they figured they were protecting him and themselves by keeping him hidden away."

"Protecting him? No way!" declared Victoria. "They were ready to believe the worst about Joshua. I don't think they ever really accepted him as their grandson. And for some strange reason, they blamed him for their daughter's death. I think they actually resented him for surviving while she died."

Phillip set his empty cup on the coffee table. "Let's hope they realize now what a mistake they made."

He smiled at her. "You see how much your influence is rubbing off on me? I've even darkened the door of my former church a few times lately. All because of you."

"Then I hope you won't be disappointed in me today."

Meaningfully he said, "I hope you won't be disappointed in *me*."

"No, Phillip. No matter what happens, I know you've done everything you could for me." She wanted to say more, remind him of how important he was to her and how much she hoped he would remain a part of her life, regardless of the outcome with Joshua. But this wasn't the time to speak of their future, not when Joshua's future was still so uncertain.

Just before noon, they arrived at the courthouse—a large, imposing building with a disconcerting mixture of architectural styles. Inside, the empty halls smelled stale with age. Victoria's heels clacked noisily on the gray tile floor as Phillip led her toward the double, thickly varnished doors. They entered the room silently, his hand reassuringly on her elbow.

"No one's here," she whispered, glancing around. The courtroom had a sallow cast, like a yellowed, antique photograph. A flag stood in one corner and a painting of George Washington graced the wall behind the judge's enormous desk. A large fan whirred overhead, its blades revolving sluggishly. The July air was desultory, clinging to the skin like a sweat-soaked shirt.

Victoria and Phillip sat down on the hard bench in the first row behind a long, narrow table. Victoria removed a handkerchief from her purse and blotted her upper lip. "I was praying for air-conditioning," she whispered.

"Let's hope that's your only prayer that doesn't get answered today," he replied as he loosened his tie slightly.

Victoria heard a rustling sound behind her. She glanced around. Maude and Sam Hewlett had entered the courtroom with a tall, slender man in a gray business suit.

"They hired themselves a good man," Phillip murmured. "That's John Cleary, one of the shrewdest lawyers around."

"And look at the Hewletts," replied Victoria. "I've never seen them look so good." She stole another glance as the couple sat down on the opposite side of the room. Maude was wearing an attractive flowered dress and her white hair had been professionally styled. Sam wore a navy blue three-piece suit that gave him an air of class in spite of his shuffling gait.

"Looks like they're going all out to get back their grandson," noted Phillip, giving Victoria's hand a sympathetic squeeze.

She shook her head in discouragement, but before she could reply, her attention was diverted by a door opening to the right of the witness stand. A man and woman emerged. The woman, middle-aged and attractive, wore a long, black robe. "Is she the judge?" whispered Victoria.

"Yes. That's Judge Rosemary Thompson. I've heard good things about her. Strict, but fair. The man with her is the bailiff."

"I expected the judge to be a man with a somber expression and a face like Father Time."

"Looks can be deceiving, Victoria. There's still no way to tell whether Judge Thompson is going to be for us or against us." Phillip glanced around as several people entered the courtroom and sat down. "Now if we just knew what the various witnesses were going to say!"

As the hearing began, Victoria's tension mounted. Sergeant Reynolds, the officer who had removed Joshua from the Hewlett home, took the stand and gave his version of what he found. "It was sort of an iffy situation," he admitted. "A borderline case. We didn't find the boy in the attic like the complaint stated. He was in an upstairs bedroom, sleeping. The attic room was there, all right, but there was no clear-cut evidence anyone had been living in it. It looked more like it could have been a playroom to me."

"Then why did you take the child into custody?" questioned Cleary, the Hewletts' attorney.

"Because the boy obviously had serious problems. He couldn't—or wouldn't—speak. He seemed retarded or emotionally disturbed. And he had a couple of bruises we figured we'd better check out."

"What did the doctors determine to be the cause of the bruises?"

"The reports are there on the judge's desk," replied the officer. "The bruises were sustained during seizures brought on by the boy's earlier head injury."

"Then, to your knowledge, the boy showed no evidence of physical abuse at the hands of another person."

"That's correct, sir."

After the policeman's testimony on the witness stand, he was followed by Mrs. Ramsey, Joshua's caseworker from the Department of Social Services. Even Phillip's cross-examination could elicit nothing to cast aspersions on the Hewletts' conduct.

When at last Maude Hewlett took the stand, Victoria felt her pulse quicken and her face flush with resentment. Maude presented herself as a selfless, doting grandmother who still grieved brokenly over her daughter's untimely death. There was little in this weeping, sad-faced woman of the petulant, sarcastic shrew Victoria had encountered.

"I don't know why they took away our little boy," cried Maude, dabbing her eyes with a tissue. "He's all we got left of our Julia. It would kill us both to lose him now."

Phillip tried to provoke Maude to reveal her belief that Joshua was possessed by the devil, but Maude was too shrewd to be baited. She answered every question with an innocence and sweetness that left Victoria shaking her head in amazement.

Sam, too, remained imperturbable on the stand. When he spoke of Joshua, his eyes grew moist. "I just want to see the little tyke back in his own room at home where he belongs," he mumbled.

When it was Victoria's turn to testify in her own behalf, she felt her throat constrict and her mouth grow dry. Even though Phillip guided her gently through her story, urging her to share whatever she was able, her hands remained clammy and her fingers trembled. Never before had she faced a public gathering and confessed that she bore an illegitimate child. A wave of painful memories surged over her as she tried to speak. I'm coming across as an emotional, unstable woman, she realized.

After Phillip's sympathetic questioning, Victoria wasn't prepared for the vociferous attack by the Hewletts' attorney. "Why do you feel it would be in the child's best interests to be with you?" John Cleary asked her pointedly.

"Because I'm his mother," she replied simply.

"Have you spent any time with the child other than when you were in the Hewlett home?"

"No."

"Has the child demonstrated in any way an attachment to you?"

"No."

"Before this summer, in the six years since your child was born, did you ever attempt to find him or get custody of him?"

"No."

"Are you prepared now to do whatever is necessary to gain custody of your child?"

"Yes," said Victoria.

"In other words, knowing that you have no legitimate case of your own, you are willing to make false claims against the Hewletts in order to win custody of your son."

"No, that's not true!" cried Victoria, her voice rising uncontrollably. "The Hewletts kept Joshua a prisoner in the attic. Don't you see? Their minds are warped and twisted. They believe my son is possessed by the devil! They think my sin put a curse on their family. They even blame Joshua for their daughter's death. If you don't believe me, just ask them!"

A murmur rose from the small audience in the courtroom. "Order! Order!" demanded Judge Thompson.

"No further questions," said Cleary, his tone clipped, almost smug.

Victoria was trembling as Phillip helped her down from the stand. She sensed that nothing anyone else said would matter now after her outburst. She had inadvertently portrayed herself as a desperate, neurotic intruder while the Hewletts had painted themselves as homely paragons of paternal virtue and stability.

Victoria saw the truth in Phillip's eyes. She had lost any chance of gaining custody of her son. "It's over, isn't it?" she whispered despairingly.

"Not until the judge announces her decision," answered Phillip.

The pleasant-faced judge with her immaculate makeup and fashionable hairdo offered no hint of a smile as she gazed first at Victoria, then at the Hewletts. "I have heard the evidence presented in this case and I am ready to announce my decision."

Victoria prayed silently over the enormous lump in her throat. Phillip gave her a reassuring glance. An expectant hush fell over the courtroom.

"Ladies and gentlemen," said Judge Thompson, her voice smooth and articulate, "I've reviewed the medical reports and psychiatric evaluations on Joshua Goodwin. I've also considered the special circumstances of this case and the testimony made in this courtroom today." She looked at Victoria. "Miss Carlin, you have shown yourself to be an earnest young woman with strong maternal instincts. As a mother myself, I can understand your deep desire to be reunited with your son."

Judge Thompson paused a moment, then turned her attention to the Hewletts. "Mr. and Mrs. Hewlett, you appear to be a sincere couple devoted to your grandson. However, you did not secure the proper medical care for the boy following his accident, nor did you investigate the possibility of therapy, rehabilitation or psychiatric counseling for the child after the death of his parents. These matters must be remedied immediately.''

She shuffled several papers on her desk. ''The testimony that has been presented to me today offers no evidence of ill intent on the part of Mr. and Mrs. Hewlett. Rather, their neglect of their grandchild apparently stems from ignorance of the proper treatment required for a brain-injured child. It is this court's duty to order proper treatment and rehabilitation to be initiated promptly by the assigned guardian.''

She sat back and breathed deeply, her gaze sweeping over Victoria and the Hewletts. ''In a case like this, the court's first concern must always be what is best for the child. Joshua Goodwin has spent much of his life with Mr. and Mrs. Hewlett, knowing them first as his grandparents and, after the accident, as his only custodial guardians. They are the only family he knows and his only link with the parents he lost. On the other hand, the child has never known Miss Carlin, his natural mother, and he has demonstrated no emotional bonding with her whatsoever.

''For these reasons, and under the condition that all court-ordered treatment be immediately instituted, the court awards custody of Joshua Goodwin to his grandparents, Mr. and Mrs. Sam Hewlett.''

Chapter Eighteen

Victoria sank back, stunned. "Oh, Phillip, no!" she moaned. It's not possible! God, You can't do this to me! I can't lose my baby again!

Phillip reached for her hand and held it firmly. "Hold on, Victoria," he whispered.

"There has to be something we can do, Phillip," she insisted, hot tears escaping. "We can appeal, can't we? Tell me there's something more we can do!"

He slipped his arm around her, his hand caressing her arm. "We'll talk outside, privately. Just come with me. You'll be okay. We'll get through this."

Moments later, as Phillip led her from the courtroom, Victoria felt numb—her mind, her senses, every part of her being. Even her body seemed somehow detached, moving automatically, as if it belonged to somebody else. She clasped Phillip's arm urgently, afraid she would sink into a whirlpool of confusion, an abyss of grief. "I've lost my son twice now," she uttered despairingly.

Just outside the courtroom, she spotted Maude and Sam Hewlett standing with their attorney. She broke away from Phillip and cried, "Mrs. Hewlett, please, let me talk to you for a moment."

Maude turned and gave her a withering glance.

"Please let me see Joshua just once before I leave town," Victoria implored. "Just for a few minutes. I beg of you!"

"Haven't you caused that boy enough trouble?" snapped Maude.

"I just want to say goodbye to him," Victoria insisted. "Let me see him, and I promise I won't ever bother you again." Her chin quivered. "Please! Those few moments with him would last me for the rest of my life."

Maude looked at her attorney. "Do we have to let her see the boy?"

He spoke cautiously as he appraised Victoria. "No, you don't, Mrs. Hewlett, but the court might be favorably impressed if you concluded your dealings with Miss Carlin on an amicable note."

Maude and Sam exchanged private glances, then looked back warily at Victoria. "We'll see," stated Maude with a lofty shake of her head. She wound her arm around Sam's and they shuffled off down the hall.

"Take good care of Joshua," Victoria cried after them. "See that he gets all the treatment he needs."

"The court will see to that, Miss Carlin," their attorney assured her.

"We'll do right by the boy, you can be sure of that, Miss Clarkin," added Sam as he craned his neck for one last glance back at her.

Victoria gave him a reluctant nod. "Thank you. I'll be in touch."

Phillip slipped his arm around her shoulders. "Come on, Victoria. Let's go home."

"Phillip, I can't," she protested. "I've got to stay in town until I see Joshua one last time. Then I promise I'll come home."

"I can't leave you alone here in Middleton," he argued.

"I'll be fine. I'll check into the Starlight Motel." She laughed mirthlessly. "I've been there so often lately, it's become like a second home to me, anyway."

Phillip shook his head disapprovingly. "You're drawing this thing out, Victoria. It's not good for you."

"Phillip, I'm not—!"

"I thought my life was over when I lost Pauline," he continued fervently, "but you've helped me see how wrong I was. Now it's your turn, Victoria. You've got to forget Joshua and get on with your life."

She pulled away, bristling. "Forget Joshua? You, of all people, should know that losing someone you love doesn't make you forget."

Impulsively he pulled her into his arms and pressed her head against his shoulder. "I know, Victoria. I know how hard it is. It's just that I can't bear to see you hurting like this."

She looked up at him, tears brimming in her eyes. "I'll be fine. I promise. I'll pull myself together. You'd better go. I'll be home in a few days."

"I'd stay over, too, if I didn't have clients lined up all day tomorrow." He wiped a tear from her cheek. "I'll drive back here and pick you up when you're ready to come home, okay?"

She shook her head. "It's not necessary, Phillip. I can take a bus."

He smiled wryly. "Are you kidding? I'll drive you. I'm not letting you out of my sight any longer than I have to."

She smiled through her tears. "You've been so good to me. Thanks again for representing me at the hearing, Phillip. You're quite a good lawyer," she said sincerely.

"I'm just sorry I wasn't good enough," he soberly replied.

"You did your best, Phillip."

He massaged her shoulder comfortingly. "I know it's too soon to talk about where things are heading with us, but one of these days, when you're up to it, we've got a lot of talking to do."

She nodded and lifted her chin bravely. "I know, but I can't think about anything right now except Joshua. You understand, don't you, Phillip?"

He leaned down and gently kissed her lips. "Yes, I understand, but that doesn't make the waiting easy. You'll be in my thoughts and prayers every day, Victoria."

"And you'll be in mine, too, Phillip." Now that they were saying goodbye, even for a few days, she wasn't sure she could let him go. But she had to. It was time for her to show some old-fashioned gumption and fortitude. If she wanted to see her son one last time, she would have to face the Hewletts again—alone.

"Now if you would just drop me off at the Starlight Motel," she said with more bravado than she felt, "you can be on your way home."

At the motel they shared a teary goodbye. There were tears even in Phillip's eyes and his voice rumbled with emotion. "I feel like I've let you down," he confessed. "Believe me, Victoria, I've never wanted to win a case so much in my life."

They kissed goodbye—a long tender kiss filled with all the bittersweet emotions they both were feeling so keenly. Victoria could see that it was as hard for Phillip to leave as it was for her to have him leave. But at last he climbed into his sleek red automobile and drove away while she stood alone in the motel parking lot, waving forlornly and wondering why on earth she was letting him go.

The next afternoon Victoria telephoned the Hewletts from her motel room. "When may I stop by to see Joshua?" she asked, her tone as forceful as she could muster.

"We ain't got him back yet," said Sam curtly.

"Then I'll call again tomorrow," she told him, swallowing the disappointment that rose in her throat.

The next day was the same. Sam insisted, "The court ain't released the boy yet."

Victoria stayed in town over the weekend, her impatience growing. Every evening Phillip telephoned wanting to know when he could come pick her up, and each time she had to tell him it would be another day before she saw her son. She telephoned the Hewletts on Saturday and Sunday and both times they told her that Joshua still wasn't there.

On Monday morning, her nerves frayed to the breaking point, Victoria telephoned Mrs. Ramsey, Joshua's caseworker, and demanded, "When will Joshua be released to the Hewletts?"

There was a moment of silence before the woman replied with a note of puzzlement, "He was released to them the day after the custody hearing, Miss Carlin."

Victoria felt a wave of shock and incredulity wash over her. "Thank you," she said numbly, and hung up. That afternoon, she took a taxi to the Hewlett house. "Wait for me," she told the driver.

She knocked soundly on the door and waited several minutes before it creaked open just enough for Sam Hewlett to crane his neck out. He stared at her, his eyes narrow with contempt.

"I've come to see Joshua," she told him, squaring her shoulders. "I've brought him a present—a little Bible—"

"He don't need your Bible," snapped Sam. "We'll raise him by the good book just fine without you. Now you git yourself outta here and don't ever bother that boy again!"

"But you said I could see him and say goodbye!"

"I said no such thing, Miss Clarkin. And if you wanna pay a mind to the good book, you read a coupla verses the missus showed me. You read John 8:44 and Hebrews 2:14. Them verses spell out the truth about you and your boy!" With that, he slammed the door in her face.

Victoria returned to her taxi, weak-kneed and trembling. Why hadn't she realized the Hewletts wouldn't keep their promise? How could she have been so stupid as to trust them after all they'd done? "The Starlight Motel," she told the driver. She rummaged in her purse for her notepad and jotted down the two scripture references Sam had thrown at her, promising herself to look them up when she had a chance.

Back at her motel, she telephoned Joshua's caseworker again. "Are you sure someone will be checking on my son regularly and making sure he's treated well? And are you certain he will receive the proper therapy and schooling?"

Mrs. Ramsey tried to be reassuring, but Victoria remained unconvinced. "I'm terribly worried about my son," said Victoria, trying to hold back a sob. "I know I can't change the judge's mind, but I don't trust the Hewletts. I don't think they have Joshua's best interests at heart."

"I'm sorry, Miss Carlin," said Mrs. Ramsey, "but we all must abide by the court's decision."

So that was that. There was nothing more Victoria could do now but hope and pray that Joshua was in good hands. As Phillip had advised, it was time for her to return home and pick up the pieces of her life.

That evening she telephoned Phillip and said, "I'm ready to come home. There's nothing more I can do here."

"I'll be there first thing in the morning," he promised.

Later that night, before slipping into the motel's lumpy double bed, Victoria took out her journal and scanned the recent entries. It had been days since she had written. Maybe she could gain some perspective about things by attempting to compress the infinite chaos of her life into finite words.

Monday, July 27

My life is in such turmoil I don't even know what to write. All the things I assumed about myself have been brought into question during these long, painful days. I am a mother without a child to love. I am a woman drawn irresistibly to a man, but I am terrified of loving him. I am a child of God who feels orphaned and abandoned by her heavenly Father. I am a doctoral candidate writing about the difference faith makes in one's life when I find my own faith slipping away.

All that I thought I was, all that grounded me and made me feel secure, is gone, like confetti in the wind. I am back at square one. I must throw out all the old assumptions and begin again, from the beginning.

But where do I begin? And how?

I am weary beyond words. I would like to lie down and sleep, and sleep, and sleep. How can I think of the future when I can hardly get through today?

God, if I haven't turned You off by my rantings, help me through this terrible labyrinth of darkness, and restore my faith in You! Help me to know where to go from here!

Once Victoria had settled back in her own condominium, she plunged obsessively into writing her thesis. Not because it was any longer something she wanted to write, but because time was slipping away. Taking serious notice of the calendar for the first time in weeks, she realized in dismay that it was nearly August already. School would be starting again in a few weeks. She hadn't begun preparation for her fall classes. And her thesis was due by September 30.

On her second day home, she telephoned Phillip and reached his answering machine. For reasons she couldn't articulate, she decided against leaving a message. It was almost as if she didn't want to talk to him now. Perhaps she and Phillip had been seeing too much of each other lately. Or perhaps seeing him reminded her too much of Joshua and the trial. Or maybe she just wasn't ready yet to deal with the emotions Phillip stirred in her. Whatever the case, she figured she would buy herself some time and wait for him to call her.

The next evening he telephoned and apologized for not calling sooner. "I've been swamped with work," he said, adding contritely, "but that's no excuse."

"You don't owe me an apology, Phillip," she insisted. "It's not like we need to see each other every day. Besides, our business association is over—"

"Maybe so, but I hope this is just the beginning of our personal relationship."

"Except, you haven't sent your bill yet," she said, preferring to focus for the moment on business.

"No charge," he said emphatically.

"I won't let you do that, Phillip. You've already done too much."

"Never too much," he assured her. "Tell me the truth. Are you okay?"

"I'm fine," she answered, too brightly. "I've been working day and night on my thesis."

"Then it's coming along well?"

She began to say yes, then stopped. She couldn't lie to him. "No, Phillip, it's not. It's not coming along at all."

"Do you want to talk about it?"

"Not now. It's too complicated. I don't even understand the problem myself."

"Listen, Victoria. I've got some free time tomorrow. Why don't we get together and talk?"

"I suppose we could. Do you want to come here?"

"I actually had something else in mind. I've been stuck in my office so much these past few days, I'm ready for some fresh air and sunshine. How about a picnic?"

She laughed. "You mean just a simple, old-fashioned picnic somewhere in the country?"

"Sure. Why not?"

"Complete with picnic basket, fried chicken, potato salad…and ants?"

"Exactly. You bring the chicken. I'll bring the ants."

"All right," she said, catching his enthusiasm, "as long as you go light on the ants."

"Deal! I'll pick you up at noon tomorrow."

Victoria was ready for the picnic well before noon the next day. This outing offered her a respite from her own dark emotions as well as a break from laboring unsuccessfully over her thesis. She was determined to enjoy this friendly little diversion. She wore a lime green, sleeveless blouse and matching shorts that flattered her long, shapely legs. For a woman accustomed to pleated skirts and tailored jackets, shorts were a bit daring. But she was ready to be a little adventuresome for a change. And my spirits could certainly use a lift, she reflected as she tied her red curls back with a silk scarf.

The picnic basket sat on the table, brimming over with chicken, assorted cheeses, fresh fruit and homemade apple pie. Victoria rarely baked for herself, but this pie was her mother's special recipe that had never failed to delight her father's taste buds. She hoped Phillip would be equally pleased.

He arrived shortly after twelve and inhaled with exaggerated pleasure as the sweet, spicy aromas filled his nostrils. "I just may unpack that picnic basket right here in your living room," he warned.

"No fair," she protested, warmed by his eagerness. "You promised green grass, sunshine, fresh air...and ants!"

"And you shall have them all," he said, gathering up the basket and picnic gear.

Phillip drove to a wooded area several miles outside of town. He led Victoria through thick foliage to a grassy spot half a mile from the gravel road, where the sun filtered in gentle rays through the towering oaks and fir trees. With ease, Phillip spread out a blanket while Victoria unpacked the picnic basket.

"How did you ever find this place?" she asked as she settled back and stretched out her legs.

"My folks used to come here when I was a kid," he said, sitting down beside her. "In fact, somewhere around here there's a tree I carved my name on. Then later, Pauline and I came to these woods a few times. We figured someday we'd bring our own kids here. I guess it was one of those rosy dreams that was never meant to be." He stopped abruptly, as if caught short by his own unexpected admission. He cleared his throat uneasily and reached for a chicken leg.

They ate in silence for several minutes. Victoria wanted to speak, but nothing seemed appropriate. She realized afresh that Phillip grieved as deeply over not having children as she grieved over losing Joshua.

As if reading her thoughts, he remarked wryly, "We make a sorry twosome, sitting here all gloomy faced on such a glorious day."

"I should have warned you I'm not at my gleeful best this week," she confessed. "I guess even a picnic can't recapture the carefree days of childhood."

"Is that what you want to do?"

She thought a moment. "Not really. As you know, my childhood wasn't all that carefree. I've told you about it."

"I know, but tell me some more. I think we've barely scratched the surface."

She shrugged. "I don't know what else there is to say. My parents were older, very well educated and extremely achievement oriented. They put a lot of pressure on me. My father, especially. He could shame me with just a word or a look. I grew up thinking my only purpose in life was to make my parents proud of me. I studied constantly and my classmates considered me a total nerd. I never had any close friends, and I certainly wouldn't have considered wasting my time by doing something frivolous.''

"Like going on a picnic?"

"Right." She laughed. "Frankly, I'm not even sure I know what 'carefree' means."

"Well, maybe we can remedy that." He glanced around, a mischievous gleam in his eyes. "We could play hide-and-seek, or maybe chase a few squirrels, or climb a tree."

She hugged her legs against her chest and rested her chin on her knees. "If you don't mind, I'd rather just relax and soak up all this peace and quiet."

He nodded. "This place has a way of making me feel like we're the only two people in the world."

She smiled grimly. "That would simplify things, wouldn't it?"

He studied her closely. "You're really down, aren't you?"

She absently traced the geometric design in the blanket they sat on. "Does that surprise you?"

"No. I had just hoped that coming home and getting back into your thesis would take your mind off things."

"You mean, off Joshua."

"It hasn't worked, huh?"

"It's not that I haven't tried, Phillip. I've spent the past couple of days struggling with my work, trying to get something written, but I keep hitting a stone wall."

"What's the problem?"

She sighed deeply. "Right now, I'm not sure my thesis statement is true—that one's relationship with God makes all the difference in the direction of one's life."

"That's quite a turnaround," he said solemnly. "You were so convinced just a few weeks ago."

"I know." She shifted her position on the blanket, feeling suddenly ill at ease.

"What happened?"

She preoccupied herself with smoothing out a corner of the blanket, straightening the frayed yarn. "Originally I was trying to show that Flannery O'Connor's faith made a positive impact on her life and that a lack of faith spelled destruction for Sylvia Plath." She cleared her throat nervously. "But now I'm not so sure I can prove that theory in my own life."

"What do you mean?"

"I mean, I have faith in Christ and it should mean something to me, especially now when everything around me is falling apart. But lately I've felt more depressed than I've ever been in my whole life. I've read Plath for hours at a time, and I identify with almost everything she says. In her poem, *Lady Lazarus,* she talks about her own suicide attempts and about dying being an art. Phillip, I feel as if I know just what she's saying. And this is what scares me out of my wits—it actually appeals to me!"

Phillip shook his head, his expression registering disapproval. "I don't think you know what you're saying—"

"Of course, I know! I'm disproving my own theory! O'Connor must have had something else—something more—to be able to go on the way she did in spite of everything."

"Are you telling me that your faith in Christ isn't enough? That God isn't the answer?"

"Has He been the answer for you? You've admitted that you have only a nodding acquaintance with God, even though years ago you made the same profession of faith I made. Maybe we were believing just what we wanted to believe. Maybe, Phillip—maybe there is no answer! Maybe Plath was right all the time!"

Phillip sat forward and ground his jaw. "Have you considered that you might be feeling this way because you just lost your son?"

She rocked mindlessly back and forth. "I've considered everything, and I just keep going around in circles. I'm ready to throw out my entire thesis."

He eyed her carefully. "And your faith?"

"I don't want to give it up, Phillip," she said quickly. "I love the idea that God Himself is vitally interested in every aspect of my life and that He loves me unconditionally. But don't you see? If it's not true, I can't bear to hold on to such a lovely illusion, such a sweet fantasy. I've got to see it proved in my own life before I can make claims about His power in anyone else's life. And right now, I just don't know what I believe!"

Phillip stood and brushed off his jeans. "I wish I had been a better example for you. I've never doubted my faith—I just haven't bothered to do much with it."

She looked up curiously at him. "What is there to do with it?"

"I don't know." He gazed into the distance for a moment as if seeking some answer in the air. "Pauline felt it was very important to exercise her faith, the same way she exercised her body so it wouldn't get weak and flabby.''

"Exercise her faith?" echoed Victoria. "What did she do?"

Phillip stooped down beside her on one knee and looked her full in the face. "Well, every day Pauline had what she called her quiet time with God. And she was involved in one of those women's Bible studies. But it was more than that. It was like she had this special relationship with God. I mean, I knew Him as a nodding acquaintance, but she seemed to know Him as an intimate friend."

"I wish I had that sort of relationship." Victoria's voice had longing in it.

Phillip's expression grew pensive. "Pauline wanted so much for me to have the same kind of commitment to Christ she had. That's one prayer she didn't see answered before she died."

Their gaze remained locked. "You know, Phillip," said Victoria softly, "I suspect you're carrying around a lot of unnecessary guilt."

He looked away and rubbed his chin thoughtfully. "I suppose so. What I've got to remember is that Pauline was at peace and content with her life even when she knew she was dying. She claimed that it was her faith in Christ that gave her the courage to face death."

"Well, Phillip," Victoria said ironically, "what I'm having a little trouble facing right now is life. At the moment, death doesn't sound like such an unreasonable option."

Phillip looked incredulous. He stood abruptly and pulled her up beside him with a harshness that left her speechless. He gripped her shoulders and glared down at her with fire in his eyes. "Don't you ever let me hear you say those words again, Victoria. No matter what happens to you, and no matter what you believe, don't you dare speak casually of life."

His voice broke over jagged waves of emotion. "Pauline fought long and hard for every last, painful breath she could manage. I watched her dying slowly, day by agonizing day. I stood there watching and I couldn't do a thing. But she never gave up. She never stopped hoping. She loved life with a passion right to the end."

Phillip pulled Victoria roughly against him and held her so close she could scarcely breathe. She felt the sobs rising from his chest as he warned, "Don't you even consider throwing away what Pauline fought so desperately to hold on to!"

Chapter Nineteen

Phillip and Victoria stood weeping together in each other's arms until their tears were spent. "Oh, Phillip, I'm sorry! I never meant that I would consider taking my life," she told him brokenly.

He held her face in his hands with a fierce intensity. "It's just...the thought of losing you, sweetheart... To hear you speak so casually of life and death——the words twisted in me like a knife."

"Dear Phillip, forgive my thoughtless remarks," she begged him. "It was stupid and selfish of me to talk that way. I didn't mean to hurt you."

He caressed her head against his chest. She could feel the pounding of his heart through his knit shirt. "I know, my darling," he whispered. "It's okay. You don't know how much you mean to me."

Even after they had curbed their emotions and composed themselves, they remained in a silent embrace, each drawing strength from the other. Finally, with the slanting rays of the afternoon sun falling across their faces, they stirred. They moved apart, looked at each other and laughed faintly.

"We're quite a pair, aren't we?" he said as he gave her his handkerchief.

She took it and impulsively wiped the tears from his face. "I trust by that you mean we're good for each other," she replied breathlessly. There was a vulnerable, boyish look in his expression that wrenched her heart and made her want to hold him and comfort him always. Surprisingly, it felt good thinking about meeting someone else's needs for a change, especially Phillip's.

Wordlessly they packed up their picnic gear and walked back to the car. It was just after dusk when Phillip turned off the narrow country road onto the sprawling freeway. As the traffic thickened, they rode in silence, listening to mood music, lost in their separate thoughts, their solitary griefs.

As they approached Victoria's neighborhood, Phillip said, "Darling, I'm sorry if I overreacted. I'm not usually such an emotional person. In fact, I keep things pretty much to myself. I hope I didn't offend you with my outburst."

"No," she said softly. "You were right to remind me how precious life is. Expressing how we really feel is more honest than pretending everything is fine when it's not. I'm glad we shared our feelings with each other, Phillip. I've never been able to do that with anyone, surely never my parents."

"I've been in the same boat," he admitted. "When Pauline was alive, she was big on sharing, but that wasn't my bag. Then, after everything I went through during Pauline's illness and death, I had all these really rocky feelings inside and nowhere to dump them. I guess I dumped a few of them on you today."

She smiled wanly. "I don't mind. You made me take a hard look at myself. Besides, it felt good being the one offering comfort this time. You've been so good about listening to all my sorrows and complaints."

He looked over at her. "I know you're thinking about Joshua."

She nodded and looked out the side window.

"Tell me what you're thinking."

"The words won't come."

"Are you wondering if you'll ever be able to reconcile yourself to the Hewletts raising your son?"

"I'm trying to accept it," she told him. "I'm trying to convince myself they'll treat him well and love him, especially now that they know his troubles are related to his head injury rather than some mysterious demon inhabiting his body."

"The authorities will keep a close eye on Joshua, too, you know. He's getting anticonvulsant medicine to prevent the seizures and therapy to help him deal with his emotional trauma. He should do okay, Victoria."

"I just can't stop feeling anxious about him. Maybe I'd feel better if Sam Hewlett had acted a little more rational when I stopped by on Monday.''

Phillip glanced at her, one eyebrow arching. ''You went to see the Hewletts?''

''I went to see Joshua, but Sam wouldn't let me in the door. He was venomous. He wouldn't even accept the present I brought Joshua.''

''You shouldn't have gone there, Victoria.''

''I know, but I had to try to see Joshua just one more time. The Hewletts had behaved rather reasonably in court. With all the doctors' reports, they must know now there's nothing evil or superstitious about Joshua's condition. And I'm no longer a threat to them, so I thought they might accept my visit.''

''I'm sorry, Victoria.''

''Me, too.'' She sighed audibly. ''You should have heard Sam ranting at me. Believe it or not, he even quoted Bible verses.''

Phillip pulled into the parking lot behind her building. ''Bible verses, you say? That's odd. What were they about?''

''I don't know. They were just the references. I jotted them down, but I never looked them up.''

''I'd be curious to know what an odd character like Sam Hewlett finds noteworthy in the Bible.''

''Come on in for a minute and we'll look them up.''

He laughed. ''Is that a new version of 'come in and see my etchings'?''

She smiled in spite of herself. ''Sorry, fella, I have no ulterior motives.''

''Too bad!'' he teased. ''But I'll come in, anyway.''

Victoria's condominium was stifling after being closed up all day in the first-of-August heat. ''You turn on the air-conditioning, Phillip,'' she suggested, ''while I fix us some iced tea.'' She served the tea with the apple pie left over from their picnic lunch.

''I don't know how it's possible, but this pie tastes even better tonight,'' he told her.

''There's more in the kitchen,'' she said, smiling.

''Don't tempt me. If I pig out on your pie, I just may not fit behind my steering wheel.''

''Then I'll have to roll you home.'' She laughed. Amazing how wonderful it felt to laugh.

''First, let's check out those verses.''

Victoria took her Bible from the buffet, then fished in her purse for her notepad. She sat down on the sofa beside Phillip and paged through the book. "I'm not very good at looking things up," she confessed.

"Don't look at me," he said. "I always depend on the table of contents at the front."

After a moment, she found the book of John. "Here's the first verse he mentioned," said Victoria. "John 8:44. It says, 'Ye are of your father the devil, and the lusts of your father ye will do.'"

She stopped and looked up quizzically at Phillip. She could read the concern in his eyes. Covering her mouth, she stifled a gasp. "Oh, Phillip, he must mean me! He still blames me for everything that happened to Joshua!"

Phillip scowled. "Not a very friendly sort, is he? Read the other verse."

Victoria's fingers fumbled with the pages. "Here it is. Hebrews 2:14."

"Read it aloud, Victoria."

Her voice trembled as she read, "'Forasmuch, then, as the children are partakers of flesh and blood, he also himself likewise took part of the same, that through death he might destroy him that had the power of death, that is, the devil.'"

Phillip looked at her. "What do you make of it?"

"I don't know. It doesn't make any sense to me."

"Let me see it." Phillip took the Bible and scanned several verses. "The entire passage is talking about Jesus conquering death by dying for us."

"But you wouldn't get that message from that one verse alone," said Victoria.

"No," Phillip agreed. "It could be talking about anyone. I don't think Sam Hewlett was thinking of Jesus' atonement when he threw these verses at you."

"No," she conceded. "In fact, Sam even said the verses were about Joshua and me."

"The first one was clearly aimed at you."

"So this one must be about Joshua."

"Here," said Phillip. "Let me read it, substituting Joshua's name for 'he.' Forasmuch, then, as Joshua is partaker of flesh and blood, Joshua also himself likewise took part of the same, that through death

Joshua might destroy him that had the power of death, that is, the devil.''

"What does it mean?" she cried.

Phillip stood and paced the floor, shaking his head ponderously. "I don't like it, Victoria. I don't like the way that sounds at all."

She took the Bible and reread the verse. As the import of the words took hold, she felt an icy chill crawl over her skin. Her mouth went dry; she looked up at Phillip and said haltingly, "Tell me it doesn't say what I think it says."

Phillip hit his fist into his palm; his dark eyes blazed. "For crying out loud, the man would have to be insane—!"

"He is, Phillip. I've tried to tell you that before. He and Maude both."

Phillip sat back down beside her and took her hand; he massaged her fingers with a disturbing intensity. "The way it looks to me, Victoria—I pray to God I'm wrong—but I've got a feeling the Hewletts have it in their head that Joshua must die in order to destroy the demon they believe possesses him."

She stared wordlessly at him as the terrible implication settled over her like a shroud. She buried her face in her hands. "No, Phillip! They can't think that! They can't be planning to hurt my son!"

"We have no proof, Victoria. But it's a possibility we've got to face."

She looked up urgently at him. "Then we've got to get Joshua out of that house!"

"Hold on. It's not that easy."

"Then we'll call the police."

"The police will want evidence."

"We'll tell them about the verses," she persisted.

He shook his head. "So Sam Hewlett mentioned a couple of Bible verses. That doesn't mean a thing, Victoria."

"But you and I know it does!"

"Listen, if we don't handle this the right way, we'll never prove that the Hewletts intend to harm Joshua."

She gripped his arm beseechingly. "But we've got to do something fast, Phillip. Who knows what is happening in that house?"

"Stay calm, Victoria." Phillip's tone held an undercurrent of authority. "I'll telephone my contacts in Middleton tomorrow and have them check things out. They'll keep an eye on the Hewletts until we can figure out our next move."

It isn't enough, thought Victoria fiercely, but she kept her opinion to herself. Even as Phillip kissed her good-night and promised to call her the next day, she remained distracted, her mind on Joshua. For several hours after Phillip had gone, Victoria mulled over ways of freeing Joshua from the clutches of the Hewletts.

After a sleepless night, she rose at dawn with a carefully formulated plan of attack. She would drive to Middleton this very day and confront the Hewletts. She would demand that they confess their devious intentions regarding her son. She would— No, no, no! It would never work! As Phillip had said, she needed proof.

But how?

Then an idea struck. With mounting excitement, she searched her purse for her key ring, examined the keys, then let out a whoop of joy. She still had the key to the Hewlett house! Sam had evicted her so swiftly that returning the key had never occurred to either of them.

Victoria gulped down a quick breakfast, then threw a few clothes into an overnight bag. She considered telephoning Phillip but dismissed the idea. He would never approve of her going alone to Middleton, especially if he knew what she was planning to do. But, before leaving, she would call Mrs. Ramsey, Joshua's caseworker in Middleton. The woman had been friendly and helpful. Perhaps she would tell Victoria how recently she had checked on Joshua and how he was doing.

But Victoria was more than a little dismayed by Mrs. Ramsey's reply. "We're really swamped with cases right now, Miss Carlin. But I'll see to it that we follow up on the boy every few weeks. Please don't worry. He'll be just fine."

Victoria thanked the woman with a polite detachment, hung up the phone and picked up her overnight bag. With renewed determination, she strode out of her apartment and climbed into her little compact.

She revved the engine and roared out into the street, veering quickly into the thick stream of traffic. Already, she was trembling with a mixture of foreboding and resolution. One thing was certain: No matter what it took, she would not return home until she was sure Joshua was safe!

Chapter Twenty

That afternoon Victoria checked in at the Starlight Motel in Middleton. "You're getting to be a regular customer," the bald manager told her with a smile.

Victoria managed a tight smile in return, but as soon as she had paid for her room, she turned and strode out. She wasn't in the mood for idle chitchat. She walked over to the coffee shop and sat in a back booth. She wasn't hungry, but she had hours to wait before she could make her move, so she ordered the veal special and picked at it, killing time.

After dinner she went to her room, sat on her bed and watched TV. The evening news, a game show, a sitcom, a police drama. As the hours crept by, she felt her stomach twist into painful knots. Her head throbbed. The tension was so tangible and terrifying, she couldn't concentrate on the television programs. Every muscle and nerve was wound too tight, ready to spring. If she didn't act on her instincts soon, it would be too late. *Dear God, I must be out of my mind doing this!*

At midnight Victoria left the motel and drove to the Hewlett home. The lights were out; everything was quiet. She parked beside the curb several houses down the street, then removed her shoes. Carrying them, she walked up the sidewalk in her stocking feet. She climbed the porch steps, taking care not to let the sagging timbers creak. With slow, precise movements, she inserted the Hewletts' key into the lock and painstakingly opened the door inch by agonizing inch.

She slipped inside. So far so good! She stole down the hall past the Hewletts' closed bedroom door and climbed the stairs to the second floor in excruciatingly slow motion. She quickly checked the first two rooms, knowing they would be empty. Then she entered the pleasant room with animal paintings on the walls. Joshua's room. She closed the door and turned on a small bedside lamp. Just as she had expected, it was empty. The youth bed was neatly made and Joshua's toys sat propped against the walls, but there was no sign of the boy.

Victoria turned to the attic door and gripped the knob. It wouldn't open. He's back in the attic! she screamed inside. She tried the knob again and again. The door wouldn't budge. Victoria began to weep. "How can they do this to you, Joshua?" she whispered. She sank against the attic door, overwhelmed by anguish and frustration. "Oh, God, please help us," she uttered despairingly.

Suddenly Victoria heard a sound on the stairs. She stepped back, her heart pounding. The bedroom door opened and Maude Hewlett stood in the doorway, her face livid with rage. "You!" she shrieked. "What are you doing here!"

Victoria shrank momentarily from the woman, then recovered her courage and said accusingly, "You locked Joshua in the attic again! How could you?"

"It ain't your business no more, lady! Never was your business." Maude turned and shouted down the hall. "Sam! Get yourself up here. We got trouble!"

Moments later, Sam scuttled into the room, tying his robe around him. His gray-streaked hair was mussed, and his glasses were askew on his nose. He took one bleary look at Victoria and his mouth gaped open. "Miss Cl-Clarkin," he stammered.

"She came here to steal the boy," said Maude. "You go call the police, Sam."

"That so, Miss Clarkin? You come here to take our grandson?"

"No, of course not!" exclaimed Victoria. Had the whole world gone crazy? She felt like the fabled Alice in Wonderland squaring off with the Mad Hatter and the loony Queen of Hearts. "I came here to see how you were treating Joshua. And I found out! You've still got him in the attic!"

"That's the best place for him," growled Maude, "no matter what the lot of them fancy doctors and social workers think."

"You won't get away with it this time, Maude," cried Victoria, her hands clenched and knees locked to hide the shaking in her limbs.

"Won't we?" Maude slipped the key off from around her neck and unlocked the attic door. "Sam, before you call the police, bring Joshua down to his room, so the officers can see how well we're taking care of him."

Sam climbed the attic stairs and returned promptly with the sleeping child in his arms. Victoria reached instinctively for the boy, but Sam elbowed her away. He laid Joshua on the bed and pulled the covers over him.

"Now go call the police," snapped Maude. "I wanna see them arrest this lady for kidnapping."

Sam nodded and left the room. Victoria knelt beside Joshua's bed and gazed yearningly at the slumbering youngster, hungrily memorizing his every feature. She wanted to gather him into her arms and kiss his pale, freckled face. She wanted to rock him and croon to him and never let him go. But she didn't dare disturb him. He looked so peaceful in his sleep, his expression relaxed, his lips partly open. "You're so beautiful," she murmured, brushing strands of red hair from his forehead. "How could anyone help but love you?"

Maude stood in the doorway, her arms folded on her chest. "Get a good look at the boy now, Miss Carlin, because the cops are going to put you away for a long, long time."

Victoria looked up at Maude, anger erupting in her throat like bile. "How dare you? You know I didn't come here to kidnap Joshua," she said unevenly. "I only came to check on him. I had to see for myself what you were doing to him, and believe me, I've seen plenty."

Maude's doughy face seemed to swell with indignation. "You ain't seen nothing, and no cop will believe a word you say. You broke the law coming in here. That's what the law's gonna see."

Minutes later, Victoria heard police sirens in the distance. She stood and leaned against the wall and put her head back wearily. *No sense in fighting this. I might as well wait for the police. Maybe they'll be the voice of reason in this mess.*

She closed her eyes and waited, listening as the front door downstairs opened and deep, male voices filtered upstairs. She heard Sam and the officers ascending the stairs in noisy clip-clops. She opened her eyes as they entered the bedroom. They stood, poised warily before her. She immediately recognized one of the officers as the patrolman who had testified in the custody hearing—the very man who had originally removed Joshua from the Hewlett home. He looked at her in surprise. "Miss Carlin?"

"You're Sergeant Reynolds, aren't you?" she exclaimed. "I remember you from the hearing."

"That's right, miss." His expression shifted slightly, as if he were somehow embarrassed. "The Hewletts have made a complaint against you. They claim they caught you trying to kidnap your son. Is that so?"

"No, sir," Victoria said quickly. Surely he would believe her!

"Did they invite you into their home tonight?"

"No, but—"

"You're saying you broke in?"

"No, I had a key," she said, holding it out to him. "I rented a room here for a while. They never took back the key."

Maude was sputtering now. "Are you cops gonna stand here all night gabbing with this woman? She broke into my house and tried to take my grandson. I call that kidnapping!"

"I wasn't kidnapping anyone!" retorted Victoria. "I just wanted to see how you were treating my son. You locked him in the attic again. How could you do that?"

"She's lying!" barked Maude. "Get her out of my house. Do your duty, officers. Arrest her!"

Sergeant Reynolds looked at his partner. "I've had dealings with Miss Carlin before. There's no evidence she tried to take the boy."

"But she's here in the house illegally," argued the other officer. "We could charge her with burglary—breaking and entering."

"She walked in with her own key," said the sergeant.

"Charge her with felony burglary," said his partner. "If the district attorney wants to, he can reduce the charge to misdemeanor trespassing."

"Misdemeanor?" exploded Maude. "I want this woman arrested for kidnapping, nothing less!"

Sergeant Reynolds heaved an exasperated sigh. "Just let us do our job the best way we know how, Mrs. Hewlett." He looked resignedly at Victoria. "We'll have to take you down to the station, Miss Carlin. You were trespassing. We'll read you your rights on the way."

"I'll go with you," replied Victoria hesitantly, "but please have someone check on my son. I really did find him in the attic again. I beg you, don't leave him in this house with the Hewletts."

The officer looked over at the sleeping child and shrugged. "He looks all right to me, miss. Don't worry. You'll have a chance to make a full statement downtown."

Victoria took a final, lingering glance at her son before the officers led her downstairs and outside to their police vehicle. She rode in silence for several minutes, her mind whirling with the events of the past hour. She felt numb, as if lightning had struck her mind and short-circuited her senses. After a while she found her voice and uttered what she hoped was a comprehensible sentence. "Will I be put in jail?"

"Looks that way, miss," said Sergeant Reynolds.

Perceiving a note of sympathy in his tone, Victoria ventured another question. "How long?"

"Depends. If you've got cash for your bail, you can get out right away. Otherwise, you stay in for seventy-two hours, until your arraignment."

"Arraignment?"

"Your court hearing where charges are filed against you. You can plead guilty or not guilty. Then the judge sets a court date for your trial."

Victoria shook her head, stunned. Hot, bitter tears rose in her eyes. "Oh, dear God, what have I done?" she murmured under her breath. "Jail—and a trial, too? I could lose my job at the university. I could lose everything!"

"Looks like you shoulda thought of that before you walked into the Hewletts' house uninvited," said the other officer.

"How much will my bail be?" asked Victoria, briskly wiping her tears.

"Two thousand dollars for a burglary charge," replied Sergeant Reynolds. "You get yourself a bail bondsman and it's two hundred dollars—cash!"

Victoria swallowed over the ache in her throat. "I don't have that kind of cash on me. I'd have to go to the bank—"

Reynolds's partner laughed involuntarily. "Bank? You don't understand, lady. You're not going nowhere for a while. You're gonna be cooling your pretty little heels in a cell."

Sergeant Reynolds cut him off with, "Listen, Miss Carlin, you better call someone here in town and see if they can't get that money for you fast."

She lowered her head. "I don't know anyone in town."

"That's a shame," said the officer softly.

Victoria stared out the window as a few, scattered multistory office and bank buildings came into view. They were downtown now, just minutes away from the police station. Victoria remembered it—a large, fortresslike building made of slate gray stones on the corner of a busy intersection. Weeks ago, she and Phillip had gone there to file their complaint against the Hewletts. Now, incredibly, the Hewletts were filing a complaint against her!

Victoria shivered involuntarily as she spotted the ominous building outlined by shards of light from the sentinellike street lamps. An unshakable coldness settled over her, penetrating the very sinews of her body. She wondered if she would be able to move, to walk, to utter a rational word in her own defense.

Fighting a debilitating numbness, Victoria managed to walk between the officers into the station house. The central office was sprawling, cluttered with desks and files everywhere, the walls lined with maps, charts and wanted posters. Victoria was led to a cubbyhole, one of the many offshoots from the main office, where an officer interrogated her for nearly an hour. Between leisurely drags on his cigarette, he wrote down her statement, word for word, then asked her to read and sign it.

The words might as well have been hieroglyphics for all the sense they made, but Victoria wearily scribbled her signature, anyway. Her hand was trembling so badly she could scarcely write. She felt as if she were slipping away, falling helplessly into a chasm of her mind's own making—a bizarre protective defense. She fought against it. And lost. Her mind went blank with terror.

The officer squashed his last cigarette in a grimy ashtray, then led her out of the cramped, smoke-filled room. He spoke to someone else. She heard the words, "Book her."

Someone took her things—her purse, her jewelry, her shoes. A woman's voice came at her from a great distance: "Come with me, Miss Carlin. This way."

The events that followed were an odious mixture of nightmare and stark reality. The incidents themselves summoned such pain that Victoria would recall them afterward—and forevermore—with a terrifying, surreal distortion. They would haunt the dark niches of her memory for the rest of her life.

She had become part of a process—ugly, sordid, humiliating. She was subjected to degradations; she saw them through her own eyes, but at the same time she felt as if she were standing off at a distance watching a helpless Victoria Carlin endure an execrable ritual of dishonor. She was fingerprinted. Photographed. Stripped of her clothing. Searched mercilessly by a rock-jawed prison matron.

Victoria steeled herself against the small atrocities of incarceration that were already dismantling her personhood, but she couldn't erect a barrier against the avalanche of shame that enveloped and numbed her. As she stepped awkwardly back into her clothes, she felt defiled. Changed. Diminished. With a captive's mindless obedience, Victoria followed the matron down a narrow hall flanked by cells. Somehow, she found her voice and uttered, "I need to make a phone call...please—"

The square-faced woman looked at her. "Didn't they let you call someone yet?"

"No," rasped Victoria. "Please, take me to a phone."

The matron relented and took Victoria to a small office nearby. "Go ahead," she said, nodding at the wall phone.

"It's long-distance, but I have a credit card in my purse," said Victoria, realizing immediately how ludicrous her explanation sounded. All of her things had been taken away.

"Go ahead. Make your call," said the woman.

Weakly Victoria dialed Phillip's number and prayed that he would be home. Her arrest was not news she could relay on an answering machine.

She sighed in relief when she heard his voice, but before she could speak, she broke into tears. "Phillip, oh, Phillip," she managed at last. "Please come. I need you!"

"Victoria, where are you? What's wrong?"

She spilled out the words in uncontrolled sobs. "Jail—Maude called the police—they arrested me. The Middleton jail. Please help me!"

"Speak more slowly, Victoria. I don't understand. We must have a bad connection. It sounded like you said you're in jail!"

"I am," she wailed.

After several minutes of urgent, emotional conversation, Phillip comprehended the situation. "How could you, Victoria?" he demanded, his voice rising. "You shouldn't have gone there alone like that."

"Please don't lecture me, Phillip. Just come get me!"

"What's your bail?"

"I don't know. Two thousand dollars, I think."

"I don't have that kind of cash on me, Victoria. I'll have to contact a bail bondsman. I'm sorry, hon. You'll have to stay there till morning."

Victoria felt every muscle in her body systematically collapsing. "Oh, Phillip—" she groaned "—please hurry! I don't think I can survive this!"

Chapter Twenty-One

Victoria was placed in a small cell in the women's section of Middleton Jail. The dank, dismal patch of space assigned to her was flanked by iron bars and contained nothing more than a cot, a sink and a toilet. The rank, musty smell revulsed her. She shuddered as the heavy barred door clanged shut, separating her from the guard and all other humanity.

Dear God, she thought wildly, I'm trapped in the center of a nightmare. Help me, I can't breathe, I can't function. The whole world has closed in on me; I'm suffocating. Please, please, get me out of here. I'll die; I'm all alone, dying inch by inch!

She stared down the narrow hall into the murkiness of other cells, her eyes hungry for the sight of another person. But it was the middle of the night. Only the random ceiling lights shone dimly along the cramped passage between the cells. Shadows loomed and fell along the corridor, but Victoria could spot no people. I feel like the last person on earth. No one will come, no one will find me! A heavy silence reverberated through the halls, echoing off the myriad bars, and mixing with distant, muted noises from other parts of the building.

Oh, God, I've never been so alone! Victoria felt the aloneness grip her from the inside out, rendering her more desolate than she had been the night her son was born or when her parents died. She lay down on the narrow cot and curled into a fetal position, hugging her body defensively. I'll close my eyes and go to sleep, and soon the nightmare will end and I'll wake up in my own bed, not this scummy one. She could feel the bedsprings through the wafer-thin mattress. The foul latrine odors made the stale air repugnant. It's not working. I can't escape, even in my mind. I'm still here in this hellish place! She turned her face toward the cement-block wall in her cell and sobbed until her chest ached, but her pain was beyond the relief of tears.

Never in her life had she stopped to consider what prison might feel like—the sudden loss of freedom, like an amputation of the spirit; the devastating sense of rejection; the overwhelming, immobilizing shame. She had been forsaken by God and man. She was worthless, condemned. This is the closest I've ever felt to being dead, she thought grimly. Maybe I am dead; I've died and they've buried me in this musty tomb!

No, this wasn't death. This was worse. Victoria's body was imprisoned, but her mind was running wild, summoning every wrongdoing she had ever committed, dredging up the past with a rabid fury. Every accusation she had ever cast at herself came back to haunt her now. She saw her parents' stricken faces the day she told them she was pregnant. She heard her father's voice blaming her for his heart attack: "You broke my heart, Victoria. You ruined all my dreams for you. Why couldn't you be perfect the way your mother and I expected you to be?"

And she heard her mother's heartbroken sobs as she wept over her husband's grave. "He shouldn't have died; it was too soon. Why did God let it happen?"

Then Victoria saw Maude Hewlett's face swelling with a purple rage and heard Maude charging her with Julia's death and Joshua's injuries. "Your sin brought death to my daughter and a sickness worse than death to your son! You deserve eternal damnation for your transgressions!"

And she heard Phillip demand, "Why did you go there tonight? Why didn't you leave things to me?"

"Oh, God, I wish I were dead," she moaned. She was still curled snaillike, hugging herself, trembling. "I've hurt everyone I've ever cared about—my parents, my son, even Phillip." She wept until nothing was left but dry, racking sobs.

Then she lay still, listening to the steady pounding of her heart, fanning her anger against God and the world. I can't be perfect! she wanted to scream at her father. All my life you made me feel inadequate, as if I were to blame for all of life's ills. Oh, Father, why did you make me feel ashamed of being just a normal little girl? You made me believe I had to please everyone else but myself!

To her mother she wanted to shout, Don't you see? I can't be everything you and Daddy were! I'm not you; I never will be! I have to learn to be myself, but I don't even know who that person is! There was so much she wanted to tell them, but her words were wasted, unheard, unnoticed, like the cries of someone lost in a wilderness. Her parents were dead and buried, beyond retaliation or rebuke. She couldn't even hit back at Rick Lancer. Irony of ironies, he had disappeared from her life without the slightest hint of the seeds of destruction he had sown.

"Oh, God, what good have You been to me?" she murmured bitterly. "I am the same person I always was, weighed down by guilt and shame. Why can I never escape? Even if I'm released from this jail, how can I escape the prison of my own soul?"

As she mulled over her silent retorts, a thought came to her from far outside herself: *Be still. Know that I am God.*

She stopped and looked around as if someone had spoken aloud to her. She wasn't about to be placated by a random Bible verse. God, You have forsaken me like all the rest, she argued silently. I have tried to be a good Christian. I have prayed and gone to church and done <u>all</u> the things a good Christian should do, but here I am still alone—and I am still guilty.

The thought came then, like a wisp of fresh air. *I am with you. I will not abandon you.*

Victoria lay on her back and stared up at the ceiling. "Are You really there, Lord?" she whispered. "Even now—in spite of all my anger and guilt?"

In the gloomy silence she heard the gentle, soundless words.
Listen, Victoria, to the stillness of your heart; hear My voice in the secret place of your mind. Know that you are not alone; My Spirit resides in you. I have carried your every heartache, borne every pain, and no matter what you do, I love you. I've always loved you, and I will love you through the eons of eternity. It's not I who judge you; I have come to forgive, not condemn. I bring peace and joy and hope. Open yourself to Me and experience my love.

Guardedly, Victoria stretched out on her cot and stared up into the darkness. Was it truly God who spoke to her? Surely it wasn't her own voice; she knew that voice all too well. No, someone else was

with her in this cell. She felt His presence as vividly as anything she
had ever known. He was here, not just in this cell, but communing
with her spirit. She waited, listening, the sound of her heart drum-
ming in her ears. She wasn't sure how long she lay still and expectant, but after a while she realized her muscles were beginning to
relax. Her anger had dissipated. The guilt, too, had ebbed away. She
felt welcome tendrils of peace—fragile buds, growing.

She recognized Him now. It was *His* presence there within her.
The personal Christ. In all the trappings of Christianity, in all the
hustle and bustle of living her new Christian life, she had nearly
missed this—the center and matrix of it all, the intimacy of communing with Jesus Himself. She realized suddenly that she had been
so filled with herself—her own guilt and self-condemnation—that she
had allowed only the smallest corner of her heart for Christ.

"I don't know how it happens," she whispered, "this intimacy
with You, Lord. I sense Your presence now more than ever before
in my life, but how do I reach You? How do You reach me?"

She sat up on her cot. "Perhaps it's enough to know we can com-
municate," she said softly. "But prayer has to be more than merely
reciting words." She shook her head, baffled. "I don't understand,
Lord. Why do some Christians seem to have so much of You, while
others like Phillip and myself seem to have so little? What makes
the difference?"

The answer was there, on the edge of Victoria's consciousness,
tantalizingly close, piquing her curiosity with such force that she
nearly forgot she was sitting in a jail cell. She sensed that if she
could grasp the answer to this question, she would have the answer
to her own life.

"Oh, God, I have studied Your Word. I have tried to obey You.
I have spent time with Your people. I have worshiped You. But we
haven't really walked and talked together, just the two of us alone,"
she whispered into the darkness. "I haven't embraced You, savored
You, enjoyed You."

She realized something else, a vital truth. "Just now, when I imagined everyone condemning me, I never once saw You condemn me,
Lord. You meant it when You said You've forgiven me. I just haven't
let myself *feel* forgiven."

She stood and paced her cell, feeling invigorated, alive, her
thoughts suddenly open to endless possibilities. "You are here, Lord.
You are real. You are mine!" she marveled. "I've caught a glimpse

of You tonight. I've touched You, Lord, and You've touched me. There's so much I want to share with You, Father. I need You. I love You!''

Victoria pulled her paper-thin mattress onto the floor, knelt beside her cot and prayed until the first fragile rays of dawn broke through the barred window down the hall.

Chapter Twenty-Two

When Victoria was released from jail the next morning, Phillip was waiting for her. She flew into his arms. He embraced her fiercely, as if she had just returned from a long, perilous journey. "Victoria, my darling," he murmured into her hair as his hands caressed her waist, her back.

"Phillip," she uttered. No other words would come.

He looked at her, his dark eyes searching hers. "Are you all right? Did they hurt you? If anyone laid a hand on you—"

"No, Phillip, I'm...I'm okay, considering where I've been."

He ran his fingers over her temple, cheekbone and chin, as if to reassure himself that she was unharmed. "You'd tell me, wouldn't you, if...if—?"

"I'm all right, Phillip. Really."

"Did they give you back all your things?"

She glanced inside her purse. "Yes, my watch, my jewelry—everything is here."

He gripped her shoulders, his eyes still probing hers. "You look...different. I was so afraid— I thought— But you're all right. You look great."

She smiled weakly. "Thanks, but I'm numb. I didn't sleep all night."

"I didn't, either. After you called, I was frantic. I knew there was nothing I could do for you until morning. I couldn't bear the idea of you being here alone, locked up—"

"I'm okay," she assured him. "Can I go home now?"

"Yes, of course. Your bail is paid. You're free to go." Phillip guided her out the door. She allowed him to help her down the steps and into his car.

As she sank back against the cushioned seat, a wave of relief washed over her. "I felt as if I'd never be free again," she murmured as he started the engine, "never be free to ride in a car in the sunshine, or walk where I pleased, or talk with whomever I wished—"

"Don't think about it, Victoria. It's over, behind you. Try to forget it ever happened."

She stared at him. "I can't forget, Phillip. I don't want to. Now that I've seen how black the darkness can be, it makes the light all the more glorious."

He gave her a puzzled glance. "Is that supposed to be some sort of riddle?"

"No. It's just that something happened to me last night—the most terrible and yet the most wonderful experience of my life."

"Now you *are* talking in riddles."

"I guess I am. I don't know how else to explain it."

"Victoria, don't even try now. We've got a long drive home. Why don't you try to sleep? Put your head on my shoulder."

She sat forward, suddenly alert. "What about my car?"

"It's okay. We'll pick it up when we come back in a couple of days for your arraignment."

Victoria groaned, her spirits suddenly deflated. "It's not over, is it? This is just the beginning. They could send me to prison."

Phillip's voice was almost gruff. "I won't let them do that, Victoria. I promise, I'll get you out of this."

"But what if you can't? I don't think I could bear another hour behind bars, Phillip. It does something to you. It crushes you from the inside out. It takes everything from you—"

"It won't happen, Victoria."

"If it hadn't been for God—"

"It'll be all right—"

"He was right there, Phillip, in that cell with me."

"Who?"

"God. It was the most incredible thing. I've never known Him quite that way before."

Phillip looked at her with a curious, anticipatory expression. "Then you weren't alone?"

"No. At first, yes—I didn't know He was there. I didn't know how real He could be. I mean, He must have been there all the time, but I kept Him at a distance."

"But you sensed Him last night? God was there with you?"

"Yes, Phillip. That's what I'm saying. Why do you look so amazed, so pleased?"

He spoke over a knot of emotion. "Because I prayed, Victoria. I prayed for the first time in ages. Desperate, urgent prayer. I haven't prayed like that since Pauline was dying. My prayers didn't help her. I wasn't sure they could help you. But there was nothing else I could do but pray."

"You really prayed like that for me?"

"I couldn't be with you. And I couldn't stand the thought of you being alone and frightened in that jail cell. I prayed God would be with you."

"Oh, Phillip!" She reached over and touched his hand. "Your prayers were answered in a wonderful way."

"Tell me."

She gazed out the car window, groping for words. "I don't know how to express it, Phillip. Even after I became a Christian, I always thought of God as being strict and aloof and demanding, like my father. But last night, He comforted me. He was so real—I felt as if I could crawl onto His lap like a little child and feel His arms embrace me. I felt His love, like something tangible, surrounding me."

"That was the way Pauline knew Him, too," reflected Phillip. "That's why she could face death the way she did."

"I'm convinced He's available to every Christian that way, but we just don't take the time or make the effort to know Him."

"I suppose you're right, Victoria. I've never really thought about it before."

"I thought about it all night, Phillip. I think we get so caught up in all the outer trappings of Christianity—traditions and rules, service and even fellowship with other Christians—that we miss real intimacy with Christ."

"But you've prayed before, Victoria—"

"Yes, of course, I've prayed. But too often my prayers were more like carefully composed letters mailed to some distant destination. I always hoped God would answer them, but the response wasn't immediate. The communication was all one-sided."

"Isn't that basically how prayer is? You tell God what you want and hope He's there somewhere in the great beyond listening?"

Victoria gazed intently at Phillip's profile as he sat in the driver's seat, his hands resting on the steering wheel. "Phillip," she said carefully, "last night, when I prayed, I felt God listening to me. I felt His Spirit communing with me in a way that went beyond words. He was there, closer to me than you are now. I can't begin to describe it. But I'm convinced that's the kind of relationship God wants with us all the time."

"That's powerful, Victoria. I caught a glimpse of that when I prayed for you. I felt a potential there I'm not sure I'm prepared to explore."

"You mean you wouldn't want to know God that well?"

Phillip chuckled mildly. "I'm not sure I'd want Him to know me that well."

"He already does, Phillip. But He doesn't condemn you. That's the other marvelous thing I discovered last night."

Phillip gave her a quizzical glance. "What are you talking about?"

"I mean, at first, when they locked me in that cell, I felt more alone and abandoned than I'd ever felt in my life. All the guilt I've ever experienced hit me afresh. I could hear my parents accusing me, and Maude Hewlett, and even you, Phillip. Then I realized that the one voice I didn't hear condemning me was God's. God forgave me the day I asked Christ to be my Savior, but all this time I've clung to my guilt. Last night, for the first time, I was really free of guilt, free to enjoy my Lord."

Phillip nodded approvingly. "You're going to need that reassurance to see you through the next few weeks."

"But you're not buying it for yourself?"

"I didn't say that."

"What is it?" she probed, sensing something more behind his words.

He cleared his throat uneasily. "I just wonder whether it was one of those once-in-a-lifetime things. I don't think people live with intense spiritual experiences like that on a daily basis."

"But if we can, we should, shouldn't we? Didn't God create us to have fellowship with Him?"

Phillip gave her a studied glance. "You know, you're sounding more like Pauline all the time."

Victoria shifted in her seat. "I'm not sure whether that's a compliment or not."

"Neither am I."

It was late afternoon when Phillip pulled up before Victoria's condo. "Do you want to come in?" she asked as he opened the door for her.

"I'd love to, but I'd better not this time," he replied. "I've got to get some work done now so I'll be free to drive you back to Middleton for the arraignment."

She shuddered. The very word left a clammy chill behind her breastbone. "It really scares me, Phillip."

He rubbed her shoulder reassuringly. "I'll be with you. I'm going to do my homework and see if I can't get the charges dropped or at least lowered to a misdemeanor."

"Do you think you can?"

He nodded. "I just wish you hadn't signed a statement without my being there—"

"I didn't know what else to do."

"They read you your rights, didn't they?"

"Yes, but I was so terrified, I went along with whatever they said. I thought I'd look even more guilty if I didn't cooperate."

"It's okay. You said earlier that one of the arresting officers seemed sympathetic?"

"Sergeant Reynolds. He was the one who testified at the custody hearing."

"Good. I'll get in touch with him. Meanwhile, you relax. I want you looking composed and confident when you face the judge."

"I'll try," she said with a little sigh. "I just hate having you leave, Phillip. I guess I'm a little skittish about being alone."

"I'll stay if you need me."

"No, you go on home and get your work done."

He pulled her over against him and kissed her goodbye—a deep, lingering kiss. Finally he released her and traced the shape of her lips with his index finger. "A few more kisses like that, my darling, and I may change my mind and stay," he said with a seductive little smile.

She matched his smile. "A few more kisses like that and I'd be afraid to have you stay."

"I'll see you soon, sweetheart. If not tomorrow, then for the—"

"I know, I know," she said solemnly. "For the arraignment!"

* * *

Two days later, Phillip picked Victoria up shortly after sunrise for their drive to Middleton. "Sorry to be so early," he told her as she slipped into his sports car, "but the arraignment is scheduled for ten sharp. We can't be late."

"Did you find out anything?" she asked as he merged with the early-morning traffic.

Phillip kept his eyes on the freeway. "I talked with your Sergeant Reynolds. A very helpful guy. He told me the district attorney has agreed to drop the charges to misdemeanor trespassing."

"But he won't drop the charges entirely?"

"According to Sergeant Reynolds, the Hewletts want to see you prosecuted to the full limits of the law. However, he did mention they're willing to drop all charges against you if you promise to stay away from Joshua."

"You know I can't make such a promise."

"Even if it means going to jail?"

"Do you think it will come to that?"

"I don't know, Victoria. I just want you to be prepared."

She shuddered involuntarily. "I couldn't bear to spend even one more hour in that jail cell."

"Then maybe you ought to consider the Hewletts' offer."

She looked skeptically at him. "Is that what you want me to do?"

"Of course not. I just want you to be aware of your options. I told Sergeant Reynolds that the district attorney doesn't have a case against you, and he agrees with me. I said you could claim that you had simply returned to the Hewlett house to pick up something you had left behind when you were staying there. After all, you walked in with your own key."

"But I didn't forget anything, Phillip. I won't lie—"

"I know. But I just wanted the district attorney to realize where things stand. At least, we know he's not going to push for felony theft or kidnapping."

"But I still may have to stand trial?"

"That's about the size of it."

"Would the Hewletts have to testify against me?"

"Right. Without them, the court has nothing against you."

Victoria sat forward with a sudden urgency. "That's it, Phillip. That's the chance I need!"

"What are you talking about?"

"It's my chance to show the Hewletts up for what they are, to make them reveal their warped attitudes toward Joshua."

"You mean, get them on the stand and—"

"Yes! Get them to slip in their testimony. Make them say something bizarre about the devil possessing Joshua."

"We tried that during the custody hearing. It didn't work."

Victoria sighed. "I know. The Hewletts were too shrewd. But this time they're not on the defensive. They're going to be so eager to get back at me, to attack me for all they're worth—"

"You may have something there. They probably won't be on their guard. I just may be able to get them this time."

"Oh, Phillip," Victoria cried excitedly, "do you really think so?"

"It's worth a try." He looked at her, one brow arching quizzically. "What about you? Think long and hard about this. Are you willing to risk a prison term for another shot at the Hewletts?"

"Yes," Victoria whispered fervently, without hesitating. "I'm willing to risk it. For Joshua!"

Chapter Twenty-Three

The arraignment went much as Phillip had anticipated. The charge against Victoria was reduced from felony burglary to misdemeanor trespassing. When Judge Bernard Smithers—a thin, thirtyish man with slick black hair and bushy brows—asked her how she pleaded, she replied, "Not guilty."

In an irritating, singsong tenor, Judge Smithers announced, "Bail is reduced from two thousand dollars to five hundred dollars." Then he asked her, in his same nasal twang, "Do you want a court or jury trial, Miss Carlin?"

She looked anxiously at Phillip. She had no idea which way to go.

"A court trial," he told her quietly. "That means you'll appear before a judge rather than an entire jury. The judge alone will decide the case."

"You're sure that's best?" It seemed like putting all her eggs in one basket. What if the judge hated her? What chance would she have?

"It'll be more private," Phillip explained in the precise, professional voice he reserved for the courtroom. "Plus, in my opinion, it's easier to deal with just one person than to predict the attitudes or prejudices of twelve different individuals."

Victoria turned back to Judge Smithers. "A court trial, your honor," she said softly. In so many ways she was entrusting her life to Phillip's care; once again she would trust that he knew best.

After hearing her preference, Judge Smithers announced, "Your court date will be set for 2:00 p.m., September 28, in Superior Court.''

Phillip spoke up immediately. ''Your honor, I move to have the court date set for two weeks from now. I have a very pressing schedule, and Miss Carlin will be resuming her teaching duties at a university out of state early in September.''

The judge studied his calendar in silence for several moments, then replied shortly, ''Very well. Your trial is scheduled for Tuesday, 2:00 p.m., August 21.''

Phillip embraced Victoria and whispered, ''We did it, hon. We've got two weeks to prepare—two weeks to nail the Hewletts.''

''I just pray that Joshua will be all right until then,'' she murmured against the nubby fabric of his double-breasted suit. For the moment, at least, she felt safe in Phillip's arms.

''Say a few prayers for the three of us,'' he urged. ''You, me and your son.''

''I intend to,'' she assured him. ''Whatever happens, Phillip, I know you'll do your best for us.''

In his eyes she read the love and concern he felt for her—and the unspoken fear that his best might not be good enough to save her and her son. She couldn't help wondering if, God forbid, she lost her day in court, would she lose Phillip, as well?

She and Phillip drove home in their separate cars. For the next three days she talked to him only briefly on the phone each evening. She didn't mind. He was behind in his work, and she herself had plenty to do. She returned to her thesis with fresh enthusiasm. She signed up for her church's weekly Bible study program. And she began scouring the libraries for medical information on Joshua's condition. She wouldn't allow herself to be guilty of gross ignorance like the Hewletts had been.

On Wednesday afternoon she telephoned Phillip. ''Are you busy tonight?'' she asked.

''Swamped,'' he replied. ''But never too busy for you. What's up?''

''I'd like you to come with me to a Bible study.''

He chuckled lightly. ''What is this—part of your new game plan to save Phillip Anders?''

''You're already saved.''

''Right. So I don't need a Bible study.''

''You might enjoy it.''

"What's so special about this particular one?"

"Nothing. It's me. My focus is different."

"I'm listening."

"It's no longer just a matter of poring over some dry, ancient texts—"

"You mean you've got a Bible teacher with some pizzazz?"

"That's not it," she scoffed.

"What, then?"

She felt almost shy saying the words. "Since my night in jail, it's like I've fallen in love with Jesus all over again. Now, when I study the Bible, I'm not just learning about someone who lived two thousand years ago. I'm getting acquainted with my closest companion who loves me and wants me to love Him back."

Phillip cleared his throat uneasily. "I'll come with you tonight, Victoria. But don't expect me to get all gung ho over this thing like you are."

"All right, Phillip, but let me share one thing I read today. Then I'll let you go."

"I'm listening," he said patiently.

"I can't recall exactly how it goes, but it's the idea that you already have all of Jesus you'll ever need. But the closeness you share together will depend on how much *He* has of *you.*"

"Sounds to me like you should be teaching that class tonight yourself," Phillip mused good-naturedly. "Keep up the high spirits. I'll see you at seven."

Victoria enjoyed the Bible study, but even more so because Phillip was beside her. It was an unexpected pleasure to introduce him to members of her congregation. She caught the knowing glances of several elderly ladies reputed to be the church's matchmakers. One tiny, gray-haired grandmother clasped Phillip's hand in both of hers and exuded, "We certainly hope to see more of you around here, young man."

Afterward, Phillip and Victoria stopped at a nearby coffee shop for dessert. "So what did you think?" she asked after they had been served generous helpings of fresh strawberry pie.

"The pie's great," said Phillip.

"Not the pie. The Bible study."

His expression grew reflective. "It felt exactly right being there with you."

She smiled spontaneously. "That's how I felt, too. Care to make it a regular thing?"

He studied her, as if trying to read precisely what she meant by the invitation. "Are you talking now about us?" he wondered. "Or the Bible study?"

She felt her face flush with embarrassment. "The Bible study, of course. I hope you'll come every week."

He smiled, a mysterious gleam in his eyes. "I'll see what I can do."

After a pleasant hour of pie and conversation, Phillip drove Victoria home and kissed her good-night at the door.

"I'd invite you in," she said tentatively, "but the condo's been closed up all evening and it's sweltering inside."

"No problem. Turn on the air conditioner and sit with me on the porch until the rooms cool off."

Victoria sat beside Phillip on the wrought-iron love seat and breathed deeply. "The air is still, but it smells so good this time of year."

Phillip nodded. "We get so busy, we don't appreciate summer. Before we know it, it's winter again."

"Don't remind me," she said with a little sigh. "Although in this heat, I wouldn't mind a little snow."

He gave her a whimsical glance. "I could probably scrounge up a few ice cubes."

"Thanks, but no thanks." She laughed.

He gave her a playful hug and kissed her forehead. "I'd better let you get inside now, and I'd better head home."

She looked up seriously at him. "Thanks for going to the Bible study with me."

"My pleasure. Same time next week?"

"Sounds good to me."

His gaze held hers for a long moment. "You know, you look absolutely gorgeous tonight, Victoria."

"Thank you, Phillip," she murmured, a flicker of modesty prompting her to lower her gaze. "You're wonderful for a girl's ego."

"It's not just flattery," he insisted. "I'm dead serious. Do you have any idea what you do to me?"

She searched her mind for something to say, but no words came. She could easily have turned the question back to him.

"Even when we're not together, you're always in my mind," he said, taking her face in his hands. She could see a struggle playing out in his eyes. "I promised myself I wouldn't start anything tonight," he murmured, "but in this moonlight you're so confounded irresistible." Before she could reply, his mouth came down on hers and he kissed her with an avid, barely suppressed passion.

She relaxed in his arms and responded with her own eager kiss. Oh, Phillip, this is what I've waited for all evening. I want your kisses as much as you want to give them. Don't you know? You're everything I've ever dreamed of.

It was true. After six long years she finally felt free to welcome a man's love without feeling fearful or guarded. She trusted Phillip with her very life. He would never hurt her, never take advantage of her.

Phillip was the one to break the embrace. "I'm sorry, Victoria," he said unevenly, sitting back and rubbing his mouth, his jaw. "I—I just can't handle this. I care about you more than you know. But I'm only human. I don't want to spoil what we have together." He stood, helped her up and opened the door for her. "If I don't leave now, I may lose all my good resolves."

She gazed up uncertainly at him. She felt a keen disappointment rising in her chest. She knew she could make him stay if she coaxed him. But he was right. Someone had to keep a clear head. "You'll call me?" she asked breathlessly.

His voice was deep, gravelly with emotion. "Of course I'll call. In fact, you'll be in my dreams tonight. And in all my waking thoughts. Good night, my darling."

That night Victoria fell asleep amid blissful reveries of Phillip's kiss, his touch, his lingering gaze. Her dreams were filled with pastel images of the two of them together—walking hand in hand down a cathedral aisle lined with exotic flowers, exchanging tender vows, then entwining in an ardent embrace while glorious chimes rang out.

Sometime after midnight she awoke and sat up in bed, startled. She had turned off the air conditioner earlier and the room was muggy and warm. "I was dreaming of Phillip," she said aloud. "It was our wedding day!" She got up and slipped into her short silk robe and went to the kitchen for a cup of tea. She turned on only a small night-light and sat at the kitchen table, her gaze straying to the window overlooking the backyard, to the vast velvet blackness of sky winking with jewels of starlight. She closed her eyes and touched her lips and replayed those tender moments with Phillip on the porch, savoring every sensation his kisses stirred.

"Lord, what do You have for Phillip and me?" she whispered into the darkness. "Do we have a future together, or is it only wishful thinking?"

As she sat in the shadows reflecting on her relationship with Phillip, fragments of memory, flashes of longing flitted through her consciousness.

She stared out the window at the sky and inhaled deeply. "Dear God," she said aloud, her voice filled with wonder, "it's really true, isn't it? I'm in love. Beyond a shadow of doubt. I've fallen in love with Phillip Anders!"

Chapter Twenty-Four

Phillip was called out of town on another case, so Victoria had several days to reflect on her feelings before seeing him again. In some ways she felt more confused than ever. Certainly she had no doubt now that she loved Phillip, but other questions pursued her relentlessly. *Should* she love him? Could she risk being vulnerable to another man? Would Phillip be able to love someone beside Pauline? The questions were endless, the answers elusive—if they existed at all.

The following Wednesday night, Phillip was back in town and escorted Victoria to her Bible study. Afterward, she invited him back to her condominium for a light supper of taco salad with fresh tomatoes and avocados and her own homemade salsa.

"This is delicious," he praised. He sat at the table, relaxed, in a short-sleeve sports shirt and khaki slacks, dipping tortilla chips into the hot sauce.

"My special south-of-the-border recipe." She smiled.

"South of the border was never like this," he teased as he scooped a mound of sour cream onto his salad.

Victoria poured him a glass of lemonade, then sat down across from him. For the first time since she had known Phillip, she felt shy in his presence. Did he see the blush in her cheeks when their eyes met? Could he hear her heart pounding earlier when he casually kissed her cheek? Did he feel the electricity in their touch?

Or hadn't his life been turned upside down this past week the way hers had? Had he already forgotten the passion of the kiss they shared last Wednesday night?

"So how's your thesis coming?" he inquired.

"My thesis?" Victoria struggled to pull her mind back from a great distance. "It's…coming along very well. I've finished the rough draft. Now it's mainly a matter of editing, revising and polishing."

"I'm glad to hear that. I know what a burden and a challenge it's been to you."

"Well, once I resolved things spiritually, it freed me to work on my thesis, as well."

Phillip nodded perfunctorily. "I'm glad you've got everything so well in hand at last," he remarked. "It simplifies things when you know where your life is going."

"Oh, but I don't know—" she began, and caught herself. Certainly she couldn't confess to Phillip how confused she felt over her feelings for him—especially when he didn't appear the least bit bothered!

"Yes, I understand," he said knowingly. "You're concerned about the trial. Since it's coming up next Tuesday, I suppose it's been on your mind a great deal this past week."

Victoria unconsciously touched the back of her neck. "I haven't thought about it as much as I expected," she murmured.

"Well, good. I'm glad you're not worried. I've been doing my homework and I think we're going to come out of this on top."

Victoria poked at a wedge of lettuce on her plate. "I hope so. It's a nightmare even to think of being sent back to jail."

"I think the risk is very remote, Victoria, although I have to stress again that no one can second-guess a judge."

She shivered involuntarily. "Oh, Phillip, I couldn't bear being locked up again."

"I'll do everything humanly possible to see that it doesn't happen."

Quietly she said, "I don't know what I'd do without you, Phillip."

He sat back in his chair and gazed appraisingly at her. "Same here." His tone lightened as he said, "Tell me what else you've been doing this week."

She thought a minute, then replied, "Well, I've spent several hours in the library researching Joshua's illness—you know, his seizures and all."

"That's good. You need to be prepared."

"Yes, I do. I learned how to care for a person during a seizure, so he won't hurt himself, and I learned what medications are available for different types of seizures."

"A good start. What else?"

"Evidently Joshua has 'grand mal' seizures. Surprisingly, the more I learn about them, the less frightening they seem to me. There's really nothing weird or supernatural about them." She paused meaningfully. "Of course, the name of Joshua's condition might alarm some people. It's known as 'post-traumatic epilepsy.'"

Phillip whistled through his teeth. "You're right. Epilepsy is a term laden with emotional innuendo."

Victoria nodded. "And I've learned some things that have disturbed me, Phillip."

"About Joshua's seizures?"

"About people's attitudes toward seizures. I'm discovering that the Hewletts aren't such a rare breed, after all."

"Meaning?"

"Well, there's a lot of prejudice out there I wasn't aware of."

"You're talking about people not understanding what epilepsy is, right?"

"Right. Let me put it this way. Granted, Joshua's seizures are a direct result of the automobile accident, but it's still epilepsy. And people's opinions about epilepsy range from the bizarre to the incredible."

"You're talking now about the Hewlett mentality?"

"Yes. The tragedy is that some otherwise sensible, knowledgeable people still hold strange prejudices against people with epilepsy."

"You mean, like thinking they're demon-possessed or insane or retarded?"

"Right—when actually epilepsy is a physical condition controllable with medication. Like hypertension or diabetes, for instance. People who have seizures can lead a normal life—if others will let them."

Phillip smiled sympathetically. "You're beginning to sound like quite a little crusader."

She smiled back. "It doesn't take much, Phillip—just seeing someone you love hurt by other people's ignorance."

"Joshua's a lucky little boy," he noted.

Victoria gazed curiously at him. "Why?"

Phillip's eyes glistened. "Because he has you pulling for him."

They ate in reflective silence for several minutes. When Phillip had finished the last of his taco salad, he sat back and folded his arms across his chest. *"Delicioso!"* he said, his voice more buoyant than it had been all evening. "You just may get yourself a repeat customer for that dish."

"My pleasure, *señor.*" She pushed back her chair. "Are you ready for dessert? Rice pudding—my mother's special recipe?"

He groaned inwardly. "Would you mind asking me again in about two hours?"

"We could make it a late-night snack if you like."

"All right. I should be hungry again by then."

She laughed. "Until then, we can relax in the living room—maybe talk a little, watch TV?"

"Sounds good to me. I haven't spent a quiet evening before the TV in months."

She gave him a calculated glance. "Do I detect a note of sarcasm in your voice?"

He raised his hands placatingly. "Not at all. I know that watching TV is considered prosaic and most people won't admit to liking anything on the tube, but Pauline and I used to be grateful for an occasional evening to relax together and catch a program or two."

Victoria's spirits sagged involuntarily. *Pauline again!* Would Phillip never stop thinking of himself as a twosome with Pauline?

In the living room, Victoria turned on the TV set and fluffed the sofa pillows. "Make yourself at home," she told him.

He sat down and automatically began removing a shoe, then he glanced up at Victoria, chagrined.

"Go ahead," she urged. "Get comfortable. Whoever heard of watching TV with your shoes on?"

"Now if you say I can prop my stocking feet on your coffee table, I'll know I've died and gone to heaven."

She laughed lightly. "Of course. What else are coffee tables for?" She kicked off her own shoes and sat down on the sofa beside Phillip. A moment later she was up, adjusting the television set.

"The faces are too red," she explained. "The color has to be just right or I can't stand to watch."

"It's perfect now," he told her. "Come sit down."

She hesitated. "What do you want to watch? I suppose you like those crime dramas, or a mystery—"

"I really don't care, Victoria. Let's watch what you want."

"I don't watch enough TV to know what's on," she said, feeling inexplicably flustered. The room was too warm. She went over to the wall and turned up the air-conditioning. "This hot August weather," she mumbled, and returned to the television set.

She fiddled with the channel selector until Phillip inquired, "Don't you have remote control?"

She stared at him, abashed. "Of course." She handed him the small unit and sat down stiffly.

As he worked the unit, the stations flashed by. "How about an old Henry Fonda movie?" he suggested. "It's in black-and-white so we don't have to worry about the color being too intense."

"Or the language, or the subject matter." Victoria chuckled.

It was satisfying to be sitting there with Phillip. Why then did she feel so nervous? When Phillip's arm casually brushed hers, she flinched slightly. He didn't seem to notice. Instead, he slipped his arm around the back of the sofa, just inches from her shoulder.

Gradually Victoria relaxed. Henry Fonda was championing some cause, but she had no idea what it was. She was more aware of Phillip's nearness than of the storyline of the show.

Phillip's arm was around her now in an offhand manner. His head nodded toward hers and finally found her shoulder. As her heart leapt at his touch, her ears revolted against an odious noise.

Phillip was dozing!

Victoria laughed aloud.

Phillip roused and gazed groggily at her.

"You were snoring," she charged, stifling her laughter.

He shook his head ponderously. "You've learned my secret. TV puts me to sleep. I don't think I've ever watched an entire show without nodding off."

"Well, I'm glad to hear it's the TV and not the company."

He pulled her close and pressed her head against his chest.

"Never the company," he murmured. "I love the company."

"I love the company, too," she said softly.

He looked down at her—a long, penetrating glance. He searched her eyes so intently she couldn't pull her gaze away. "I love you, Victoria Carlin," he said.

Her voice was as light as air. "I love you, too, Phillip Anders. With all my heart."

A pleased, surprised look flickered in his eyes. "You do? You really love me?"

"Yes." She laughed mirthfully. "I really do!"

He bent his head to hers and whispered against her lips, "Now I know the good Lord's smiling down on me!" His mouth moved over her lips, leisurely at first, then with a growing urgency. She wound her arms around his back and clung to him as if she would never let him go. He held her so close she could scarcely breathe; she could feel their hearts beating as one.

When at last he released her, she felt light-headed, breathless. She knew she could be content spending the rest of her life in this man's arms, savoring his kisses.

"Do you know what this means?" he said with an edge of excitement, his own breathing ragged.

"You mean, our loving each other? I know what it means to me," she said softly. "I've finally found the man of my dreams. What does it mean to you?"

He held her tight against him and stroked her hair. "I never knew I could feel this way again. In fact, I'm not sure I ever felt this way before."

"Are you talking about...Pauline?" she asked, knowing he was.

He shifted his position and gazed off into space. "I have to be honest with you, Victoria. I guess I've hinted at this before, but I wasn't the kind of husband I should have been. I took my marriage for granted. I was too involved with my career to pay much attention to Pauline. We weren't close the way she wanted to be. I considered myself the strong, silent type. It seemed like a sign of weakness to open up and bare my soul, so I rarely did."

Victoria ran her fingers over his arm. "But you've changed, Phillip. You're baring your soul right now."

He grinned sheepishly at her. "So I am. I guess you bring out the best in me. So maybe I'm husband material, after all?"

"I think you're wonderful husband material."

He gazed shrewdly at her. "Miss Carlin, is that a proposal?"

She felt her face redden. "Really, Mr. Anders, a proper lady doesn't make proposals."

He laughed. "Are you saying the ball's in my court?"

She grew pensive. "I'm saying my head is still spinning with the fact that you love me. I can't begin to think where we go from here."

"I want us to have a future together," said Phillip, "but I know we have a lot to work out before we can make plans."

"Do we even want the same things, Phillip?" she asked.

"I want you," he said simply.

"And I want you, too," she agreed. "But there's so much more to consider."

"I want a family," he told her. "You know how I feel about kids."

"And I want Joshua," she said softly.

"He's a kid," said Phillip. "I could love him."

"Really? With all of his problems?"

"He'll need a dad, someone to help him over the hard spots."

"And you'd be willing?"

"More than willing."

"Oh, Phillip!" Her expression slackened. "But I don't know if Joshua will ever be mine. And with the trial ahead, my life is so uncertain. How can I even think about our future?"

"It's okay," he assured her. "We've got time. All the time in the world. Meanwhile, my darling, we can both be praying that God will show us what He wants for us." He pulled her back into his arms and kissed the tip of her nose. "And just between you and me, I'm going to be rooting for a wedding one of these days."

Chapter Twenty-Five

Phillip picked Victoria up early Tuesday morning for the trip to Middleton. "The trial's not till two, but I thought we should get an early start," he told her as he took the southbound freeway on-ramp.

"I was up at five, anyway," she replied. "I couldn't sleep."

"Nervous?"

"Terrified." She managed a smile. "But I'm not alone. I've got reinforcements."

He looked curiously at her.

"You and the Lord," she explained.

"I've had a few conversations with the Lord about this matter myself," he admitted. "And I intend to have a few more."

She patted his hand. "Thank you, Phillip. You don't know how pleased that makes me."

"This case is very important to me," he continued. He paused. "*You're* very important to me. I think you know that by now. There's nothing I want more than to see you cleared of all charges and re-united with your son."

She sighed. "It sounds almost too good to be true."

"Well, if I know human nature, the Hewletts will be so intent on revenge, they'll let their guard down. All I need to find is one chink in their armor, and I'll attack."

"You make it sound so easy."

"It's not easy at all. But I've done it before and I believe I can do it again."

"I just pray the Hewletts will slip up. If they don't, they'll get to keep Joshua and I'll face a prison term."

"Don't let yourself think that way," cautioned Phillip. "This is where your faith will make a difference. You can't let the Hewletts or the judge think you're defeated."

"You're right," said Victoria, her voice brightening. "I've got God Himself on my side—and you, my darling, are defending me. What more could I ask for?"

It was after 11:00 a.m. when Phillip pulled up before the courthouse. "There's a place down the block where we can pick up some lunch," he told Victoria.

"I'm really not hungry," she said. She stared out the windshield at the imposing gray building that towered above them. "I just want to go in and get this over with."

He nodded. "I know you do. But you need some soup or something to keep your strength up."

"I'll try, but I'm not promising anything."

He reached for her hand. "Before we get out of the car, I'd like us to..."

She looked quizzically at him. "What, Phillip?"

He chuckled uneasily. "I never did this with Pauline—I mean, she wanted us to, but I felt like I was this rough-and-ready guy..."

"What are you talking about, Phillip?"

In little more than a whisper, he said, "I'd like us to pray together, Victoria."

She smiled. "I'd like that, too, Phillip."

"Don't expect—"

"I don't expect anything," she assured him. "I just want us to pray together."

He moved his lanky legs away from the steering wheel and took both her hands in his. Bowing his head, he said earnestly, "Lord, Victoria and I need You in that courtroom today. There's a little boy—Joshua—who needs to be with his mother, and that's what I'm going to work on. But I could sure use some help. And Victoria here is pretty tense about this whole thing. She could use a boost of confidence from You. I guess that covers it for now. Thanks, Lord."

Victoria prayed, too, in a soft, urgent voice. "Thank you, Father, for loving us. Thank you for Phillip. Give him wisdom today. Help me to stay calm and know what to say. Whatever happens, I know

You are in charge, Lord. I know you will give us your best. Help me to trust You. In Jesus' name, amen.''

After a quick lunch of soup and sandwiches, Victoria and Phillip went directly to Superior Court. They were the first ones in the courtroom. Victoria sat quietly with her head bowed until several other people began to filter in.

''Who are all those people, Phillip?'' she whispered.

''Trials are public hearings, Victoria. Since anyone can come in, you always have a few curious onlookers.''

When the Hewletts arrived, Victoria sat up, alert, suddenly tense. Their presence changed the entire atmosphere in the room. She could feel the undercurrent of hostility already. Maude gave Victoria a withering glance as she settled her voluminous frame on the hardwood bench. Victoria met her gaze and held it, offering a tight smile in return. Maude was wearing a red polka-dot dress and bright flowered hat. ''Lovely hat,'' Victoria told her levelly.

Maude shuddered with indignation and looked away.

Sam was wearing the same navy blue suit. It looked rumpled on his stooped frame, and his wide paisley tie was askew. He refused to look in Victoria's direction.

Judge Bernard Smithers, who had presided over Victoria's arraignment, would decide her case today. With his narrow face and pointed chin, he reminded Victoria of a weasel. Still, he seemed sincere enough. Victoria prayed that he would be fair.

After both attorneys had delivered their opening statements, Roger Maxwell, the prosecuting attorney, called Maude Hewlett to the stand. She sat down smugly, adjusted her hat and smoothed her dress over her thick knees. As a witness, she was imperturbable. She answered every question in a voice as smooth as glass.

Even under Phillip's strenuous cross-examination, she never faltered, never wavered for an instant. She managed to dodge every issue Phillip introduced regarding Joshua.

Victoria's hopes ebbed. She realized that every plus for Maude was a minus for herself. Phillip must have realized it, too, because he didn't keep Maude on the stand for long. After just a few minutes of intensive interrogation, he announced, ''No further questions.''

As Maude triumphantly took her seat, Phillip glanced at Victoria. His expression said it all: The case isn't going the way I hoped. He sat back down beside Victoria and whispered, ''I may not even cross-examine Sam. If he's anything like Maude, he could seal the case against you.''

"You've got to question him," insisted Victoria. "He's our last chance to save Joshua."

"It's a risk," whispered Phillip.

"I'm willing to take it," she replied.

Maxwell, the prosecuting attorney, was already summoning Sam Hewlett to the stand. Sam sat slunk in his seat with his knobby fingers gripping the chair arms. His eyes bulged behind his spectacles and a tendon in his cheek twitched nervously. After Sam was sworn in, Maxwell inquired, "What is your name, sir."

Sam looked up, startled. "Don't you know?"

"Yes, I do," said the attorney patiently. "But please tell us anyway, for the record."

"Sam Hewlett. That's with two *t*'s," he told the court stenographer.

"Where do you live, Mr. Hewlett?"

Sam worked his mouth into a smile. "Maude and I live at 1045 Blackberry Street. Been there since the place was built. Maude's folks built the—''

"Just answer the questions, Mr. Hewlett," instructed Judge Smithers in his slow, nasal twang.

"How long have you lived at 1045 Blackberry?" questioned Maxwell.

"Twenty-five years," replied Sam. "Like I told you, Maude's folks—'' He stopped and peered out of the corner of his eye at Judge Smithers. Judge Smithers peered back.

"Were you in your residence on the evening of August third, Mr. Hewlett?"

"I sure was."

"Did anything unusual occur that evening?"

Sam gave the attorney a puzzled glance. "Maude already told you what happened."

"I know, Mr. Hewlett, but would you please describe the events of that evening in your own words?"

"Well, let me think," muttered Sam. "It's kinda hard to remember everything. As I recollect, Maude and I had pork chops for dinner. We watched 'Wheel of Fortune' on TV—or was it a 'Lucy' rerun, Maude?"

"Mr. Hewlett," interrupted Maxwell, "would you please confine your testimony to the unusual events that occurred."

"Oh, sure." Sam snorted. "What happened was that that lady schoolteacher sitting over there broke into our place and tried to kidnap our grandson."

"Objection," declared Phillip. "There's no evidence of a kidnapping attempt or a break-in."

"Objection sustained," replied Judge Smithers. "Mr. Hewlett, please limit your response to actual, verifiable facts."

"Tell us again, please, Mr. Hewlett, whom you encountered in your home on the evening of August third," persisted the prosecuting attorney.

"That lady there," snapped Sam. "Victoria Clarkin."

Maxwell stared in astonishment at Sam. "*Who*, Mr. Hewlett?"

Maude stood up and barked at Sam, "It's *Carlin*, you old goat! You never could remember that name!"

"Order, order!" demanded Judge Smithers.

"Carlin—yep, that's what it is," said Sam, nodding.

"Did Miss Carlin have your permission to be in your home that evening, Mr. Hewlett?" asked Maxwell.

"No, sir. Maude would rather croak than let that woman near our place."

"Go on," coaxed Maxwell. "What was Miss Carlin doing in your home?"

"She was in the upstairs bedroom, trying to get into the attic. Maude found her and called me. Then I called the cops."

"Did Miss Carlin remove anything from the premises?"

"No, but she would have if we hadn't stopped her. She was after the boy—"

"Objection!" declared Phillip. "That's pure conjecture on the witness's part."

"Objection sustained," droned Judge Smithers.

The questioning went on, but Victoria tried to shut it all out of her mind. The questions seemed so pointless, so trivial, so redundant. But she sat up attentively when it was finally Phillip's turn to cross-examine Sam Hewlett.

"Mr. Hewlett, you said something that Mrs. Hewlett neglected to mention in her testimony. You stated that Miss Carlin was in the upstairs bedroom trying to get into the attic. What did you mean by that?"

"Just what I said. The door was locked. She was trying to force it open."

"What was she after, Mr. Hewlett?"

Sam looked flustered. "I don't know. I didn't ask her."

"Where was your grandson, Joshua, while Miss Carlin was trying to break open the attic door?"

"Objection," protested Maxwell. "Your honor, that question is irrelevant."

"No, it isn't, your honor," insisted Phillip. "Mr. and Mrs. Hewlett have accused my client of entering their home to kidnap their grandson. I think it's pertinent that the court know where the boy was when Mr. Hewlett first saw Miss Carlin."

"Objection overruled," said Smithers.

"Where was Joshua, Mr. Hewlett?"

Sam looked helplessly at Maude. She glared back mercilessly.

"The boy was in his bed, asleep," said Sam.

"In what room, Mr. Hewlett?"

"Why, right there in the room where we found Miss Clarkin—uh, Carlin. That's Joshua's bedroom, and a right nice room it is."

Phillip shook his head slowly. "Mr. Hewlett, are you trying to tell the court that Miss Carlin entered your home to take your grandson? Yet, when she found him in the upstairs bedroom, she wasted valuable time trying to break into your attic?"

Sam buried his chin in his neck. "That's about the size of it."

Phillip eyed Sam closely. "Do you keep anything valuable in the attic, Mr. Hewlett—like a child?"

"Objection!"

"Strike the last part of that question, 'like a child,' from the record," said Judge Smithers.

"Your honor," protested Phillip, "it's vital to my client's case that we establish the whereabouts of Joshua Goodwin the night Miss Carlin was found in the Hewlett home."

"Very well. Rephrase your question, Mr. Anders."

"Mr. Hewlett, was your grandson sleeping in the attic the night Miss Carlin entered your home?"

"No," asserted Sam defensively. His Adam's apple bobbed and his voice cracked. "The boy wasn't in the attic. Like I said, he was in his bedroom asleep."

"Then doesn't it strike you as extremely foolhardy that Miss Carlin—who you yourself claim was after the child—was trying to break into your attic?"

"Who can figure a woman?" grumped Sam. He fidgeted with his collar, craning his neck as he poked a long finger between his collarbone and his starched shirt.

Phillip leaned down close to Sam and stared him squarely in the eye. "Isn't it true, Mr. Hewlett, that the reason Miss Carlin came to your house that night, and the reason she was trying to force open the attic door, was because she knew you had locked your grandson in the attic like a caged animal?"

Sam began to sweat profusely. "No, it wasn't that way. We treated the boy good. We kept him clean and fed."

"But you did lock him up like an animal, didn't you, Mr. Hewlett!" persisted Phillip.

"Objection!" shouted Maxwell.

Sam began to whimper. "The boy acted like an animal. Ever since the accident, he had fits like a mad dog. What else could we do?"

Maude erupted from her seat. "You crazy old man! Listen to yourself! You're ruining everything!"

"Order, order!" demanded Judge Smithers.

"Mrs. Hewlett, sit down!" commanded the prosecuting attorney.

"Crazy old man!" Maude stormed at Sam. "Shut up!"

Amid the uproar, Phillip pushed on with his questioning. "Was it your idea, Mr. Hewlett, to lock the boy in the attic?"

"It was Maude's," twittered Sam shakily. "She said we had to get the devil out of the boy. She said it was the only way—"

"You're saying your wife locked your grandson in the attic because she believed he was possessed by the devil?"

"Objection!" shouted Maxwell.

"Oh, shut up," demanded Judge Smithers. "I want to hear this one, myself."

Sam was cowering now under Maude's fierce glare. Victoria sat spellbound. Phillip pressed on relentlessly. "Answer the question, Mr. Hewlett. You're under oath. Did your wife lock your grandson in the attic because she believed he was possessed by the devil?"

Maude glowered at Phillip, her eyes venomous slits. Her face was as red as raw meat and seemed to swell with every breath she took. "Yes, the devil's in that boy," she shrieked from the other side of the room, "and ain't no doctors or social workers or no fancy lawyers gonna get the devil out!"

Chapter Twenty-Six

Pandemonium broke out in the courtroom.

"Order! I demand order!" bellowed Judge Smithers, pounding his gavel on his desk.

Maude turned imploringly to the judge. "You gotta understand, your honor, that boy is Sam's and me's responsibility, no one else's. Things was fine—we had things right in hand—before that woman, that scarlet hussy who bore that child in sin, came along. We was managing all right, keeping the boy under control, keeping the devil at bay—"

Judge Smithers stood. "Bailiff, remove this woman from the courtroom!"

"Your honor," wailed Maude, "it's because of her the whole world knows our shame. It's her sin that cursed us, that killed my daughter and left us with that boy!"

The bailiff gripped Maude's arms tentatively and began to tug. Maude shook the young man off and stood her ground. "Don't anybody here see how things are?" she railed. "Sam and me got to make things right. The only way we can get the curse off us is to get the evil out of that child!"

The bailiff tried again, forcefully seizing Maude's forearm. Sam clambered down off the witness stand and took Maude's other arm. "Come on, Maude," he whined, "the judge don't want to hear no more." Together the two men managed to lead the ranting woman out of the courtroom.

Judge Smithers wiped his brow and sat back down. Clearing his throat, he instructed, "Attorneys Maxwell and Anders, please approach the bench."

Phillip quickly squeezed Victoria's hand, then strode to the front and stood beside Roger Maxwell.

Judge Smithers looked wearily at the two men. "Under the circumstances, gentlemen, I recommend that the charges against Miss Victoria Carlin be dismissed. Any problem with that, Maxwell?"

"None, your honor. I was about to move for dismissal myself."

Judge Smithers banged his gavel and declared in relief, "Case dismissed." To his aid, he murmured, "Hold the next case. I need a break."

Victoria stood excitedly and nearly flew into Phillip's arms. "You did it!" she cried.

"*We* did it," he replied, kissing her cheeks and hair. "Praise the Lord, darling, we did it."

She nodded wordlessly, fighting back tears, savoring the warmth of his embrace.

"You ready to go home?" he asked, offering her his handkerchief.

She blotted her tears and replied, "As soon as we get Joshua."

His expression clouded. "It's not a done deal yet, honey."

She stared at him in alarm. "But after what Maude said—"

"Let's talk outside, okay?"

She gave him a troubled glance, then a reluctant nod. Why after such a stunning victory was he already putting doubts in her mind? Surely everything would go their way now. It was just a matter of time before Joshua would be hers. God willing, *theirs!*

Phillip slipped his arm around her waist as they left the courtroom. Just outside the door, Sergeant Reynolds stopped them and said, "Congratulations, folks."

"Thank you," Victoria said breathlessly.

The sergeant managed an awkward grin. "I was scheduled to testify against you, Miss Carlin, but I'm glad I didn't have to."

"So are we," said Phillip.

Victoria looked up questioningly at the sergeant. She needed his reassurance. "You heard the things Mrs. Hewlett said. Tell me, are they evidence enough to have Joshua removed from her care?"

"Oh, yes," replied the officer. "Psychological abuse is one of the hardest kinds to prove, but Mrs. Hewlett made it clear that's what she's subjected the boy to. And I suspect physical abuse isn't out of the question, as disturbed as that woman is.''

"Then we can go get Joshua now, can't we?" urged Victoria, casting a triumphant little glance at Phillip.

"Hold on, sweetheart," said Phillip. "Like I was trying to tell you, it's not quite that easy."

Alarms went off again in her head, her heart. "What do you mean?"

"Your lawyer's right," said Sergeant Reynolds. "We need to get a warrant to have Joshua removed from the Hewletts' home."

"You mean, just like before?" Victoria cried incredulously. She had emerged from one black pit just to be flung into an even darker one.

"That's right," replied Sergeant Reynolds. "The police need a court order to take the boy into custody and make him a ward of the court. That's the law."

Victoria was trembling now. She had come so far, broken down so many barriers and overcome so many obstacles, and it still wasn't enough. "How long will it take?" she asked, the words thick in her throat.

"A while," replied the officer.

Victoria felt as if she'd been struck by a battering ram. "You mean, after everything that just happened—after Maude's insane outburst—you're going to leave my son in her care for even a few more hours?"

Phillip slipped his arm around her shoulders and pulled her close. "I'll see what I can do to speed things along, honey."

"Me, too," said Sergeant Reynolds. "Maybe we can get the warrant early in the morning."

Victoria began to weep—large, rolling sobs that caught in her chest. "Dear God in heaven, no! I can't bear to think of my baby with that horrible woman. Please, Phillip, do something! Can't we go get him now?"

He massaged her shoulder consolingly. "I'm sorry, darling. We can't. We're too close to getting the boy back. We can't muddy the waters now. We've got to follow legal protocol to the letter. But I give you my word, you'll get your son."

Victoria inhaled sharply and squared her shoulders. "All right, Phillip, but until I get Joshua, I'm staying right here in Middleton. I'm not leaving town without my son."

"All right, we're in this together. We'll both stay until Joshua is safely back in police custody. Come on, let's go get ourselves a couple of rooms for the night at our favorite haunt."

She took his arm. "You mean, the Starlight Motel?"

"Where else?" he asked with a small smile.

They drove directly to the motel and registered for their rooms, then walked over to the little coffee shop and had dinner together. Victoria wasn't hungry, but she found comfort in Phillip's company. Still, even he couldn't keep her mind off Joshua. After dinner, as they headed back to their rooms, she told him, "I hope you don't mind if I say an early good-night. I'm really exhausted, and I need some time alone."

Phillip looked disappointed but he managed a smile, anyway. "I guess it was sort of a hollow victory today, wasn't it?"

Victoria's lower lip quivered. "Yes, as long as Joshua's still with the Hewletts." She reached up and touched Phillip's cheek endearingly. "It's not that I don't appreciate all you've done, Phillip. I do. You were wonderful! And later we'll be able to celebrate this victory together in a special way. But right now, I'm just so worried about my boy."

"Sure, I understand, sweetheart," he replied. "You get a good night's sleep, okay? Lord willing, Joshua will be safely in the court's hands by tomorrow."

Victoria held on desperately to that thought later that evening as she drifted into a restless slumber. But her dreams were filled with garish images of the Hewletts laughing and taunting her, mixed with heartbreaking images of Joshua lying alone in his little attic bed. She saw herself running from room to room in the Hewlett house, shouting, "I'll save you, Joshua! Don't be afraid! Mommy's coming! You'll be okay, darling!" But every room was empty; she never found her boy.

When she awoke at dawn, Victoria felt physically exhausted, as if she had been running a marathon all night—and as far as she was concerned, she had!—but she was determined to tackle the day with new hope and vigor. At breakfast, she asked Phillip if they could follow the squad car to the Hewlett house when the officers went to pick up Joshua.

"Maybe, as long as no one sees us," he told her between bites of scrambled egg, "and providing Sergeant Reynolds is kind enough to tell us when they're going."

She grabbed her purse. "What are we waiting for? Come on, Phillip!"

His fork clattered on his plate. "Where are you going?"

"To the police station!" she said, pushing back her chair. "They could already be on their way to the Hewletts'!"

After a tense, breakneck drive, Victoria and Phillip ended up spending two hours at the police station, waiting. "We could have finished breakfast," said Phillip as he pumped coins into the money slot of a candy machine. He offered her half of a chocolate bar, but she shook her head. She wasn't hungry. Her stomach was in knots and the sour taste of anxiety filled her throat.

At ten, Sergeant Reynolds came striding toward them with a hearty grin. "We got the warrant," he said eagerly. "Officer Hughes and I are on our way now to pick up the boy."

"Thank God!" Victoria sighed.

She and Phillip followed the patrol car at a discreet distance and parked down the block as the police vehicle pulled to a stop at 1045 Blackberry Street. Victoria's heart hammered in her chest as she watched the officers briskly mount the steps and knock soundly on the Hewletts' door. They waited. There was no response. They knocked again.

"Why aren't the Hewletts answering?" Victoria asked Phillip. She clutched her purse strap, twisting it back and forth around her icy fingers.

"Maybe they know who's knocking," said Phillip.

The iciness crept through her veins to her heart. She couldn't endure the suspense much longer. "What will the police do if no one answers?"

Phillip remained insufferably calm. "They'll probably force the door open."

Victoria looked back at the house and realized that's just what the officers were doing. After a minute, the door flew open and the policemen entered.

She clutched Phillip's arm, her anxiety mounting. "Is there going to be trouble? I don't want Joshua hurt."

Phillip moved suddenly, startling her. With a quick sweep of his arm, he opened his car door and stepped out into the street. "Come on, Victoria," he said brusquely.

She hurriedly climbed out after him. "What is it, Phillip? What's happening?"

He caught her hand and they ran down the street toward the Hewlett house, her stacked heels clattering on the pavement. They scaled the porch steps just as the officers came back outside. Sergeant Reynolds's brow was furrowed. He looked at Phillip and slowly shook his head.

The iciness in Victoria's chest turned to stone, heavy, choking her windpipe. "What is it?" she cried, breathless, paralyzed with dread. "Tell me! Please! In the name of heaven, what's wrong?"

"They're gone," reported the sergeant darkly, swatting the side of his thigh. "Man, they got us good. They took the boy and ran!"

Chapter Twenty-Seven

Victoria pushed past Sergeant Reynolds and rushed into the Hewlett home. The shadowed nightmares of a thousand troubled nights merged into one horrifying reality: Her son was gone; she might never see him again.

"Wait up, Miss Carlin," the sergeant ordered, but Victoria was already dashing up the hall stairs toward Joshua's room. Phillip and Sergeant Reynolds followed, their heavy shoes pummeling the creaking floorboards.

"They've taken everything!" Victoria exclaimed, pulling open one dresser drawer after another. "Look, his toys, his clothes, everything—gone!"

The attic door stood open. Victoria raced breathlessly up the steep, narrow steps, the stifling warmth of the airless room already drawing out beads of moisture on her forehead and upper lip. Her eyes, adjusting to the darkness, swept over the weathered timbers and sparse furnishings, proving what she had already feared. The room was empty, stripped of every last scrap or clue that might lead to Joshua.

"Miss Carlin," shouted Sergeant Reynolds, a few steps behind her, "you can't just go looking around this house on your own. You go back outside and let Officer Hughes and me handle this."

Victoria came slowly down the stairs, her shoulders sagging. "It's too late," she cried, tears moistening her eyes. "They've taken his bedding, his clothes, all his toys. They're not coming back."

Phillip led Victoria down to the living room. "Come on, hon. I'm sorry. It shouldn't have turned out this way. But there's no use in us sticking around here now. Let's let the police do their job.''

''That's right, miss,'' said Sergeant Reynolds. ''We'll take over. If they left any clues at all, we'll find them.''

Victoria nodded numbly and allowed Phillip to escort her back down the street to the car. She couldn't think straight now; her thoughts kept short-circuiting, replaying the past half hour as if there might be something she had missed, some clue she had overlooked or a riddle waiting to be guessed. There had to be something she could do to change this outcome. This day wasn't supposed to have gone this way; Joshua should have been safe by now. She must have failed, or neglected some important detail. Someone failed; if not she, then who? Someone had to have an answer to this insanity! Please, God, help me to understand! What are You trying to do to me? Kill me, if You must, but please don't punish my helpless little boy!

As Phillip drove back to the Starlight Motel, Victoria sat beside him in silence, motionless, her mind paralyzed by grief and fear. It was as if she were watching herself from a great distance; she could see herself, hear her own thoughts churning away in her head, could even feel her fierce heartbeat, but somehow she couldn't bring herself to move or respond, to lift a finger or flex a toe. She was disconnected from her body, watching, enduring the engulfing pain and disappointment, and yet she remained detached, immobilized.

''I'm so sorry,'' Phillip ventured after several minutes. He reached over and clasped her hand tightly in his. ''I would have done anything in my power to spare you this heartache, Victoria.''

She stared wordlessly out the window, her hand limp in his.

''They'll find him, Victoria. I know they will.''

Silence.

Phillip spoke again, this time addressing someone else. Victoria realized with a start that he was praying aloud even as he drove. ''Lord, help us,'' he said urgently. ''Lead us to the Hewletts. Don't let them harm Joshua.'' He continued over unaccustomed emotion. ''Father, this prayer business is still new to me, and I know that I, for one, don't deserve any special favors from You. But for Victoria's sake, please come through for us. Please help us find Joshua.''

Victoria felt as if she were stirring from a muggy dream, slowly finding herself, testing the languid muscles in her hands and feet. She began to weep. Haltingly she said, ''Help me to trust You, Lord—

even now when all I want to do is blame You. If You never answer another prayer, please watch over my son.''

She felt a little better after they had prayed—not so helpless or frantic or numb. Somewhere in her heart of hearts she recognized that God was in charge.

''I know—I've got to believe—God won't let anyone hurt Joshua,'' she said softly, with growing conviction.

Phillip nodded. His voice was charged with feeling as he said, ''I believe that, too, Victoria. With all my heart.''

It wasn't until Phillip and Victoria were alone in her motel room that she allowed her pent-up feelings to surface. ''Phillip, where could Joshua be?'' she agonized, twisting a tissue into shreds. ''Where could the Hewletts have taken him? I can't bear this. I can't sit and wait and do nothing. Help me, Phillip. Tell me what we can do!''

He took her in his arms and held her tight, as if by the solid strength of his body he would calm her tremulous frame. ''I know how upset you are,'' he soothed, ''but we've got to compose ourselves and think this out rationally. It's the only way we can help Joshua. Can you do that, darling? Relax, take a deep breath, maybe even splash some water on your face, okay?''

''I—I'll try, Phillip,'' she murmured. Already she could feel his strength permeating her, his loving concern buoying her spirits. ''I'll be all right,'' she assured him. ''Just give me a few minutes.''

Phillip removed his sport coat, turned on the air conditioner and sat down in the chair by the TV set while she checked her tearstained face in the bathroom mirror. She pressed a wet washcloth against her forehead and cheeks, and the coolness revived her. ''I look terrible,'' she murmured at last, wiping the smeared mascara from under her eyes. When she had cleansed her face, she came back out and sat down on the edge of the bed. ''What do we do now, Phillip—go home, stay here, what?''

He loosened his tie and rubbed the back of his neck. ''I don't know, Victoria. There must be something we can do, but at the moment I'm as baffled as you are.''

She studied his dark eyes for answers. ''What will the police do now?''

''They'll put out an APB—all points bulletin—for the Hewletts. The authorities have a court order to pick up Joshua, so I imagine they'll begin a statewide search for him.''

The tendrils of anxiety were returning, tightening her nerves into knots. "And what are we supposed to do in the meantime—just sit back and wait?"

Phillip stood and paced the room. "No, Victoria. I've been thinking—"

"What, Phillip?" she pressed. "Do you have an idea? Please think of something, anything. I can't sit here waiting."

His voice took on an edge of excitement, as if he were immersing himself in some sort of game and the stakes were high. "I've been trying to guess where the Hewletts might have gone. Do they have other relatives that you know of?"

"No. They just had their daughter, and she's dead. I don't think they have any friends. They always kept to themselves."

"Did they ever mention any place they liked to visit—another town or state, or a favorite vacation spot?"

"No, Phillip, not that I recall. This is getting us nowhere. Who knows where on earth people like the Hewletts would go on vacation?" Victoria paused. Something rang a bell. What was it? Something Maude had once said. Victoria looked up, suddenly alert. "Wait a minute. Vacation spot? Yes, Phillip. Why didn't I think of it before? The Hewletts have a cabin up north somewhere. They go there sometimes during the summer."

Phillip clasped her hands in his. "Where, Victoria? Did they give you any idea where it is—what town it's near?"

She shook her head, flustered. "No, or if they did, I never paid attention."

"There must be some way to find out where it is—old letters, postcards, photographs..."

"I've never seen any. We'd have to search the house from top to bottom to find anything."

"And I doubt the police would let us do that."

"Wait. There are the paintings—"

"Paintings?"

"Maude's daughter was an artist. She made several paintings of the cabin. I remember, it was in a lush, wooded area. There were mountains in the background, too. Not huge mountains, but they were more than foothills."

Phillip sounded aggravated. "You could be describing Mountain View or Crestwild or even Summitville. They're all easily a couple of hours' drive from here. Maybe less."

"Oh, Phillip," she urged, "couldn't we drive up north and try to find the cabin? Please. I've got to be doing something."

He shook his head. "It would be an impossible task, Victoria. There are thousands of little cabins surrounding those towns. We'd never be able to check them all out."

Her shoulders slumped. "Oh, Phillip, just when I was starting to see a ray of hope."

He gave her a solacing embrace. "I'm sorry, Victoria. It's just not feasible. If we had anything else to go on..."

She gazed intently at him. "Something else to go on? Wait. Maybe there is something."

"What it is?" he exhorted. "Do you remember something else?"

Victoria clasped her hands to her face and closed her eyes. "Something Maude said... Not a location—something else... Something she did when she went to the cabin..."

Phillip's face was close to hers, his breath warm on her cheek. "What, Victoria? Try to remember!"

"Soap. Something about soap."

"Soap?" he echoed dubiously. "What about soap?"

"I don't know. I can't remember."

"What kind of soap?" He tried several possibilities in a mildly disparaging tone. "Soft soap, lye soap, no soap?"

"Stop it, Phillip—you're confusing me."

"Keep thinking, Victoria. Hand soap, face soap, fancy soap?"

"Yes, fancy soaps! That's it!" she said excitedly. "Maude sold her crocheted soaps to the little souvenir and craft shops in several towns around here."

Phillip looked puzzled. "Crocheted soaps? So what?"

"Think about it, Phillip. If we can find one of those little shops that carries Maude's crocheted fish and turtles, they'll surely have her address!"

He looked skeptical. "So instead of looking for a needle in the haystack, we go out looking for crocheted soap?"

"Exactly!" Victoria was beaming now. "Maude gave me a couple to keep, Phillip. I think they're still in my overnight bag. All we have to do is drive around and show them to the shopkeepers and ask if they carry them."

Phillip drummed his fingers on the bedspread. "I think you're being overly optimistic, Victoria. Those homey little shops are everywhere. It would take us weeks to cover them all."

"Please, Phillip. It can't hurt to try." She drew in a determined breath. "And maybe God will lead us to just the right one."

He shrugged relentingly. "Who am I to argue against you...and the Lord?" He leaned over and kissed her cheek, then stood and ambled to the door.

"Where are you going?" she asked.

He flashed a sardonic smile. "To my room. I'm going to get my overnight bag and shaving gear. Get your things ready. We'll hit the road as soon as we're packed."

She gave him an impulsive hug. "Thank you, Phillip. You're wonderful! I adore you!"

"I love you, too, darling, but save the compliments," he advised, "until we can prove we're not embarking on one real wild and incredible goose chase."

Chapter Twenty-Eight

Before Victoria and Phillip began their drive up north, he telephoned Sergeant Reynolds and told him of their plan. After Phillip had hung up the receiver, Victoria asked eagerly, "What did he say?"

Phillip massaged his jaw thoughtfully. "He said we should stay out of this and let his men do their job. He says they'll find the Hewletts without our help."

This was the last thing Victoria wanted to hear. "Did you tell him my theory about the crocheted soaps?"

"Yes. He thinks we're crazy, but harmless."

She seized Phillip's arm with sudden concern. "You didn't let him talk you out of looking for the cabin!"

"No, but he made me promise to call the police immediately if by some fluke we find the Hewletts before they do."

She sighed with relief. "Of course we'll let them know." She lifted her chin resolutely and tossed back her long, burnished curls. "Well, come on, Phillip, what are we waiting for?"

With a little flourish he opened the motel door for her and feigned a gallant bow. "After you, sweetheart."

It was a deceptively quiet, uneventful drive; both Victoria and Phillip were preoccupied, lost in separate worlds of thought. She knew they were both functioning on an undercurrent of tension and anxiety, but neither chose to admit it.

They arrived in the little town of Crestwild at three. Phillip was suddenly all business, studying his map, carefully plotting exactly what they would do, but Victoria found his take-charge manner comforting, reassuring. It kept her mind off the relentless terrors over Joshua that struck at the core of her heart.

"There are a dozen shops along Blue Jay Street," Phillip was saying. "Shall we each take one side of the street and meet back at the car in an hour?"

"Sounds good to me," said Victoria, forcing her mind to focus on Phillip's instructions. She handed him one of the crocheted soaps. "This is what we're looking for."

He gingerly accepted the dainty, fragrant soap-turtle and slipped it into his pocket. "What a guy won't do for love," he murmured under his breath.

At 4:15, Phillip was already standing by his sports car, waiting. "Find anything?" said Victoria as she approached the vehicle.

"Not a thing," he replied. "But you should have seen all the frilly gadgets and trinkets they tried to sell me instead."

She nodded wearily. "I know. I was shown every line of fancy soap in the book."

He took her hand and swung it almost jauntily. "Listen, honey, we need a little break. What do you say we stop now and grab some supper and then head out toward Summitville?"

She managed a faint smile. "Sure. I could use a break."

They arrived in Summitville shortly before six. Again they separated and scoured the little shops along the narrow, old-fashioned main street. Again, they came up empty-handed.

"Let's try the shops outside of town," suggested Phillip as they hit the road again.

They stopped at every craft and souvenir shop along the highway to Mountain View. No one had ever seen Maude's crocheted soaps before, but every shopkeeper was eager to sell them something else. "We don't carry those, but we do have these darling little—"

"Thanks, but no thanks," Victoria had learned to say quickly as she edged out the door.

They arrived in Mountain View just before the shops closed. "Let's check out what we can for the next twenty minutes and meet back at the car at eight," Phillip suggested.

A half hour later, when Victoria arrived back at the car, she could tell by Phillip's expression that he had had no success. "Another dead end," he said flatly.

Her heart sank. "Me, too."

Phillip scratched his head; he looked baffled, beleaguered. "Of course, we haven't tried the outlying areas."

"But everything's closed now." She could hear the hopelessness in her own voice.

"Well, sweetheart, we could find ourselves a motel, get a good night's sleep and try again tomorrow."

Victoria nodded. "I guess so," she said, even though tomorrow seemed a hundred years away.

"I know you feel down, Victoria. But things will look better after a good night's sleep. Who knows, maybe by tomorrow morning the police will have found Joshua," he added. He took her hand, pressed it against his cheek and smiled. "You know, I don't know what there is about this mountain air, but I'm famished again. Let's go have some dessert."

She shook her head with mock disapproval. "Has anyone ever told you, you're always thinking of food! How can anyone eat so well and stay so trim!"

"Running, my dear. I run off every extra pound."

"Is that so? I may have to take up jogging myself."

He winked. "You, Victoria, are perfect just the way you are."

She laughed in spite of herself. "And you're an old sweet talker." It was amazing the way he could turn her emotions around with just a word or a smile. "All right, if I'm so perfect, then lead the way to the gooey desserts."

Victoria and Phillip had fresh strawberry pie at a nearby diner, then drove to Mountain View Lodge and secured two rooms for the night. For a long while they stood outside their doors halfway between the two rooms, talking quietly as they gazed up at the moonlight. Neither of them wanted to say good-night; neither wanted to break the spell of the moment by going off to their separate rooms. But at last Phillip said reluctantly, "I'd better let you get to bed, or we'll never get up in the morning."

They embraced, but neither broke away. Victoria had never imagined it could be so hard to let Phillip go. We should be together, she realized. We should fall asleep in each other's arms and wake up looking into each other's eyes. He should be my husband; I should be his wife. We should be together for the rest of our lives. Do you feel that, Phillip, as keenly as I do? Will you ever be ready to make such a commitment again?

Before she could read the answer in his eyes, he broke away and made a little nervous sound low in his throat. With sudden resolve he took her arm and led her over to her door. "If I don't get you into your room right now, my lady, we'll spend all night in the moonlight and we'll both be zombies tomorrow."

She knew he was right, but she couldn't resist having the last word. Just before she slipped into bed that night, she tapped lightly on Phillip's wall and called out, "Good night, darling. I love you. I'll always love you!"

Phillip tapped back, and even though she couldn't hear his voice, she knew he was telling her he loved her, and somehow that made him seem very close as she lay in the darkness of that lonely, anonymous motel room.

Early the next morning, feeling just a bit worse for wear for lack of sleep, she and Phillip were on their way again.

"I telephoned Sergeant Reynolds just before we checked out," he said, "and there's still no news."

She swallowed her discouragement. "Every time you call him, my heart leaps with hope, then plunges just as rapidly."

He cast her a consoling glance. "I'm sorry, Victoria. I really thought they might have found Joshua by now."

"Well, we certainly aren't any closer to finding him, either." She sighed.

Phillip pulled onto the highway heading north. "Maybe today, sweetheart."

She eyed him intently. "You don't really believe that, do you, Phillip? This whole search is crazy, isn't it? You're just humoring me in my lunacy."

He kept his gaze on the road ahead. "I'm not humoring you, Victoria. We're following the only lead we have. Sure, it's slim, but it's all we've got."

With resignation, she asked, "Where do we go today?"

Phillip handed her a map from the dashboard. "I've circled several vacation areas that have handy access from the freeways out of Middleton."

Victoria opened the map. "You've marked Ridgeway, Pine City and Red Bluff. Why these towns?"

"Because you've told me before that Maude doesn't drive, and I can't imagine Sam being much of a navigator. I think their cabin would have to be somewhere easy for them to get to."

"I hadn't thought of that, but you're right, Phillip. The more direct the route from Middleton, the better."

Victoria and Phillip tried Ridgeway first, but there was only a handful of stores, and no one carried Maude's soaps. They drove directly to Pine City—a tiny, western-style town nestled amid towering pines. Main Street was a narrow gravel road, and several of the unpainted clapboard buildings were boarded up. "Doesn't look like there's much here," mused Phillip as they headed for the lone general store—a weather-beaten structure with the unlikely name Buttons and Bows.

The proprietor was a stooped, spindly man with a week's growth of gray whiskers. When Victoria showed him the crocheted soap, he put his hand to his ear and said, "Eh?"

She repeated her question, drawing out each word for emphasis. "Do you carry these handmade, decorated soaps?"

"No, we just got the regular kind. Nothing fancy."

Victoria nodded automatically. It was the answer she expected. She and Phillip turned to go.

"But I got one of them doodads at home," rasped the man.

Victoria pivoted sharply. "You have one of these—just like this?"

"Yeah, sitting pretty as you please on the bathroom shelf. Except it's a fish, not a turtle. And it's green, not pink."

"But it is handmade, just like this one?" pressed Victoria excitedly.

"Where did you buy it?" asked Phillip.

"Didn't. The missus did."

"Could we talk to her—ask her where she got it?" urged Victoria.

The old man shook his head. "Flo's been dead about a year, God rest her soul."

A moan escaped Victoria's lips.

"Then you have no idea where she purchased the soap?" Phillip questioned.

The man shrugged. "Somewhere in these here parts. Flo always stuck pretty close to home."

"Thank you, sir, for your help and your time," said Phillip. He purchased a bag of apples, then he and Victoria were on their way again.

"If only we could have found out where his wife bought Maude's soap," Victoria lamented as Phillip took the fork to Red Bluff.

But Phillip was upbeat. "Don't despair, hon. We've got our first real clue in two days. We know now that Maude peddled her soaps somewhere around here. It's just a matter of time...''

Victoria handed him an apple. ''But just how much time do we have?''

He looked curiously at her. ''What are you thinking?''

''I was remembering those Bible references Sam quoted,'' she admitted in a shaky voice. ''What if Sam and Maude intend to harm Joshua—especially now that their hand has been forced? I know I'm probably being irrational, but—''

''No, Victoria, you're not,'' he conceded. ''I'm worried, too.''

She stared at him. ''You think they may hurt him, too, don't you?'' She gasped. ''Maybe even...kill him?''

Phillip gripped her hand tightly. ''Don't, Victoria. There's no sense in letting our imaginations run wild. We can't afford to give in to despair. We've got to keep trusting!''

''I'm trying, Phillip,'' she whispered. ''God knows I'm trying!''

Just outside Red Bluff, they stopped at a gas station for a local map. ''Looks like the shops are spread out in this little burg,'' said Phillip, ''so we'll drive around and visit them together.''

After an hour, Victoria shook her head dejectedly. ''It's another dead end. There's nothing here.''

''Don't give up,'' said Phillip, giving her knee an encouraging squeeze. ''We've only covered half the town.''

''But it's already after two. We have only a few more hours before it's dark again. Then what?''

''Let me telephone Sergeant Reynolds once more, then we'll do what we can before the shops close.''

After verifying with the sergeant that there was no news, Victoria and Phillip drove to a nearby store boasting a flowery, hand-painted sign that read Happenstance Boutique. The rustic little shop was jammed with novelty items—everything from kitchen utensils and frilly aprons to homemade toys and antique books. A plain woman in a gingham dress stood behind the counter and smiled congenially as Victoria and Phillip approached. ''May I help you?'' she asked in a lyrical, singsong voice.

Victoria removed the crocheted turtle from her purse and held it out to the woman. She had repeated her lines so many times to so many clerks in so many shops, the words were starting to sound mechanical, almost meaningless. ''I'm looking for one of these handmade soaps," she said, already anticipating the woman's negative reply. "Have you ever carried them in your store?"

The clerk examined the soap. "Yes, I've seen these around, but I'm not sure we still carry them."

Victoria's pulse quickened. Had she heard right? "You've seen them, you say?"

"Oh, yes," replied the woman. "We've stocked them off and on for years. But it's been a while since the lady who makes them has been in." She walked over to a nearby counter. "Have you looked around? We may still have one or two."

"About the lady who makes them," interrupted Phillip, his tone insistent, yet controlled. "Is there some way we could get in touch with her?"

The clerk shrugged. "She doesn't live in the area, but she and her husband have a summer cottage near here. Every vacation she'll come in with a big basket of her crocheted soaps. But, like I said, I haven't seen her for a while."

"Do you have her address?" asked Phillip.

The woman thought a moment. "It's probably in our files, but I'm not sure it would be proper for me to give it out."

"You would be doing the right thing, believe me," urged Victoria.

"Are you interested in doing business with her? I'm sure she would welcome new customers."

"Our business with her is urgent," said Phillip.

"I just don't know if she would appreciate my sending strangers her way," replied the woman uncertainly. "She's a very private woman."

"We're not strangers," explained Victoria quickly. "In fact, I know her quite well. Her name is Maude Hewlett and I lived in her home for a while this summer. We tried to contact her in Middleton, but she had already gone. Our problem is, she neglected to give us her address here in Red Bluff."

The clerk brightened. "Oh, well, why didn't you say you were friends? And now I bet you want to surprise her! How sweet of you! You wait right here and I'll get her address."

Phillip squeezed Victoria's arm and whispered, "Couldn't have done better myself."

The clerk returned and handed Victoria a slip of paper. "Mrs. Hewlett's cabin is on Evergreen Road, just a mile or two north of here. It shouldn't be hard to find."

"Thank you," said Phillip, steering Victoria toward the door.

"You tell her the lady at Happenstance Boutique is out of her soaps," trilled the woman. "Those pretty little things sell real well. You tell her to bring me in some more real soon now."

As Phillip pulled back onto the narrow, winding highway heading north, Victoria's excitement mounted. "We did it, Phillip! We found Maude! Praise God!"

"We've still got to find the cabin," said Phillip, "and even then, Victoria, there's a chance they aren't there."

"Phillip Anders," she chided, "don't you dare dampen my spirits now. I know we're going to find Joshua today. I just know it."

He smiled reassuringly, then pointed to a desolate, tree-shrouded fork in the highway. "Here's Evergreen Road. Hold on, it's going to be bumpy."

Victoria glanced around. "This is more like a dirt path than a road."

"Watch for a cabin on the right."

"They're too far back from the road to see any house numbers."

"And the few cabins I see are surrounded by trees and bushes," complained Phillip.

"I hope Evergreen Road doesn't go on for miles," fretted Victoria, "or we'll never find the Hewletts by dark."

Phillip clutched her arm. "Look! There ahead—through that clump of trees. See the car parked beside that cabin?"

Victoria strained forward. "It's the Hewletts' car!"

"Right. I'd know that old heap anywhere."

Her heart hammered. "What do we do now? Just go up to the door and demand Joshua?"

"No, Victoria." He spoke in a low, no-nonsense tone. "Right now we hightail it to a phone booth and call Sergeant Reynolds."

"But what if the Hewletts leave?" she cried. "We could lose Joshua again just when we've found him."

"I promised the sergeant I'd call," said Phillip. "This is a police matter now, Victoria."

In spite of her protests, Phillip drove back into Red Bluff and stopped at a service station. He made his call and was back behind the wheel within minutes.

"What now?" she asked as he pulled back onto the highway.

Phillip patted her hand. "We go back to the cabin and keep an eye on things until the police arrive."

She tried to keep the cynicism out of her voice. "You mean Sergeant Reynolds actually agreed to let us be there when they serve the warrant to pick up Joshua?"

"No," replied Phillip. "The fact is, he told us to go home and wait for his call."

She stared incredulously at him. "You agreed to that?"

"No, I just said we'd stay out of the way. I figure we can park down the road and be available, just in case."

Victoria shivered. "Available for what, I wonder?"

This time, it seemed to take only minutes to reach the Hewlett cabin. The small redwood cottage sat back from the road between two enormous pines. A spindly fence surrounded the place. Phillip pulled off to one side and stopped behind a clump of overgrown foliage.

"How soon do you think the police will arrive?" she asked.

He adjusted his seat to give his legs more room. "The local authorities may arrive anytime. Sergeant Reynolds said he's driving up, too. It'll take him a couple of hours."

She shivered. "Everything will be over by then."

Phillip nodded. "He wants to be the one to drive Joshua back to the state children's home."

Victoria was silent a moment, then asked, "How soon can I petition the court for custody of Joshua?"

"Immediately," he answered with a smile. He took her hand and rubbed it gently. "And I don't see any reason why you shouldn't get him."

Victoria felt tears glisten in her eyes. "Oh, Phillip, how I pray you're right."

For several minutes, neither of them spoke. Phillip still held Victoria's hand. Lightly he kissed her fingertips. Their eyes met. "When this is all over," he said huskily, "we've got to talk...about us. Our future."

Victoria interlocked her fingers with his. "Oh, Phillip—" she sighed "—you don't know how much I want that, too, but I'm not sure we have all the answers we need."

"Answers?" he quipped. "I don't even know the questions." When she didn't respond, he cleared his throat uneasily. "It's just that we keep saying we love each other, Victoria, and yet neither of us is brave enough to talk in specific terms about our future."

She stared down at their interlaced fingers. "I know how much you loved Pauline,'' she said softly. ''I don't want you feeling forced to make a commitment before you're ready.''

''Forced? Is that how you think I feel? I just want you to be sure *you're* ready for a commitment.''

Before she could reply, the roar of a police vehicle severed her thoughts. The patrol car passed them and swerved into the Hewlett driveway. Two uniformed officers emerged, stalked to the front door and knocked.

Victoria's fingers tightened around Phillip's hand as they watched intently from his automobile. It feels as if my entire life has come down to this moment, she thought as her heart drummed fiercely. What happens in these next few seconds could spell the difference between bliss and despair. Lord, watch over Joshua. And help me, God, to hold on to You, no matter what.

She sucked in a breath as the officers knocked a second time, then a third. Finally she heard their deep, urgent voices, sounding powerful even from a distance. ''Sheriff's deputies. Open up!''

An eerie silence settled over the cabin and the surrounding woods as the officers stood tensely poised, waiting. Through the open car windows, Victoria could hear only the rustling of leaves and the echoing song of birds overhead.

Then, before she could speak or react, a hunting rifle protruded from the front window of the Hewlett cabin and a shot rang out, violently shattering the afternoon calm.

Chapter Twenty-Nine

Instinctively Phillip pulled Victoria down, away from the windshield. "You okay?" he whispered.

"Yes," she said shakily. It wasn't quite true. Her heart was throbbing and her head reeling. "Were the officers hit?"

Phillip peered cautiously out the window. "No, they're running back to their squad car. They'll call for reinforcements."

Victoria sat up, trembling, and brushed her hair back from her forehead. Her breathing was labored and her wrists and ankles felt like jelly. "I can't believe it... The Hewletts—how could they become violent like this?"

"I think it was a warning shot," said Phillip.

She clutched his arm as the frightful implications struck home. "What about Joshua? If there's a shoot-out, he could be hurt—oh, Phillip, if they haven't harmed him already!"

"Don't even think that, Victoria. We've got to believe Joshua is okay." He drew her into his arms. "Right now let's just pray that the police can settle this whole thing peacefully."

Victoria heard sirens in the distance. "Praise God!" she breathed. "Backups must be arriving already."

Three police vehicles slammed to a stop along the narrow dirt road. In moments the officers were out of their cars and surrounding the little cabin. The deputies who had sent for help stooped behind their car and conferred with three of the men. Another officer set up a loudspeaker on the automobile hood. His voice boomed, "Mr. and

Mrs. Hewlett, release the little boy—your grandson, Joshua Goodwin. Then come out of the cabin with your hands up!''

Victoria heard Maude's voice burst venomously from the half-open window. ''Nobody takes my grandson away from me! We'll all die first!'' She jabbed the rifle out the window and fired into the air again.

Victoria's apprehension mounted as the policemen attempted to reason with Maude. There's no reasoning with that woman, she wanted to cry out as she strained to hear the distant interchange between Maude and the officers. The deputies tried every possible argument, every conceivable tactic, but Maude railed back with a steady stream of abusive, vituperative barbs. A long, agonizing hour passed with the volatile stalemate no closer to resolution.

''We can't just sit here waiting for something to happen,'' implored Victoria. ''Joshua could be killed.''

''That's the point, Victoria. That's why the police are proceeding with caution. One wrong move could push Maude over the edge. The police don't want that and neither do we.''

Another hour passed. Victoria's legs felt unbearably cramped in Phillip's sports car. ''Couldn't we slip over to the squad car and watch from there?'' she asked Phillip.

''No way, hon. If Maude gets one glimpse of you, who knows what she might do?''

''But maybe I could reason with her, persuade her to put Joshua's safety first—''

''From the way she's talking to those officers, she's in no mood to listen to reason, you know that.''

Another police vehicle arrived. Victoria's hopes soared momentarily as she recognized Sergeant Reynolds. He strode over to Phillip's car and peered inside. ''I told you two to stay away from here,'' he charged icily.

Phillip raised his hands in a conciliatory gesture. ''We're watching from the sidelines, Sergeant, and like I promised, we're staying out of everybody's way.''

The sergeant grunted, obviously unconvinced. ''Keep it that way, Anders.''

''But if there's anything we can do,'' added Phillip firmly, ''just say the word.''

Sergeant Reynolds's brows furrowed over his troubled eyes. ''Yeah. Figure out how we can get that crazy dame outta that cabin without force. I don't wanna see anything happen to that kid.''

Sergeant Reynolds took his turn at the bullhorn, too, his voice friendly and casual at first, then growing progressively firm. To no avail. Maude spewed out a hateful, contemptuous reply, then there was silence in the cabin for almost a half hour.

Victoria's anxiety grew; she could feel the tension prickling her skin like barbed wire. The officers were growing weary and irritated. They paced restlessly out of range of the cabin. This isn't working, she thought frantically. Someone's going to get hurt before this is over. It could be my son!

At last Sergeant Reynolds returned to Phillip's car, mopping his forehead. "Got any ideas, Mr. Anders?" he asked dryly.

"Is Sam in there?" questioned Victoria. She was grasping at straws. What difference did it make whether Sam was there or not? Maude always held the upper hand.

"If he's in there, he hasn't said a word," replied the sergeant.

"What about Joshua? Are we sure he's even in there with her?"

The sergeant stuffed his handkerchief into his back pocket. "At this point, we're not sure of anything, except we're dealing with a lady whose elevator doesn't go all the way to the top. A real psycho, you know?"

Victoria gazed back at the Hewlett cabin. Shadows from the towering pines stretched across the little cottage, shrouding it in a dusky haze. "It's already getting dark!" she exclaimed. She looked around, squinting against the orange wedge of sun hugging the horizon. "Once it's dark, Phillip, no one will ever budge Maude out of that cabin."

"Our men have thought of that, Miss Carlin," said the sergeant. "That's why we've got to come up with something now, some plan of attack. Otherwise this standoff could go on all night."

"You can't let that happen," entreated Victoria. "Please, let me talk to Maude."

"No," said Phillip, his fingers tightening on her shoulder. "You'd only be putting yourself in danger."

"I don't care," she said with unaccustomed defiance. "Joshua's already in danger. I'd trade places with him in a minute."

"We aren't looking for heroes, Miss Carlin," said Sergeant Reynolds.

"Please, just ask Maude if she'll talk with me," persisted Victoria. "What harm can it do to ask?"

The sergeant rubbed his chin thoughtfully. "She has a point, Mr.

Anders. If Mrs. Hewlett says she'll talk to Miss Carlin, it's worth a try."

Phillip scowled, concern evident in his voice. "Go ask Maude, but I can't imagine the woman wanting to talk to Victoria."

The sergeant returned to the bullhorn. Victoria listened as he spoke conversationally with Maude for a minute, and then brought up Victoria's name. "What would you say, Mrs. Hewlett, if I told you Victoria Carlin is here and would like to speak to you?"

"I'd say you're full of beans!" snarled Maude from behind the open window.

"Would you talk to her, Mrs. Hewlett?"

A long silence. Then came the reply. "Sure. Why not? I got plenty to say to that woman."

Sergeant Reynolds signaled privately for Victoria and Phillip to join him behind the parked squad car. Now that she was committed to this foolhardy showdown, Victoria had second thoughts. Why had she volunteered to face Maude? It was a stupid idea; what did she think—that she could march in and single-handedly save her son? Playing the dauntless heroine might only endanger Joshua further. Searching Phillip's eyes for an answer, she mouthed the words, "What should I do?"

"Talk to her, if you think it'll help," said Phillip, "but in the name of heaven be careful!"

"Stay with me," she whispered.

"Always," he told her fervently. "I won't leave your side."

They climbed out of the car, crouched down and ran stealthily, hand in hand, through the underbrush until they reached the police vehicle. Victoria's side ached and the air seemed thin in her lungs. The roof of her mouth felt like tar paper. More doubts assailed her. What was she thinking of, confronting Maude Hewlett? Victoria was the last person who should try to reason with that madwoman. Surely her presence would only incite Maude to new levels of lunacy and rage.

The sergeant ducked over beside Victoria. His face was sweating, the moisture running in little streams down his ruddy forehead and beading in his shaggy brows. "Now listen, Miss Carlin," he ordered, "I don't want any heroics, you understand?"

"I understand," Victoria replied, trying to keep her voice calm.

Sergeant Reynolds was still giving her a laundry list of instructions. "Now you go ahead and talk to the Hewlett woman," he said, "but keep things nice and calm, okay? No surprises, no emotions, no hysterics, you got that? And if I say that's enough, then you and Mr. Anders get yourselves out of here fast. You got that clear and plain?"

Victoria nodded, although she couldn't have repeated a word the sergeant said. Her mind felt stymied, blocked, paralyzed. She knew now how her students felt when they were called upon to comment on some assignment they'd never bothered to read.

"You got something to say, Miss Carlin," prompted the sergeant. "This is your chance. You say it."

Victoria took the bullhorn, her hands shaking, her lips stiff as cardboard. Tentatively she called out, "Maude, are you listening? It's Victoria Carlin."

"I hear you" came the clipped response, the tone surly and combative.

Victoria pressed on, her voice growing stronger. "Is Joshua with you, Maude? Is he okay? Please, Maude, tell me about Joshua."

"The boy's none of your business!"

Victoria decided to try another tactic. "What about Sam? Is he there with you?"

There was no reply. Then, after a minute, Sam's voice quavered, "I'm here, Miss Clarkin. Me and the boy's right here." He paused and Victoria suspected that Maude was coaching him. "Why don't you all go home now and let us be," he continued, his voice cracking nervously. "Just let Maude and the boy and me have some peace!"

"I can't go home yet," cried Victoria. "Not until I've told you something very important."

Maude was back. "You got nothing to tell us we don't already know, Miss Carlin. You're an evil, conniving woman. You've brought us nothing but misery!"

"Listen, Maude," Victoria pleaded. She paused, forcing herself to concentrate on her own words, not the insults Maude was hurtling. "I understand how you feel, Maude. You're hurting. You're still mourning the death of your daughter. I know how hard that is for you."

"How can you know? You'll never understand!" Maude retorted hotly.

"Yes, I do," persisted Victoria. "I lost someone, too—my mother—not long ago, and I miss her terribly. I know that's how you feel about losing Julia."

"Don't waste your pity on me," shouted Maude. "Pity yourself and this boy. The devil's got his hand on the two of you! Julia would still be alive if it wasn't for you!"

"You're wrong, Maude." Victoria's voice rose with conviction. "Julia died in a tragic accident. It had nothing to do with Joshua or me."

"Liar!" Maude yelled back. "Joshua was cursed by your sin!"

"No, Maude! Joshua's an innocent little boy," declared Victoria, riding the edge of her emotions. "Your daughter loved him. She would never want you to blame him for her death!"

"Then I blame you!" shouted Maude. "You conceived that boy in sin! You opened the way for the curse on us and our house!" Her voice grew shrill and uncontrolled. "It was your sin that killed my Julia and destroyed this poor boy's mind!"

Victoria swayed against Phillip. Her knees were buckling. Immediately his arms circled her, offering support. She hadn't realized until now how close she was to collapsing. "Don't do this to yourself, Victoria," he whispered. "Don't subject yourself to her venom."

She laid her head against his shoulder and inhaled deeply. "I must, Phillip. I've got to have it out with Maude once and for all." Victoria straightened and spoke again into the mouthpiece. "Maude, listen to me. You're right about one thing. It was my sin that brought Joshua into the world. I've lived with that fact for over six long years. But you see only half the truth, just as I did for so many years. You're thinking only about the wrong that was done."

"What else is there?" challenged Maude bitterly.

"There's a greater power," exclaimed Victoria. "It's God's power, for good and blessing and love. What you don't understand, Maude— what I didn't understand for so long—is that God can forgive the sin and make us clean and pure in His sight."

When Maude didn't reply, Victoria continued urgently, "That's what God did for me, Maude. He forgave me and made me a new person. God loves me! And He loves you, too, Maude! And Sam! And Joshua!"

"You're lying!" shrieked Maude. "Don't you think I know the truth? God's turned His back on us!"

"No, Maude," Victoria persisted. "God's Son died for our sins— yours and mine. Christ has won the victory over the devil!" She paused, catching her breath. "You can choose who will control your life. If you choose God, you can be free!"

"Lies! All lies!" retorted Maude. "There's a verse in the good book that proves you're lying!"

"What verse?" coaxed Victoria. "Tell me!"

After a minute, Maude called out, "It's I John 3:8. 'He that committeth sin is of the devil; for the devil sinneth from the beginning.'"

Victoria took her New Testament from her purse while Phillip held Sergeant Reynolds's flashlight. She quickly found the reference. "You've got to finish the verse, Maude!" she challenged. "Listen to the rest of it! 'For this purpose the Son of God was manifested, that He might destroy the works of the devil.' Don't you see, Maude? Jesus has the power to destroy evil. If you want to be free from the curse of sin, you must trust in Jesus. That's what I did. He set me free. He can do that for you, if you'll let Him!"

"Get out of here!" screamed Maude, "and get the police out of here, too, or I'll shoot us all!"

If Victoria had ever thought about a defining moment in her life when all that mattered could be won or lost, this had to be that moment. She had to do something bold, extreme, unexpected, if she was ever going to catch Maude Hewlett off guard. With a prayer on her lips, she squared her shoulders and summoned the courage to take the only action she could think of. She sprang to her feet, darted around the police vehicle and stood in full view of Maude, her hands at her side. "I don't believe you want to hurt anyone, Maude," she said evenly.

Phillip lunged for her, but she sidestepped him. "Get back out of sight, Victoria!" he said urgently.

She ignored him and took several slow-motion steps toward the cabin. She could hear the officers around her muttering in alarm. "Hey, get her back here!" "What in blazes is she trying to do, get herself killed?" "What cockamamie stunt is she pulling?"

She shut out their voices and focused all her concentration on Maude. "If you want to punish someone, Maude, punish me," she said solemnly. "Let Joshua go. Let me take his place."

"Don't come no closer," Maude cautioned from inside the house.

From the corner of her eye Victoria could see Phillip edging closer, just out of Maude's range of vision. "Victoria," he whispered desperately, "get back here now!"

"Let me do this, Phillip," she whispered back. "It's the only way."

"You're risking your life," he argued fiercely.

Victoria closed her eyes, shutting him out, shutting out everyone and everything except Maude and herself. A terrified voice in a corner of her mind told her she had to be as crazy as Maude to be standing here like this; she could never pull off this travesty of a hero act. Maybe she should listen to the voice. What made her think she was so brave? Her head was splitting and her skin crawling with nervous jitters. But another voice said, You've started this; now finish it. You're not alone.

She steeled herself, inhaled sharply and took another step. The gun barrel in the window lowered toward her. Her stomach knotted, shooting a sour taste into her throat. She heard Sergeant Reynolds order, "Get that woman back here before she gets her fool head blown off!"

But no one moved.

Victoria waited, her limbs so tense the pain shot through her muscles like lightning bolts.

Nearly a minute passed. Then a sudden noise broke the stillness. Victoria flinched, then recovered. It wasn't the gun. The cabin door creaked open. Sam stood in the doorway with Joshua. "Don't shoot, officers!" he called hoarsely. "I'm bringing the boy out!"

"Get back in here, Sam!" howled Maude. "Don't you dare cross me like this, you old fool. I'll shoot you both!"

Sam took the boy's hand and shuffled toward Victoria. It was a sight that wrenched her heart—a doddering, disheveled old man and a frightened, confused little boy, all freckles and carrot red curls. She waited, breathless, tearful, the air electric with tension.

Maude emerged from the doorway, seething, her rifle aimed at Sam. "You crazy old man," she screamed. "Bring that boy back here!"

Sam shambled on.

Victoria held out her hand to Joshua. Sam scooted the reticent, wide-eyed boy toward her. Weeping now, with salty tears coursing down her cheeks, Victoria gathered her son into her arms and rocked him against her breast. Dear God, he's flesh and blood real, warm as sunshine, hair and skin soft as silk, a breathing, squirming boy smelling of new-mown grass and peppermint candy!

Then suddenly, like a videotape spinning out on fast forward, everything happened at once, too fast, the images blurred, the voices garbled, the sequence of events seemingly jumbled. In one great surge, the police converged around Victoria and the child and whisked them away to a waiting squad car. In the bewildering confusion of the moment, Victoria was aware only of Joshua's nearness and Phillip's protective embrace.

Chapter Thirty

More than a month after the volatile confrontation at the Hewlett cabin, Victoria was granted temporary custody of her son. Phillip drove Victoria to Middleton to pick up the boy. After several hours of conferring with Joshua's social worker, his therapist and his physician, Victoria was escorted to her son's room.

She had been imagining this day for weeks, playing out in her thoughts what it would feel like to be given her son, to be told she could finally be his mother. She had had only those brief minutes with him in the patrol car after the confrontation with Maude. But those few minutes had been enough to whet her maternal appetite and to convince her she would have more than enough love to see her son through the hard days ahead. As she remembered those tender moments with Joshua, her arms ached to hold him again, to kiss his freckled cheeks and breathe in the fragrance of his burnished, downy-fine hair. And now she was on her way to his room where those desires would become reality.

As soon as she entered her son's room, her eyes went immediately to the tiny figure sitting cross-legged on the large bed. Joshua was wearing a new T-shirt and jeans, and his hair had been neatly combed. He sat waiting patiently, turning a plastic action figure over and over in his hands.

Victoria approached the bed slowly, lest she alarm him. When she reached him she put a tentative hand out and touched his tennis shoe.

"What handsome shoes," she said, struggling to speak over the lump in her throat. "Are they new, Joshua?"

His gaze remained on the figure in his hands.

"I'm very happy to see you again, Joshua," she said, moving her hand cautiously to his hair. Gently she stroked his shiny auburn curls. He continued to play with his action figure, seemingly oblivious of her presence. She yearned desperately to gather him into her arms and shower him with the affection she had waited six years to bestow. But she knew it would be a slow process, that she must proceed with utmost care. She couldn't risk frightening the boy; somehow, in time, she would win his trust.

"Are you ready to go home, Joshua?" she asked brightly. "I have a bedroom for you filled with toys and books and a rocking horse, and there are colorful cartoon animals on the walls."

Joshua turned his gaze to the window, his fingers still fidgeting with the action toy. Victoria looked helplessly at Mrs. Ramsey, his caseworker.

"It'll take time, Miss Carlin," the woman murmured. She nodded toward two worn suitcases, an overnight bag, several blankets and a box of toys by the door. "We brought all of Joshua's things from the Hewlett home," she explained. "And please don't forget this old teddy bear with one eye. It's Joshua's favorite, along with that old flannel blanket he sleeps with, the rumpled one there on the suitcase."

Victoria took the stuffed animal from Mrs. Ramsey and handed it to her son. "Is this your favorite teddy, Joshua?"

The boy ignored her.

She laid the animal on his lap. "Would you like to carry Teddy when we go for our long drive in the car?"

Joshua dropped the action figure and hugged the animal, burying his face in the bear's furry head.

Victoria looked at Mrs. Ramsey and shrugged, as if to ask, What do I do now?

"Like I said, give him time, Miss Carlin," said Mrs. Ramsey. "He's coming around, a little more every day."

"It's just that I—I feel so inadequate."

Phillip stepped forward and slipped his arm around Victoria's waist. "You'll be a wonderful mother—don't you doubt it."

She looked up at him, her eyes filling. "I hope so, Phillip. I want that more than anything."

"Don't you have something you want to give Joshua?" he said, his gaze going to her purse.

"Yes, I do," she said with sudden excitement. She reached into her purse and pulled out a small metal car and handed it to the boy. "This belongs to you, Joshua. Someone once told me if I had enough faith I'd be able to return it to you personally someday. He was right. God has been very good to both of us."

Joshua's fingers closed around the tiny car; he lifted it to his chest and held it there for a long minute, then ran the wheels over his knee and made a low, guttural sound.

"I think he remembers it," said Victoria, a new wave of emotion overtaking her.

"And now that Joshua is happy with his toy car, maybe we'd better get him into my car," suggested Phillip, "and head home."

Victoria turned to Mrs. Ramsey. "Is there anything else I need to know before we go?"

"You just follow the doctor's instructions," Mrs. Ramsey said kindly, "and make sure Joshua has his checkups on schedule. And, oh, yes, be sure to feed Joshua that high-fat diet we gave you. I know some doctors still consider it experimental, but it's helped a lot of children with epilepsy."

"I'll follow it to the letter," said Victoria. "But I'm wondering—when will I be talking with you again, Mrs. Ramsey?"

"Oh, don't you worry. I'll be in touch. And if you have any questions, you be sure to call me or Joshua's doctor."

"I can't thank you enough…"

"Don't thank me. I just want to see you and that little boy have a good life together."

Phillip squeezed her shoulder and said, "My car's waiting at the entrance door. Are we ready to go?"

She nodded. "You can carry Joshua's things out."

Mrs. Ramsey went over and took Joshua's hand. "Come on, honey. We're going for a nice ride with someone who loves you very much."

After Joshua was buckled in comfortably with his teddy in the back seat of Phillip's car, Victoria turned to Mrs. Ramsey. "I can't seem to find anything else to say, except thank you."

The two women clasped hands. "I'll see you back in Middleton in about six months." Mrs. Ramsey smiled.

"You mean, for the final custody hearing?"

"That's right. And if all goes as we expect, Joshua will be legally yours."

Victoria blinked rapidly. "I am so grateful..." She slipped into the back seat beside Joshua, dabbed her eyes and waved goodbye to Mrs. Ramsey.

For most of the ride home, Joshua sat gazing silently out the window. Once, when a huge semi rolled past, he pointed out the window and said, "Truck!"

Phillip looked back in amazement.

"Isn't it wonderful?" said Victoria. "Mrs. Ramsey told me he's talking a little now—an occasional word here and there."

"It's a beginning," said Phillip.

"Yes. A wonderful beginning."

Joshua grew sleepy the last hour of the journey home and relaxed against Victoria, his eyes heavy; then he cuddled up, drawing his knees against his chest, and fell asleep with his head in her lap. She reached for the flannel blanket Mrs. Ramsey had said was his favorite, a tattered holdover from infancy.

It struck Victoria suddenly that it was a blanket she recognized. Yes, of course, it was the receiving blanket with little puppies that she had given to her newborn son; she had asked that it go with him to his new home, and so it had. Not only had he kept it, it had been his favorite! And now after all these years she had it back, just as she had her child back. "Yes, God is so good," she murmured as she tucked the velvety blanket around his shoulders.

For the rest of the drive home she stroked Joshua's forehead while he slept. He looked so vulnerable in the passing lights and shadows of the automobile. She couldn't help thinking about the profound responsibility that was hers now. It was her place to watch over and protect her son, to help him grow strong in spite of life's hurts and disappointments. Was she up to the task? Only with God's help. If love mattered most, she had an abundant supply.

It was dark when Phillip finally pulled up beside Victoria's condominium. Phillip gathered the boy in his arms and carried him inside.

"Take him to the guest room—the second door on the left," Victoria told him.

Phillip laid the sleeping youngster on the youth bed in the pleasant room brightened by cartoon characters on the walls.

"As you can see," she said softly, "I redecorated the room the way I thought a little boy would like it."

"Looks great to me," replied Phillip. "Winnie the Pooh sheets and a Mickey Mouse lamp—what more can a kid ask for?"

Phillip brought in Joshua's things while Victoria helped the sleepy child into his pajamas and tucked him into bed. It was the ritual thousands of parents went through every night, often perfunctorily, without thinking; but for Victoria the ritual felt sacrosanct, imbued with a rare enchantment. She had never felt so blessed. She leaned down and kissed Joshua's smooth, warm cheek, caressed his tousled hair and whispered a little prayer. "My Father, thank You for giving me back my son. Help me to be everything he needs me to be. Please make him healthy and whole again. Show him how much I love him, and how much You love him, too." Victoria's voice cracked and she brushed away a tear. She didn't want to wake her slumbering child, so she stood and tiptoed away from the bed before her emotions overcame her.

She realized then that Phillip was standing in the doorway, watching, the golden glow of the hall light framing his dark, towering silhouette. "That's the most beautiful sight I've ever seen," he murmured as he embraced her and led her from the room. "I'd love to see that little scene with you and the boy played out every night."

"I think that could be arranged," she said with a wistful little smile.

"I think I'd like to hear what you have in mind," he said with a roguish wink.

"First, you tell me what *you* have in mind."

"How long do you have?" he asked.

She shrugged. "I don't know. Maybe a hundred years?"

He nodded. "That might do."

They settled on the living room sofa, and he picked up two glasses of iced tea from the coffee table and handed her one.

"Thanks," she said.

"I guess Joshua was exhausted from the trip," he noted.

"Yes. He hardly stirred when I undressed him for bed."

Phillip studied her for a long minute.

"What is it?" she asked. "What are you thinking?"

"Just wondering how you feel now that it's all over and you finally have your son."

She rested her head back against his shoulder. "I feel—I don't know—everything at once. Happy, scared, grateful... I just pray I'll be able to make him happy."

"You will, Victoria."

"I'm going to do everything I can for him, Phillip. I've enrolled him in a special school. He'll attend every day while I'm at the university teaching. And I've signed him up for physical therapy and speech rehabilitation. I've even made an appointment for Joshua and myself with a child psychiatrist."

Phillip squeezed the back of her neck affectionately. "Just don't get so involved in all you're doing for the boy that you forget to simply enjoy him."

She smiled. "Don't worry. I've got six long years of stored-up love to give him."

"He's a lucky little guy."

"No, Phillip, I'm lucky—and, oh, I know it's not luck at all. It's God's providence. I'm so grateful to Him and to you."

He chuckled lightly. "You weren't so bad yourself, you know. I keep remembering the way you stood up to Maude Hewlett at the cabin. I never would have let you face her like that, but I must admit, it did the trick."

"I didn't budge Maude," she replied, "but somehow I reached Sam. I still can't believe he set Joshua free."

"I bet that's the only brave thing that man has ever done," mused Phillip.

"I'm sure it's the first time he ever crossed Maude," she agreed. "And you're right—that does take courage." After a minute, she asked, "What do you think will happen to Sam and Maude?"

"I don't know," replied Phillip. "Sam will probably get off with probation or a light sentence. I know one thing. For the first time, he'll be free of Maude."

"What do you mean?"

"Let's just say that after the stunt she pulled at the cabin, Maude will have time over the next couple of years to make all the crocheted soaps her heart desires."

Victoria elbowed Phillip playfully. "You're awful!"

He pulled her into his arms. "I know, but I love you, anyway."

She looked at him. "I love you, too."

He kissed her gently, with a sweet wistfulness that sparked her own yearnings. He pressed her head against his shoulder and absently stroked her back. Neither spoke for a long while.

Finally she stirred and looked up at him. "Now tell me what you're thinking."

He chuckled. "Yes, I intend to."

"All right, I'm listening. Tell me."

"Where should I begin?" he said teasingly.

"Is it about us?"

He grinned. "Yes. What else?"

"Then I'm ready to hear every word."

He relaxed his embrace, but his hand still caressed her arm. "Our lives have been so busy lately, Victoria, but we can't talk around it anymore. We have decisions to make."

"What decisions?" she prompted. She refused to make this easy for him.

"You know, our future. What I'm trying to say is..." He paused and drew in a deep breath. "God has been teaching me what love really is, Victoria—forgiveness, acceptance, sacrifice, trust, even a leap of faith. I can't promise I'll be the world's greatest husband, but I'd be honored—no, I'd be overjoyed—if you'd let me try."

She gazed warmly up at him, wanting to shout to the heavens that of course she'd marry him. But she was determined to play this scenario out all the way. "Is this a marriage proposal, Phillip?" she inquired.

He took her face in his hands and searched her eyes, looking a bit baffled and yet amused. "That's the idea, Victoria. Do you want me to get down on one knee?"

His eyes held her spellbound. "No, Phillip," she assured him, "this is good, just the way you are."

"Then will you do me the honor of becoming Mrs. Phillip Anders?"

"What about Joshua?" she asked. She had to know beyond a doubt how he felt about her son. "It may take years of hard work and special care before he becomes a normal little boy."

Phillip ran his fingertips over her mouth, her chin. He was smiling the most disarming smile. "Joshua needs a father and I want very much to have a son," he said, as if it were the most obvious and suitable arrangement in the world.

"Oh, Phillip!" she said through sudden tears, but no other words would come.

"I hope you'll let me adopt Joshua," he went on seriously. "You know how I've always wanted a family. I promise I'll love him as my own and raise him to be a strong, godly man.''

"I know you will, Phillip," she said, her hand going to his sturdy face, his russet hair. "I hope he's just like you."

"Better than me," said Phillip. A mischievous gleam flashed in his eyes. "But I warn you, my darling, I plan on getting the rest of our children the natural way."

She gave him a whimsical smile. "My goodness, you're talking about our children, and I haven't even given you my answer."

He playfully kissed the tip of her nose. "When did you learn to be such a tease?"

"I'm not teasing. I just want to hear the question again."

He drew her into his arms, held her close and kissed her with a slow, tender passion. Then he said huskily, "Will you marry me, Victoria?"

"Yes, Phillip," she said, her voice light with joy. "Yes, yes, yes!"

He reached into his jacket pocket and produced a small black velvet box. With a gallant little flourish he took her left hand and slipped a diamond ring on her finger. "I brought this with me just in case," he told her lightly. "I was hoping it might come in handy."

"It's beautiful," she said, holding it up to the lamplight. She felt tears brimming in her eyes. "Oh, Phillip, I want to share our happiness with my son," she said softly. "*Our* son! Come. I won't wake him, but I want to say the words in his presence—that the three of us are going to be a family."

Quietly she and Phillip stole into Joshua's room and stood by his bed, watching the moonlight cast a soft glow across his peaceful, sleeping face. "It's not going to be just you and me for long, my darling boy," she whispered adoringly. "Very soon now, it's going to be the *three* of us—your mommy and your daddy and you, Joshua. And no matter what happens, we'll never be alone, because our heavenly Father will be with us and watching over us forever."

Epilogue

December 5

Dear family and friends:
Just a note in our Christmas card to share the wonderful news with you. Phillip and I are expecting a baby around Easter. We're so excited, especially Phillip. He's already decorating the nursery in our vintage colonial house that we bought and fixed up last summer. The house has plenty of rooms, and I think Phillip plans to fill each one—not all of them with children, of course. We're accommodating a menagerie of kittens and puppies that Joshua has brought home for us to adopt. As you know, we're big on adoption around here, especially since Phillip's adoption of Joshua became official last year. If we keep up this pace, you can call us "Anders's Ark."

But, of course, much of our attention lately is focused on the new baby. Both Joshua and Daddy love to feel the baby wiggle and kick in Mommy's tummy. Phillip's sure we're going to have a little girl with flaming red hair like her mother's, but I think it'll be a little boy with gorgeous dark eyes like Phillip's. Joshua doesn't care whether he has a brother or a sister; he's just so excited about having a real little playmate instead of another puppy!

You'd be amazed at how well Joshua is doing. He's still on medication, but the diet has worked wonders. His seizures are rare and usually mild, for which we're thankful. He's in third grade at a reg-

ular school now, making friends and doing well. He's come such a long way these past two years, it's hard to remember what he was like when I first found him. Sometimes I let my mind go back to those painful days just so I won't get complacent and take for granted all the good things God has given us.

Would you believe, I'm a full professor now at the university, and my students call me Dr. Anders, which tickles Phillip to no end. He says his father always wanted a doctor in the family; he's glad it's me and not him.

Actually, Phillip has made a career change, as well. Except for especially needy cases, he's given up his detective work and gone back to practicing law. I guess my case against the Hewletts gave him a taste for the courtroom again. He's working with Legal Aid and representing poor families who need an attorney to protect their rights. He's become quite the crusader, and I can't tell you how proud I am of him.

Phillip and I celebrated our second anniversary last month. We talked about taking a cruise to Hawaii, but after so many months of morning sickness, I decided a boat rolling on the ocean wasn't for me. So, instead, we drove down the coast to the Starlight Motel in Middleton for the weekend, a nondescript little place that has special significance for us. And for any of you who are wondering, yes, we're just as much in love as we were on our wedding day!

I thank God for Phillip and my son and the baby I'm carrying. Every day I realize how blessed I am by this ordinary, routine life that shines with an eloquence only God can bestow.

If any of you are ever in our neighborhood, please drop in for a chat. We'll sit by the fireplace and sip hot chocolate. Phillip might try to show you the videotapes of our wedding... But Joshua will truly entertain you, introducing you to all his pets. Needless to say, we'll relax, have fun and be grateful for every moment that God gives us to love and enjoy one another.

* * * * *

Dear Reader,

As a fan of authors Flannery O'Connor and Sylvia Plath, I was fascinated by their very different lives and approaches to faith in God. I thought what an interesting thesis it would make if I ever pursued my master's degree. Instead, I gave my character Victoria the chance to explore the role faith plays in our everyday choices, including the choice to live or die.

But, of course, Victoria's story is mostly a love story—her love for her son, for Philip and for God. I love writing romances about people of faith, because it gives me a chance to explore the ideal romance—not just two people deeply in love, but God's boundless love for his people who've strayed from his side. God knew we could never be strong enough to find our way back to him, so he came to us in the person of his Son. Jesus, the most romantic figure in history, left the glory of heaven to take the form of a man so he could bear our sorrows and pay the price for our sins. He expressed the ultimate love, laying down his life for us and offering eternal fellowship with him. No wonder Scriptures refer to Christ as the Groom and his rescued people as his Bride. We are his beloved, his pearl of great price. And what does Jesus ask in return? Only that we accept him and love him with all our hearts. Dear reader, like Victoria, please open your heart and let him love you. And remember, I love and appreciate you, too!

Warmly,

Carole Gift Page

Available in October from

 *Love Inspired*™

VOWS

a brand-new miniseries by
Irene Hannon

Don't miss this deeply emotional series
about three close friends....

Each has a secret hidden in her past.
Each will experience the love of her own special man.
But will they be able to conquer the shadows
which still haunt them...and look to the
future with renewed faith?

The series begins in October with...

HOME FOR THE HOLIDAYS

A woman who hides her beauty from the world
meets a man who desperately wants to know
everything about her. Can she accept his strength
and spirit? Dare she reveal all she fears and allow
them the chance at an extraordinary love?

And look for **A HUSBAND OF HER OWN**, available
in February 1998.

Follow the lives and loves of the residents of
Duncan, Oklahoma, in a heartwarming series from
Love Inspired...

*by
Arlene
James*

*Every day brings new challenges for young
Reverend Bolton Charles and his congregation.
But together they are sure to gain the strength to
overcome all obstacles—and find love along the way!*

**Watch for these titles in the
EVERYDAY MIRACLES series:**

THE PERFECT WEDDING
(September 1997)

AN OLD-FASHIONED LOVE
(November 1997)

A WIFE WORTH WAITING FOR
(January 1998)

WITH BABY IN MIND
(March 1998)

Don't miss any of these wonderful books,
available from

Love Inspired™

Dear Reader,

Thank you for reading this selection from the *Love Inspired* series. Please take a few moments to tell us your thoughts on this book. Your answers will help us in choosing future books for this series. When you have finished answering the survey, please mail it to the appropriate address listed below.

1. How would you rate this book?

   1.1 ❑ Excellent   4 ❑ Fair
   .2 ❑ Very good   5 ❑ Poor
   .3 ❑ Satisfactory

2. What prompted you to buy this particular book?

_____

_____ 2,7

3. Will you purchase another book from the
   Love Inspired **series in the future?**

   8.1 ❑ Yes—Why?_____

_____ 9,14

   .2 ❑ No—Why not? _____

_____ 15,20

4. Did you find the spiritual/faith elements in this
   story to be:

   21.1 ❑ Too strong? 2 ❑ Too weak? 3 ❑ Just right?

   Comments _____

_____

_____ 22,27

5. Did you find the romance elements in this story
   to be:

   28.1 ❑ Too strong? 2 ❑ Too weak? 3 ❑ Just right?

6. **What other types of inspirational stories would you like to read?**

29 ❏ Mystery   30 ❏ Historical   31 ❏ Anthologies
32 ❏ Humor   33 ❏ Nonfiction
34 ❏ Other _____

7. **Where did you purchase this book? (choose one)**

35.1 ❏ National chain bookstore (e.g. Waldenbooks)
.2 ❏ Christian bookseller
.3 ❏ Supermarket
.4 ❏ General or discount merchandise store (e.g. K mart)
.5 ❏ Secondhand bookstore
.6 ❏ Other _____ 36,41

8. **Which of the following types of paperback books have you read in the past 12 months?**

42 ❏ Contemporary popular women's fiction
    (e.g. Danielle Steel, Sandra Brown)
43 ❏ Romance series books (e.g. Harlequin,
    Silhouette, Loveswept)
44 ❏ Historical romance books
45 ❏ Mystery
46 ❏ Inspirational fiction
47 ❏ Inspirational nonfiction
48 ❏ Other _____ 52,57

Inspirational Romance Fiction

49 ❏ Heartsong   50 ❏ Palisades   51 ❏ Other _____ 58,63

9. **Please indicate your age range:**

64.1 ❏ Under 18 years   .4 ❏ 35 to 49 years
.2 ❏ 18 to 24 years   .5 ❏ 50 to 64 years
.3 ❏ 25 to 34 years   .6 ❏ 65 years or older

Mail To:
In U.S.: "Love Inspired", P.O. Box 1387,
       Buffalo, NY 14240-1387
In Canada: "Love Inspired", P.O. Box 609,
       Fort Erie, Ontario, L2A 5X3   LIOCT1B